aganets and the Mortimers

pa of Hainault

Gaunt m Blanche

Six daughters

Two other sons

Henry IV
Earl of Bolingbroke

Sir Edmund Mortimer
m
Catherine Glyn Dŵr

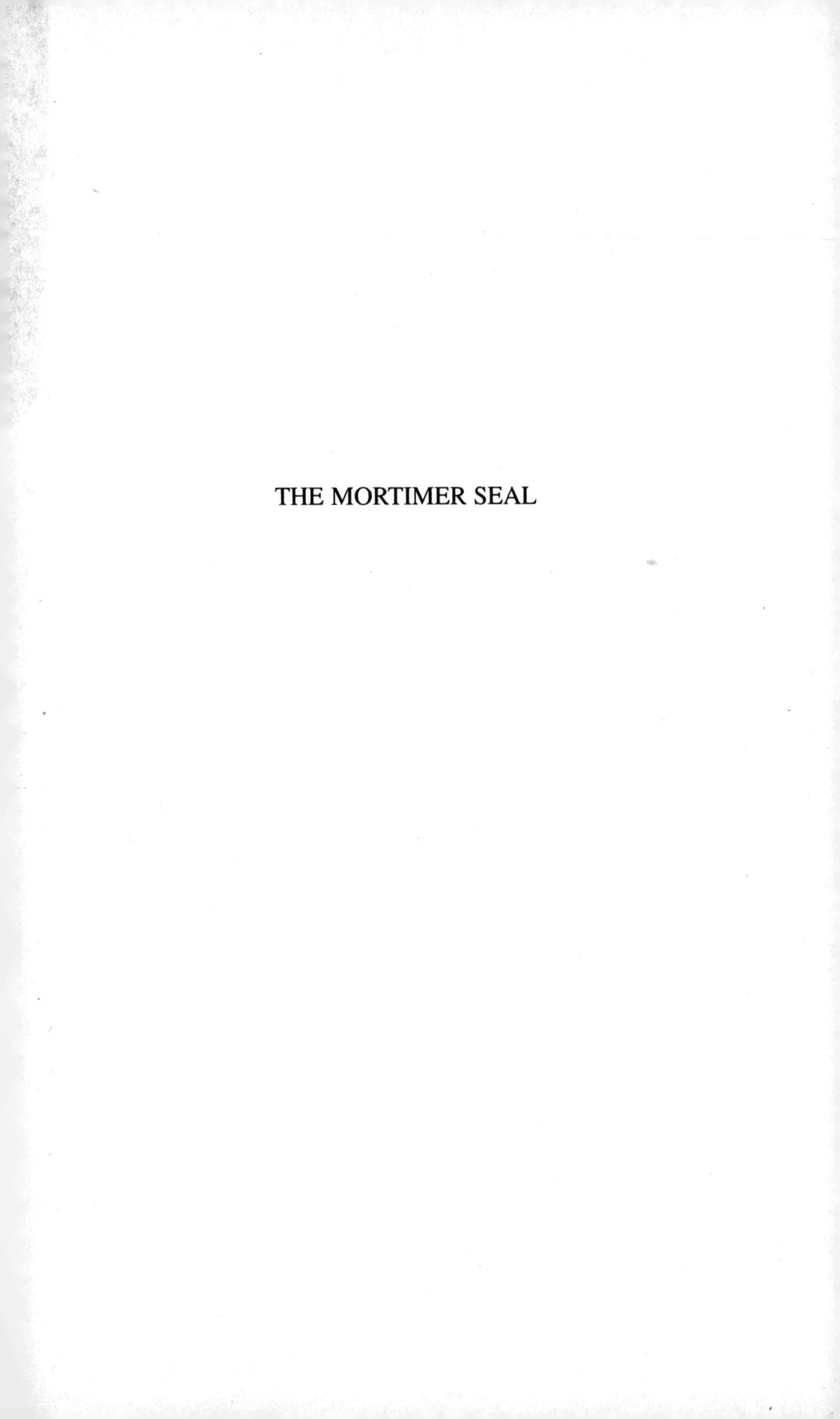

THE MORTIMER SEAL

Also by Bill Bailey:

A Ha'porth of God Help
The Glyn Dŵr Legacy

The Mortimer Seal

Bill Bailey

UNITED WRITERS
Cornwall

UNITED WRITERS PUBLICATIONS LTD
Ailsa, Castle Gate, Penzance, Cornwall.

British Library Cataloguing in Publication Data:
A catalogue record for this book is available from the British Library.

ISBN 1 85200 114 3

Printed in Great Britain by
United Writers Publications Ltd
Cornwall.

Author's Note

Whilst this is a work of fiction, the historical characters portrayed in its pages were real people whose dramatic lives shaped the times in which they lived. Sir Edmund Mortimer was killed at Harlech Castle in 1409 when it finally fell to Prince Henry after a long siege. His wife Catrin and their three children, together with Owain Glyn Dŵr's wife, Margaret, were all taken as prisoners to London where they died in captivity and were buried at St. Swithin's. Owain Glyn Dŵr's son, Gruffydd, captured at the battle of Pwll Melyn, was never freed and died in the Tower of London.

Despite the loss of the western castles and with little hope of gaining new allies, Owain Glyn Dŵr continued to fight on, but with diminishing hope of gaining the independence he sought for Wales. Always refusing the King's pardon, he became a fugitive. It is believed he died in 1415, at the home of his daughter Alice who was then married to Sir John Scudamore of Monnington. His son Maredudd, however, accepted the King's pardon for his part in the rebellion.

Glyn Dŵr's cousins Ednyfed and Rhys Tudur of Anglesey were both captured by the English, and executed at Chester in 1412. It is ironic that Henry Tudor, a direct descendant of Rhys Tudur, landed at Dale in Pembrokeshire in 1485 to seize the throne from Richard III and founded the Tudor dynasty as King Henry VII.

Glendower: *I am afraid my daughter will run mad,*
So much does she dote on her Mortimer . . .

My daughter weeps: she will not part with you . . .

She is desperate here, a peevish, self willed harlotry,
One that no persuasion can do good upon.

Shakespeare: Henry IV Act III Sc. 1

Chapter One

April 1999

Eddie sat by the side of the river at Tintern despondently searching the pockets of his rucksack for the last time, but there was no sign of that which he so desperately needed. He was sweating now, but it wasn't caused by the evening sun that cast long shadows from the ancient ruins of the Abbey. He needed a fix. Needed it badly, but with only a few coins in the pockets of his jeans there was no way he was going to get one, especially here. Even if he had the bread, there was not a dealer in sight – or even out of sight.

He ran his hand through his long, untidy blond hair, his blue eyes mirroring the despair he felt. Then, hands trembling, he took the makings from his worn jeans and made himself a roll-up and lit up. Of course, it didn't help but it kept his right hand occupied, eased the tremors, just a bit.

It was then that he saw her staring at him. As he looked at her she smiled, a knowing look in the blue eyes that seemed strangely out of place in contrast to her dark hair. She walked hesitantly towards him, her short denim skirt emphasising her long shapely legs, a small rucksack slung carelessly over her shoulder. Still smiling that knowing smile, she came and sat beside him. Then, head on one side, she asked, 'Bad, is it?'

If there was sympathy in her voice it was edged with sarcasm and he took a drag on his roll-up before glancing sideways at her. Trying to control his shaking hand, he looked at her for a moment, eyes blank, without interest. Then, brusquely, 'What is?'

She gave a cheeky grin. 'I know all about it,' she replied just a shade smugly. 'Bin there, done that!'

'Done what?' His hands were clenched, knuckles white. Even in his present state though he could see that she was attractive. No, more than that, but he didn't know her and he was not about to admit anything to her.

'Come off it, you know what!' She was still grinning though, as she looked at him, then, as she got up, she added softly, seducingly, 'I've got something that might help!'

Startled, he said eagerly, too eagerly, 'You a dealer then? You got a fix?' Then the despair came flooding back into his voice, 'It doesn't matter, I've got no bread anyway!' His hands trembling again, he took another drag on his roll-up before looking at it with something akin to disgust then throwing it violently away from him. No it didn't help, it was a fix he needed. Now!

There was mockery now both in those blue eyes and in her voice. 'No!' she said scornfully, 'I'm not a dealer, do I look like one?'

He looked up at her as she stood there, waiting for him it seemed. Rubbing his forehead he shook his head then said reluctantly, 'I don't know. What do dealers look like anyway?'

'Whatever,' she replied curtly. 'I'm not one, but I think I can help.'

He shook his head again. 'Oh, I see! Trying to save my soul are you?'

Exasperated, she snapped, 'No, nor that either but if you're not interested then just sit there feeling sorry for yourself!' Then she turned and began to walk away.

A note of desperation in his voice, he called out after her, 'Wait, I *am* interested! If you've got something, then let me have it for God's sake!'

Hesitantly she turned back towards him and, serious faced, shook her head slowly. 'No not here,' she said quietly. 'You'll have to come with me.'

Desperate again, sweating, he almost spat out the words, 'For God's sake, why not?' but even as he spoke he stood up, scrabbling to pick up his rucksack. Then, as she turned away again, he was hurrying after her. As they walked away from Tintern Abbey, his tall form almost towering over her, he asked anxiously, 'Where are we going then?'

Glancing up at him, she smiled saying, 'Not far!' Then she turned away again, her pace quickening. They were out of the village, walking quickly along the Hereford road, before he spoke again: 'How much further for goodness sake?' Then, seeing the exasperation in her face added, more gently now, 'I don't even know your name!'

She grinned. 'You never asked, did you? More interested in what I had, I suppose!'

Shamefaced, he nodded. 'Yes, I'm sorry!

'I know, it doesn't matter, as I said, bin there! It's Cathy. What's yours?'

'Eddie, Eddie Mortimer.'

She grinned. 'That's nice! We're introduced now. Where were you going, Eddie, before . . . you know . . ?'

He grinned back. 'Before I had the shakes you mean? Ludlow.' Then the desperation was there again, pleading almost: 'I've still got them!'

He didn't need to tell her that though, the signs were all there: his whole body seemed to be quivering, even in the cool of the evening his face was bathed in sweat. As if to emphasise his point his right forearm went across his stomach, pressing hard to contain the griping pains that racked him.

Cathy looked at him, concern in her eyes, and urged him on. 'It really isn't far now, Eddie,' she murmured sympathetically. 'Not far at all!'

'God, I hope so,' he muttered through clenched teeth. 'We seem to be taking forever!'

It wasn't long either before they came to a derelict barn by the side of the road. Cathy smiled at him but there was an anxious look in her eyes as she said cheerfully, 'Here we are then, home at last!'

He looked at her in surprise. 'Home?'

Cathy grinned again as she led the way to a gap in the wall that had once been the doorway of the barn. 'That's right. At least, this is where I slept last night!'

As they entered the barn, Eddie could see that the inside held as little promise as its exterior. Moss grew from the bottom of its walls which were open to the skies and the floor was scattered with well trodden straw. Evidently the barn had been used for shelter by generations of sheep. The only sign of human habitation was a rolled up sleeping bag in one corner. Pointing to it, he asked incredulously, 'That yours?' And, as she nodded, added, 'That was trusting, wasn't it?'

Cathy laughed. 'Well the sheep weren't going to steal it, were they?'

He shook his head then, with a touch of disbelief in his voice said, 'Well, it doesn't seem so, anyway!' Pleading again now, he added, 'Have you got it then, whatever it is?'

She nodded as she walked over to the sleeping bag and began unrolling it. 'I hope so!' Fumbling around in the bottom of the sleeping bag, she pulled out a small plastic bag and smiled. 'Yes, here it is, still safe!'

He looked at it for a moment then closed his eyes before saying in a voice taut with exasperation, 'What a bloody stupid thing to do! Anyone could have walked in here and taken that!'

Cathy shrugged her shoulders. 'Well, I didn't need it any more!'

'But I do, what is it for God's sake?' Such was his desperation that he didn't even realise what that sounded like – he wanted it whatever it was!

Cathy realised though and he sensed a touch of scorn in her voice now as she asked, 'Don't you even want to know what it is then?'

'Of course I do!' But even as he spoke his hand was held out towards her.

Ignoring him, she slowly opened the plastic bag whilst he looked open-mouthed at the pills inside. Then taking one out of the bag, she offered it to him, saying, 'It's methadone.'

He took a step back from her and repeated almost in disgust, 'Methadone! Have I come all this way for that?'

Lips tight, she nodded. 'Yes, that's right. I only said that I had something that would help – and it will. Go on, take it!'

Grudgingly he moved towards her again, hand held out, asking as he took the pill, 'Where did you get them?'

Eyes veiled now, she replied quietly, 'I had a friend who helped me. He was a doctor.' She turned away from him to rummage in her rucksack before handing him a small bottle of spring water.

As he took it from her he mumbled, 'Thanks,' but she was already kneeling down and rolling up the sleeping bag as if not anxious to pursue the conversation.

The plastic water bottle in his hand, Eddie turned, to see Cathy sitting cross legged on her sleeping bag, looking at him appraisingly. Somehow, he felt a sense of shame and lowered his eyes. Her question was innocent enough though. Her voice soft with sympathy, she asked, 'Better now?'

He looked up at her, shook his head and gave a sheepish smile. 'I don't know, not yet. I'm sure it will help though. Thanks.'

Her smile lit up the elfin face, which, even in the dim light of the barn he could see was tanned brown as though she spent much of her time in the open air. It was she who lowered her eyes now and he realised that he had been staring at her. They were silent for a moment, an uncomfortable silence and he walked over to the doorway to lean on its broken wall. The road was empty, no sign of life. It was as though no one had passed that way since some farmer had used it to cart his goods to market in days long since gone.

As he stood there, he felt the inner tensions ease. Perhaps it was the pill, he thought, perhaps the peacefulness of the isolated barn. He smiled to himself, perhaps it was the company! Whatever it was, he felt better; better than since . . . The smile fled and he turned towards Cathy. 'Sorry if I was staring at you just now, I didn't mean to, just lost for words for a moment, that's all!'

Impishly, she grinned. 'I'm not sure that that's a compliment! It doesn't matter, it's OK!'

'Where are you going, Cathy?' he asked, anxious somehow that there should not be another uncomfortable silence.

She shrugged. 'Nowhere in particular! Where are any of us going? Staying here tonight anyway!'

The aimlessness of her answer struck a chord but he brushed the half formed thought aside as he asked again, 'Do you mind if I stay too?'

Smiling, she waved a hand around. 'Be my guest, there's room enough. That's your corner, over there!'

He smiled in understanding, the corner to which she had pointed was the one furthest from where she was sitting on her sleeping bag. As he went over to pick up his rucksack she had that appraising look in her eyes again. When she spoke it was more of a statement than a question: 'You in the army, were you?'

He nodded then, non-committally. 'Yes, for a while.'

'Thought so . . . the rucksack!'

One could get that in almost any army surplus store he thought but, shrinking away from the subject, kept his silence. Not so Cathy.

'Officer were you?' she asked, head on one side.

Eddie sighed before saying curtly, 'Yes! For a while.' He turned away to look out on the road again, hoping she would take the hint and drop the subject. Not Cathy. It seemed she was nothing if not persistent!

'Why did you leave, was it the drugs?'

Tight lipped now, he turned his head towards her to say angrily, 'No! I didn't want to leave the regiment. That came after! What does it matter to you, anyway? It's over, done with!'

For a moment she seemed taken aback by his vehemence but soon rallied. 'Just curious that's all, you don't look like the usual drop out junkie.' She paused and he hoped that was the end of her quizzing. She was frowning now though, looking puzzled and before he could stop her she asked, 'Why did you leave then, I mean if you didn't want to?'

He stood there in the doorway, glowering, his left arm across his chest, hand massaging his right shoulder. As if suddenly conscious of what he was doing, his left arm dropped away to his side and with a sigh he just said quietly, 'As I said, Cathy, it's over, done with, best left in the past.'

Getting up she looked at him for a moment, a far away look in her eyes, then nodded in agreement. 'Yes it usually is, isn't it?' Walking slowly over to him, she linked her arm in his, saying, 'I'm sorry! I wasn't being nosey, just interested, that's all!'

Looking down at her, he smiled. 'That's all right. Sorry I was a bit short with you, it's just something I'd rather not talk about.'

As he looked in her eyes, he became conscious of the warmth of her body next to his, the seductive smell of her perfume, yes, and the soft look in her eyes. Bending his head, he felt her hair brush his cheek but as he went to kiss her she turned her head away quickly so that he only succeeded in kissing her cheek. Then her flat palm was on his right shoulder, pushing him away from her.

Her face flushed now, she said angrily, 'Stop that! What do you think I am, an easy lay?' She stopped abruptly, for his face was distorted in pain and his hand had gone to his shoulder again. 'What's the matter?' she asked, suddenly contrite. 'I only gave you a little push! Have you hurt your arm or something?'

Eddie gave a wry grin. 'Yeah, sort of. Don't worry though, you didn't do anything. Anyway it's I who should be sorry.'

Cathy brushed aside his apology. 'Forget it!' she said but her eyes had a speculative look now and he sensed another question coming. It was. Hardly pausing for breath, she asked, 'What is it with the arm, anyway? Was that why you left the army?'

Sighing, he gave in to the inevitable. 'Yes, I got wounded, then when I was well enough, I got invalided.'

Cathy, her hand to her mouth, looked horrified then. 'Oh! That's awful! You poor thing!'

He shrugged, hoping to bring the conversation to an end. 'Well it happens! You can't join the boy scouts and not go camping, can you?'

Cathy though was not so easily deterred. 'So that's why you got on to drugs?'

Bemused, he gaped at her, seldom had he met anyone quite so persistent! 'I don't know . . . they fed me a lot of painkillers when I was in hospital, but I don't think it was that. Anyway, let's drop it, shall we?'

Cathy nodded. 'Yes, OK! Got the message!' Then said cheerfully, 'Would you like a mug of tea? I've got the makings.'

He grinned. 'I have too, but all I want to do now is go to bed.'

As she walked to her sleeping bag, she looked over her shoulder, smiled and there was irony in her voice now as she replied, 'Yeah, I know!'

He glanced at her, but she was already kneeling down, unrolling her sleeping bag, unaware that he was staring at her again. He began unrolling his own then stripped off with his back to her, thinking wryly as he did so: Yes, I really would, but there's no chance there!

After the short silence her sudden cry startled him and he turned his head to see her standing there, frowning, staring with shocked eyes at the ugly scar on his shoulder. Then, her voice almost a whisper, she said, 'That must have been awful! It still hurts, doesn't it?'

He turned to face her, quickly holding his shirt up to his chest to conceal the scar of the exit wound. Then with a wry smile and a toss of his head he said, 'Only when I laugh, as they say!'

Hesitantly she came towards him and putting her hand gently on his she took the shirt away from his shoulder to see the scar. Looking up into his eyes, she shook her head. 'Oh, Eddie, I'm sorry, I didn't know! No wonder . . .' but her voice tailed off as though she couldn't bring herself to finish the sentence.

He finished it for her: ' . . . I'm a junkie!' He sighed before adding, 'It's no excuse, Cathy, none at all!' He smiled as he put his hand on her shoulder. 'I know it's a dragon I have to kill. Must kill . . . and I will!'

Her eyes softened as she said quietly, 'I know!' then her hand was on his left shoulder, her body pressing close to him and there was no resistance now as, with his arms around her, he bent his head and kissed her.

Eddie stirred and turned his head to avoid the sunlight streaming into the barn through the open doorway. Still half asleep he reached out his hand to feel only the dirt and straw of the barn floor beside him. Eyes closed to shield himself from the sunlight, he felt around him but still there was nothing, no one. Suddenly awake, he sat up and looked around but there was no sleeping bag beside his, no Cathy. Frowning now, he called out, 'Cathy!' but there was no reply, nothing, just a depressing silence. Unzipping his sleeping bag, he stood up, running his hand through his tousled blond hair and, fully awake now, looked around the barn yet again but there was no sign of anyone other than he having been there! It was empty and he was alone . . . again.

Confused, he stood there for a moment wondering whether it had all been a dream, a drug induced dream. He shook his head as he tried to think back over the night, but it was all there, as clear in his mind and as tangible, as if Cathy were beside him now. He could still feel her touching his scars, their bodies melting together. No, it was no dream! He was sure that it had all happened, really happened. As surely as she had gone! Disconsolate, he looked down at the solitary sleeping bag and irritably kicked it aside.

He smiled in relief. It had not been a dream, for there on the dirt floor was the evidence. The plastic bag of methadone pills was lying there, glistening in the morning sun. It was no dream, Cathy was real, she *had* been there with him. His heart sank. Yes, but why had she gone? He shook his head in exasperation, after all that had happened how could she have left like that, without a word of explanation.

The momentary elation he had felt on seeing the bag of pills fled and he just stood there for a second, then with a sigh, went over to his rucksack and took out a bottle of water. Using it sparingly he washed his face and cleaned his teeth before taking out a battery shaver and shaving himself, thinking all the while, with no little amazement, of all that had happened the night before. All that had really happened!

There was a movement outside and his heart lifted. 'Cathy!' he called anxiously, but the only response was a sheep looking inquisitively through the doorway of the barn, hesitating a moment, then turning away again.

Dressing, Eddie brewed himself a mug of tea on his diminutive gas stove before rolling up his sleeping bag and packing his rucksack. Picking up the bag of pills, he suddenly realised there was a slip of paper inside. Thinking it was a note from Cathy, he tore open the bag only to realise that it was merely instructions for taking the pills. He scanned through it, to see from the instructions that it appeared he was overdue to take another. He took one, still wondering, worrying, where Cathy could have gone . . . but gone she had, he realised and taken her sleeping bag and rucksack with her.

Strapping his sleeping bag to the rucksack, he carefully hoisted it onto his shoulders after placing a folded towel there under his shirt. With a last glance around the barn he sighed and stepped out onto the road to Hereford.

As the lorry pulled in ahead of him, Eddie hurried towards it and opened the nearside door to peer hopefully inside. The heavily built driver looked about forty-five and unlike Eddie, hadn't bothered to shave that morning or even the one before. 'Where are you going mate?' he asked impassively.

Hoping he was not being too ingratiating, Eddie smiled as he answered, 'Ludlow.'

With a toss of his head the driver said, 'You're in luck then, I'm going there, 'though I'm stopping in Worcester for a couple of hours. Jump in!'

Flinging his rucksack ahead of him, Eddie clambered into the passenger seat. He was still trying to sort himself out as the driver slipped into gear and drove on. As he got into top gear he turned to Eddie, to say conversationally, 'Yeah, I'm stopping in Worcester for a bit, if you hang about there I'll take you on to Ludlow.'

Eddie smiled again. 'Oh, yes please, that'll be splendid. Thank you very much!'

The driver nodded. 'That's OK. What you going there for then, the Shakespeare do at the castle? Have one there every year, they do. Busy, Ludlow is then. Lot o' visitors.' He nodded again, satisfied with his own cultural knowledge.

Eddie hesitated, then nodded vigorously. 'Yes, that's right! Going there for the Shakespeare play.'

He wasn't really. He was going there because he had a ring he had to sell. The heavy gold signet ring with the Mortimer coat of arms that he'd been given by his father. The Earls of March had held the castle at Ludlow and their family name was Mortimer, or so he believed. He had been told by a jeweller in London that the ring was antique and that with its crest he'd likely get a better price for it in Ludlow. In any case, it was all that he had left now and it would help if it fetched a couple of hundred or so. In his present financial state he was hoping that it might be 'or so'!

Keeping his eye on the road, the driver nodded, content it seemed with his evaluation of his passenger's intentions. He was silent for a moment then, with a quick sideways glance, asked, 'Army, were you?'

Eddie nodded, his eyebrows arched, surprised as much by the driver's use of the past tense as by his assessment of occupation.

The driver, eyes on the road again, nodded comfortably. 'Yeah, I can always tell! In it myself, see. RASC I was.' He paused, frowned, then said, 'No, don't tell me!'

Eddie sighed inaudibly thinking that he hadn't been about to do so but the driver, deep in concentration seemed not to notice. Then, with that quick sideways glance again, he continued with his assessment: 'Now I reckon you were a Para, am I right?'

Very nearly thought Eddie, I was in the Paras . . . before I joined the Regiment. He only nodded though as, smiling, he asked, 'How did you guess?'

The driver snorted. 'Guess, mate? Me, I don't have to guess, not after twenty years in the mob. I can always tell!' As he manoeuvred to avoid a couple of cyclists, he delivered his coup de grâce, saying with the confidence of an orderly sergeant, 'Officer too, weren't you?' He grinned as Eddie nodded weakly. 'OAD that was see, mate, not guessing! What we were always taught. Observe, Assess, Decide!'

Eddie sighed inwardly, thinking that it was going to be a long ride to Worcester. He shuddered at the thought of going on to Ludlow with the driver making his self satisfied assessments all the way. At the thought of the alternative though he braced himself as he admitted his offence.

He hadn't needed to do so, for as the lorry lumbered around a bend in the road, the driver pouted his lips. 'Yeah, I can always tell! Captain, weren't you?' Without waiting for Eddie's confirmation he continued, 'Yeah, Captain! Too young for major see and seen too much action for lieutenant!'

That succeeded in surprising Eddie and despite himself he was forced to ask, 'Why do you say that?'

The driver grinned confidently. 'It's always there in the eyes, mate! You see as much in other people's eyes as you see with your own!'

Eddie defensively closed his eyes at this piece of wisdom, wondering how far he would have to walk to Worcester if he were to get off now. Too far, he decided as he settled himself back in his seat. Then, attack being the best method of defence, he asked curtly, 'How far to Worcester now then, Staff Sergeant?'

Eyes to the front, head up, chin pressed into his chest, the driver answered smartly, 'About fifteen miles, sir!'

There was a moment's silence before the driver turned his head sharply and, frowning now, asked, 'How did you know that?'

Grinning, Eddie replied, 'It's all in the eyes, mate, remember?'

Momentarily subdued, the driver nodded then, fumbling in the top pocket of his shirt he took out a packet of cigarettes and offered it to Eddie: 'Have a fag?' And as Eddie nodded added, 'Light one up for me too, will you?

They drove on in silence after that exchange and as he drew on his cigarette Eddie's thoughts drifted back to the barn and to wondering why Cathy had left so abruptly, so secretively. Finding no answer, he sighed and the driver turned to him to say almost apologetically, 'It's all right guv, not far to Worcester now, about another ten minutes or so.'

Feeling that it should be he who apologised, Eddie smiled. 'Great, I'll buy you a drink when we get there, I could do with one myself, too!' Yes, but not a drink he thought as his hand went to his jeans' pocket to make sure the bag of pills were still there. Without turning his head the driver said impassively, 'Not while I'm driving, sir! More than my job's worth, that is!'

It sounded like a rebuke but, knowing that he had barely the price of a drink in his pocket let alone two, it only left Eddie feeling relieved. 'Of course!' he said. 'Sorry about that! Perhaps in Ludlow then?' Perhaps he'd have enough money by then too!

The driver nodded. 'Perhaps, but it'll have to be after I unload there.' He changed the subject. 'Here we are then! Outskirts of Worcester. The place I'm delivering to is on City Walls Road. Not far from the canal that is. City centre's not far either, plenty o' places there where you can get a pint and a pie or whatever.'

He was silent after that, concentrating on his driving as they drove into the city and the traffic got busier. Soon they were driving along a busy main road in the city and it was not long before he was turning off it to pull in alongside a red brick warehouse cum workshop. With a 'Here we are then!' he gave a nod to Eddie, stretched and got out of the cab. By the time Eddie had picked up his rucksack and got out also, the driver was already undoing the lacings of the lorry's canvas sides. The driver turned his head. 'Back here one o'clock sharp if you want to go on to Ludlow, guv!'

With a smile and a wave, Eddie said, 'Great! Thanks, I'll be here!' Then seeing a glint of water at the rear of the workshop, he set off towards it and quickly found himself on the towpath of the canal. Ahead of him he could see a group of people sitting there eating and drinking. It must be a pub, he thought and set off towards it wondering as he went whether he had enough for both a drink and a sandwich. As he drew near he could see that there were only three people sitting at a wooden table by the lock gate although from the babble of noisy talk and laughter one would have thought it was a much larger group.

Suddenly he stopped in his tracks as he saw the girl looking at him, a glass of red wine raised to her lips, the laughter still there in her eyes. Then raising her glass to him, Cathy, the laughter in her voice now too, said, 'Hello Eddie! Come and join us!'

Chapter Two

He stood there dumbfounded for a moment, hardly able to believe his eyes. It was Cathy. It was not her presence there though that took him aback so much as her total lack of surprise at their meeting, that and her familiarity with her companions. The group's laughter was stilled now and the stocky young man with his arm around Cathy affectionately, looked at Eddie warily as though sensing an opponent. The other man just sat there, his great bulk leant back in his chair, a hand like a ham almost hiding the glass it held. Cathy, however, looked totally relaxed, as she sat between the two men with that protective arm around her shoulder.

Eddie stood uncertainly for a moment, wondering what on earth Cathy was doing there, how she had got there. Then, as she smiled and waved him towards the table with the glass held negligently in her hand, he walked hesitantly towards the table. The younger man was pulling out a chair for him now and, with what Eddie felt could be resignation, said, 'Yes, come and join us won't you?'

It seemed though that they had been expecting someone to join them, for the table was already set for four. It was a well laden table, with platters of meat and salad, bread and bottles of wine, and Eddie suddenly realised that he was hungry as well as thirsty.

As he took the offered chair there was silence for a moment, broken at last by Cathy who introduced him to her companions: 'Eddie,' she began, waving a hand towards the younger of the two men, 'this is my friend Idris, Dr Idris Bowen . . .' then with the same imperious wave of her hand towards the other man, ' . . . and his friend, David.'

As David nodded, Eddie sensed a look of recognition in his eyes as if they had met before. No, he thought, more like one soldier meeting another. The recognition was still there in the man's eyes as he picked up a bottle of red wine and raising it asked, 'A glass of wine, Eddie?'

Eddie didn't hear him for a moment for he was looking at Cathy who was sitting there still smiling at him happily, apparently completely unfazed by his surprise appearance. Suddenly aware that David was waiting for an answer, Eddie turned back to him. 'Oh yes, that would be fine, thank you.'

There was amusement now in David's eyes as he filled the glass that Eddie held towards him, then putting the bottle down, he raised his own saying as he did so, 'Iach i dda!' As the others raised their glasses, they too echoed the toast, whilst Eddie raised his and responded with, 'And good health to you all!'

There was a guffaw from David at this response, the amusement still there in his eyes as he asked, 'You understand Welsh then, Eddie?'

Eddie shook his head, and smiled as he replied, 'Only that bit! I've drunk with a few Welshmen before.'

David pursed his lips and, head on one side enquiringly asked, 'That would be in the army, would it, Eddie?' It was a statement though, not a question and Eddie just nodded, hoping this was not going to be a repeat of the driver's questioning.

David still looked as if he were awaiting confirmation so Eddie gave in at last, saying tersely, 'Yes, the Paras.' He left out the bit about the Regiment thinking it was all in the past tense anyway.

'Good mob, the Paras,' David acknowledged, still leaning back in his chair comfortably, confidently. Then said proudly, 'Welsh Guards I was!'

Yes, that figures, thought Eddie, senior NCO probably, but it was not a conversation that he wanted to pursue, so he just nodded and took a sip of his wine. As he put his glass down he saw Idris gazing at him with a professional eye, a doctor assessing a patient. Avoiding eye contact, Eddie turned his head away to look at Cathy, thinking as he did so, this must be the doctor who gave Cathy the methadone. He was still registering that fact when Cathy inclined her head towards him and calmly announced to the others, 'Eddie and I met at Tintern on my way here yesterday.'

Still not knowing the relationship between Cathy and the others, he just nodded in agreement, but avoided her eyes now as he thought: You forgot to mention the bit about the barn, Cathy! If she were aware at all of what he might be thinking though, she gave no sign of it as she smiled at him innocently.

Nor was this a subject that Eddie wanted to talk about either, at least not in the present company, so he changed the subject and asked Idris, 'Do you live here, Idris, or just passing through?'

Idris's brown eyes held that appraising look again as he paused before replying, 'I live here, I have a practice in a village nearby.'

Even in those few words Eddie could detect the sing song accent. With raised eyebrows he asked, 'You're Welsh too then Idris?'

Idris laughed but there was irony rather than humour in the laughter, as though a child had asked a silly question of an adult, then he said, 'With a name like Idris, what else?' He paused before adding slyly, 'You're English of course; with a name like Mortimer what else?'

Eddie just grinned as he agreed: 'Of course, what else!'

It almost killed the conversation stone dead but Cathy broke what could have been a difficult silence by saying brightly, 'Isn't any one going to eat? I'm starving!'

Eddie smiled to himself as he thought that she probably was, having been up since the crack of dawn. Cathy wasn't looking at him but instead was busy putting meat on plates and passing them around. David was sitting upright now, filling up glasses with wine, but Idris quietly put a hand over his glass. Cathy was passing a full plate to Eddie now but, wondering how he was going to pay for it, he put a hand up, saying apologetically, 'No Cathy, I'm fine, thank you.'

With a firm gesture of the fork she was holding she brushed aside his refusal saying firmly, 'Don't be silly, there's plenty here for the four of us!'

He didn't persist with his refusal, for having had no breakfast he really was hungry and the food looked tempting enough. It was only when Cathy pushed the salad bowl towards him that he remembered about the table having been set for four. He looked at Cathy as she served Idris. 'I hope I'm not sitting in someone's place, were you expecting someone?'

The other men smiled and Cathy, eyebrows raised, laughed. 'Why, yes! You of course!'

Incredulous now Eddie sat back in his chair as he asked, 'You were expecting me?'

Big David laughed as he said in high good humour, 'Pulling your leg she is Eddie, they always lay these pub tables for as many as they can hold!' To emphasise the humour of it all he leaned across and patted Eddie on the shoulder with that enormous hand of his.

It was David's turn to be surprised now though as, obviously in pain, Eddie clapped a hand to his shoulder, his face white. Immediately there was concern all around: David mortified that he might have hurt Eddie; Idris, all professional, was on his feet beside Eddie. Only Cathy remained quietly in her seat, not anxious it seemed to reveal that she already knew the cause of Eddie's pain. Nor how she knew!

A moment later Eddie was explaining it all to Idris: 'No! My shoulder's all right, really! It's just bruised, that's all it is.' It was not quite true but the last thing he wanted was this stranger conducting an examination here by the lock gate, doctor or no! He thought then of the methadone. No! He especially didn't want this doctor examining him!

As the colour came back to his cheeks and he reaffirmed that everything was all right, they all settled down again to eat their meal. As Cathy glanced at him though, Eddie was not entirely sure whether it was a look of commiseration on her face or one seeking his silence!

Unwittingly, he grimaced, thinking that all he had to be silent about was a one night stand with someone she had helped who needed help. It had not gone unnoticed though, for Idris was leaning forward and with concern in his voice, asked, 'The shoulder's still hurting then, Eddie? You must let me have a look at it!'

No way, thought Eddie, but he just smiled, saying lightly, 'No, it's all right, really! I'm just embarrassed at making such a fuss about nothing.'

There was a momentary look of disbelief on Idris's face but he didn't press the matter any further and Eddie gave a silent sigh of relief. In the silence that followed Eddie saw Cathy, fork to her mouth, glance at Idris as though she were wishing that he would insist but she didn't say anything. Then, her eyes softening, she continued eating and Eddie felt a pang of jealousy as he realised that Idris was more than just a friend to her.

He pulled himself up with a jerk. What on earth have I got to feel jealous about he thought, this is the chap who saved her from a drug habit, and me? She just helped me, that's all! He thought of the laughter and chatter there had been as he had walked along the canal bank towards them and suddenly felt as if he were intruding on a happy family party. He took a surreptitious look at his watch and saw to his surprise that it was already half past twelve, still half an hour before he had to get back to the lorry. Still half an hour, but he felt torn between staying there with Cathy, seeing that soft look in her eyes whenever she glanced at Idris and getting the hell away from them all. He picked up his wine glass and, emptying it in one gulp, dabbed his mouth with his napkin. He smiled, as he stood up. 'You'll all have to excuse me!' he said. 'It's been very kind of you all, but I really must go. I've got a lift to Ludlow and it won't wait for me!'

Cathy frowned as she held a hand out to him, palm down. 'No, stay Eddie and finish your meal! We'll get you to Ludlow . . .' She looked at the others for support as she added, 'Won't we?'

David though was just sitting there smiling non-committally as he stroked his black, drooping moustache. Idris too, was somewhat less than enthusiastic as with a polite smile he nodded his agreement before saying, 'Yes, of course, you must finish your lunch!' He paused, then said, 'There's a bus this afternoon that will get you to Ludlow!'

With a depreciating smile Eddie shook his head saying, 'No! It's been most kind of you all but I really must get on. Thanks for the lunch!'

They all got up now as he picked up his rucksack and, without thinking, carelessly slung it over his shoulder. He winced as he did so but was somehow pleased to see the momentary concern in Cathy's eyes. If he could see anything at all in the expression on Idris's face though it could only have been 'I told you so!'

As he turned to go Cathy, smiling now, said quietly, 'See you!'

He nodded. 'Yes, see you!' Then turning away he set off back the way he came along the canal bank. He had not gone far before he glanced back over his shoulder to see them all still standing there watching him, Idris and Cathy hand in hand. With a final wave he turned away, thinking with some regret as he did so that Cathy, like the Regiment, was in his past.

He did not go straight back to the warehouse where he hoped the lorry would be waiting for him but walked across a bridge over the canal towards the town. Lost in thought over the lunch-time's events he soon found himself in what seemed to be the town's high street. Suddenly he found himself sweating, his hands trembling. It must be the wine he thought for a moment, but even as the thought crossed his mind he knew really that it was not that . . . knew that he needed a fix.

Seeing a pub across the road, he crossed the busy street and went into the bar where he ordered a half of beer. Going to a table in a quiet corner of the bar, he put the glass down and fumbled in his pocket for the precious plastic bag of pills. He panicked for a moment when he couldn't find it in either of his jeans pockets, then remembered zipping up one of the rucksack's pockets after placing it there.

All fingers and thumbs in his haste, he eventually managed to retrieve it and, after a quick glance around the bar, popped a pill in his mouth and took a hasty swig of his beer to wash it down. He grinned then as he thought that Dr. Idris wouldn't have approved of that! He had a quick mental picture then of Idris and Cathy standing hand in hand by the table on the canal bank and thought, sod him, who cares what he likes!

He sat there for a few minutes sipping his beer as he tried to calm down, but all he succeeded in doing was picturing Cathy as she was in the barn last night with that soft look in her eyes as she had caressed his wound, wanting to take the pain away. He remembered her farewell after lunch then and finished his beer in one draught, almost slamming the glass down on the table as he thought, yeah, *see you!*

It was five to one by the time he got to the warehouse and the driver had just finished securing the canvas sides of his lorry. As he saw Eddie he looked at his watch then, with a grin said, 'Always tell a soldier, can't you? As my old sar'n't major always used to say, " 'Them's as keen gets fell in previous!" '

Eddie smiled. 'Yes, I know,' he replied. 'I think his brother was in my regiment!' It surprised him really that he could take the driver's comment with such equanimity. It must be the pill he thought, then it dawned on him that in a way it was probably relief, for he had found the lunchtime stressful. Cathy had seemed anxious; anxious perhaps that he should keep their secret. Idris had certainly been wary, his brown eyes always assessing; probably seeing yet another junkie; wondering too no doubt, about his and Cathy's relationship. David, whilst friendly enough on the surface, had been watchful all the time, as though he wanted to know more about Eddie before he was satisfied.

The driver walked around to the offside of the cab, saying, 'Climb aboard then, guv!'

Eddie shrugged as he did so, thinking again, sod them! He wouldn't be seeing them again anyway! As he settled himself in the passenger seat though, he found himself thinking with regret, no, nor Cathy either!

He was left to his own thoughts for a while as the driver concentrated on his driving whilst he got out onto the City Walls Road, then through the busy traffic onto the road that led north. That surprised Eddy and he asked, 'You're not going through Leominster then?'

The driver shook his head and said tersely, 'No! We'll turn west in a few miles. It's a bit shorter this way.'

They were on the open road before the driver spoke again to interrupt his thoughts: 'You had a good lunch then, guv?'

It startled Eddie, for he had been back at the canal-side again, watching Cathy smiling at him, seeing her with Idris's arm draped around her shoulder, feeling the pangs of envy all over again. 'What?' he asked.

'A good lunch, guv, was it?' the driver repeated. Then with a quick sideways glance he grinned. 'Yes! It must have been, you were miles away! Meet some girl, did you?'

Eddie gave a wry grin. 'Chance would be a fine thing!'

The driver snorted. 'What, a young feller like you? Why when I was your age and in the army . . .' he paused and left the rest to Eddie's imagination. After a moment he continued reflectively, almost regretfully, 'O' course it's different for me now, what with being married and having things like mortgages and so on.'

Most of the way to Ludlow seemed to pass after that with the driver regaling Eddie with the marital problems of the long distance lorry driver through most of which Eddie managed to doze, rousing himself to mutter an occasional sympathetic 'Really?' or 'Yes, it must be very difficult!' During a short break in the saga he consoled himself by thinking that at least it was a change from the Brain of Britain quiz on military service!

He looked at his watch, it was ten to two, must be nearly there he thought and looking around him he could see that they were already approaching the outskirts of the town.

As if reading his mind the driver glanced at him. 'Nearly there!' he said. 'Where would you like me to drop you off?'

Eddie shrugged. 'Oh, anywhere really!'

'Well, I'm going to an industrial estate,' the driver replied casually. 'Probably best if I drop you off after we cross over Ludford Bridge. Broad Street will take you right into the town centre then, that OK?'

Nodding, Eddie smiled. 'Yes, that'll be fine, thank you!'

Minutes later they were crossing over a bridge and turning right alongside the river bank. They had gone a couple of hundred yards before the driver could pull in. 'Back to the bridge, guv, then turn right, will take you into town!' He was obviously anxious to get away, so scrabbling for his rucksack and opening the cab door, Eddie got out quickly. On the ground now he looked up at the driver and said, 'Thanks for the lift, it's been very kind of you!' He was about to shut the door when he remembered: 'Oh, and about that drink?'

The driver, already getting into gear again, grinned. 'Shan't be stopping guv, got to get back to base!' Then, with a wave of his hand: 'See you!'

As Eddie shut the cab door he seemed to hear the echo of Cathy's words, but smiling, waved, thinking that it was most unlikely he would see either of them again!

Picking up his rucksack, he slung it over his shoulder, carefully this time, then set off to find the centre of the town and hopefully an accommodating jeweller's shop. He gave a rueful grin, thinking that he needed the money if he was going to sleep in a comfortable bed tonight. It did not take him long before he found himself in the town centre and, in no great hurry, he wandered around looking for jewellers' shops, discounting the ones that looked to him to be too flash. Eventually he found one that seemed to strike the right note with him.

The black painted woodwork had the owner's name in gilt lettering above the window which seemed to contain rather more old fashioned jewellery than modern lines. He hesitated a moment, feeling in his pocket to make sure the small velvet covered box was still there then, taking a deep breath, he opened the door. For a moment the loud ringing of the bell startled him but the elderly, grey haired man already behind the counter just smiled as he explained, 'Yes, it is a bit loud, isn't it? I'm working in the back room sometimes, you see! What can I do for you, sir?'

Taking the ring box from his pocket, Eddie opened it and placed it on the counter, saying confidently, 'I've got this ring that I thought you might be interested in.'

The jeweller gave him an appraising look over the top of his half rimmed spectacles without saying a word for a moment, then sighed as he looked down at the ring lying in its bed of blue velvet. He pursed his lips. 'Not a lot of demand for old rings these days I'm afraid!' Then, somewhat reluctantly, he picked the ring from its box, at the same time lifting his glasses on to the top of his head and placing a magnifying glass in his right eye. He twisted the ring this way and that as he inspected it thoroughly without saying a word. At last he put it back in its box and looked at Eddie straight-faced. 'It's gold,' he said at last, nodding as if to confirm his own assessment. Taking the magnifying glass from his eye, he added, 'Quite old too, but it's not just a ring, it's a seal.' He tapped the ring with his forefinger. 'That's the Mortimer crest, you see!'

Eddie agreed tersely, 'Yes, I know!'

The jeweller drummed his fingers on the counter for a moment and dropped his spectacles back into position, before asking, still straight-faced, 'Could I ask how you came by it?'

Eddie's eyes narrowed before replying brusquely, 'My father gave it to me! Been in the family for years!'

The jeweller nodded and smiled as if satisfied. 'Yes, that's fine!' Then, picking up the ring again he added, 'Well, if you'll excuse me for a moment, I need to take some advice before I can give you a valuation, it won't take long!'

As Eddie nodded his agreement, the jeweller walked quickly into the back room of the shop. He appeared to be talking to someone on the phone, but Eddie couldn't hear what he was saying. Whatever it was, it did not seem to take long before the jeweller came back behind his counter. He smiled apologetically. 'I'm sorry,' he explained, 'my friend isn't there at the moment, but if you care to wait, he'll ring me back in a few minutes.'

As Eddie hesitated, the jeweller smiled encouragingly saying, 'I was just going to make myself a cup of coffee, would you like to wait and have one with me?'

The man seemed to be taking so much trouble it seemed to be churlish to refuse so, a bit reluctantly, Eddie nodded and said politely, 'Yes thank you, I'll wait.'

He sensed a look of relief in the jeweller's eyes before the man turned and scuttled away into the back room again. He seemed to be taking some time to make the coffee and at last Eddie sat down on a chair by the counter, hoping to hear the telephone ring rather more than for the appearance of the coffee.

With his back to the shop door he was startled to hear the door bell's loud ringing, which served its purpose by bringing the jeweller scurrying out of the back room to stand behind the counter expectantly.

Eddie turned his head towards the doorway, to see a policeman standing there, the door now shut behind him. It was only when he spoke that Eddie registered the significance of his appearance. 'Sergeant Edmonds, sir,' he said briskly to the jeweller. 'You have a problem I believe, sir?'

Chapter Three

The bastard, thought Eddie, as he looked in surprise at the jeweller, he thinks I've nicked the ring!

The policeman still stood there in the doorway as he waited for the jeweller to reply, blocking any hope of Eddie making his escape. Not that he wanted to, he'd done nothing wrong, just wanted to flog the ring and be on his way. The jeweller avoided Eddie's eyes as he said quietly, 'Well, this gentleman wanted to sell me this ring, constable, and I just thought that I ought to check with you first.'

The sergeant looked Eddie up and down before answering: 'I see sir, is it on the list of stolen property you'll have, sir?'

'No, but it's worth . . . it's quite unusual, quite old, a seal of the Mortimers, the old Earls of March, not the sort of thing that's very often on the market and the provenance . . .'

The policeman interrupted and smiled understandingly: 'A bit iffy is it sir?' Evidently he had heard of the Mortimers. Turning to Eddie he asked, 'Could I have your name, sir?'

Exasperated, Eddie sighed. 'Yes, it's Mortimer, Eddie Mortimer!'

Expressionless now, the sergeant said, 'I see Mr Mortimer. May I ask how you came to possess the ring, sir?'

Eddie took a deep breath, trying to remain cool, polite, then said, 'Yes, as I told him,' he nodded towards the jeweller, 'it's been in the family for years. My father gave it to me.'

All understanding again, the sergeant smiled. 'I see sir. Your father then, Mr Mortimer, he'd have been the Earl of March, would he?'

It was then that Eddie lost his cool! 'If he'd been the Earl of March he wouldn't have been called bloody Mister, would he?'

If Eddie had lost his cool, the policeman had not. 'Just trying to establish the facts, sir,' he said quietly. Then asked reasonably, 'Do you have any proof of ownership?'

Eddie shook his head. 'None with me, my father's solicitor will have a copy of his will, it's probably mentioned in that.'

'No receipts, or anything like that?' asked the policeman.

Exasperated again, Eddie shook his head. 'I wouldn't, would I? It's probably a few hundred years old . . .' then said, with a nod towards the jeweller, 'you can ask him!'

Seemingly at something of a loss, the policeman paused before coming up with: 'Do you have any means of identity with you, sir?'

Exasperated by the whole frustrating business, Eddie ran his hand through his fair hair, then said, 'Identity, oh yes . . .' and reaching into the back pocket of his jeans, fished out his wallet. After shuffling a few bits of paper in it he pulled out a card and handed it to the policeman who, after studying it for a moment, jotted something down in his notebook, then turned to the jeweller.

'Well sir, the item's not on any of our lists of missing property and I have Captain Mortimer's details, so I can't see any reason why he shouldn't sell it.' He paused and Eddie gave a quiet sigh of relief but the policeman went on to add, 'I suppose you could check with the museum, but unless they've lost it without telling anyone I shouldn't think they'd be able to do anything more than confirm if it's genuine or a fake!'

Giving his hands a dry wash the jeweller glanced anxiously at Eddie, then, averting his eyes, he thanked the policeman, who smiled as he replied, 'That's all right, sir. Glad to be of help.'

He was already at the door as grinning, he turned towards Eddie saying, 'And goodbye Captain Mortimer, or is it the Earl of March?'

Eddie shook his head. 'No, I don't think so! I believe the last one's been dead for a few hundred years!'

The policeman grinned his acknowledgement: 'Yes, so I believe! Hope I don't have to see you again.'

There was something of resignation in Eddie's smile as he thought that that made a change!

As the shop door shut behind the sergeant, Eddie turned grim faced towards the jeweller. 'What the hell was all that about?' he asked angrily. Then, pointing at the ring which still lay in its box on the counter, he said, 'Don't I look respectable enough to have something like that? God, it's only a bloody ring!'

The jeweller just stood there for a moment, shame faced, hands clasped together nervously. Then, head on one side he said, almost pleaded, 'No, of course not Mr er . . . Captain Mortimer, it's just that we have to be so careful, so very careful, these days. Perhaps if you'd given me your name . . .'

Looking at the man standing there hunch-backed, his face lined and grey, Eddie's anger cooled, just an old man trying to stay the right side of the law, I suppose, he thought. He was silent for a moment as they both stood there looking at one another. At last, with a toss of his head, he said, 'Oh all right, forget it! Just tell me what you think it might be worth!'

A little more confident now, the jeweller adjusted his spectacles and picked up the ring to examine it once again. At last he replaced it carefully in its box and gave a little sigh; 'Well,' he said hesitantly, 'as I said, not a lot of call for old jewellery these days, I'm afraid . . .' Thoughtful now, he stroked his chin then pursed his lips, thinking, calculating whilst Eddie waited, thinking of his empty pockets.

At last, after what seemed to Eddie to be an age, the jeweller said as if reluctant to make an offer at all, 'Well I suppose I could let you have . . . let's say a hundred and fifty . . . but only because of our little misunderstanding, you understand.'

Eddie's face fell, after what he'd been told in London he had been hoping for at least two hundred, perhaps a bit more. He hesitated, thinking better than nothing, I suppose. Then he remembered the jeweller telling the sergeant, *'No, but it's worth . . . quite unusual . . . not the sort of thing that's very often on the market . . .'* 'No!' Eddie said firmly. 'It's not just old! It's an antique and it's worth more than a hundred and fifty, much more!'

The sorrowful look on the jeweller's face was belied by the calculating look in the eyes behind those half rimmed glasses. Shaking his head now, he reached out and, snapping the lid of the ring box shut, pushed it across the counter towards Eddie, saying firmly, 'No, I'm afraid not!'

Disappointed, Eddie picked it up and turned towards the door, wondering whether he would have any better luck at any other jeweller's in the town. As he put his hand on the door handle he thought, somewhat bitterly, that he didn't want to go through all that again . . . nor meet Sergeant Edmonds again either! That reminded him of the museum, perhaps they might be interested there!

As he turned the handle, he heard the jeweller call him, 'Ah, Captain Mortimer, just a moment!' He turned, to see the jeweller, hands clasped together, a conciliatory smile on his face.

Without taking his hands from the door handle, Eddie snapped, 'Yes?'

The jeweller gestured Eddie towards the counter, 'Perhaps in view of the circumstances I could stretch my offer a little further!'

Eddie hesitated, and walking slowly back to the counter, he asked tersely, 'How much is a little?'

All businesslike now the jeweller said with conviction, 'Two hundred pounds, Captain Mortimer, and that's a very good offer I can assure you, normally you'd only get its scrap gold value!'

Again Eddie shook his head. 'It would be worth more than that to the museum!'

The jeweller gave a confident smile. 'Not at the moment, Captain Mortimer, their budget for this year is overspent already!'

Eddie ignored that, saying with a shake of his head, 'I wouldn't accept less than two fifty!'

The jeweller hesitated then said, 'Now if you had proof of ownership . . .' he stroked his chin, 'even then . . .' he paused as Eddie fumbled for his wallet and pulled out a business card.

Putting it on the counter he snapped, 'That's my father's solicitor, he'll confirm it's mine!'

Minutes later Eddie was walking up Broad Street again, two hundred and fifty pounds the richer, looking for a decent pub: after the events of the afternoon he needed a drink. What he really needed of course was . . . well perhaps a methadone would do . . . it would have to, he didn't fancy trying to trawl around in this strange town for some sleazy dealer!

An hour later he strode confidently out of the pub and walked up to the Castle Square thinking that after he had a look at the castle, he'd find somewhere to stay for the night and plan. Plan where he was going to go from here, what he was going to do with the rest of his life, how he was going to kick the habit. Yes, he'd do that tonight, but now he was just going to enjoy the rest of the afternoon.

Walking through the main gate of the castle, he paid his entrance fee then went through to the outer bailey of the castle, surprised at first, not only at the size of the outer bailey but also at how familiar it all seemed. He shrugged, thinking that it was not surprising really, after all, it was not the first castle he'd seen. Traversing the outer bailey he crossed a wooden bridge over the dry moat and going through the gatehouse stepped into the inner bailey. He paused there for a moment, a feeling of disappointment sweeping over him at the incongruity of the wooden stage being erected in front of the great hall. He shrugged off the feeling, realising that the stage must be for the Shakespeare play the lorry driver had told him about.

As he wandered through the accommodation part of the castle and then up onto the Garderobe Tower, the feeling of familiarity grew. Standing there looking out over the River Teme and the river plain beyond he imagined for a moment that he was watching, waiting for

Welsh rebels to advance upon the castle. He smiled to himself, Welsh rebels! When had the Welsh ever threatened such powerful fortresses as Ludlow! What was it to him anyway? Such threats as Ludlow Castle had ever faced were ancient history. With a last look westward, he turned away and climbed down from the tower, following in the footsteps of many an ancient lookout who had looked across the Teme with more anxious eyes than his.

Despite himself however, the feeling of familiarity persisted as he walked back across the outer bailey and when he went into the gate-house where he browsed around the tourist shop there for a while, eventually impulsively buying a book about the Mortimers. As he walked out of the main gate he smiled at himself, thinking that with such profligacy, his new found wealth would not last very long. Clutching the book he had bought he went out into the town, deciding that he had better find himself somewhere to stay for the night.

That evening found him ensconced in a guest house he had come across in a side street. Not very grand he thought as, after a shower, he climbed into bed. Looking around at the room, he acknowledged that, even though it was all chintz and threadbare carpet, it was rather more comfortable than the barn he had slept in the previous night. He smiled to himself then as he thought of Cathy, but the smile quickly disappeared as he remembered her standing by the canal-side, holding hands with Idris. Thrusting the image from his mind, he picked up the book he had bought at the tourist shop and began reading about the Mortimers, the Earls of March. He had only read a few pages before he put the book down, suddenly remembering Idris commenting *'and you're English . . . with a name like Mortimer, what else!'* How on earth did he know that? thought Eddie, Cathy only introduced me as 'Eddie'! He worried about that for a minute or two, like a dog with a bone, but could find no answer.

Thinking at last that Cathy must have talked about him before he had met them, he put the thought aside and picked up the book again, but as he continued reading his mind kept straying to the strangely assorted trio. So much so in fact that by the time that he had got as far into the history of the Mortimers as 1400, when one of them had married Owain Glyn Dŵr's daughter, he again put the book down and switched off the bedside lamp.

Even though the bed was far more comfortable than the earth floor of the barn, it was a fitful sleep he found, disturbed by dreams of battles long since fought, of rebellion, sieges and royal intrigue. Throughout the night too, the faces of Cathy, Idris and David came flitting through his dreams as though to haunt him. *'You're English!'* Idris kept saying and

Cathy, smiling provocatively, kept whispering, *'See you!'*

It was five o'clock when he woke up, feverish, his hands trembling, his mouth like the bottom of a bird cage. He looked around the room, almost surprised to find that he was alone, that there was no Cathy or Idris there with him, smiling, taunting him.

Getting out of bed he made himself a roll up, but as he was about to light up, he saw the notice: 'No smoking!' Putting the roll-up back in the tin he walked across the room, switched on the electric kettle and made himself a coffee. As he picked up the cup and saucer though, they rattled so much that he could see that he needed more than just caffeine, much more than that!

It took a little while for the pill to work, but it did eventually. By then he was far too wide awake to sleep again, so he just sat up in the bed, back against the head rest, a cold cup of coffee in his hand, trying to plan the rest of his life. I must sort it all out he thought, I'm just twenty-six, I must sort myself out!

He sat there, trying to think, to plan, but his mind wandered as he thought of his life so far, of his time in the army, his service with the Regiment and then the fierce fire fight when he had been wounded and carried away lifeless by his men, those who were left. It was not the first time he had lived through it all again and now, as then, he broke out into a cold sweat as he relived the fear of it all. Not just the fear, but the guilt too, of having led his men into the ambush, seeing them fall in the hail of fire, of having survived himself.

That's what had started it all he thought, not the painkillers, but the guilt. That and not being able to live with himself whilst remembering the bodies he had seen lying there before finally, mercifully, passing out. His recovery had taken months before at last he had been able to use his arm again. The doctors had told him that it would never be the same, that he'd never regain its full use. He'd have been discharged from the service then had it not been for the court martial. It was months too, before that took place. Months of anguish during which he went over and over again the events of the raid, believing in his own guilt long before the court delivered its verdict.

Nor did he find any absolution when that was given, when he was found innocent of any blame, for he had already found himself guilty. Sighing now, he put the coffee cup on the bedside table, realising fully for the first time that that was the cause of his drug habit: He had passed a sentence on himself more severe than any court martial would have passed: self destruction.

He gave a wry grin. Yes, he thought, passed sentence and very nearly carried it out. Leaning his head back against the headboard, he sighed. Perhaps the court was right he thought, perhaps it was time for a remission of sentence. He sighed again, knowing in his heart that he had no appeal system that would ever fully overturn his own verdict.

As his thoughts drifted on, he thought of Cathy, wondering whether she would have been so sympathetic if she had known the cause of his wound. He smiled ironically then, sure that her friends Idris and David would have little sympathy for him. He closed his eyes, thinking that he could not really blame them. His eyes closed at last and the images blurred, his thoughts became hazier and hazier until at last he found, if not peace, at least sleep and a temporary remission of his guilt.

A motorcycle revving up outside woke him and, quickly alert, he looked around him, wondering for a moment where he was. Looking at his watch he saw that it was half past eight and he scrambled out of bed, breakfast in the guest house finished at nine!

Over breakfast he found that, despite the disturbed night, he had come to some conclusions about his future. The first was that, whatever the cost, he was going to kick the habit. The second was that he was going to find some sort, any sort, of job and from what he had seen of Ludlow this would be as good a place as any to start. He grinned as he put a forkful of bacon to his mouth, perhaps the jeweller needed an assistant! After breakfast he would scout around the town, carry out a reconnaissance. His fingers tightened on the fork as he thought, no, that's all in the past and the past was something he was determined to put behind him, had to put behind him!

Having told the landlady that he might want to stay another night, she agreed that he could leave his rucksack there whilst he looked around the town. A few minutes later he was walking down Broad Street again, wondering where he could start, where he could hope to find a job. His heart sank then, who on earth would want to take me on, he thought, an ex-soldier with no qualifications other than to kill, especially if they ever found out that he was a drug addict to boot!

If he was to survive though, he had to find a job, the few pounds he had got from selling the ring weren't going to last for ever! By ten o'clock he found himself in the street where he had found the jeweller's and frowned as he saw that there was some commotion outside the shop. Quickening his pace he got there just as two men came rushing out, one of them holding a small canvas bag. Through the open door he could see the old jeweller lying on the floor of his shop, blood trickling from his head onto the floor beside him.

For a moment he was back in the ambush seeing, not the jeweller, but his own men lying where they fell in pools of their own blood. It wasn't guilt he felt now, but an all consuming anger. Clasping his hands together he brought them down in a vicious swipe on the neck of the nearest fleeing thief and heard without pity, the crack of breaking bone as the thief fell to the ground without a cry.

He turned to pursue the other man, when the door of a waiting car opened and two men rushed out brandishing baseball bats. Facing them, arms spread out, daring them to attack, he moved towards the one on his right, weaving, his feet dancing lightly, ready to avoid the swinging club. As the first man rushed in to the attack, Eddie ducked his head aside, but only to find the second man's baseball bat come crashing down on his wounded shoulder. He let out a cry of agony as, knees buckling, he fell to the ground, his hand clutching his injured shoulder.

As his eyes glazed over, he saw her then as through the mist already enveloping him. It was Cathy, standing amongst the small group of onlookers, a look of horror on her face, she was frowning now, her hand stretched out towards him but though her lips moved he could not hear her call out to him nor even hear her speak at all.

His voice barely a whisper he called out to her, 'Cathy!' but his head fell to one side and her face disappeared from view. Then, as he tried to focus on her again, he thought he saw Idris standing beside her, his hand on her arm, holding her back. For a moment he heard a babble of indistinct sound, then it faded. Suddenly there was only silence, the light fading into complete blackness as the peace that had eluded him for so long finally embraced him like a lover's arms.

Clutching Idris's arm, Cathy looked up at him. 'Help him!' she said urgently. 'For God's sake, Idris, help him!'

The sound of a siren was getting louder as Idris put his hand on hers and patted it gently. 'The ambulance is almost here, Cathy,' he said quietly. 'The paramedics can be of as much help to him as I now, he needs to get to hospital . . . ' He looked at Eddie lying there, completely still, his face ashen white, then added quietly, ' . . . and quickly too!'

Cathy looked at him shocked. 'He'll be all right, won't he, Idris? I'll go with him in the ambulance!'

Idris shook his head. 'No, Cathy, not now. Best if we go and check up on him later, I know where they'll be taking him.'

Then, holding Cathy by the arm, he led her gently but firmly away. As he did so, Cathy, eyes streaming, looked over her shoulder, to see the paramedics loading Eddie and the jeweller into the ambulance on stretchers and then, sirens screaming, it was racing away again. 'He'll be all right, won't he?' she asked Idris again. Then the tears came once more as, without answering her question, he just patted her arm.

Chapter Four

Ludlow 1399

Robert the goldsmith stood in the spring sunshine outside the doorway of his shop off Broad Street and looked at the horse and cart still standing there, the horse nervously pawing the compacted earth of the lane. The carter should never have come down here he thought angrily, not with such a large cart. That was the cause of the accident and of the trouble it would bring, for trouble it would surely bring to someone.

The old goldsmith wrung his hands as he stood there, unsure for a moment of what he should do next, fearful too of the consequences when he broke the news to Sir Edmund's steward, Geoffrey de Lacey, at the castle. Yet tell him he must, for Sir Edmund lay close to death, it seemed, in the bed above the shop where he had been carried after the accident. Robert had already called the apothecary, but he knew that Sir Edmund needed the attention of a physician.

Old Robert pulled himself together. Yes, he must tell the steward, he thought, for Sir Edmund needed a physician and that right urgently if he were to live. Hunch backed, his leather apron still around his waist, he set off on his way to the castle as quickly as his old legs would carry him. A few steps took him out from the lane onto the cobbles of Broad Street and that slowed his progress, for he was still wearing the slippers he always wore in his shop.

Barely noticing the merchants' houses, all oak beams and white plaster, that lined the street, he hurried as best he could to the market square and thence to the castle that dominated the town, anxious to give his message and be relieved of the responsibility for Sir Edmund's life. By the time he arrived at the gateway to the castle though he was less sure of his errand, thinking that the bearer of bad news sometimes bore the brunt of the displeasure of those to whom it was given. An anxious frown on his face now, he thought hopefully that there was no fault that could be placed at his door. Indeed if there were fault at all, then it was the carter's and he was being kept safe enough in the back room of the shop, guarded by Robert's assistant. He shook his head as he hurried on, hoping that his worst fears would not be realised and that there would be no trouble over the accident to Sir Edmund.

Of course Robert had been to the castle before, for occasionally he had been called there to display his wares to the nobility, but this errand was far different and it was with some diffidence that he approached the burly man at arms at the gate-house. He need not have worried though, for the man at arms recognised him from his previous visits and, smiling, asked, 'Is your visit here today so urgent, smith, that you come to visit my lord in your workaday clothes? You could have saved your old legs the journey, for Sir Edmund is in the town!'

Puffing, the goldsmith gasped, 'I must see the steward! 'Tis about Sir Edmund I come! He lies close to death in my shop!' His message delivered, he leant back against the stone walls of the gate-house, panting for breath, his face grey.

Despite his great bulk and his chain mail, the man at arms showed himself to be a man of quick action and minutes later the steward was hurrying into the gate-house where the goldsmith was now seated on a wooden stool. He was a tall, muscular man whose fair moustache only served to emphasise his lantern jaw, his plain grey attire more suited to a cleric than the soldier he so obviously was. He glared at the goldsmith and there was disbelief in his voice as he asked, 'What's this news you bring of Sir Edmund, man? Close to death? Why, only hours ago he was fitter than you ever were in your youth!'

Urgently now, the goldsmith blurted out his message again: ' 'Tis true sir, on my oath 'tis true!' Then the fear was back and he stammered, 'There was an accident sir, I swear it was an accident and he was injured, needs a physician.'

For a moment the steward stared at him, his eyes calculating, then he said curtly, 'A physician is at your shop by now, or I'll have his head! Now you get back there and stay close by 'til I am satisfied that you had nought to do with whatever it is that's happened there this day!' He paused and there was a threat now in his voice as he continued. 'Yes, stay close by, for you'll never run so far my arm will not reach you!'

Ashen faced with fear now, the goldsmith nodded. 'Of course, sir steward! I dare not leave my shop, for thieves are ever anxious to gain entry there!'

The steward's lips curled, then he said contemptuously, 'Thieves, smith? They are your least of worries 'til this matter's settled!'

Turning on his heels he left the gate-house, leaving the goldsmith sitting there hands clasped nervously together, eyes raised to the ceiling thinking of what might await the carter when he met the steward. Old Robert rose from the stool and putting out a hand to the table to steady himself he glanced at the man at arms who stood there now unsmiling, obviously seeing the goldsmith in a new light: a possible offender, one with whom he might have to deal with in the way of all such men. Robert blanched, then averting his eyes, walked slowly out of the gate-house and through the town, fearful now of what he might find when he reached his shop.

He was not kept long in uncertainty for, as he reached the shop, it was to see an obviously terrified carter being led away, a man at arms on either side. His fear was not without cause thought Robert for Sir Edmund Mortimer was guardian of the young Earl of March and as such was virtually Lord of the March. To injure him, let alone cause his death, would lead to the carter's neck being stretched and not without some unpleasant preliminaries! His heart in his throat, he entered his shop, to find another man at arms at the foot of the stairway, barring his entry there.

'Is the physician here?' he asked. 'I live here, I must see what's happening!'

The man at arms, hand on sword hilt now and unmoved by his pleading, put his other hand on Robert's shoulder and pushed him back, then with eyes hard as flint said, 'No one goes up there 'til the physician's done his work.' He grinned, baring his discoloured teeth. 'And I have a feeling, goldsmith, that you'd better hope he does it well!'

Robert's stomach churned as he thought of the carter being led away in shackles. The mere thought of what the castle's dungeons might hold for him too, made him turn away to seek the temporary, illusory, safety of his work bench. He must have sat there for some time before an elderly man dressed in black, a white neckerchief at his throat, came tut tutting down the stairs, shaking his head all the way. The goldsmith listened anxiously as the white haired man spoke to the guard, but he could hear only the odd word, none of which made any sense to him. Then the man at arms was rushing, heavy footed, out of the door as though the devil himself was on his tail and within minutes four men were bringing a litter into the shop and up the stairs.

There were sounds of a commotion in the bedroom before, with many muttered oaths and cautions over the difficulty of it all, the litter was carefully brought down into the shop. There the men rested it for a moment, catching their breath, but the physician urged them on; 'Not a moment to lose!' he was saying; 'We must get him to the castle!' The men picked up the litter again, but not before the goldsmith could see the inert body lying on it, oblivious to all that was taking place. Poor Sir Edmund, he thought, then thinking of the strange attire the knight had been wearing wondered if it was indeed Sir Edmund! He looked again at the litter as the men carried it out of the shop, to see that a hand hung limply from the litter on a finger of which was a ring that he recognised immediately. It was the Mortimer seal that he had made himself only last year: so it was indeed Sir Edmund. Pray God he lives, thought Old Robert. Then, thinking of the carter being led away in shackles, pray God for both our sakes!

The lantern jawed steward was waiting at the gate-house when the litter arrived accompanied by an anxious looking physician. One look at Sir Edmund lying ashen faced on the litter and the steward's face clouded with concern. Turning to the physician, he asked tersely, 'Will he live?'

The physician motioned the litter bearers on with a wave of his hand and they continued at a trot across the wide expanse of the outer bailey towards the entrance to the inner courtyard. Only then did he look at the steward to reply almost petulantly, 'This is no time for questions that I cannot answer, sir steward! We must get him to his chamber with all haste!' With that he was hurrying after the litter and the steward, his feathers, if not his neat grey tunic, ruffled, hastened to catch up with him.

The news of the accident to Sir Edmund had obviously spread quickly for there were groups of people standing around the outer bailey talking in hushed voices as they watched their lord's progress in the litter. The steward turned to the man at arms by his side to say irritably, 'Get these people about their business, this is no holiday!' The physician may have charge of his patient, but the steward knew who was in command of the castle whilst Sir Edmund was sick!

As he caught up with the litter the physician, relenting it seemed, turned to him the steward. 'In truth, steward, I know not yet what ails Sir Edmund, he has some serious bruising but no broken bones. An old shoulder wound is suffused, as though he were hit there by the cart, but none of this could be the reason for such loss of spirit, I doubt not though that he struck his head in the fall. If such be the cause, his body will mend soon enough but it will take much time and patience if he is to recover whole in mind.'

They were crossing the bridge over the dry moat now and going through the gateway to the inner bailey. The steward, who had been looking increasingly worried as he listened to the prognosis, was frowning. Glancing at de Lacey, the physician, as if to safeguard himself, hurriedly added the corollary, 'All this, of course, is if we can rouse him from his stupor.' He looked across the bailey towards the chapel of St. Mary Magdalen and crossed himself before continuing: 'And that, as you well know, steward, is in God's hands as much as mine!'

Nodding, the steward also crossed himself but even as he did so he looked askance at the physician and there was quiet menace in his voice as he agreed, 'Quite so, doctor! It is but sad that He may not share the blame!'

There was a stiff silence between them as they hurried on for a few moments, then turning to the physician, the steward smiled but there was no softening of his eyes when he spoke: 'I must get me back to the gate-house, doctor, and leave you to your work, for I have business there with the carter.' The menace was back in his voice now as he added, 'With him perhaps blame may be more readily attributed!'

The physician did not reply, just averted his eyes, thinking perhaps that it would indeed be as well for the carter and himself if Sir Edmund were to recover whole in body and mind.

Geoffrey de Lacey rested his tall frame against the back of the chair in the guard room of the gate-house, drumming his fingers on the table as he waited impatiently for the carter to be brought to him. What on earth had possessed Sir Edmund to go wandering around the town without an escort, he asked himself. He shook his head in irritation at the thought that the knight had done it often enough before, had even been heard of drinking in a tavern there, for God's sake! 'Broadens the mind, man!' he had replied more than once when de Lacey had remonstrated with him. The steward thought of the trouble all this would cause him if the knight did not survive, perhaps even the loss of his own office as a new knight brought a favourite with him! Who might command here he wondered, not the young Earl, that was certain, he was but a child!

He brushed the thought aside as the heavily shackled carter was brought in by two men at arms. This was more certain stuff than his conjecturings! As the carter stood there at the foot of the table unwashed, unshaven, his tattered clothing hanging loosely about him, the steward remained silent and his narrowed eyes bored into the man, assessing him as he would have a horse.

Under his gaze the carter lowered his eyes, then, looking up at the steward again, tried to raise a hand as if to touch his brow but it got no further than his waist, held there by the weight of his shackles. The gesture registered with the steward, the man's been a soldier he thought. He almost smiled for a moment thinking: Good! He'll know how a soldier earns his pay!

It seemed that the carter, a heavily built man in his middle years, could bear the silence no longer, for with that ineffective gesture of his hand again, he spoke, his voice a pleading whisper, 'An' it please your lordship, it was an accident, I didn't mean the gen'man no harm, it was an accident!'

Unmoved by the flattery of the title, the steward listened in silence to the man's pleading, thinking, that's interesting, how does he know that he struck a gentleman. Not from Sir Edmund's dress it appears, or so the physician says! At last he spoke, an inflection of surprise there as he asked, 'A gentleman you say?'

More certain of himself now, the carter nodded. 'Of course, your lordship, I could tell by the way he carried hisself. He was clean an' he'd shaved hisself too . . . or been shaved more'n likely!'

Observant, thought the steward, then said abruptly, 'Who did you serve with?'

The carter looked surprised by the question and hesitated for a moment as if wondering how best to please his inquisitor. 'Serve with, my lord?' he repeated.

'Yes!' snapped the steward. 'Serve with! You were a soldier once, weren't you?'

There was a touch of pride there now as the carter's shoulders braced back but he hesitated before replying, as if anxious to give the right answer and aware that in these troubled times one's survival could depend upon for whom you fought. 'Twenty years, man and boy, I served the king,' he said at last.

'In the baggage train, no doubt!' the steward sneered.

The carter nodded. 'Aye, some of the time, your lordship . . .' Then said defiantly, 'But I carried my lance too, 'til I was wounded!'

The steward thought that seemed right enough, a lanceman relegated to the baggage train on injury, then following his new trade when too old to stand the rigours of war.

The carter had the bit between his teeth now though and anxiously tried to impress the steward, blurting out, 'Aye, my lord, served the king for twenty years I did, in France, Scotland and Ireland!'

'Silence!' snapped the steward. 'Just answer my questions, don't try and tell me your worthless life's story! How did you come to knock down Sir Edmund?'

The carter looked at him aghast, a look of fear in his eyes now, his voice a whisper again as he asked, 'Sir Edmund, my lord, I . . . I did not know . . .' then he fell silent.

'Just answer the question!' the steward snapped again.

Obviously the man knew of Sir Edmund well enough, knew now the enormity of his offence too, for he took a deep breath before he began his story. 'I took my cart up Broad Street, my lord, then turned off to deliver my load at the far end of the lane. It's a narrow lane, your honour, and I had a heavy load on board, so my horse was only going at a walk. I was just by the goldsmith's shop there, when I saw this gen'man was waving to a woman across the lane. Waving and calling out to her he was . . .'

'A woman, you say?' interrupted the Steward, eyebrows raised.

The carter nodded vigorously as he answered, 'Yes, your honour, it must have been someone he knew too, for he called to her by name.'

'By name, you say?' asked the steward. Mystified now, he wondered what woman there was in the town that Sir Edmund would know by name. He stifled a sigh, that must be the reason for Sir Edmund's excursions into the town alone he thought: a woman in some bawdy house there, no doubt!

From his silence now, the carter obviously thought that the steward's question was not rhetorical for he was nodding again. 'Yes my lord, he called her by name, I can hear him calling her now, "Cathy" he called, "Cathy!" ' He paused, then explained, 'Twice he called her, your honour.'

Exasperated, the steward sighed, before saying, 'Yes, I understand that. Now what happened then?'

'Well, my lord, the woman couldn't have heard him, though young enough she was, for she did not even turn her head, just walked on for a yard or two . . .' He frowned and fell silent as if not knowing what to say next.

Exasperated, the steward pressed him: 'And then what!'

Whilst the steward waited impatiently the carter was still frowning, thinking, unsure it seemed of what had happened next. The frown clearing at last, the carter continued: 'Well, it all happened so fast then my lord, but when the gen'man called her again I turned to him and saw him stepping into the lane without looking, almost under my wheels he went my lord . . .' there was a momentary pause in his tale before he added hastily, 'but he didn't go under them my lord, I saw to that! I reined up hard and hauled on my brake! Only walked into my cart he had, but I could see him lying on the ground so I looked for the woman, thinking that she might help, know who he was like, but she had gone your honour, just vanished she had. It was then I called the goldsmith, seeing as he might know who could help the gen'man.' He spread his hands open palmed as far as his chains would allow, before saying finally, 'It were an accident, my lord, as God is my judge, it were an accident!'

There was no trace of emotion on the Steward's face nor in his reply. 'He may well be your judge and that sooner than you think, unless Sir Edmund arises speedily from his bed!' Then, with a nod to the men at arms he issued a curt command: 'Take him away!'

There was a rattle of chains as the carter was led away. As he was led out through the doorway, he turned his head to cry out, pleading, 'It were an accident, my lord, an accident . . .' his cry was cut short and then there was only the sound of the men at arms' footsteps as he was dragged away.

Left alone the steward sat there stroking his fair moustache and thinking, still with some surprise, of Sir Edmund visiting the town's bawdy houses. Wondering too, if Sir Edmund did not recover, whether he might be given command of the castle himself, a knighthood perhaps. He sat there for a moment longer relishing that thought, then rising, he walked out of the gate-house and over to the great chamber block to see if the physician had succeeded in bringing Sir Edmund out of his stupor. He grinned as he crossed over the dry moat, if Sir Edmund had indeed been visiting a bawdy house, the stupor might not be all the physician would have to deal with!

As he strode across the inner bailey the eyes of the few people working or loitering there followed him, wondering no doubt as he did, what he would find when he got to Sir Edmund's chamber. Passing the chapel of St. Mary Magdalen he saw a few women hurrying into it. Going to pray for Sir Edmund's recovery he thought and, thinking as much of his own tenure in office as of Sir Edmund, he called one over to him. Loosening the drawstring of the leather pouch at his belt, he took out a coin and offered it to her. She was a young serving maid who often served at table in the great hall and she stood there timidly, evidently in awe of the castle's chief officer. Her pink cheeks flushed as she clutched her shawl tighter around her thin shoulders, the ends of a plain cotton scarf fluttering in the light breeze, but she made no move to take the coin. He smiled at her. 'Come, take it, Rose!' he said quietly. 'Take it and light a candle for Sir Edmund's recovery for me.'

Her eyes lit up as she reached out a hand to take the coin. 'Oh, I will sir, I will,' she said eagerly, then with a quick curtsy, hurried away to follow the others into the chapel.

He stood watching her go for a moment, and as her trim figure disappeared into the church he wondered why on earth the handsome young Sir Edmund took to wandering around the town with, no doubt, many such admirers so close to home! Then shaking his head he walked on to enter the chamber block and climb the stone staircase to Sir Edmund's chamber.

As he entered the room, the physician standing by the bedside looked up at him and shook his head slowly in answer to the unspoken question of the steward's raised eyebrows.

The steward sighed, no change then, not even nigh on two hours after Sir Edmund had been struck down! Why, he'd seen men struck down on the battlefield from apparently worse blows than that which Sir Edmund had suffered, only to rise and fight on! Running after some doxy and bumping into a cart! What a way to go, if go you must, he thought as he walked over to the window. Down below him the River Teme was placid, glinting in the spring sunshine with a few cattle grazing in the fields of the river plain, beyond. He turned his head to ask quietly, 'No change at all then?'

The physician came over and stood beside him and answered in a low voice, 'He stirred once, his lips moved, but I heard nothing. His pulse is strong enough, his breathing too, but still the stupor holds, I fear. He sweats, as though in the grip of some fever . . . which seems unusual,' he sighed. 'I've salved his wounds and tried to cool the fever with cold compresses, nought else can I do till he is with us once again.'

The steward looked at him steadily for a moment, then said, 'How long may that be?'

The physician returned his gaze before saying firmly, ' 'Til he is ready to return!'

The steward having no answer to that, looked around the room for a moment thinking how strange it was that this room he knew so well from his many talks with Sir Edmund there looked so different now. The sunlight still streamed in through the tall window, the wall hangings that covered the stone walls were still there, the high bed, the good oak furniture. All this was the same and yet it was all different. Suddenly he realised what the difference was, for now it had the smell, the feel, of a sick room.

Feeling a need now to get out into the open and breathe fresh air again, he turned to the physician. 'Stay by him doctor and watch him well.' He nodded towards the anteroom. 'The man at arms out there will get you anything, anything at all, you need. Aye and he will bring me word too, on the instant, of any news you might have for me.' With that he walked out of the chamber, anxious now to shed himself of the all pervading feeling of sickness

Chapter Five

Back in his own quarters, the steward, Geoffrey de Lacey sat thoughtfully drinking a glass of good red wine. Loyal as he was to Sir Edmund to whom he was esquire and owed his present station, he envied the knighthood that Sir Edmund held and yearned for such rank and station for himself. With the Welsh border lands being as peaceful as they were though and the knight's duty of keeping the marches secure for King Richard holding them both at Ludlow, he saw little hope of achieving his ambition. Now, were Sir Edmund not to recover, he thought as he sipped his wine, all that might change.

He grimaced, change indeed but not necessarily for the better! True he might gain knighthood, might even be made seneschal of Ludlow and hold it for the young Earl, another Edmund, were fortune to favour him. More likely though, the Mortimers would put one of their own in command. He sighed, that would leave him to seek preferment from some other lord and despite the ancient lineage of his name, he was unknown at court, had never even met the king.

There was a knock on his door and a man at arms walked in, an old retainer he knew well, one not used to standing on ceremony with any man, who announced in a gruff unmannered voice, 'The physician sent me to tell you that Sir Edmund stirs, sir!'

Roused from his thoughts, his ambitions, he rose with a wry grin on his long face now as he thought fleetingly of the bawdy houses of Ludlow. 'I never doubted it Evans! His stirring was the cause of all this trouble!' The man at arms looked at him blankly for a moment without understanding, then without a word led the way out of the Steward's chamber.

When they got to Sir Edmund's chambers, the man at arms stayed in the anteroom, leaving the steward to go on alone into Sir

Edmund's apartment.

The room was as Geoffrey had left it: airless, stuffy, with that all pervading smell of sickness still lingering there like a harbinger of death itself. The physician was still standing by the bed as though he had never left it, but Sir Edmund was sitting up in bed now, propped up by pillows, a clammy sweat about his forehead. The steward's eyes widened in relief and he smiled. 'Sir Edmund!' he said, but the physician raised a hand to silence him and there was no reaction at all from Sir Edmund, who only lay there, his eyes blank, unseeing.

The physician motioned the steward to the window and bending his head towards him, whispered, 'He is out of his stupor, thanks be, but his spirit is not fully restored and I doubt that . . .' he glanced quickly towards Sir Edmund, 'he hears or comprehends ought that we might say.' A glance towards the bed again, then he said, 'He is still feverish too and look, his hands shake as though with a palsy!'

Following his gaze, the steward looked towards the bed and he could see the knight's hands trembling uncontrollably as they lay on top of the blanket. The steward frowned as he asked quietly of the doctor, 'What ails him?'

The physician shook his head. 'Nought that I have ever met before, sir steward! Whatever it might be, it has nought to do with his fall!' The steward stood there, stroking his chin, wondering whether he should tell the doctor of the possibility of Sir Edmund visiting a bawdy house but quickly cast the thought aside. If the knight had caught a fever somewhere, he might have caught it anywhere.

Sir Edmund spoke indistinctly then and their heads turned quickly towards him and de Lacey heard him call again: 'Cathy!'

The steward heard him clearly enough but when the physician turned to him and asked, 'What did he say?' the steward shook his head.

'I don't know,' he replied, 'I heard him not!'

Even as he answered the doctor though, he was thinking, it's that damned woman's name again! Who in God's name is she?

There was a look of disbelief in the physician's eyes as he replied, 'Well whatever it might be, it is a good sign, an omen I believe of his recovery!' With that, he was ushering the steward from the room, saying as he did so, 'I must cool that fever again, give him a potion to clear the blood of his confusion!'

Without understanding a word the physician said, the steward nodded thinking as he did so, the man speaks a language beyond the understanding of a poor soldier! He was still thinking in the same vein as he stomped down the stone staircase. Now, if he tells me he has to cut off an arm or a leg or splint a broken limb, he thought, then that I understand! But all this talk of clearing the blood, then it's but the stuff of magic and beyond my comprehension. Often enough I've cleared blood, but as often as not it leads to death!

Arriving at the doorway of the chamber block he stood there irresolutely looking around the inner bailey, then shrugged his shoulders. The work of the castle had to go on, little thanks he'd get from Sir Edmund if there was ought amiss when the knight came out of whatever ailed him. Thinking that in any case, the physician knew well enough to inform him of any change in Sir Edmund's condition, he strode off about his duties.

So engrossed was he in these that it was evening before the steward thought of Sir Edmund's nephew, the young Earl of March and walked thoughtfully back to the chamber block. The Earl is but seven, or is it eight years old, thought de Lacey, too young at all events to be bothered with such matters: no doubt his nurse will have apprised him of such as he should know . . . or should have, he excused himself. His pace quickening now, he was soon climbing the stone staircase again only to find the Earl's chamber empty when he arrived there. He paused for a moment then with a sigh thought, well, whilst I'm here . . . and turning, went to Sir Edmund's chamber. He was at the door of the chamber when it opened to reveal the young Earl Edmund accompanied by his nurse.

The Earl looked at the steward, his eyes brimming with tears. 'You didn't tell me my uncle was ill, sir steward!' he complained petulantly. The tears came then and the nurse patted him on the shoulder.

'There, my lord,' she said soothingly, Sir Edmund will soon be better, just like the physician told you.'

Even as she said it her eyes were on de Lacey as if seeking his confirmation, his support. The steward nodded his agreement readily. 'Of course my lord,' he said, smiling. 'Nurse Mary tells you truly; a day, perhaps two and Sir Edmund will be out of his bed and riding with you again! Why,' he added gruffly, 'he's had no worse a knock than when you fell off your horse a week back!'

The steward's words seemed to reassure the young Earl for his face cleared, but evidently his fall was not something he wanted to discuss. With a hand to his eye to brush away a tear still lingering there, he turned to his nurse to say, 'Come Mary, I want to go back to my chamber now!'

Smiling in sympathy, the steward stepped aside to allow the Earl and his nurse to pass, but the smile quickly disappeared for, as the Earl passed, he looked up at de Lacey to say petulantly, 'You should have told me, sir steward!'

Geoffrey de Lacey just bowed his head in acknowledgement of the rebuke, thinking as he did so, the little brat should learn some manners, some respect for his elders! A pity he didn't break his neck in that fall last week! de Lacey grinned then, thinking that were that to have happened, despite the bond of kinship between the two of them, Sir Edmund's sorrow might then have been tinged with hope! He still stood there as he thought, Sir Edmund's no different from me, he must envy young Earl Edmund the earldom as much as I envy him his knighthood! Brushing the thought aside, he went on into the room, to see the physician standing, his back to the window, wiping his hands on a towel. The man looks tired thought de Lacey and, eyebrows raised as before, he asked, 'What news, doctor?'

The physician seemed in low spirits as he sighed and listlessly dropped the towel onto a chair. 'Little enough, I fear,' he said quietly. 'He speaks clearly enough now and then, but it is unintelligible to me. He is yet plagued with the fever and suffers the gripes it seems. He frowns a deal and seems to know not where he might be.' He stood there thoughtfully for a few moments then, with a wan smile on his lips, he added, 'I wish I shared the optimism you imparted to the Earl just now, for I fear that it will be many days before Sir Edmund rises from his bed!'

His words proved true enough for it was five days before, on another of his many visits to the knight's chamber the steward saw much improvement in the knight's condition. Sir Edmund was sitting up in bed when de Lacey got there and though his eyes were bright and there was some colour in his cheeks again, he gave no sign of recognition when the steward entered the room. Although the physician was smiling, he still looked tired, exhausted even and signalled the steward over to the window and stood there looking out over the Teme and the fields beyond. His head bent towards the steward now as he whispered, 'He is much improved, sir steward, but when I addressed him, as is only proper, as Sir Edmund, he did but laugh and whilst thanking me for my care of him, told me to call him Eddie!

The steward grinned. 'That's not like our lord and master. Pleasant enough he may be and often speaks too freely with the peasantry yet he is rightly conscious of his rank and station!'

Geoffrey de Lacey turned towards the bed to see Sir Edmund watching them, his eyes apparently bright with curiosity. They looked at each other in silence for a moment, a silence only broken when the knight, frowning now, asked, 'Who are you?'

The steward was taken aback at this abrupt question, and gave a sharp intake of breath before, frowning, he answered, 'Why, I'm de Lacey, my lord, your steward as ever!'

The invalid grinned. 'Now that's quick promotion! Only a few minutes ago,' he gave a nod towards the physician, 'he was telling me I was a Sir!' He swung his legs out of the bed and the physician went towards him, hand outstretched, but he was standing now, still grinning. 'It's been very kind of you all and I'm very sorry to have been such trouble . . .' then, tired after his exertion it seemed, he sat back on the bed and his hands fell back beside him. Looking up at them now, he said wearily, 'God, I could do with a drink!'

Amazed at all this, the steward looked at the doctor, an unspoken question in his eyes but the doctor was already hurrying to a cupboard. 'A little red wine perhaps,' he was saying, then added cautiously, 'with a little water.'

Handed the goblet, Sir Edmund drank greedily of the watered wine before looking up at them again, resting the goblet on his knee. His eyes clouded now, he asked, 'How long have I been here? What happened?'

Uncertain what to tell him, they looked at each other, wordless. It was the steward who spoke first, he coughed and tried to choose his words carefully: 'A few days, Sir Edmund. There was an accident outside the goldsmith's in the town and you were brought back here to the castle whilst the physician here took care of you.' He left out the bit about the knight waving to some damned woman, thinking, better to discuss that privily when he was well enough.

There was understanding in Sir Edmund's eyes now, and he nodded slowly. 'That's right! There were a couple of thieves coming out of the jeweller's and I tackled them!'

The steward remained silent thinking, better he remembers it like that, than being knocked down by a carter whilst calling out to some doxy! Hand to mouth, he coughed again before saying, 'Yes, of course my lord, perhaps it's best if you get some rest now, we can talk about it all again on the morrow.'

Turning now, he glanced at the physician and gave a slight shake of his head, before walking quickly out of the chamber. Thieves indeed, he thought as he walked slowly down the staircase, the physician will have to clear a lot more confusion from his blood before ought of Sir Edmund's talk makes sense!

Geoffrey de Lacey was a worried man that afternoon as he stood on Mortimer's tower above the curtain wall of the outer bailey. From his vantage point there he could see across the Teme and the fields beyond to the distant, blue hazed hills. He was seeing none of this however but only his own equally hazy future if Sir Edmund did not come to his right mind and that quickly too! The Countess Eleanor, Earl Edmund's mother and strong willed matriarch of the Mortimer family, was due at the castle any day now and he shuddered at what she might say and do if she found Sir Edmund in his present state. Sighing, he turned and made his way down to the outer bailey, thinking as he went that the damnable thing about it all was that there was nought he could do to help himself, or indeed Sir Edmund. Only the physician could do that and little enough success he had had thus far.

It was past the time of the midday meal the next day before his duties would allow him to visit Sir Edmund's chamber again. As he entered, he saw the knight sitting up in bed a bowl of broth in his hand, but the physician came quickly towards de Lacey and, taking him by the elbow, led him back into the antechamber. Irritably shaking off the physician's hand de Lacey asked curtly, 'What is it, man? How fares Sir Edmund?'

Black shadows under his eyes, the lines on his forehead etched deeper now, the physician shook his head. 'He had a most troubled night, sir steward, the ague and fever with him again. Delirium was there too, in which he seemed to talk of battles and cried out at times as if in pain!' He paused, then said more hopefully, 'This morning though the fever has abated somewhat, his mind seems a little clearer too and he did not demur when I addressed him, as is proper, as Sir Edmund.'

As the steward made to enter the chamber again, the physician stopped him with a hand on his forearm, saying quietly, yet with authority, 'It were best to leave him yet, sir steward and not add to the confusion his fevered mind yet suffers.'

The steward hesitated then turned and began to leave the anteroom, as he got to the door he turned his head to say, 'Let us both hope his confusion clears as the rising sun clears the morning mist, doctor, ere Countess Eleanor arrives!' His eyes boring now into the physician's, he added in a whisper, 'Pray God he does, for all our sakes!' With that he hurried off, his footsteps echoing on the stone staircase as he went.

The invalid had indeed suffered a troubled night, plagued as it was not only by a fever that drenched him with sweat, but with nightmares that seemed to last the whole night long. Images and sounds of battles raced before his eyes as he fought amongst strange warriors armed with even stranger, fearsome, weapons. It was only with the dawn, when he had felt a stabbing, burning pain in his shoulder that he had awoken, running with the sweat of fear, still clutching his shoulder and knowing that only the awakening had saved him from dying there on that strange battlefield.

He looked at the old, white-haired man standing by the window, amongst an array of bottles and basins and said urgently, 'My shoulder, look at my shoulder man, I'm wounded!' The pain easing then, he had taken his hand away, expecting to see it running with his life's blood and was amazed to see nothing there, his hand clean, if wet with sweat.

The old man smiled as he looked at him. 'I fear you've had a nightmare, Sir Edmund, that and the fever have brought back old memories, best left behind! The wound is an old one, where you were pricked by a lance I calculate. 'Tis well healed now and the anguish I saw there when you were first brought here has now been dissipated by my salves.' The doctor walked towards him and, as Sir Edmund winced in anticipation of what he might see, gently pulled the nightshirt aside. 'There,' he said, 'as you can see, just an old wound long since healed! Nought there for you to worry over.' With that he took hold of Sir Edmund's hand and raised the arm, moving it around in a small circle. 'You see, nought wrong, is there?'

To Sir Edmund's surprise he felt nothing, no pain, just a little embarrassment at feeling the old man's cool fingers against his own sweaty hand. As the doctor laid his hand back on the bed, Sir Edmund shook his head and confused now, unbelieving, said quietly, 'No doctor, it's fine!'

Resting his head back on the headboard he looked around the room, as familiar as though he had spent a lifetime there, yet oddly unreal. The doctor was looking at him thoughtfully and after a moment smiled and said softly, as if to reassure him, ' 'Tis not that old wound that concerned me, Sir Edmund, but the blow to your head you suffered when you were struck by the carter's wagon! These past few days you did indeed give reason for that concern. Now though you seem to have sweated out the fever and the ills it caused which bodes well for your recovery!' He nodded, as much to reassure himself it seemed as Sir Edmund, then continued: 'I'll help you to this chair here by the window whilst I have your linen changed.' He stroked his chin before adding, 'And then a little broth with perhaps a small measure of wine, eh?'

A little later, whilst the bed was being changed, Sir Edmund sat looking out of the window at the River Teme flowing softly by and the cattle grazing calmly in the fields beyond. The peaceful scene gave him a sense of permanence, of tranquillity, and eased the turmoil in his mind. This is reality he thought, all else was but a dream, a nightmare.

As he was helped back to his bed though he thought of the doctor saying something about a carter and a blow to the head, he frowned as he realised he could remember nothing of that. Back in bed, he was supping his broth when the door opened and he heard Geoffrey de Lacey talking with the doctor but their voices were hushed and he could not hear what they were saying. With a sigh he listlessly put down the empty bowl on the chest beside the bed and laid his head back on the pillow. His eyes slowly closed, and Sir Edmund Mortimer fell into a deep sleep.

Chapter Six

Over the next few days, Sir Edmund made rapid recovery, so much so that he was soon able to leave his bed, although as yet only to sit in the chair by the window. He was clearer in his mind too, with fewer and fewer lapses into the hazy miasma that had clouded his thoughts. Fewer too were the nightmares that disturbed his sleep and the incidence of the fever and trembling ague gradually became less frequent. As the knight's condition improved, the physician became less anxious, less weary too, now that he was able to get more rest during the night.

When Geoffrey de Lacey made his daily visit, Sir Edmund was able to talk reasonably now about the affairs of the castle, only becoming hazy again when the steward raised the subject of the events surrounding the accident. He became perplexed then, always saying, 'I remember not!'

On one such occasion, when the steward tried too hard to prompt his memory by saying with a sly smile, 'Oh you must remember, Sir Edmund! You were by the goldsmith's in the town, a carter passing there with his wagon and you called out to some doxy across the lane.'

Sir Edmund flushed and replied angrily, 'Some doxy you say! Think you I go a'whoring in the town?'

The steward flinched under his angry gaze. 'Why no, my lord, of a certainty, not that! 'Tis just that the carter thought he heard you call out to some woman passing by.'

Sir Edmund's eyes clouded, then shaking his head he said a little uncertainly, 'No, Geoffrey, I recall none of this.' Frowning, he asked, 'This carter you tell me of, where is he now?'

Sure of his ground, the steward answered firmly, 'Kept safe, my lord, till you are well enough to deal with him!'

Sir Edmund nodded. 'Good! I will speak with him!' He half rose then as if to put the action to the words, before slowly sitting back in the chair. 'Yes! I will speak to him . . . tomorrow.' Looking perplexed again, he rested his head back on the chair before repeating more firmly, 'Yes, I will speak to him tomorrow and hear what he might have to say.'

He was silent now, his eyes clouded, his brow furrowed in thought and the steward stood there, uncertain whether to go or stay. At last Sir Edmund looked at him and asked, his eyes clear again, 'Is there ought else you would have me deal with, Geoffrey?'

The steward almost smiled for a moment, thinking that the knight had 'dealt' with nought for over a week, then with a quick shake of his head replied, 'No, my lord, there is nought of great import.'

Sir Edmund waved a hand in dismissal. 'Then leave me now, Geoffrey,' he said and, as the steward turned to go, added more firmly, 'but I shall see this carter you told me of on the morrow!'

Climbing the stone staircase to Sir Edmund's chamber the next morning, the steward wondered whether the knight would remember any of that which had passed between them the previous day. When he entered the chamber he was surprised to find the knight standing at the window fully dressed. Not only was he dressed, but in his plum red tunic with its flounced sleeves, high necked cream shirt and matching hose he looked every inch the nobleman, to which the gold hilted sword belted about his waist gave added emphasis.

He turned as Geoffrey entered the apartment and, the tone of his voice matching his attire, demanded: 'The carter fellow, you have him ready?'

Unblinking, the steward answered readily enough, 'Yes, my lord!'

In fact when he had had the carter fetched from the dungeon that morning the wretch had not been fit to be seen by anyone, much less Sir Edmund. Geoffrey de Lacey's nose twitched as he remembered the prison stench, the filth, which had met him that morning when he had had the carter brought to the gate-house guard-room. Yes, ready enough now he thought, remembering the many buckets of water that had brought the carter to that condition. His voice revealed none of this though as he answered, 'Yes, my lord, he is in the gate-house guard-room!'

There was a touch of the old hauteur, arrogance, now as Sir Edmund turned, to say curtly, 'Good! Well lead on! Let us see what this man has to say for himself, hey?'

Leading the way out of the chamber, the steward smiled to himself, wondering what his lord and master would have to say when the carter told him about that damned doxy he had called Cathy!

As they walked through the inner and outer baileys the steward noted, indeed was almost surprised, to see that Sir Edmund walked as briskly and purposefully as was his wont. It seemed as if no trace of his illness remained. He nodded too as castle folk smiled and touched their hats as he went by, acknowledging some by name.

As they entered the guard-room the two men at arms, holding the prisoner by his arms brought him to some semblance of erectness. The carter was less odorous now than when the steward had seen him earlier that morning and though his hair was still damp and dishevelled, his clothing, such as it was, passed as being dry enough. Both it and he, it seemed, had benefited for the wetting. Nothing though, it seemed, had changed the pallor of his skin and if he had been frightened when the steward had interviewed him, it was nothing to the abject fear with which he now gazed at Sir Edmund.

As de Lacey looked from the carter to Sir Edmund he was surprised to see not anger on the knight's face but rather, he imagined, a flicker of recognition in the blue eyes. Strangely, the steward's heart lifted as he thought there's hope now, if Sir Edmund recognises the carter, he must be well again.

The brisk walk across the baileys seemed to have tired the knight though, for pulling a chair back from the head of the table, he sat down heavily. He just sat there for a moment without a word, just looking at the carter, those blue eyes boring into him as though he would see into the man's inner soul.

There was silence and all eyes were on Sir Edmund as he sat there, hands resting palms down on the table, just gazing at the carter. When he spoke at last it was quietly, reasonably, but all eyes swivelled onto the carter standing there in chains, pitifully anxious to please this nobleman, whom he had hurt. When he replied it sounded as though he recognised his life might hang in the balance. He had little to say though that the steward had not heard before but the steward smiled as he noticed that the carter put less emphasis on his tale about Sir Edmund calling out to the woman, for now it was just ' 'I heard you call to someone across the lane.'

Sir Edmund's next question registered with the steward however, thinking as he heard it, nought wrong with his memory now, it seems!

'I called to someone?' Sir Edmund asked, then continued, 'Did I call a name? Was it a woman?'

Frowning, the carter hesitated before he said at last, 'I don't rightly remember that, my lord.'

The steward interrupted impatiently: 'You remembered it well enough when I spoke to you! You said Sir Edmund called her Cathy.'

The carter shook his head, then said stubbornly, 'No, I don't rightly remember your honour! I remember my lord call out a name, or some such like as that, but I can't bring it back to mind.'

The steward's lips stretched thin as, flint eyed, he stared at the man. Ten minutes, he thought, just ten minutes it would take me to improve your memory! He said nothing however, just glanced from the man to Sir Edmund who, eyes clouded again, seemed as if he too had lapsed into loss of memory.

Smiling now, as though it were not only he who had imagined things, Sir Edmund averted his eyes from the steward and, suddenly alert again, pronounced sentence on the hapless carter.

'My steward tells me you served in King Richard's army, carter, and that you were wounded in his service . . . ' his hand involuntarily stroked his own shoulder. 'Were it not for that, less leniency you'd find with me, for your wagon is ill suited to such lanes. It is for that and not for my injury that I fine you one mark!' He nodded to the men at arms, saying firmly, 'Unshackle him!'

If the carter looked relieved, the steward was livid. He was still sore with the carter at the doubt he had cast on all the steward had told Sir Edmund of his accident.

The carter's pleasure at being set free was short lived however, for apparently he had suddenly realised the size of the fine Sir Edmund had imposed. Freed of his chains, he stood there rubbing his wrists where the shackles had chafed them, his eyes pleading as he looked at the knight.

'A mark, my lord?' he said, a whine in his voice. 'A mark! Why 'tis more than I ever earn by many a day's hard labour. Pennies is what I get, my lord, pennies! Aye and precious few of them, each one hard earned.'

The steward's eyes widened, obviously astounded by the carter's impudence and he watched as Sir Edmund sat back in the chair, his clasped hands on his lap. The knight sat there for a moment without speaking and when he spoke at last, it only served to irritate the steward even more.

'I gather you have been my unwilling guest these few days past . . .' Sir Edmund said with a smile of understatement ' . . .for what I judge to have been an accident caused more by ill judgement than ill will. I shall therefore remit the mark against your enforced stay, but for two days you shall use your cart at the steward's bidding.'

The carter's face lit up, overjoyed it seemed at such remission of his sentence. He touched his forehead, backing away from the table as he did so. Bowing his head now, he said humbly, 'Thank you my lord! God's blessing on you my lord!' One glance at the glowering steward though and his look changed to one of gloom, as if knowing that there would be many demands made upon his service during those two days.

The change in the carter's demeanour had not passed unnoticed by Sir Edmund and there was amusement in his eyes as, nodding to the men at arms, he told them, 'Take him away, and have him fed before he starts his labours, he looks as though his board has been but leanly spread these past few days!'

One of the men at arms touched the carter on the shoulder and nodding towards the door began to lead him out of the guard house. As the carter got to the door, Sir Edmund, his eyes narrowed, called after him, 'Carter!'

The man turned, a look of apprehension on his face, as though fearing that his good fortune was about to change for the worse again. Nor was his anxiety eased at seeing the frown on Sir Edmund's face and the eyes that bore into his own, stripping him of the veils of innocence. The worry was there in his voice too, as he replied, 'Yes, my lord?'

His eyes widened in surprise as the knight asked quietly, 'Do you ever take your cart to Worcester town, carter?'

Nor was he alone in his surprise, for the steward took a step back at the question, to look at Sir Edmund in apparent disbelief as if about to ask *'What on earth . . ?'*

Seemingly dumbfounded, the carter hesitated, then nodded slowly. 'But rarely do I go as far, my lord,' he replied. Then hesitating again as though fearing some hidden trap, he finally admitted, 'I did go there last week my lord, but 'tis a long journey for my poor old nag and the road . . .' his voice failed him and he just spread his hands, leaving the state of the road to Sir Edmund's imagination.

There was a distant look in Sir Edmund's eyes now as he almost whispered his reply, 'Quite so.' Suddenly he grinned as he added, 'With such a long journey on so rough a road, it is as well your arse is so well padded!' Then, with a wave of his hand he dismissed the carter and his attendant men at arms.

The steward watched as the heavily built carter, looking offended now, muttered, 'Aye, my lord,' then turned and followed his guards out of the gate-house. The steward glanced at Sir Edmund thinking, he knows the man! 'Twas that and nought to do with the carter's service with King Richard that led to his leniency today.

The knight was standing now, the amusement still there in his eyes and the steward realised that in his present humour, it would be pointless to remonstrate with him over the man's light sentence. It was as well, for Sir Edmund said briskly, as if recognising the steward's unspoken irritation, 'Perhaps the man's a fool, Geoffrey, but an honest one I have no doubt and no knave, I wager! He'll serve you well enough the next two days.'

The steward nodded reluctantly. 'As you say, my lord.' And there was a touch of iron in his voice now as he added, 'He'll serve well enough, indeed!'

Sir Edmund's eyes narrowed as he said firmly, 'Aye, he'll serve and labour for an honest day's work each day of those two days my sentence is upon him!' Then, his authority established, he softened and touched the steward lightly on the arm to say, 'Come Geoffrey, we must both be about our business, for the Countess Eleanor visits us tomorrow and she'll expect a tidy house!'

The countess was the relict of the late Earl Roger and mother of the young Earl Edmund, coming there to take the Earl and his younger brother, Roger, to Berkhamsted Castle, there to be brought up under King Richard's protection by Sir Hugh Waterton. Reluctant as he was to see the boy's visit end, Sir Edmund recognised that it was well for the boy, now in line to the throne as heir general, to dwell nearer to the king and thus more readily be educated in the ways of kingship.

Sir Edmund watched from the outer gate-house tower as Countess Eleanor's retinue entered the town. More like a royal progression than ought else he thought and indeed it was, for over two score knights, men at arms and lancemen formed her escort. It was a colourful procession too with the sun glinting on the polished armour, the chinking of harness and the light breeze ruffling the pennants borne by the lancemen's weapons. Many of the townsfolk lined the street to watch it pass by, their mouths agape at the knights in their armour and the chain mailed men at arms. Evidently the Countess was not one to take lightly her own security on such a journey. The main body of her train was followed by her baggage carts escorted by a dozen or so lightly armed servants, a few mounted, the remainder trotting on foot alongside the carts.

Turning, Sir Edmund made his way down to the main gate-house, smiling as he thought of his steward, worrying now no doubt both as to how all these people would be accommodated and at the cost of it all!

Geoffrey de Laccy was indeed worried and it showed on his face, in his words too, as he greeted Sir Edmund at the gate-house: 'Good God, my lord, your sister-in-law does not travel light! King Richard himself would have brought no greater a retinue than this!' Thinking then of the cost of it all, no doubt, he asked anxiously, 'How long will this tribe be with us, my lord?'

Sir Edmund grinned. 'Have a care, Geoffrey,' he replied, 'it is of my kinsfolk you speak! I doubt that the Countess will linger here more than it takes to rest herself after her journey, a week perhaps, I doubt that it will be more than that. I wager that the bare furnishing of our border fortress will make her yearn for the greater comfort of her own estates, more suited to her gentility.'

The steward looked at him askance, thinking, her gentility indeed! That was not a word she understood from all that he had heard of her! He opened his mouth to reply and perhaps it was as well that before he could there was a clatter of horses' hooves as the vanguard of the Countess's retinue entered through the gateway to the castle.

Minutes later the Countess herself entered, seated on a white palfrey and looking as regal as if she were indeed a queen. Not without some reason thought Sir Edmund. For had not her husband Roger, his own brother but so lately the Earl of March, been nominated by King Richard as his successor to the throne? Her own son, young Earl Edmund was now the heir general unless King Richard determined otherwise.

She was through the gate now, and taking off his befeathered velvet hat he made low obeisance before rising, to say with a smile, 'Welcome, sister, our castle here may not have all the comfort to which you are accustomed, but our welcome is warm indeed!'

With a nod, she replied graciously enough, 'Your hospitality is always welcoming, Sir Edmund.' Condescendingly she added, 'More so, than I feared one might expect in this wild borderland!' She straightened her back as though fatigued by the journey, then offering him her hand said imperiously, 'Come, help me down from this wretched horse! I will walk to my apartment, the roads you have here have nigh on killed me!'

Reaching up, he smiled as he helped her down from her side saddle, thinking as he did so, you should have a word with a carter I know of, my lady, he might have sound advice for you! She stood there for a moment, irritably brushing travel dust from her dress then straightening up stood there imperiously waiting for him to lead the way. Looking at her, he thought that her plain black dress embellished with only a heavy gold necklace made her a commanding figure. She seemed taller too, than he remembered, tall and thin. The scarf over her wide brimmed bonnet that held it in place against the breeze was tied under her chin making an oval of her face. The long nose and piercing blue eyes gave the pale face the look of a bird of prey. A determined woman, no softness there at all he was thinking when she interrupted his thoughts: 'Come, Sir Edmund, would you have me wait at your gate like some supplicant? Lead on, I pray!'

Smiling again, he apologised. 'Forgive me, my lady! I was lost in thought, impressed that you should ride when you could have been borne here more comfortably in a carriage!'

'What? More comfortable, tossed this way and that as the carriage lurched with each and every rut and bend in your damnable roads?' she replied acerbically. 'Come! I must walk my aches and stiffness away before I can rest!'

The banquet in the great hall that night was such as to satisfy even the Countess's regal aspirations. The great hall of the castle was full, every seat taken with her retainers, the castle's officers or the local gentry. There was music from the minstrels' gallery above the hall, whilst in the hall itself jesters and tumblers provided entertainment for the guests. The tables were well laden with fruit and wholesome bread and cheeses and there were ewers of wine and tankards of ale for all according to their station whilst servants scurried hither and thither with platters of rich meats all of which could well have adorned a king's table. Sir Edmund was anxious to show the Countess that his castle here on the wild borderland that she had referred to on her arrival, would not be outdone by the king's palace at Westminster!

Seated at the high table, Geoffrey de Lacey bit his lip, anxiously hoping that all went well at the night's festivities and worrying even more about the drain on the exchequer that all this would incur. He glanced across to where the Countess sat on Sir Edmund's right hand at the head of the table, disdainfully picking at her meal, and quite impervious to his concerns.

The Steward's ears pricked up as he heard the Countess tell Sir Edmund, 'We cannot linger here, much as we would wish Sir Edmund. A day, perhaps two, to rest us from the journey.' Her long nose lifted as she continued, 'The king's command brooks no delay in the Earl's arrival at Berkhamsted! A day perhaps two at most is all that we can spare.'

Praise be for that, thought Geoffrey de Lacey and one day better than two!

It was in the early afternoon on the second day however, that the

Countess and her retinue set out for Berkhamsted, this time accompanied by the young Earl Edmund and his brother. Brought up from an early age to know that tears were not for such as he, Earl Edmund's face was nevertheless a melancholy picture indeed as he sat on his richly caparisoned pony by Ludlow Castle's gate-house ready to embark upon this new adventure.

During the Earl's short stay at Ludlow a strong bond had formed between him and his uncle, Sir Edmund, who felt a pang of sympathy for the young Earl now setting off with his mother, to be left in the care of strangers in far away Berkhamsted Castle.

Sir Edmund waved as he watched the diminutive horse alongside the Countess's palfrey carry away the slight figure of the young Earl and turning to Geoffrey de Lacey asked, 'Why so long a face, Geoffrey? Be glad that Earl Edmund will remember you as a friend, for there goes our future king!'

The steward nodded. 'Aye, my lord,' he replied before adding with a grimace, 'but I fear we shall both be old men before he sits on the throne!'

Sir Edmund grinned. 'In these uncertain times, Geoffrey, for us to live to be old men may be a benison itself!'

Chapter Seven

Life was peaceful enough at Ludlow Castle as spring turned to summer and Sir Edmund gradually regained his health both bodily and mentally. One day in June he and Geoffrey de Lacey were sitting at table in the great hall, lingering over a glass of wine after their midday meal, when a messenger entered. Sir Edmund's eyebrows rose as he saw that the man, the dust of a long journey about him, wore the king's device of a white hart on his tabard and wondered, as the man walked hesitantly towards them, what news he brought from the king. He was not left long in doubt for the messenger was beside him now and bowing handed him a parchment scroll, saying, 'My liege lord, King Richard bade me bring this to you with all haste, Sir Edmund!'

Untying the red silk ribbon that held the parchment scroll, Sir Edmund saw by its seal that it was indeed from the king.

Geoffrey de Lacey had edged closer to him now, looking wide-eyed, hopefully, at the parchment as he asked, 'What news, my lord?'

The letter did not take long to read and when he had finished, Sir Edmund turned to de Lacey, a look of disappointment on his face. 'The news is as it ever is, Geoffrey! Fresh rebellion in Ireland and the king hastens there with all his power. We are, as ever, enjoined to stay at home and guard the marches well.'

The steward tossed his head, then said bitterly, 'Aye, as ever, my lord, when honour might be found in Ireland!'

Sir Edmund gave a smile of resignation. 'If fortune favoured you, honour indeed might be found in that misbegotten island, Geoffrey, and but little else, for it is a poor place and you'd find no booty there!' He waved the parchment. 'At all events, our duty's here and 'tis here that we must do the king's bidding.'

Nodding, the steward sighed. ' 'Tis a pity my lord that duty but so rarely brings renown!' A toss of the head again. 'Guard the marches! Why, all's been quiet here these many years!'

Sir Edmund laughed at his steward's disappointment. 'That's the truth, Geoffrey, but a king must guard against that which might never happen or, taken unawares, he might lose his crown!'

Seeing the steward still not convinced he said quietly, 'Hopes of great honour, great rank, do not always materialise, Geoffrey, even when they appear within one's grasp! Think on Henry Bolingbroke: already an Earl himself, he was heir to the greatest magnate in the land, John o' Gaunt, Duke of Lancaster. Did he inherit though, when the great man died this past February? Why no! For the title and all that great estate, all that power, ran through his fingers like so much sand, when it was confiscated by the king on John o' Gaunt's death!

Geoffrey de Lacey frowned and interrupted dismissively: 'Yes but all his misfortune was inflicted by himself. It was his involvement with the Lords Appellant that first caused him to lose the king's favour. Fortunate indeed he was then to keep his head upon his shoulder, Gloucester and Arundel were not so lucky! Why, he was only exiled to France over that brawl with Lord Mowbray, his fellow Appellant!'

Sir Edmund gave him a knowing smile. 'Truly said Geoffrey, and then his exile was for but six years. But why think you did the king extend the period of that exile to one of life, when John o' Gaunt died?'

The steward shrugged. 'Why, to make it equal justice with Lord Mowbray's exile, I suppose.'

Sir Edmund sighed as he shook his head. 'You have much to learn about the politics of kingship, Geoffrey! The king was guarding his borders as we must guard them here!'

Geoffrey de Lacey looked mystified as he asked, 'Guarding his borders, my lord?'

Sir Edmund nodded. 'Aye, borders,' he repeated, then added in explanation, 'or more properly, the balance of power in his realm. Do you think that King Richard could let Bolingbroke, a man no doubt disgruntled over the Appellant affair and his exile, to return to his Lancastrian estates and all the power they represented? Return there when not only disgruntled over that affair and his exile, but moreover in lineage to the throne. I think not Geoffrey, and that is why Bolingbroke's inheritance was confiscated, his exile extended.'

There was silence after that for a moment, the steward sitting there frowning, Sir Edmund smiling quietly like a tutor well satisfied with his lesson.

Sir Edmund said thoughtfully, 'Aye, Geoffrey, honour on the field of battle sometimes brings rank and rank its power and privileges but possessing them may be seen as a threat to some and therein lies the danger! Whilst we sit here o'er long at our meal, no doubt Henry Bolingbroke thinks on these things.' He grinned as he added, 'We though, have not the luxury to sit here and think, for we must be about our duty and guard the march! Quiet it may be on the marches now but the temper of the Welsh is ever unpredictable.'

The next few weeks passed by uneventfully as Sir Edmund waited to hear news of the king's progress on his campaign in Ireland. During those weeks he often thought of Henry Bolingbroke and his father, John of Gaunt. The Duke was much like me in many ways he thought, for he was a younger brother of the Black Prince, the eldest son of Edward III and thus it was that Richard gained the crown. A year after his son the Black Prince was killed in battle back in 1376, King Edward also died and the ten year old Richard of Bordeaux, was crowned King Richard II! Yes, so much alike we are, he thought, my brother Roger dies in Ireland and his son, young Edmund, a lad just six year's old, dons the ermine mantle of Earldom and has the prospect of a throne to boot! Whilst I, he thought with more than a touch of envy, remain a knight with nought but that which I hold for young Edmund!

Thinking of his nephew brought the image of the lad to his mind and the envious thoughts were driven away by the picture of the innocent child for whom he held the castle. Seeing in his mind's eye again the despondent young Earl as he left for Berkhamsted and an uncertain future, he was left feeling only sadness and pity for the young Earl. Suddenly he smiled, God's blood, he thought, Geoffrey would give his right hand for what I have and hold!

One afternoon nearly a month after the Countess had taken the young Earl away, Sir Edmund looked up in surprise as the steward burst unceremoniously into his chamber. His eyebrows arched and he asked somewhat curtly, 'What news do you bring so urgently that you have no time to knock upon my door, Geoffrey?'

The steward flushed at the rebuke and breathlessly replied, 'A messenger, my lord . . .'

Sir Edmund sighed. 'A messenger! What, does he bring stale news of the king's campaign in Ireland?'

There was a hint of triumph in the steward's eyes as he paused, then shook his head. 'No, my lord, he comes not from Ireland, but from Northumberland, from your brother-in-law Harry Hotspur!'

Sir Edmund was clearly taken aback by this information for it was seldom indeed that there was such urgency of communication between

Harry Hotspur and himself. There was the sound of footsteps on the stone staircase now and the steward smiled as he asked, 'Shall I bring him to your presence, my lord?'

Irritated at the thinly veiled sarcasm, Sir Edmund snapped, 'Of course man, get him in here!'

As soon as the man entered the room it was apparent to Sir Edmund that he was near to exhaustion, something that had already been signalled by the weariness of his footsteps as he had climbed the staircase. He swayed now as he stood in front of Sir Edmund, who turned quickly to the steward to say curtly, 'A goblet of wine for the man, Geoffrey, before he falls!' Then to the messenger, 'What news do you bring from Northumberland?'

The messenger, already reaching for the proffered goblet, said in a voice that was a mere croak, 'Fearful news, my lord!' then gulped greedily at the wine

Sir Edmund stood up, his face flushed with anger, as much directed at the steward as at the messenger, saying curtly to de Lacey now, 'You should have brought him here fit to tell his tale for God's sake, Geoffrey!'

The man had lowered the glass now though and Sir Edmund turned to him, asking, 'What is this "fearful news" that you have you brought?'

'Why sir,' replied the man, who seemed to have recovered somewhat, ' 'tis of rebellion that I speak!'

Astonished, Sir Edmund and Geoffrey de Lacey said in unison: 'Rebellion?'

The messenger looked fearful himself now as he repeated, 'Aye my lord, rebellion, though I do but bring you my lord's message.'

Sir Edmund understood the man's fear, the penalty for rebellion was to be hanged, drawn and quartered, enough to make any man tremble at the mere thought.

Whilst he might understand the fear, it was even more urgent that he should hear the message, so he demanded, 'Get on with it man, who the devil is it that rebels?'

'Why my lord,' replied the messenger in more measured tones, ' 'tis Henry Bolingbroke! He landed at Ravenspur but a few days back with a force brought there in three ships from Boulogne. As he marched on Lancaster his force grew 'til it was indeed an army, my lord!'

Sir Edmund and the steward looked at each other, eyes widening as the man told his tale, then Sir Edmund spoke quietly, 'He has come to regain his inheritance, Geoffrey!' he sighed in relief. 'That need not be rebellion!'

The messenger nodded, then continued, 'Aye, so many said, my lord, until he sent word to my lord, the Earl of Northumberland.'

His patience waning, Sir Edmund said with growing irritation, 'Do I have to wring your message out of you, like blood from a stone, man! What word did he send to your lord?'

Stony-faced the man spoke again, hesitantly as if not anxious to utter the words of treason, 'He sought my lord the Earl's aid, sir, to wrest the crown from King Richard!'

If Sir Edmund had been able to take the news of Henry Bolinbroke's return from exile with some equanimity, what the messenger had just said destroyed all that. He knew too that it had destroyed the peace they had known on the borders for the past few years. No man remained untouched by rebellion, no matter on whose side he fought.

He knew though that the man's errand had not yet been fulfilled and he had a feeling of foreboding as he quietly asked the messenger, 'What answer did the Earl give Bolingbroke and why have you ridden hard this far?'

The messenger gulped. 'Why, my lord, the Earl and my lord Henry Percy have joined him with their power and . . .' he hesitated again, then blurted out, 'and they would have you join them too!'

Sir Edmund did not just have a sense of foreboding now, it was all pervading, enveloped him, for he knew that whatever his decision, there would be no turning back. Whatever he decided there could be only success or utter defeat!

His face pale and suddenly looking older than his twenty-five years, he looked at the messenger then turned to Geoffrey to say, his voice a whisper now, 'We must think on this, Geoffrey, aye, think hard indeed!' He nodded at the messenger. 'The steward here will have you taken to your quarters where you may recover from your journey, whilst we ponder on the burden of your message and give you honest answer for your lord when we have so deliberated.'

A minute later Geoffrey de Lacey reappeared, anxious it seemed to hear what his lord and master thought about the portentous message he had received, the answer to which could well change their lives dramatically. The steward found Sir Edmund standing by the window gazing out towards the distant hills, lost in thought.

The steward smiled. 'It seems my lord,' he said cheerfully, 'that Henry Bolingbroke was not prepared to suffer the loss of his estates and now seeks bigger game whilst King Richard is away!'

Sir Edmund looked at him thoughtfully for a moment before saying firmly, 'This is no deer chase, Geoffrey, and were it so the game that

Bolingbroke hunts rightfully belongs to my nephew, the Earl Edmund!' He paused and as the steward flushed at the reprimand, said, 'Yes, not only is Earl Edmund designated as the king's heir general but he has stronger rights by virtue of lineage than Bolingbroke, for he is descended from Lionel, Duke of Clarence, King Edward's second son.' He continued with dismissive emphasis: 'Bolingbroke's father, John o'Gaunt, was the third son.'

Evidently diplomacy was not the steward's greatest strength, for frowning now, he queried, 'But is he not heir general for that his lineage is through the female line, his grandmother Philippa, and therefore Bolingbroke's claim the stronger?'

'That matters not!' snapped Sir Edmund. 'He has been designated to succeed!' Forefinger to his lip now, he was silent for a moment, before saying, 'All this talk of lineage is of less consequence than that King Richard is our undoubted king. Were we to join my sister's husband, Hotspur, not only do I rob my nephew of his rightful hope of kingship, but I take up the sword against my liege lord.'

It seemed the steward was not swayed by these arguments for he said persuasively, 'Henry Bolingbroke is no fool my lord, he would not embark on this venture lightly, nor yet without promise of support from magnates other than the Earl of Northumberland. Richard is away in Ireland and no doubt will be met on his return by Bolingbroke with all his power. If the rebel prevails and wins the crown, what then? He will surely remember those who offered him cool welcome on his return from exile!'

Sir Edmund looked at him as though he were Lucifer tempting Eve before the Tree of Life. 'Is this how you would find your honours, Geoffrey, your preferment? By siding with a rebel?'

Geoffrey de Lacey smiled. 'Why no, my lord, I do but put the devil's case! My sword stays here,' he tapped its scabbard, 'until you tell me to draw it, be that gainst king or usurper!'

His hand rubbing his chin, Sir Edmund looked at his steward steadily for a moment, then reached out and slapped him on the shoulder, to say, 'Well said, Geoffrey! Let it rest there the while, now is a time for deep deliberation for by tomorrow's light I must have an answer for Harry Hotspur and his father!'

Sir Edmund stood on the Garderobe tower of Ludlow Castle looking out towards the Welsh hills wondering whether King Richard was even now crossing the Irish Sea to challenge the audacious Bolingbroke. Wondering too which magnates had already joined the rebel's banner.

Undoubtedly the knights and retainers of his great Lancastrian estates would support him and that, together with the powerful Earl of Northumberland already being pledged to give him aid, meant that he would indeed be strong enough to challenge the king. He sighed, to challenge yes, but to prevail?

From what the messenger had said, it seemed that Bolingbroke was already marching towards Cheshire, for it was there and in North Wales that Richard had his power base and no doubt to where he would head on his return from Ireland. Sir Edmund smiled, that would be a convenient place to rendezvous with whichever side he chose to join! He knew that he could quickly muster some three thousand men, even five thousand given a little more time. A force that could well tilt the balance in such a confrontation. He gave a wry smile, thinking that had he but time he could perhaps strike a profitable bargain with Richard . . . or with Henry; but there was no time!

In a matter of weeks, perhaps even days, the fate of Richard and Henry would be decided. Not only their fate, but that of those who chose to join one or the other. Looking at the hills made hazy by distance he wished to God that he could see the future more clearly than he could the hills, could see which way the balance could best be tipped. He knew that his duty, loyalty, lay on the king's side and thus with his nephew the Earl. On the other hand, if Bolingbroke prevailed, then the Earl, whilst having lost all hope of kingship, would still be Earl, whilst for himself there would only be the new king's displeasure for not having gone to his aid!

He sighed, trying to weigh the potential displeasure of Bolingbroke against the certainty of punishment by King Richard if Bolingbroke were to be defeated and he had not supported the king. The sun was sinking beyond the hills, the night air chilled and he had still failed to resolve the imponderable when at last he went down from the tower to his chamber thinking that this was a matter to be slept on. Sleep however was not an ally to him, for all night he tossed and turned as he went over and over the problem that he had failed to resolve up there on the tower. Images of a reproachful Earl Edmund, of an angry King Richard and a menacing Bolingbroke peopled the night. His sister and her husband, the impetuous Hotspur, were there too, his sister imploring him to help her husband. The imperious Countess Eleanor was there at the last berating him for betraying her son the young Earl. When finally he fell into a troubled sleep it was to see himself lying on a bloody battlefield with the victors marching off, triumphant. Strain as he might though he could not see whether their banner bore the king's white hart or Bolingbroke's Lancastrian rose.

He felt only gratitude when sunlight streaming through the tall window of the chamber at last aroused him. Perhaps though it was the loud knocking on his chamber door that had brought him back to consciousness. As he sat up, the bed in disarray, Geoffrey de Lacey entered the room. The steward smiled and, as if pre-empting a rebuke, said apologetically, 'You did not answer my lord and so I thought you might already be about the castle!'

Sir Edmund shook his head and, still half asleep, replied, 'No, Geoffrey, 'twas late before I slept at all and even then it was but fitful sleep I had!'

The steward favoured him with a sympathetic smile. 'Aye my lord, you had much to think on, of that I have little doubt!'

It was not until they were seated in the great hall, breaking their fast, that the steward asked the question that had obviously been on the tip of his tongue since he had awoken Sir Edmund. He began somewhat hesitantly: 'Do you call upon the knights who owe the Earl their homage to muster their men, my lord?'

Tactfully, he had not put the important question as to whether Sir Edmund had decided to support Henry Bolingbroke. Sir Edmund looked at him without speaking for a moment, thinking as he did that so arraying his force would give him the opportunity to act without having made a final decision. He nodded before saying firmly, 'Yes Geoffrey! We must send out an array to the knights Devereux, Whitney, de la Bere and Clanvowe immediately! Arrange for messengers to go to them this morning. I want them mustered and ready in all respects to march at my command by two days hence!'

Since the knights all held their castles as tenants of the Mortimers, the Earl was their liege lord and Sir Edmund as his guardian could with all right order the array.

With raised eyebrows the steward asked, 'Two days, my lord? They will be hard pressed to meet such an array!'

Sir Edmund brushed the comment aside. 'For long enough they have managed their estates without having to meet their feudal duty, 'tis time they paid their due! Tell them I will brook no delay, or they will pay their forfeit!'

The steward nodded. 'Aye my lord. What then? Do we support Bolingbroke, or rally to the king?'

That was the question that Sir Edmund had thrashed around all night. Thrashed around but thus far without resolution. He avoided giving a direct answer, saying instead, 'I calculate Bolingbroke and King Richard will join battle near Chester. We shall march there with our forces . . . when the time is right. We must be prepared though for a speedy response for any call for aid! In the meantime I shall send men, experienced in the art of war, to reconnoitre and bring back news of ought that transpires there.'

The steward nodded as if in agreement but asked doubtfully, 'Does time permit such delay before we cast the die, my lord?'

Sir Edmund looked at him sharply and there was irritation in his voice as he replied: '*We* permit delay, Geoffrey? If there is delay at all, it is mine, for it is I who have to weigh such things in the balance and upon my head the blood guilt of those of our men who fall . . .' The image of the body strewn battlefield he had seen in his dream flashed before his eyes as he added, ' . . . whichever cause we aid!'

Seeing the torment in the knight's eyes now, the steward asked hesitantly, 'What . . . what will you tell Hotspur's messenger, my lord? He says that he must depart today.'

'Tell him?' asked Sir Edmund innocently. 'Why, I shall tell him that I have arrayed my power and shall march on Chester in good time to meet his good lord there!'

The steward's eyes lit up. 'We march on Chester to give aid to Bolingbroke then, my lord?'

Sir Edmund shook his head and gave a quiet smile. 'That I have not yet decided upon!' Then he added dryly: 'Yet I have no doubt that if we march on Chester we shall undoubtedly meet Northumberland there, either in his vanguard . . . or the king's!'

The steward raised his eyes ceilingward, then with a sigh said, 'But we . . . you must decide, my lord!'

Sir Edmund smiled, but his voice was sharp enough as he answered the steward: 'True indeed, Geoffrey, *I* must decide! Too many men will shed their blood needlessly if I hasten to make the wrong decision.'

An hour later as Geoffrey de Lacey watched the Northumbrian messenger ride smartly out of the castle's main gateway, he wondered what Hotspur and his father would make of the ambiguous wording of Sir Edmund's message. Nearby, his hand casually resting on his sword hilt then raised in farewell salute to the messenger, Sir Edmund frowned as he pondered over the same question.

Nor were they alone for the outer Bailey seemed full of people, with news of Bolingbroke's rebellion having quickly spread after the messenger's arrival. The castle was in many ways like a village, where someone's secret was everybody's news. Men at arms, archers, lancemen, servants and womenfolk were all there, serious faced, as though wondering what the messenger's departure portended for them and whose hopes of life he took with him too!

* * * *

One man who had not waited in the castle for the Northumbrian messenger's departure was one of the Mortimers' Welsh archers. His indenture having expired the previous day, he had left the castle and the Mortimers' service earlier that morning and now stood leaning on his longbow in the market square as the messenger left the castle. Of an age with Sir Edmund, the archer's stocky build and muscular arms matched well the cut of his chin and set of his shoulders, which told all that he was no man's servant. That was true also of his apparel, for his plain leather jerkin now bore the arms of no lord. He was a free man and rather than renew his indenture with the Mortimers had decided to seek service in North Wales with Owain Glyn Dŵr, for he had been told that his unknown father had hailed from that part of North Wales.

He turned his head as he heard the clatter of hooves and saw the messenger ride out of the main gate. Beyond the gate he caught a glimpse of Sir Edmund and the steward and as he did, gave a toss of his head, thinking that he was well out of there. From what he'd heard it seemed the knight was as yet barely recovered from his accident. If indeed there was to be rebellion it was as well to have fit men to lead you, whichever side they chose to support. Aye, he thought, as well out of there, for in rebellion there was little quarter given and even less booty to be gained. Slinging his bow across his shoulder, he turned and headed for the Dinham Bridge across the River Teme knowing that did he linger in the square, he might yet be pressed back into service with the Mortimers. Idris the Archer was on his way to Wales.

Chapter Eight

Whilst Sir Edmund waited for his men to return with news from Cheshire, Geoffrey de Lacey, eager to join in the inevitable battle between Henry Bolingbroke and the king, was becoming increasingly impatient. Each day he pressed Sir Edmund ever more urgently to set out with all his knights and soldiers. Such was his impatience that he seemed to care little which side Sir Edmund chose to join, although himself favouring Henry Bolingbroke. Each day, however, Sir Edmund bade him be patient until they gained news from Cheshire.

Four days after the Northumbrian messenger had ridden off, Sir Edmund and the steward stood on the Garderobe tower watching for the return of the men Sir Edmund had sent to Cheshire when de Lacey turned to him to say urgently, 'Time is fleeting, my lord, and still no news, we must act now!'

'Why, Geoffrey?' asked Sir Edmund a little cynically. 'Do you fear the battle will be joined and you not there to gain your knighthood? We must have intelligence before we march or your shoulder may be tapped harder with the sword than you may wish!'

His face flushed, de Lacey replied angrily, 'I fear that not, my lord!' Then pointing to the northwest added, 'Even whilst we stand here, history is in the making there, are we not to be a part of it?'

Sir Edmund smiled before saying dryly, 'History can wait a little longer for our part, Geoffrey!' He frowned, then added quietly, 'We must be sure!'

'Sure, my lord?' asked the steward impatiently.

'Aye, sure!' replied the knight. 'By now my nephew sits vulnerably in Berkhamsted, a pawn between a king and he who would be one.' There was a tortured expression on his face as he continued, 'My sister too, is she not vulnerable if Bolingbroke's rebellion fails, wedded as she is to Hotspur who marches at his side? I must be sure, Geoffrey, beyond all doubt, so I may use my good offices to protect them both, whoever wins this battle you would have us join.'

Evidently de Lacey's eagerness to join the fray was not so easily quenched for he replied adamantly, 'We have no choice my lord, for fight we must! Richard and Henry both will say, "he who is not for me, is against me". We cannot be friend to both, but I doubt not that Bolingbroke shall win, for you will know that he is well favoured by many magnates for his piety and his learning. He has travelled far, learnt many tongues and is an able knight who has well used his skill at arms: did he not fight with honour alongside the Teutonic Knights in their Baltic Crusade?

'Why must we wait for news, my lord? Travellers have already told of how greatly his army has been increased by the many lords who join his banner and of his fast footed advance on Cheshire. Nor, by all they say, has his advance been in anyway impeded by the little resistance he has met thus far.'

Sir Edmund snapped icily, 'I shall not risk my kin nor yet my men on traveller's tales, Geoffrey! We wait!' With that he turned and stomped angrily down from the tower to his chamber leaving the steward standing there, his hands spread wide in his exasperation.

Whilst at Ludlow Sir Edmund delayed making his decision, elsewhere in the kingdom events were moving apace. Henry Bolingbroke was indeed gaining increasing support whilst making a triumphant progress through the middle of England. Nor was he meeting great resistance in his speedy advance and when he arrived in Cheshire, even King Richard's ardent supporters there fled before him.

By the time Henry arrived in Chester, it became irrelevant whether Sir Edmund took his relatively small force to join the rebel. Irrelevant except perhaps for the favour he might have gained. Whilst Sir Edmund hung back out of loyalty both to the king and to his own nephew Earl Edmund, King Richard had no such restraints. Rather, borne out of the necessity for his own survival on the throne, he left Ireland in all haste to meet and challenge the would-be usurper. It was a brave attempt and no one could accuse Richard of cowardice, for the force he had taken with him to Ireland was far smaller than that which Henry now commanded. It was all too late however, for if he had had any hope of defeating Henry it would have been at Ravenspur on the Humber when Henry had first landed.

It was on the morning following the steward's outburst to Sir

Edmund on the Garderobe tower of Ludlow Castle that one of the experienced men at arms sent out by the knight came riding into the castle, his horse all lathered from his hard ride. By the time he had reached the gate to the inner bailey, Sir Edmund and the steward were both anxiously waiting for him on the drawbridge over the dry moat.

As the man at arms reined up, the sweat glistening on his horse's flanks, its breath like steam in the cool morning air, the man's gloomy face and his despondent demeanour told all that he did not bring good news to Ludlow. Without even waiting for him to dismount, Sir Edmund asked urgently, 'What news, man?'

The man at arms remained silent for a moment, as though reluctant to impart bad news to his lord. Then, as Sir Edmund opened his mouth to repeat his question, the man at arms shook his head and anticipated him: 'Bad news I fear my lord, there was a battle near the Welsh town of Flint and the king, o'erwhelmed by Lord Henry's greater army, was defeated there.'

Sir Edmund's face paled at the man's terse report whilst alongside him, the steward rolled his eyes skywards in silent exasperation. Shaken by the news, Sir Edmund asked in a hushed voice, 'What of the king, did he survive?'

Dismounted now, the man replied, 'Aye my lord, the king survived but I know not for how long. Some say that, captured by Lord Henry, he left the field a prisoner, but I learnt not whither he was taken.'

Solemn faced, Sir Edmund quietly dismissed the man, then turning to the Steward, said with a sigh of relief, 'At least the king is safe, Geoffrey!'

All hopes of knighthood dashed, the steward snorted. 'Safe my lord? He is a prisoner and for how long the king?'

'He is alive and our anointed king, Geoffrey,' stated Sir Edmund flatly before adding: 'Henry Bolingbroke may have won the battle and thus regained his Lancastrian estates by duress . . .' he paused, then said hopefully, ' . . . yet he is no regicide!'

Geoffrey de Lacey, who was looking thoughtfully at the man at arms now wearily leading his horse away to the stables, turned his head to glance at Sir Edmund before saying softly, 'I pray that that is so, my lord . . . for Earl Edmund's sake!'

Angrily now, Sir Edmund snapped, 'Henry is no regicide!' Then turning on his heel, stalked briskly towards the castle's main chambers on the far side of the inner bailey.

He had a bitter taste in his mouth as he looked out of his chamber's window, wondering what was happening to Henry Bolingbroke's prisoner, the king. Surely he thought, if Richard rescinds his confiscation of the Lancastrian estates and restores them to Henry, all will be well. His face clouded though as he wondered how the king might hold his crown with Henry having thus shown his true power in the realm. Pray God he does, thought Sir Edmund, for in that lies the young Earl's safety.

An air of tension prevailed in the castle in the days that followed, with all there wondering what dire news the next visitor to the castle might bring. Uncertainty gave rise to rumour but there was no firm news although some gossip had it that the the king had been taken to the Tower of London. Rumour growing on rumour, it was even bruited abroad that he was held there awaiting execution, though few believed that tale.

Often enough anxious eyes were cast up to the Garderobe tower, for Sir Edmund could be seen there, pacing to and fro atop the tower for hours. Up there in his solitary eyrie, Sir Edmund worried over Earl Edmund's precarious position and how he might be best protected. Were Henry somehow to depose King Richard, how would he then regard another, more legitimate, claimant to the throne, one well known to be Richard's heir? More importantly how would he use him?

'Twere better had I supported Henry even at the cost of a broken oath of fealty, he thought bitterly. As he looked northwards in his pacing it brought his sister to his mind, at least Elizabeth is safe, he thought, for Hotspur fought for Henry. His mind ran on, trying to find consolation. Yes, Elizabeth is safe and Cathy too . . . he stopped dead in his pacing, a bewildered look in his eyes as he thought, Cathy? Who is Cathy? His eyes cleared, as he remembered the carter saying something about him calling after some woman and he smiled to himself, the carter would have said anything to get himself out of trouble!

He turned to go down the stairway to the inner bailey and there, in the dim light of the stairway the fleeting image of a woman came to his mind's eye, a young dark haired woman with surprisingly blue eyes, her moist lips parted in a provocative smile. Clutching the handrail tightly he stopped there for a moment, beads of perspiration on his brow and something inside him wanting to cry out to her, but she was gone . . . again.

Shaking his head in bewilderment, he went on down the staircase and into his chamber wondering what had made him suddenly imagine having seen this woman, whoever she might be, wondering too, why he had thought that she had gone again! Still wondering about that he fell into a troubled sleep, for the nightmares were back again and with them came the fever too. Flitting always through his tortured dreams of bloody battles, of leading his men into deadly ambush, was the figure of a slim young girl. Always too, as he reached out and called to her she smiled, saying tantalisingly in a voice that was almost a song, 'I can help you!' Then, like the wraith she had to be, she was gone.

The noisy clash of arms in battle was so great that it brought him to sudden wakefulness and, finding sunlight streaming in through the window, he sat up in the bed, sweat streaming from him. Strangely, the noise of battle was still around him though and gradually it dawned on him that it was the sound of someone hammering on the chamber's door. His throat dry, rasping, he called out 'Enter!'

The steward came into the room, looking as gloomy as he had been indeed the last few days. There was concern in his voice now though as, frowning, he asked, 'Is all well, my lord?'

'Well enough!' Sir Edmund replied curtly, as he swung his legs off the bed, anxious not to allow de Lacey the satisfaction of saying, I told you so! Then cocking his head at the steward he said, 'From the way you nearly beat my door down, Geoffrey, you must have news for me!'

The steward nodded, then stated sombrely, 'Aye, my lord, though not good news I fear! A messenger from the Countess Eleanor has arrived but minutes since, to tell you that Henry Bolingbroke has taken the king from London to his own castle at Lancaster and that she fears for the young Earl's safety!'

Wide-eyed in horror, Sir Edmund gasped, 'To Lancaster?' Then shaking his head: 'That is bad news indeed, Geoffrey!'

Looking perplexed, de Lacey asked, 'Why so, my lord? The king was held prisoner in London's Tower, is it so different he now languishes in Lancaster?'

'Therein lies a whole wide world of difference, Geoffrey! Do you not see that? Whilst the king was being held in London, I was sure that did the king but rescind his confiscation of Henry's inheritance, all would be well and he would keep his crown. Henry holding him now in Lancaster is evidence enough that the king refused him that concession. 'Tis that, or else that Henry seeks a bigger prize and will indeed be satisfied with nought else but the crown itself!' Sir Edmund paused. Then, his brow furrowed in his anxiety, continued, 'And how can he gain that whilst Richard lives?'

Geoffrey de Lacey shrugged, then head on one side, replied, 'You said yourself, my lord, that Henry is no regicide but how can Richard reign when Henry has defeated him in battle. How can he reign when magnates from across the realm supported Henry in the king's defeat?'

Sir Edmund had no answer to that question nor, it seemed, did anyone else for there was an uneasy peace in the land over the next few months. With or without the king's approval, Henry Bolingbroke appeared to have regained his Lancastrian estates, whilst the king remained incarcerated in Lancaster and the question of who wore the crown seemed to be in limbo.

Messages from the Countess Eleanor were encouraging enough though: the young Earl Edmund, it appeared, was still safe in Berkhamsted Castle although there was a stony silence from Northumbria and Sir Edmund could only assume that all was well with his sister Elizabeth now that the rebellion was over.

This uneasy peace continued as summer gave way to autumn and the trees alongside the Teme below Sir Edmund's chamber first changed from green to russet gold, then gradually shed their leaves. A cold wind was blowing flurries of fallen leaves around when a messenger arrived again bringing news that sent an even colder shiver down Sir Edmund's spine.

Geoffrey de Lacey was alongside him when he read the letter from the Countess, and as he came to its end, he shared the concern that the Countess had evidenced. Nor could he shield the anxiety he felt from the steward, for it was there in his eyes for anyone to see.

'What is it my lord?' asked de Lacey anxiously, for the news was obviously of some import.

Wordlessly, Sir Edmund handed him the letter to read. As he came to the end, de Lacey looked at Sir Edmund wide-eyed, his mouth half open, his face a picture of astonishment, before handing the letter back to Sir Edmund without a word. There was incredulity in his eyes, his voice, when at last he asked, 'The king has *abdicated*, my lord?'

Sir Edmund nodded. 'It seems so, Geoffrey, though I would not have believed it were that letter not in the Countess's own hand! She is not one to mince her words, nor yet exaggerate!' Sighing now he added, 'At least the king still lives, though I wonder what pressure Bolingbroke placed upon him before he thus gave up the crown?'

If de Lacey was shaken by the news, he was not so subdued by it as his lord and master, for with a thin smile he replied, 'Why, much the same as that placed upon Richard's forebear, Edward, the second of that name, that caused him also to abdicate, my lord!'

Sir Edmund looked at him askance for a moment, then realised that he had but spoken the truth, for some hundred and fifty years before, Edward II had also abdicated after being defeated in 1326 by his estranged Queen, Isabella and her lover Roger Mortimer.

He gave a wry smile. 'You were wrong then, Geoffrey, history was not in the making up there in Flint, it was but being repeated!'

* * * *

It was undoubtedly a feat of arms and indeed shrewd strategy that only some six weeks after landing at Ravenspur, Henry Bolingbroke had succeeded in regaining his confiscated estates. There was also an element of opportunism in his seizing on that early success to defeat King Richard in North Wales and become the de facto ruler of England. A living king, even one held as prisoner, makes poor company for a de facto ruler providing, as he does, a focus for renewed support and it was a problem that Henry had had to resolve.

It took months rather than weeks, however, for him to persuade a reluctant King Richard to abdicate and then present his own somewhat tenuous claim to the throne to Parliament. So it was not until the middle of October 1399, some four months after returning from exile, that Henry was anointed king as King Henry IV with all the traditional pomp and ceremony. Some felt that it was a good omen of clemency for Richard that Henry, Earl of Monmouth, the new king's son, carried the Sword of Mercy at his father's coronation.

In Ludlow Castle, Sir Edmund Mortimer hoped that this would prove to be true. Hoped it would be true also for that other claimant to the throne, the young Earl of March. The interregnum following Richard's defeat had indeed been an anxious time for Sir Edmund, concerned as he was not only for his nephew's claim to the throne, but increasingly for the young Earl's safety. So far, his fears had been shown to be unjustified, at least as far as the boy's safety was concerned, for he still stayed at Berkhamsted untouched, it seemed, by the momentous happenings elsewhere in the realm.

Sir Edmund had not attended the coronation, but was not alone in that, nor was his rank such as to make his attendance imperative. Time enough to pay my homage when needs must, he thought now, as he mounted his horse in the outer bailey ready to set out on a day's hunting.

Nearby, de Lacey, already mounted, gazed at him with calculating eyes, but averted them when Sir Edmund turned to him.

Sir Edmund smiled thinly, for he had seen the look in the steward's eyes and wondered how far he could now trust the ambitious de Lacey. Was it possible that his own lack of enthusiasm for Henry's enthronement, his loyalty to Richard, might be used to further the steward's ambition? He pushed the thought aside, it was something that he would have to deal with, but it could wait.

He was about to order the hunting party to set off, when a rider came through the castle's outer gate-house and seeing Sir Edmund, came riding smartly towards him. From his livery, Sir Edmund knew that he came from the Countess Eleanor at Wigmore and his heart sank as he wondered what news the man brought. Touching his helmet in salute, his face revealing nothing, the messenger said, 'I bring you word from the Countess Eleanor, my lord.'

Repressing a sigh, Sir Edmund took the offered parchment scroll and thanking the man he began to read it sitting there on his horse. Out of the corner of his eye, he saw the steward walk his horse slowly towards him.

The letter was brief and, as always with the Countess, to the point and by the time the steward was at his side Sir Edmund was rolling up the parchment again.

'Good news, my lord?' asked the steward smiling innocently, head on one side.

Sir Edmund shrugged, then, without emphasis, replied, 'The king has taken Earl Edmund into his wardship, Geoffrey.'

Geoffrey de Lacey smiled. 'Then that is good news indeed, my lord!'

Straight-faced, Sir Edmund nodded. 'Aye, good enough.' Then turning to the messenger said, 'Thank your noble lady for her letter and tell her that I share her pleasure that Earl Edmund is now safe in the king's wardship.' He turned to de Lacey, 'Geoffrey, see this man is fed and well rested before his leaves tomorrow!'

Whilst the steward was busy arranging for the messenger's care, Sir Edmund wondered whether he should continue with the hunt, for Countess Eleanor's letter had not been as bland as that which he had conveyed to de Lacey. Rather she had been even more concerned now for her son's safety as a ward of the man she described as 'the usurper'!

Smiling to himself, he thought that that was a letter best burned when he had the opportunity, certainly not one to be shared with de Lacey, over whose loyalty he was now beginning to have reservations.

By the time de Lacey was remounted though, Sir Edmund had decided to continue with the hunt believing that there was little that he could do that demanded instant action. It was a somewhat dispirited hunting party that returned that evening though, for the game had proved elusive. Nor had Sir Edmund, his mind more on problems other than those of the hunt, shown his usual enthusiasm for the chase, and the steward's surly demeanour had dampened what residual enthusiasm he might have had.

The hunting party dispersed quickly after its return therefore, and Sir Edmund retired to his chamber. His servant having ensured that there was hot water and a change of clothes awaiting his return, he washed and changed into clean clothing before sitting at his table. Carefully selecting a quill he began to pen a letter to the Lady Eleanor, a letter to which he did not wish de Lacey to be privy.

When it was finished, he read the letter and, satisfied, put a blob of melted wax beneath his signature and impressed his seal upon it. There, he thought, that is the best that she or I can do for Earl Edmund, little enough though it might be! Our self interest is such that our intercession with Henry will be of little help to him, but Hotspur's plea will sound stronger in his ears, for he supported Henry, support he'll yet need again against the Scots! He called his servant and when the man entered told him, 'Give this letter to the messenger.' Then added, 'Give it only to him and give it privily!' As the man left, he leant back in his chair, looking thoughtfully into the leaping flames of the wood fire burning in the hearth. He poured himself a goblet of wine from the ewer on the table and as he sipped it, remembered the calculating look in his steward's eyes after the messenger had arrived that morning.

Yes, he thought, I shall have to do something about de Lacey! He shuddered as he thought of the contents of the Countess's letter, of her referring to King Henry as 'the usurper'. That he is, truly enough, thought Sir Edmund but mischievous minds could turn such words passed between the Countess and himself as conspiracy. A new king, unsure of his security on his newly won throne was apt to deal severely with such an offence, be it even imaginary! He grimaced, especially when it was alleged to have been between such as the Countess Eleanor and himself, kin to a rival claimant to the throne!

Being aware that there was a problem and being able to take action about it, were very different matters though. Were he to rid himself of de Lacey, he thought, why, he would run fast footed to the king and spread such gossip that, even though it be without foundation, would cast such suspicion that would make the Earl's safety precarious, not only his, but that of all the Mortimers!

He gave an irritable toss of his head, no, he could not just get rid of de Lacey, he either had to be kept at Ludlow and watched well at that . . . or his silence ensured! Rising, Sir Edmund glanced out of the window, thinking as he did so, best keep him happy here, I suppose. Then, with a shrug of his shoulders, he left his chamber for the great hall.

On arriving there he went to his accustomed place at the head of the table and sat down, then turning to de Lacey on his right hand, said affably as he picked up a goblet, 'A glass of wine, if you please, Geoffrey!'

Chapter Nine

By the spring of the year of our Lord 1400 it appeared, on the surface at least, that little had changed in England with the ascension to the throne of King Henry. The war in Scotland continued, with the Earl of Northumberland and his fiery son Hotspur taking the field there for the new king. With hostilities continuing too in Ireland and the French, as ever, harassing the ports in Southern England it appeared that Henry had little time to spare to take retribution on the Mortimers for their failure to support him in his rebellion.

Life went on normally too at Ludlow Castle where Sir Edmund was carrying out an inspection of the castle's defences, when de Lacey turned to him to say, 'Little changes it seems here, my lord, our new king vents no spleen on those who did not rally to his banner. All we have heard from London is to guard his borders well!'

Sir Edmund looked at him thoughtfully for a moment thinking that the steward seemed to have settled down into his old ways since the coronation, being courteous, punctilious in his duties and no longer so overtly ambitious. He smiled as he replied, 'Some eggs take a while to hatch, Geoffrey! Yet I think that King Henry, as all new kings, needs friends rather than enemies within his realm, for he has enough who wish him harm outside his borders. Were not the Scots and Irish enough to keep him occupied, the French cast envious eyes upon his possessions in Calais and Aquitaine and their ships of war raid our southern ports. With such drains on his exchequer, he needs no strife within his realm!'

Geoffrey de Lacey smiled but there was irony in his voice as he replied, 'True indeed my lord, nor need he fear any disloyalty within whilst he holds hostages to fortune!'

Sir Edmund turned on him angrily. 'Earl Edmund is no hostage! He is the king's ward and so ensured of the king's protection!'

Eyebrows raised in apparent surprise at Sir Edmund's vehemence, de Lacey nodded saying, 'Of course, my lord! As indeed are all his loyal subjects!'

Sir Edmund looked at him for a moment, wondering whether it was only in his imagination that he had detected an emphasis on the word 'loyal', wondered fleetingly too, whether it was possible that the steward had had sight of that letter from the Countess Eleanor. He brushed the thought aside knowing that was impossible, for the servant had been told to give the letter privily to the Countess's messenger. The momentary suspicion fading, he smiled again and saying, 'Just so, Geoffrey!' led the way as they continued the inspection.

They were walking along the western battlements when de Lacey nodded towards the distant hills: 'The king may have problems with the Scots and the Irish, my lord, but the Welsh are quiet enough!' He paused before adding reflectively, 'As they have been since the death of their Prince Llewellyn who gained them a short lived independence some hundred and fifty years since!'

Sir Edmund smiled and said, 'Long may the dragon sleep, Geoffrey, for many a town here on the marches would feel its fiery breath were it to waken once again!' He shrugged. 'I fear though that you will have to travel further for hopes of honour on the field of battle, for the Welsh are pacified, they have no leaders of great renown and hardly a knight amongst all their gentry. There are more castles there than in all of England and those all English held. The towns too, are English, for the Welsh have no rights of citizenship in them! Pacified did I say, Geoffrey? No, the Welsh are subdued! The dragon will sleep on yet awhile!'

Even as he spoke though the dark clouds on the western horizon seemed to hold a more ominous message for them than that of the heavy rain which fell on Ludlow later that night.

Throughout that spring and into the summer of that year, murmurs of discontent in Wales were reaching Ludlow Castle, murmurs to which strength was lent by the knowledge that King Richard had been favourably regarded in Wales, at least for an English king. By the summer though there were still only murmurings and although Sir Edmund had the watch strengthened there was nothing to give rise to any alarm. In their conversations both Sir Edmund and the steward were in accord that there was little to give them concern. Nor were they unduly concerned when a report reached them towards the end of the summer that a Welsh squire had raided Ruthin town where Lord Grey, another marcher lord, had his castle.

'It seems, Geoffrey,' Sir Edmund told de Lacey over an evening meal in the great hall, 'that this Owain Glyn Dŵr had a dispute with Lord Grey over some common land that the squire held to be his, but both king and Parliament sent him packing when he appealed to them.' He shrugged and gave a dismissive laugh. 'He is skilled at arms by all repute and fought in Scotland and France for Richard, from whom he held his manors. Yet he is but a squire and must be mad to risk combat with Lord Grey, a marcher lord, over a parcel of common land! No, the next we'll hear of this, Geoffrey, is when we learn his neck has been stretched!'

Seeing the disappointment on de Lacey's face, Sir Edmund laughed. 'Charge your glass, Geoffrey,' he said, passing him the ewer of wine. 'You'll have time to drink that and yet another before you have to don your mail!'

Geoffrey de Lacey gazed gloomily into his goblet of wine, then taking a deep draught, put it back on the table and with a toss of his head replied, 'I fear so, my lord, 'tis but another border raid, though how Lord Grey let this Welsh ruffian escape after ravaging Ruthin town and putting it to the torch, I'll never understand!'

Sir Edmund smiled. 'Squire Glyn Dŵr chose his timing well, Geoffrey! A quick raid into the town on market day when the streets were choked with people, cattle and market stalls. That was no place for pitched battle had Ruthin sallied out from his castle. No! Better to let Glyn Dŵr ride off with a few cattle and mete retribution upon him at a time and place of Lord Grey's choosing. Why, Glyn Dŵr's seat at Sycharth is but a fortified manor and is no place to withstand a siege. He'll yet pay heavily for his impudence, Lord Grey will hang him on Sycharth's motte amongst the ruins of his manor!

Even whilst Sir Edmund was speaking, messengers were riding out from Owain Glyn Dŵr's manor at Sycharth calling for a council of war to be held at one of his other manors at Glyndyfrdwy. Now, in the middle of September, it was assembled and gathered around the table in the manor's great hall. At the head of the table sat Owain Glyn Dŵr, his son Gruffydd on his right, his brother Tudor on his left. Around the table sat his cousins, the Tudurs of Ynys Môn, which the English knew as the Isle of Anglesey. His brothers-in-law the Hanmers were there too as was Hywel Cyffin, Dean of St. Asaph who sat far enough away from the renowned seer, Crach Ffynant, of whom he disapproved.

There was no doubt whose was the dominant figure there, for Owain Glyn Dŵr's heavily built figure seemed to exude power and vigour. There was silence now as he gazed around the room for a moment, his brown, deep set eyes seeming to pierce into each man's soul.

Plainly dressed, with only a gold medallion on its heavy gold chain for adornment, he was clearly no courtier, but a man of action. They all knew that, for they knew him well and the news of his audacious attack on Ruthin town had only served to confirm that knowledge.

As he looked around the table he was thinking, trying to choose his words carefully before he spoke. Even though they had all come to Glyndyfrdwy at his bidding, he needed their support and, kin though most of them were, the hazards of what he was about to propose weighed heavily in the balance against any reward he might offer them.

When he spoke all heads were bent towards him, as each man, grave faced, listened intently to each word he uttered. For all there knew that what he proposed could change their lives for ever. There was silence in the hall when at last he finished and, leaning back in his chair took the goblet of wine in front of him and sipped at it thoughtfully as he glanced around the table, assessing the reaction to his words.

When Owain had finished, his cousin, Ednyfed Tudur, was sitting head bowed, hands resting on the table in front of him. It was he who, raising his head, broke the silence now as in quiet, measured tones he addressed Owain, 'We came here at your bidding Owain, because of kinship and of your present and real danger after your success against the marcher, Lord Grey of Ruthin.' As he paused to take a deep breath there were heads nodding around the table and Owain gripped the stem of his goblet tightly, fearing rejection. 'Yet what you speak of here, Owain,' continued Ednyfed, 'is not to seek our aid 'gainst a rapacious and powerful neighbour but rebellion against an anointed king!

'You speak of heavy taxes and of only the English being citizens in our towns.' He shrugged. 'Have not we Welsh lived with this and worse since our good Prince Llewellyn's death?' He grinned suddenly. 'None here 'cept our learned Crach Ffynant seems o'er thin because of it and towns we never had until the English came here with their castles!'

There were more heads nodding around the table now and before Owain could reply, Ednyfed's bluff, bearded brother Rhys Tudur, broke in: 'Aye, Owain, Ednyfed, though ever cautious, speaks truly! We pay our taxes, as little as we can and when we must, but you and I live well enough in our manors and care little who lives in squalor in their English towns! I came here with my power to help ensure Lord Grey steals no more of your common land and treats not Sycharth as you treated Ruthin town!' Grinning now, he added, 'And were I to gain some little booty on the way, why t'would not go amiss and be some recompense for my journey here, but as brother Ednyfed says, rebellion 'gainst the king smacks of great hazard for little gain! Little care I which king sits on England's throne.'

Owain listened thoughtfully whilst his cousins had their say then, smiling, replied quietly, 'Hazard there is enough in that which I propose, cousin! More blood than booty too, I wager. Yet Richard favoured us Welsh more than most English kings who held rule over us and it is he who is our anointed king, for we can only guess under what duress the usurper Henry gained his crown. Were Richard dead then it is Edmund, Earl of March who should be king, by right of lineage and Richard's given word: but Richard lives! It is from him I hold my manors, not this usurper, Henry!

'You talk of hazards greater than the gain, yet what might Richard grant us were we to unseat the usurper from his precarious throne, his hold 'pon which Robert of Scotland, the Irish and the French already threaten. Nor can the Mortimers lie happily in their beds whilst Bolingbroke holds the Earl of March as ward or more likely, hostage. Were we to rise, we should not be alone and if we are ever to rise, to regain the sovereignty for Wales that is its right, now is the time, for Henry will never be weaker than he is now!'

He paused to take a sip of wine, then continued, with fervour, hwyl, 'We here, who all have the blood of Welsh Princes in our veins, hold our lands under sufferance from our English masters when it is we who should exercise that rule.' He punched the air in emphasis. 'Aye, and 'tis we who should hold the castles, the towns in Wales and in our wisdom decide who should dwell therein!'

The arguments continued until daylight failed and the torches in their cressets were lit when at last Owain's brother Tudor stood up, a goblet of red wine in his hand, to say sharply, 'Enough of all these carping words! I say be damned to hazard and Henry Bolingbroke too! Let those who have no stomach for the odds depart! I am for Lord Owain!'

Gruffydd, Owain's son was on his feet now too and raising his goblet cried out, 'I am for *Prince* Owain!' One by one, the others rose to their feet and raising their glasses acclaimed Owain as their Prince.

Owain rose to his feet slowly and looked around the table. He smiled, satisfied now that there were no dissentients, then raised his glass to them before taking a sip of wine. He was smiling in relief, release of tension, as he spoke, 'Ere you call me "Prince", I think you should tell Henry of Monmouth that he's lost his coronet, but . . .' he shrugged, 'if his father is not rightful king then it be doubtful if he were ever Prince!' There were smiles around the table at that, heads nodding in agreement with him at last and he continued, 'You do me great honour this night in agreeing to support me in this venture but think well on the hazards whilst your heads rest on your pillows tonight, for we shall have a long furrow to plough and some here may never reach its end. Think well ere you put your hand to the plough for only death will release your hold!'

Following Owain Glyn Dŵr's council of war at Glyndyfrdwy it was not long before news was reaching Ludlow Castle of English held towns in north-east Wales being sacked by the rebels. Flint, Denbigh, Holt, Harwarden and Ruddlan it seemed had all suffered from their depredations, and Oswestry and Welshpool put to the torch. After leaving Welshpool in flames however, he had suffered a defeat on the banks of the River Vyrnwy near Welshpool at the hands of a local squire, who left the field of battle with much of the booty that Glyn Dŵr had gained on his campaign.

Sir Edmund laughed when he read the letter about Glyn Dŵr's defeat at Welshpool. 'That will put an end to his rampage!' he told de Lacey. 'If Squire Burnett can so defeat him, what chance of success can he hope for 'gainst the king's forces?'

Marching south towards London from campaigning against the Scots however, it seemed that King Henry did not view this burgeoning rebellion so lightly. Having already sent Lord Grey of Ruthin to deal with Glyn Dŵr, he now delayed his own return to London and set off with his already weary army on a forced march to confront the rebel himself. By the time he arrived in Shrewsbury he received news, strengthened by Glyn Dŵr's defeat on the River Vyrnwy, that the rebellion was over. Before his army had time to resume its long march to London however, news reached him that Glyn Dŵr's cousins, the Tudurs, had seized Anglesey or Ynys Môn as the Welsh knew it. Infuriated, Henry turned his army and set off on a punitive march through North Wales, a chevauchee, in which everything was burned or pillaged as the army went its way.

Anglesey was not to be the scene of a great victory for Henry, however, for there the Tudurs forced him to seek refuge in Beaumaris Castle. After an ignominious escape to the mainland again, he retreated through Caernarvon and the mountains of North Wales, harassed by Glyn Dŵr's rebels as he made his way to the safety of England.

The news of Henry's repulse in Anglesey spread quickly along the Welsh marches and Sir Edmund was not alone amongst the marcher lords to ensure his defences were secure. There could be no doubt now that the Welsh were in rebellion, or at least sufficient of them to put the king himself to flight.

There were many serious faces in Ludlow Castle in October, not least of which were those of Sir Edmund and de Lacey. Sir Edmund turned to his steward as they stood on the Garderobe Tower: 'Well, Geoffrey, we have done all that which can be done, the knights who owe their fealty to the Earl now hold their forces at readiness lest I should I call upon them to march against Glyn Dŵr.' He turned to look around the castle. 'All is secure here, though I doubt that the Welsh rebel has engines to help him gain entrance here and the watch will not treat him civilly if he does but knock upon our door!'

Geoffrey de Lacey was silent for a moment, as though giving thought to what his lord and master had just said then, eyes narrowed, replied, 'True, my lord, sobeit the watch are English!'

Sir Edmund frowned, then said irritably, 'Of course the watch are English, Geoffrey! What else?'

The steward gave a humourless smile and said, 'Why, my lord, most of our archers are indentured men and Welsh to boot! One left the day before my Lady Eleanor's messenger came and I doubt not that he now fights alongside the rebel Glyn Dŵr even whilst we talk.' He shook his head saying, 'I trust them not, my lord!' He pointed towards the town. 'Tomorrow is market day and I wager there'll be Welshmen bringing sheep and cattle there to trade with honest Englishmen.'

Sir Edmund laughed. 'Come, Geoffrey, you tilt your lance at ghosts! Would you have me send our archers all away? Bar all Welshmen from our market day? Our archers are all indentured men and fight for whoever pays their wage, they and their kin have fought for us Mortimers a hundred years or more!' He sighed then and waved a hand, before adding, 'But, if 'twill satisfy your doubts of them, let us agree that until this rebellion dies, as soon it must, the guards at our gates are English men at arms and that they keep watch from all our towers too!' He laughed again. 'We'll have such men about the town and market place as well, though I fear it will please them less than it might you!

*   *   *   *

It was only a few hours after the steward issued the order to put Sir Edmund's decision into effect that the captain of the men at arms, a giant of a man, was bending his head to make his entrance through the doorway of Sir Edmund's chamber. He stood hesitantly in the doorway for a moment, his helmet under his arm. Smiling, Sir Edmund asked, 'What ails you, Richard, you have a face like thunder?'

The man at arms shifted his feet uncomfortably then, clearing his throat, began, 'Well my lord, 'tis the steward's order! He says that the watch at the gates and on the towers must be from the men at arms! Why sir, that spreads them thinly enough, but he says they have to patrol the town as well, whilst the archers sit in their quarters drinking ale! My men will not be happy with that my lord, nor yet will the archers, for it tells them they are not trusted here, where many have lived all their lives!'

Sir Edmund remained silent for a moment, for whilst sympathising with the captain's problem, he could not now undermine the steward's authority. Rising, he squared his shoulders back to say sternly, 'There is good reason for the steward's order, Richard, and 'tis one you should understand!' He walked over to the window and pointed to the west. 'Over there the Welsh are in rebellion 'gainst our, and their, liege lord the king! I doubt that it will be long ere it is over, but, 'til it is we must watch our backs as well we guard the march. 'Tis long enough since your men have had to earn their pay and now they grumble over keeping watch! Thanks they should be giving that they pay not their dues in blood! As for the archers, 'tis well we guard 'gainst treachery from anyone, although I doubt not that they will earn their pay as well as any other if needs must. There's yet enough to occupy them around the castle and busy hands have less chance to do mischief, eh? I'll so tell the steward, Richard.'

Looking less than enthusiastic the man at arms murmured, 'Aye my lord.' Then, eyes brightening, he asked, 'Do we march on Wales my lord, to take this rebel, Glendower?'

Sir Edmund smiled. 'Not yet, I fear, Richard. His raids have all been, thus far, in North Wales and in the marches to the north. I doubt that his so-called rebellion will last long enough for him to venture this far south!' Then, seeing the disappointment on the man at arm's face, he added, 'But we must ever be on guard lest he is not checked, eh, Richard?'

Glum faced now, the man at arms nodded and replied, 'Aye, my lord, but I'd rather the cut and thrust than all this watch and wait!'

Sir Edmund grinned. 'Aye, for with the cut and thrust there sometimes comes a little booty and none with watch and wait!'

The man at arms just nodded and turning, bent his head again as he went out of the door. He was still in the doorway when Sir Edmund called after him, 'Oh, Richard!'

In turning quickly, the man at arms cracked his head on the lintel and, eyes half closed, stood there rubbing his head for a moment before replying, 'Aye, my lord?'

Trying hard not to laugh at the man's pain, the laughter was still there in Sir Edmund's eyes and his voice, as he told the man at arms, 'When you send out the first patrol into the town, Richard, I shall go with them!'

Eyebrows arched and surprise evident in his voice the captain asked, 'You'll go with them, my lord?'

Still amused, Sir Edmund nodded. 'Aye, Richard, I shall go with them. I want no disgruntled man at arms venting his ill humour on the townsfolk!'

The captain shook his head as though doubting the wisdom of Sir Edmund venturing into the town then, reluctantly said, 'Well, 'tis market day tomorrow, my lord, and I send out four men when the market has assembled.

'I shall be with them, Richard,' said Sir Edmund smiling, 'and do not fear, little harm can come to me in the market square!'

Chapter Ten

The two men were standing in the outer bailey near the gate-house when Geoffrey de Lacey glared at the burly captain of men at arms, and asked angrily, 'What mean you, that you wait for Sir Edmund?'

Unmoved by de Lacey's anger the captain replied straight-faced, 'I wait here on his instruction, sir steward, for he said he would accompany us into town today.' He shrugged. 'So wait I must!'

Face flushed the steward was about to make a sharp retort, when the captain said with an amused smile as he nodded towards the gateway to the inner bailey, 'I shall not have long to wait now, sir steward, for my lord approaches!'

Geoffrey de Lacey could see that the captain was right, for striding towards them, unencumbered by any armour or even mail, came Sir Edmund. The knight cut a noble figure with his tall, slim figure, his rich blue cloak adorned with a heavy gold chain, his blond hair showing beneath the low crowned blue velvet hat. The steward saw none of this, but only his lord about to embark upon another imprudent venture into the town. With an irritable glance at the man at arms, the steward hurried across the outer bailey to meet the knight.

At the approach of his steward, Sir Edmund paused in his stride, his hand resting casually on the hilt of his light court sword. Smiling, he greeted the steward, 'Goodmorrow, Geoffrey!' Then with raised eyebrows, he asked, 'Does your glum face tell me you bring ill news?'

Geoffrey de Lacey brushed the question aside as he nodded towards the man at arms, to ask instead, 'Richard there tells me you go with him into the town today, Sir Edmund. Is that wise my lord,' he waved a hand expressively at the knight before adding, 'and to go thus attired?'

Sir Edmund grinned and, head on one side, said in mock reproof, 'Why, Geoffrey, 'tis not long since you chided me for venturing into town without an escort befitting my rank and station! What better escort would you wish for me than Richard and his men?' Then, more seriously he said, 'I do but go to see for myself, Geoffrey, the temper of the townsfolk and how they bear the news of this Welsh revolt. As to my attire, what need have I for armour in my own town and what might I learn there, booted and spurred, my visor down?' Seeing that the steward still frowned, he laughed and said cheerfully, 'Come, Geoffrey, if there are any men from Wales in town today they've come to sell their sheep or cattle here, not bring rebellion to our door!'

With that he took the steward by the arm and walked with him towards the waiting captain of men at arms. Minutes later de Lacey was touching his hat in salute as Sir Edmund led his escort out of the castle and into the castle square. Still frowning, de Lacey watched the small group merge into the crowded market place and shook his head, thinking morosely that it was not the Welshmen who might be in town today that he was concerned about but rather that wretched doxy, Cathy, whoever she might be. The frown clearing, he smiled thinly as he thought, at least Richard and his men at arms will make sure Sir Edmund falls under no wagon's wheels!

If the late autumn sun brought little warmth to the busy market place, it did not appear to affect the mood of the bustling crowd as women called out to friends or neighbours and tradesmen cried their wares. There was much jostling and shoving too as farmers tried to get their bleating sheep or lowing, wide-eyed cattle into pens. Sir Edmund had little difficulty in making his way through the market however, as his escort ensured that his path was clear, although he had to walk with care lest, unwittingly, he befouled his footwear. His progress caused no ill humour though, but rather smiles as women gave little curtsies and men touched their head-wear in salute to their lord. Nor could he detect apprehension amongst the crowd even though here and there he heard some stocky, dark haired men, speaking amongst themselves in the alien Welsh tongue.

If ever he heard them speak, he could not understand what they might have said, but it mattered not, for they paid him little heed. Ill mannered men they were it seemed, for amongst all the crowd, they alone did not touch their hat or forelock to him or make way unless obliged to do so by Richard or his men. Not rebels though, but cattle drovers, thought Sir Edmund grudgingly, for he could see that they were unarmed, carrying little other than a stave or whip to drive their beasts.

Sir Edmund was nearly through the market and about to lead his men into the High Street, when he saw two or three Welshmen from across a market stall. A woman with them was bargaining it seemed with the stall-holder over some trinket she held in her hand. Like her companions she was obviously Welsh, with her dark hair, the grey woollen cloak around her shoulders, yet even from across the stall he could hear that she spoke English well enough, albeit with that strange Welsh lilt.

He was about to turn away and lead on into the High Street when she looked up at him, laughter in her startling blue eyes. He stood there for a moment, mesmerised, confusing images flashing through his mind, then finally recognition as he remembered seeing her, or one so like her they might be sisters, across the lane from the goldsmith's.

It seemed that Richard, the man at arms, had seen the object of his lord's interest for without waiting for any order he sent two men at arms to either end of the stall, barring the way of escape of the Welsh party and, standing beside Sir Edmund now, asked, 'You want them held, my lord?'

Looking across the stall, Sir Edmund could see that the Welshmen were standing with their backs to the girl now and scowling, were holding their staves defensively, prepared to do battle it seemed with the men at arms. Local people though were backing away from the stall apprehensively whilst the worried stall holder was standing there holding his hand out to Sir Edmund and saying, 'There's no trouble here, my lord! Why, she can have the bauble!'

Sir Edmund put his hand on the captain's arm and said quietly, 'Gently Richard! I do but want to talk to the woman!'

Richard nodded as though in understanding. 'Aye, my lord, gently it is!' he replied, then added firmly, 'You'll talk with her or ought else an' so it be your wish, with but a broken stave or two if needs must!'

Sir Edmund turned on him to say sharply, 'Gently, I said Richard. I want no violence offered to these people. They've done no harm here today, nor shall they be harmed!' With that he turned and walked around the stall but, as he made his way towards the girl, one of the Welshmen holding his stave two handed, barred his way.

One of the men at arms was quickly at Sir Edmund's side, sword raised as though to strike, but the knight raised a hand, saying quietly, 'Put down your sword, man, would you use it on an unarmed man, prepared to protect his lady with a stick?' Then turning to the Welshman, he said, 'I do but wish to ask a question of your lady!'

It seemed he might as well have spoken to a wall for, still scowling, the man stood there, his stave raised defensively. After a moment the girl said something to the man, apparently in Welsh for Sir Edmund, whilst hearing well enough, understood not a word of it, except perhaps the name Dafydd. Reluctantly, it seemed, the man stood aside still clutching his stave as though prepared to strike and watching Sir Edmund through narrowed eyes.

Sir Edmund could see now that which he had felt since he had glimpsed sight of her across the market stall. This was no drover's woman nor yet a serving wench. Proudly she stood there facing him, the mockery still there in those sea blue eyes of hers. The laughter lingered in her voice too as she asked mockingly, 'What would you have of a poor Welsh girl, Sir Knight, now that my 'man at arms' has put up his stave?'

Whilst Sir Edmund could tell from her lilting accent and her dress that she was undoubtedly Welsh, she was certainly not poor, nor yet was she a drover's woman. Underneath that grey woollen cloak she wore a green linen dress that fell to her ankles, a silver clasp was at her throat and her voice held the tone of one well used to command rather than be bidden.

Sir Edmund touched a finger to his hat in salute and smiling now, said quietly, 'I meant to cause you and your men no alarm, madam. I fear I mistook you for a friend called Cathy.'

Those blue eyes widened as the Welshwoman shook her head, then lowered them demurely as she replied quietly, 'I fear I cannot help you, my lord, for I know no Cathy and we are strangers here, come to market for the day with our few sheep and cattle from my father's farm.'

There was something in the young girl's voice, her eyes, that seemed to be mocking him as she stood there, head on one side as though anxious to help but unable to do so. Sir Edmund stood there uncertainly for a moment then sighed and, touching his hat lightly, said, 'I am sorry to have troubled you, madam, I bid you good-day!'

He turned to his captain of men at arms, saying briskly, 'Come, Richard, we have disturbed these poor people long enough, let us be on our way and let them get on with their honest business!'

With a wave of his hand, the captain called his few men to him and, led by Sir Edmund, the group made their way the few yards to the entrance of the High Street. They were almost there when Sir Edmund turned to look back at the market to see the Welsh girl and her companions still standing there as if watching him depart. At that distance though it could only have been in his imagination that he thought that there was something akin to mockery in the way she smiled as she waved to him. Then she turned away to talk to the big

Welshman she had called Dafydd, who turned his head to look steadily at Sir Edmund as though to ensure he would remember the knight should they meet again. Turning back to the woman, the big Welshman said something to her, no doubt in their strange tongue and they both laughed.

Feeling strangely irritated, Sir Edmund turned to lead the way along the High Street, annoyed with himself that the laughter of the strangely assorted Welsh pair should be its cause. It was just as he entered King Street with his escort that he realised the real cause of his irritation. It was rejection. That woman *was* Cathy and with every step he took, he was more sure of that!

The conviction grew until he knew that he had to go back, to find her and to find out who she might be, this woman who had been a part of his fevered dreams. Suddenly turning to Richard, he said sharply, 'We're going back to the market!' With that he turned about smartly and was hurrying back along the High Street towards the market with his escort's chain-mail chinking as they sought to keep up with him.

As they came to the end of High Street by the Castle Square he could see the stall where Cathy and her Welsh companions had been, but they were not there. The stall-holder was crying his wares and a few local people were standing there laughing and talking amongst themselves but of the Welsh group there was no sign. The few people around the stall quickly found other interests as Sir Edmund approached with his escort and there was a look of resignation on the stall-holder's face as Sir Edmund walked up to him and demanded urgently, 'Where have those Welsh people gone?'

A worried frown on his brow, the stall-holder spread his hands. 'Why, my lord, I do not know, they were here for but a minute or two after you left, then they went their way.' He gave a toss of his head and complained, 'Nor did the woman buy the trinket after all the trouble she had caused!

Captain Richard interrupted his complaint to ask sternly, 'You have eyes in your head, man, which way did they go!'

The stall-holder's face paled, but he shrugged. 'I am not sure, Captain, but I believe they went towards the cattle pens.'

It was past noon when, a search of the market place for the woman and her Welsh companions having proved fruitless, a disgruntled Sir Edmund returned to the castle. Nor were patrols sent out along the roads to Wales, much to the disapproval of de Lacey, any more successful. Cathy, if indeed it was she to whom Sir Edmund had spoken in the marketplace, had disappeared like a wraith. Yet Sir Edmund knew that she was real and not merely some figment of his imagination.

Richard, the man at arms, a man not given to great flights of fantasy, knew that too and so he told the steward.

'Saw her with my own eyes, sir steward,' he told de Lacey. 'Stood as close to her as I am to you. A lady she was too and no Welsh farmer's daughter as she would have us believe. Pretty enough she was for a slip of a girl, no more'n seventeen or so she'd be, I'd say.'

Geoffrey de Lacey snorted. 'Welsh and a lady too! Those words share the same yoke as well as horse and oxen might! The woman's some doxy that Sir Edmund knew and was the cause of that accident that befell him in the town! Put out the word to all your men that there's a mark in't for any man who apprehends her and brings her to the castle!'

Richard grinned. 'A whole mark, sir steward?' he queried. 'Why, my men will fill the outer bailey with doxies from the town so that by happenchance they'll bring one in that looks like her!'

Still grinning and shaking his head in amusement at that thought, the burly man at arms turned and went off to pass the word to his men of the steward's largesse that awaited the lucky man who found the Welsh girl.

Over the next few weeks a few women were indeed brought back to the castle struggling and complaining loudly but as none passed the scrutiny of Captain Richard, their numbers quickly declined as the men at arms' enthusiasm for the hunt waned. Events on the Welsh borders were in any case increasingly the subject of everyone's conversation and attention. Contrary to Sir Edmund's prediction the depredations of the supporters of the rebel Owain Glyn Dŵr continued unabated. Raids along the border by cattle thieves which had been endemic for many years were now giving way to forays by armed war parties which terrorised the English side of the border.

It seemed too that following his retreat from Anglesey, King Henry was taking the Welsh rising seriously, for barely had he returned safely to London than he confiscated the estates of Squire Glyn Dŵr and gave them to his own bastard half brother, the Earl of Somerset. The Earl it appeared though was not over anxious to claim his newly acquired lands, for he made no haste to oust Glyn Dŵr, now acclaimed as Prince of Wales by many Welsh, from his manor at Sycharth.

There were reports too that Welsh students were leaving Oxford

University to return to Wales, something confirmed by Bishop Trefor of St. Asaph when explaining to the king the dangerous state of affairs within Wales. Gossip had it too that Welsh labourers were deserting their employment in England to return to their own country to take up arms.

Despite all these tales, Sir Edmund was encouraged by the fact that his Welsh archers did not desert but continued with their indentures, not only at Ludlow but with the other knights who owed fealty to the Earl of March.

It appeared, however, that Bishop Trefor's advice to the king had some effect, for in February of 1401 King Henry issued a pardon to all Welshmen involved in the rebellion. All that is, except Owain Glyn Dŵr and his cousins the Tudurs of Anglesey, who had humiliated Henry there.

Surprisingly, this news was received enthusiastically by de Lacey, when he joined Sir Edmund one day for the midday meal. 'The king's generosity will stifle the rebellion, Sir Edmund,' he said cheerfully, 'the Welsh will find the choice between freedom and being hanged, drawn and quartered not a difficult one to make!'

Unsmiling, Sir Edmund looked at the steward over the top of his goblet of wine and shook his head, saying, 'I fear not, Geoffrey,' he replied quietly. 'It is the ringleaders of this rebellion who need to be appeased, or hanged, if it is to be quelled. If you but scrape away the ash and leave the embers aglow, the fire will burst into flame anew! 'Tis the heart of the fire you need to quench if you would have it out.' He sipped his wine meditatively then added, 'Nor does it seem that the Earl of Somerset is over eager to pull the hot coals from the fire for the king, he has not yet taken his power to Sycharth manor to unseat the rebel Glyn Dŵr!'

It was nothing to do with the king's amnesty for the rebels that caused Sir Edmund's ill humour though, but rather the news that had reached him from the Countess Eleanor that King Richard was dead, killed or so she said, at Henry's command. In her letter she had urged Sir Edmund to guard the marches well for Henry until, she wrote, 'the time is right.' What she meant by that he knew not, nor would he have any other find the treasonable letter so, having read it, he burnt it, putting its strange message down to a mother's anguish for her son, the Earl of March.

Looking at the steward, busily chewing on a piece of mutton, he wondered yet again whether de Lacey had really been privy to that other letter from the Countess, if so, he thought this last one at least would be read by no other than himself. He bit his lip as he watched the other man gorge himself on mutton, thinking that that first letter from the Countess would be damning enough, for both the Countess and himself. There'd be no amnesty from King Henry for conspiracy, not now, if what the Countess said was true, that Richard was dead. If that were indeed true, then all that held Henry from legitimacy for the crown he wore was the Earl of March and what better excuse to remove that threat than to hold his kin as having conspired to gain the throne for him.

In between mouthfuls, the grease running on his chin, the steward looked up at him and leaning back in his chair smiled as he said, 'You are deep in thought my lord, your food uneaten before you, you are not yet pining for that Welsh girl . . .'

He had not finished before Sir Edmund interrupted him angrily: 'Damn your insolence, Geoffrey, I pine for no one! I do but have a care for the king's borders in these troubled times and wish I had such loyal men around me as he has in me!'

Taken aback by the forcefulness of Sir Edmund's rebuke, de Lacey's face flushed and suddenly contrite, said quietly, 'I crave your pardon my lord, it was but a feeble jest, I meant no harm!'

Sir Edmund glowered at him for a moment then relenting, said softly, 'Aye, but no more such jests and you value your bed and board at Ludlow, Geoffrey!' Then, pushing his plate away, Sir Edmund rose from the table adding as he did so, 'And Geoffrey, wipe your chin, you slobber grease!'

The next day was Good Friday and Sir Edmund and his steward were at prayers in the Chapel of St. Mary Magdalene in the inner bailey of Ludlow Castle. In Conwy Castle in North Wales its constable, Sir John Massey, was similarly at the service of Tenebrae in his castle's chapel together with all the garrison of some hundred men or so. It was unfortunate for him that he had so denuded the castle's defences, unfortunate too, that a local man employed as a carpenter within its walls, followed more trades than one. Whilst the constable and his men were still at their devotions, he opened the gate and Rhys and Gruffydd Tudur with some forty men swarmed into the castle. Shortly afterwards Sir John and the castle's disarmed garrison were making their dejected way out of the castle leaving the Tudurs in proud possession of the first of King Henry's castles to fall to Owain Glyn Dŵr's rebels.

Over the months that followed Sir Edmund was to receive many letters from his brother-in-law, Hotspur, now in North Wales to regain

Conwy Castle for the king by negotiation or force. The letters were not such as Sir Edmund could share with de Lacey, for they contained many complaints of the king's parsimony. In them, Hotspur complained that he could not bear the cost of the siege of Conwy for much longer unless the great expense he had incurred on the king's behalf, not only at Conwy, but in Scotland against the Scots, was soon repaid.

As he burnt Hotspur's latest epistle, Sir Edmund smiled to himself in his chamber, thinking that it seemed his brother-in-law was now less than enamoured with the king whose rebellion he had supported only some eighteen months or so ago! He sat back in his chair and stroked his chin reflectively. If such erstwhile supporters of Henry as Hotspur and his father the Earl of Northumberland were thus disenchanted with the king, there was yet hope that the young Earl of March might gain the throne.

For nearly four months the Tudurs held on to Conwy Castle against both Hotspur and the young Prince Henry but towards the end of June 1401, starvation forced them to surrender to Sir Hugh Despenser who had taken command of the siege after Hotspur had left to campaign in Scotland again. Whilst the Tudur brothers escaped with their lives, they had to surrender nine of their men to Despenser who promptly executed them as traitors.

When de Lacey went to Sir Edmund's chamber all agog with the news that Conwy had been retaken he found the knight less than enthusiastic. 'Hanged, drawn and quartered you say they were, Geoffrey?' he replied quietly, 'when Despenser took the castle with hardly a blow being struck? Why, with such incentive to surrender, we'll not have the Welsh lay down their arms in droves!'

'They were traitors, my lord!' expostulated de Lacey.

'Aye, truly said, Geoffrey,' agreed Sir Edmund, 'but to treat them so and let the men who led them to their treason go free? Where is the justice in that? No, better to hang the leaders as an example to all such men and let their foot soldiers free to go back to their land and till the soil. What Despenser has done will but encourage stubbornness even in defeat, for such men would rather die on their feet, a sword in their hand, than by hanging from a rope!'

Chapter Eleven

Not all in the castle shared Sir Edmund's views on the treatment of the surrendered men at Conwy. When de Lacey spoke with Captain Richard, the man at arms was philosophical enough about the news of the executions: ' 'Twill do no harm, sir steward,' he said in his plain, matter of fact way of speaking, 'to show these rebels there's no such thing as quarter given in rebellion. Why, do you think the Flemings from Pembroke that Glyn Dŵr defeated near Plynlimon but last month would have taken many prisoners when he had killed nigh on two hundred of them in the battle? Neither do you show any mercy to a wolf when it's at your throat. It will do no harm for our own men to know the rebels have been so treated. Rather will it stiffen their backs, for they will know the rebels will exact revenge for Conwy!'

It was not long before the man at arms' words were to be seen as prophecy, for news soon reached Ludlow from the monks at Abbey Cwm Hir that Owain Glyn Dŵr's rebels were on the march in Radnorshire. The warning came too late, however, to save the Abbey for within days it was learnt that it had been looted and put to the torch by Glyn Dŵr. The depredations of the Welsh rebels did not stop there for, spurred on no doubt by the Tudur's original success in taking Conwy, they went on to lay siege to Radnor Castle.

What happened when the castle at last fell to the rebels caused even the cynical de Lacey to say in disgust to Captain Richard, 'They put the axe to the necks of all three score of the castle guard when the castle fell, Richard! Why, they are but barbarians, for 'tis gainst all the rules of war!' He turned on the stolid man at arms, to add bitterly, 'There! Will that stiffen the backs of our men enough for you?'

The man at arms nodded, then replied quietly, 'Aye, that will be sufficient, sir steward! I doubt our men will surrender readily to the rebels now. Yet do not speak of rules, nor yet of courtesies of war, for this is rebellion, where the only rule is to succeed and where in failure you can expect nought but death for all else is but largesse!'

He turned to look around the castle for a moment and pursed his lips, before adding, 'I doubt that Glyn Dŵr will have the stomach to venture this far East, sir steward, but success at times breeds overweening audacity. I must do my rounds and speak to my men,' he grinned as he added, 'my words to them will stiffen their backs enough, for my sword will be at his neck 'fore any man of mine cries "Quarter"!'

If de Lacey was disgusted at the news of the massacre at Radnor, his surprise that Sir Edmund had not ordered an array of his forces to march into Radnorshire and seek out the rebel was even greater.

The knight was standing by the window looking out to the Welsh hills but turned his head when the steward entered the chamber and seeing de Lacey's solemn face said softly, 'Sad news, Geoffrey! Those poor men at Radnor should have expected better from their victors than that!'

His words seemed only to exasperate the steward, who snorted before replying, 'Aye, my lord! Sad news indeed, but when do we march to exact a blood price for their deaths? Your power should already be arrayed and on the march!'

Sir Edmund smiled understandingly. 'Your anger is well justified, Geoffrey. Yet anger of itself seldom gives rise to prudent action. I do not care to uselessly expend my power in chasing will o' the wisps around the Welsh countryside. Were we to march into Radnorshire now, think you that Glyn Dŵr would wait there to meet us in battle? No, he'd melt away like snow before the sun and months we'd spend in fruitless chase. Patience is what is called for now, Geoffrey, and readiness to strike when he o'er reaches himself!'

Evidently de Lacey was not convinced by Sir Edmund's argument, for there was a touch of bitterness in the steward's reply: 'I fear my lord, that King Henry might see such patience as unwillingness to take the sword to the rebel when he is even now within our reach.'

Sir Edmund smiled again then, head on one side said, 'Indeed Geoffrey, I might share your views as to the king's reaction, were I not sure that he had learnt a little from his foray to the Isle of Anglesey. From his bitter experience there I wager he has learnt the wisdom of patience, for this Glyn Dŵr and his kin are are no 'prentices in the art of war. Nor do they seek to confront us on a field of battle, but seize each opportunity to attack and then swiftly seek the safety of some mountain fastness. We wait, Geoffrey, and when we strike it shall be with the mailed fist of men fresh and ready for battle, not weary from some useless search!'

It must have been the chill of Sir Edmund's chamber, for de Lacey sniffed before replying stiffly, 'Sobeit, my lord, though I doubt we'll ever meet this Welsh rebel whilst we sit here at Ludlow waiting for him to lay siege!'

His reply stretched Sir Edmund's tolerance too far, for the knight snapped, 'If it is a siege you fear, Geoffrey, then you'd best be about your business and see the castle is well prepared. Speak to Richard, for he's experienced in the art of war and has survived a siege or two!'

Geoffrey de Lacey flushed at the rebuke, for though a squire to Sir Edmund he had not as yet proved his mettle in battle and the knight's comment had touched him on the raw. With a terse, 'Aye, my lord!' the steward turned on his heel and left the chamber.

Grinning at the steward's discomfiture, Sir Edmund sat on a wooden stool by the window, but the grin quickly faded as he began to feel a little guilty at what he saw now as a cheap jibe at the steward's inexperience. Guilty too, knowing that there was more than a measure of truth in the steward's reaction to his own failure to respond to Glyn Dŵr's depredations.

As he sat there alone, he knew that he should have made a more immediate response to the attack on the Abbey Cwm Hir and the sacking of Radnor town and its castle by the rebels. Knew too that the capture of Glyn Dŵr or even inflicting a defeat upon the rebel would have gained him the king's favour. He looked out of the window with unseeing eyes. Yes, he thought, gained the king's favour and in so doing helped ensure that he remained king. What then of Earl Edmund, for it would not help the Earl to gain the crown that was rightfully his!

If this rebellion of the Welsh could yet aid Henry's overthrow, why, 'twere better then to let Squire Glyn Dŵr be a thorn under Henry's saddle, perchance the king might thus be unseated!

He nodded thoughtfully as he allowed his train of thought to develop. 'Twould do no great harm to be seen by Henry as being cautious, but the Mortimers must not be seen to aid the rebel, for that could put the young Earl's very life in danger.

In the beginning of July even this tenuous loyalty of Sir Edmund's was stretched to breaking point when he received another letter from the Countess Eleanor. From it Sir Edmund learnt that the king had given Prince Henry a thousand pounds from the issues and profits of the Earl of March's estates to finance the prince in relieving Harlech and Aberystwyth castles now besieged by Glyn Dŵr. Whilst Sir Edmund was angry at this news, the Countess was evidently infuriated at what she described as this theft from her son's patrimony by 'the usurper'. It was another of the Countess's letters that Sir Edmund had hurriedly and secretly burnt for what else it contained could only be seen as even more treasonable.

By the autumn it seemed from all the news that reached Ludlow Castle, that whilst the sieges of Harlech and Aberystwyth continued, Glyn Dŵr must have left the conduct of the sieges to his kin. His force now swollen by men who had flocked to his banner in North Wales, he attacked the towns and castles of Montgomery and Welshpool. His attacks seemed, however, to have met with mixed success, for whilst Welshpool town was sacked and burnt, Lord Charlton beat off the attack on the castle there as did Sir Brian Hurley the attack on Montgomery Castle.

This news was of great interest to Sir Edmund, for Sir Brian also held the lordship of the manor of Brampton Bryan from the Earl of March. In defending the king's castle at Montgomery, Sir Brian had given a show of allegiance to King Henry that was essential for the Mortimers. Essential at least until, as the Countess had said, the time was right.

Responding to the apparently growing support for the rebels in Wales, King Henry assembled an army at Worcester at the beginning of October and marched through South Wales. Whilst it was said that Glyn Dŵr was active in Pembroke until the king arrived at Carmarthen, he was not discovered by searches of the king's men, having once again retreated into the mountains to the north. Having failed to bring Glyn Dŵr to battle, King Henry vented his frustration upon the monks of Strata Florida, who he believed to have supported the rebels, before beginning the long march back to England.

Sir Edmund was unable to resist pointing out to de Lacey the futility of such expeditions. When news reached Ludlow Castle that the king's army had arrived back at Hereford, Sir Edmund was standing in the inner bailey with the steward and turned to him. 'Do you not wish, Geoffrey,' he remarked innocently, 'that you were with the king on his chevauchee through South Wales? Much honour you may have gained in sacking an Abbey here, or an execution or two there! Why, I have little doubt that you'd have come back wearing the ermine!'

Unsmiling, de Lacey replied, 'Aye, my lord, I might have done indeed, for had I been there, I might have found the Welsh fox myself! As it is, the king has but rid himself of a few traitors along the way!'

News, but more often rumours about the activities of Glyn Dŵr, the self acclaimed Prince of Wales', came to Ludlow almost daily over the next few weeks, some claiming that he had attacked the great castle at Caernarvon, others that he had met with the Earl of Northumberland and wished to return to the king's grace. It was even rumoured that the elderly Earl of Northumberland had suggested to the king that the rebel's manors be restored to him. Conflicting rumours though suggested that the king was proposing to send out an array to all the lords of the marches and muster a great army at Welshpool for a march into Wales to finally crush the rebellion.

With news of a fresh unrest in Ireland, suggestions of any concession to the Welsh rebels were soon forgotten, as all along the marches men prepared for war. Messengers went out from Ludlow to all the knights under Sir Edmund's command to ready themselves to meet the king's array, now expected daily.

With the imminence of his own involvement in this assault on Wales, Sir Edmund held daily councils with his steward and his captains to ensure that Ludlow and its dependent knights would be prepared to meet the king's array. It was after one such meeting that de Lacey, as ever eager to embark on an expedition into Wales, said enthusiastically, 'I trust we shall have not long to wait before we march, Sir Edmund, else our men's ardour will quickly cool. Why does the king delay?'

Sir Edmund smiled. 'Perhaps because Glyn Dŵr is not foremost amongst his many foes, Geoffrey! The Scots and French have ever allied themselves 'gainst the English and as the war with Scotland continues he cannot afford to array all his power 'gainst Glyn Dŵr lest he is exposed to two fold assault from France and Robert of Scotland. With the Irish lords in rebellion again and rumours of Glyn Dŵr seeking alliance with both the Scots and Irish, he has to choose carefully which assault he must meet first.' He smiled, not entirely sympathetically, before adding, 'I fear King Henry must sometimes yearn for his carefree days of exile in France and often wish that he had made more friends there than it now appears he has!'

Geoffrey de Lacey snorted, saying, 'He must deal with Glyn Dŵr and that right speedily. The man already sees himself as a sovereign prince thus seeking to make alliances with foreign powers! I hear the French King Charles has already acknowledged him as such and sent him a golden princely helmet! The king must crush these enemies within his realm to then the more effectively pursue his foreign foes.'

Sir Edmund grinned as he replied ironically, 'Your time is wasted here at Ludlow, Geoffrey, the king has need of counsel such as yours in London, but 'til he calls upon you, I fear that you must be about your duties!'

Sir Edmund stroked his chin thoughtfully as he watched the steward leave the chamber wondering as he did so, that whilst Henry had enemies enough within and outside his realm, what others were there within England, like the Countess Eleanor, who merely waited 'until the time was right'?

With the coming of spring in fourteen hundred and two a comet sped across the night skies leaving its fiery trail behind. Across England and Wales men saw it as an omen of victory, their hopes of whose that victory might be dependent upon which side of the Welsh marches they stood. For Lord Grey of Ruthin, Owain Glyn Dŵr's arch enemy, it was to be an omen of disaster. Throughout the spring Glyn Dŵr and his rebels had harried Lord Grey's lands and in April Lord Grey sallied out from his castle with all his power, intent upon finally crushing the insolent Welshman. Such an outcome, however, could not have been in his stars that spring for the wily Glyn Dŵr declined the confrontation of a set piece battle against a superior force. Instead he waited in ambush for Lord Grey and in the ensuing mêlée many of Lord Grey's men fell to the hail of arrows from Glyn Dŵr's archers. The Welsh took few prisoners that day and fortunate indeed were the lucky survivors of Lord Grey's force who finally reached the safety of Ruthin Castle again.

Lord Grey was not amongst them, for when Glyn Dŵr left the field of battle, he took his enemy with him in chains to Snowdonia. The marcher lord was a rich prize for Glyn Dŵr, for not only was he a wealthy man himself, but he was an ardent supporter of King Henry and therefore, quite literally, worth a king's ransom. If Lord Grey could still see the comet from the mountain cave in which he was now held prisoner, he must have viewed it in a very different light from when he had last seen it from the ramparts of Ruthin Castle.

Lord Grey's misfortune gave rise to another outburst from de Lacey when he rushed to Sir Edmund with the news. 'A Welsh squire taking a marcher lord prisoner, my lord, why 'tis infamous! Is there no limit to the man's arrogance?'

Sir Edmund smiled. 'Arrogance, Geoffrey? Why, Glyn Dŵr is no squire now, as you should know, for he is Prince of Wales and tells us so himself! If it was arrogance that made Lord Grey a captive why then, it was his own. Now it is he who must pay the price of his impetuosity and that, I fear, will be high enough for Glyn Dŵr has old scores to settle with my Lord of Ruthin! Think on that Geoffrey when you would have us chase this squire through the Welsh hills, for I have no wish to keep Lord Grey company in his prison!'

It seemed that, unlike Lord Grey, Owain Glyn Dŵr now saw his star in the ascendant, for his attacks on the English held towns and castles in North Wales continued unabated and were apparently unaffected by his negotiations for the ransoming of Lord Grey. Although perhaps it was these negotiations that held him back from attacking Denbigh, one of the wealthiest of the Mortimer lordships.

No doubt too, he was aware that the Earl of March was held hostage by the king for the good conduct of the Mortimers and perhaps saw them as potential allies in the future. Furthermore Denbigh was under the control of Hotspur, with whom Glyn Dŵr was conducting negotiations for Lord Grey's release.

Much to Lord Grey's dismay, the negotiations for his release were prolonged, not due solely to the fact that he could not himself raise the enormous ransom demanded by Glyn Dŵr. In London, King Henry, upon whose help Lord Grey relied, had much to worry over other than Lord Grey's captivity. Embattled on all fronts, the king now discovered a conspiracy to depose him, led by King Richard's half brother Sir Roger of Clarendon. It was a conspiracy doomed to failure from the outset, for Richard, who the conspirators wished to restore to the throne, was no longer a prisoner but had been secretly killed at Henry's command.

That fact, of which they were unaware, did not save the conspirators for one of the Friars Minor involved in the plot accused Henry to his face of being a usurper, which served only to hasten their executions.

In North Wales Glyn Dŵr's negotiations with Hotspur continued on a friendly basis borne, it seemed, out of mutual respect. Friendly they may well have been but, because of the pressures, both financial and military, on King Henry, they were certainly ineffectual. Whilst they continued desultorily over the next few months, Hotspur busily reinforced the defences of Ruthin and even sent ships to support the English held castles on the North Wales coast.

Neither was Glyn Dŵr idly awaiting the result of the negotiations, for by the middle of the year he had gathered a great army around him from both North and South Wales and, it was rumoured, was marching towards Radnorshire again with his host.

Could it be that with his victory over the Flemings at Hyddgen near Plynlimon and now his more recent victory at Ruthin and his capture of Lord Grey he felt bold enough to attack the Mortimers at Ludlow, the seat of their power? Even now, with the tramp of Glyn Dŵr's army echoing in his ears, mentally if not physically, Sir Edmund found it difficult to believe that that was so.

Geoffrey de Lacey and Richard, the captain of men at arms, were with Sir Edmund on the battlements when a messenger from the Mortimer castle at Maelienydd brought him the news that Glyn Dŵr had set out from Llanidloes and was marching eastwards with a great army. The steward was almost exultant at the news. Eyes bright with ambition and the eagerness for battle of one who has seen little of its reality, he exclaimed enthusiastically, 'He is coming here, my lord! No need now to chase him through the mountains, he is coming to us and it will be his undoing!'

Lips pursed, Sir Edmund looked at him steadily for a moment before saying quietly, 'Coming here, Geoffrey? Why should he choose to attack Ludlow when he has left Denbigh unassailed? At Denbigh his lines of communication would be shorter, his way of escape surer. His men too would be fresh, not weary after a long march. No, Geoffrey, he is an experienced soldier, who knows well enough his strength lies not in great battles or long sieges but in nip and tuck, he'll not come here!

'Not once in either of King Henry's forays into Wales did Glyn Dŵr confront the king in battle, but faded away into the hills wherein his safety lay! I grant you that he is marching east, nor do I doubt that he will pillage and torch towns and churches along his way, for he needs to fill his war chest.' Seeing the look of disappointment on the young squire's face, Sir Edmund smiled. 'Fear not, Geoffrey, for whilst he will not come here, the time has come when I must meet this man who calls himself the Prince of Wales and you shall have your chance to find honour on the field of battle,' he paused and, sounding a little less confident, added, 'if I can but bring the rebel to do battle!'

Wide-eyed now, de Lacey asked, 'You mean we march, my lord?'

Grave faced, Sir Edmund nodded. 'Aye Geoffrey, we march and all the Mortimer retainers shall be marching with us! If Glyn Dŵr's army is as great as rumour has it, we shall need all of them around us when we meet this warlike prince. Pray God that they're all with us yet and we with them, when it is done!'

When the others left him, Sir Edmund paced the battlements pondering the reason behind Glyn Dŵr's march towards Radnorshire and the Mortimer's territory. From the letters he had received from Hotspur, it appeared that Glyn Dŵr and Hotspur, Sir Edmund's brother-in-law, had been on friendly enough terms. Glyn Dŵr also would surely be aware that young Earl Edmund, an alternative claimant to the throne, was held hostage by the king. Reason enough surely, to cultivate rather than attack the Mortimers. Prince he might be, thought Sir Edmund, but if he rules his people at all, he rules by consent and the Mortimers have enemies enough amongst the Welsh gentry.

He smiled a little bitterly to himself as he thought, it is they who have persuaded him upon this enterprise for they have old scores to settle with us Mortimers, as he did with Lord Grey! At least, he thought, the Countess is no longer at Wigmore, is no longer Countess either, for she is safe with her new husband, Lord Despenser's brother.

As they went down the steps of the tower from the battlements, de Lacey said in exasperation to Richard, 'He still does not believe the Welsh rebel has the impudence to assault Ludlow, Richard! At last though he is now prepared to seek out Glyn Dŵr and with the forces Sir Edmund can muster 'twill not be long ere we send the rebel's head to the king in a silver casket!'

The man at arms grinned. 'The Welshman, sir steward, is no capon ready for the pot! More than one head, I wager, will fall do we but chance upon him and it will take a large casket to send them all to Henry. Have a care that yours be not amongst them! Now I must be about my business, for it is no outing for maidens that we are about to embark upon, 'tis war and that you'll find can be a bloody business.'

Chapter Twelve

It was a jubilant army that set out from Llanidloes with their prince at their head. Jubilant, for this was Wales resurgent, nor was it mere rebellion now, it was war and they were marching to take the battle for Welsh sovereignty to the English! Riding with Owain Glyn Dŵr were his brother Tudor, his son Gruffydd and his cousins, the Tudurs of Ynys Môn. Half the uchelwyr, the gentry, of Wales were there too, many of whom had old scores to settle with the Mortimers from generations of oppression.

Often as they rested along the way, Prince Owain and his lords discussed their strategy for this new campaign, with some supporting an attack on the major Mortimer strongholds of Wigmore or Ludlow whilst the more cautious favoured raiding the lesser towns and castles. It was to those who sought to assault Wigmore or Ludlow that Owain addressed himself as they were halted some way from Maelienydd. 'We are here, my lords,' he said, 'to show the English that we may attack where and when we will and that there is no safety for them in Wales nor yet along its marches! Yet castles such as Ludlow we may only gain by long siege or by stratagem such as that which gained our cousins Castle Conwy.

No long siege could we maintain along the marches, for Henry would fall upon us with men drawn from all his kingdom. No long siege therefore I say, but let us show our presence along the Mortimer's march and ensure they long remember we passed their way! No pitched battle either should we seek for, as ever, the English will outnumber us and can afford the attrition that will bleed us to death! Then, when we have done in the marches, we go westwards by way of Wye into South Wales, where our successes will gain us yet more support.'

The arguments on either side were long and heated before at last the more adventurous were persuaded of the wisdom of Owain's strategy. When the leaders were mounted again, the army separated into bands led by their own lords which set off, intent now upon wreaking havoc on the towns and villages of the Mortimer lands before they were to unite again near Knighton.

As he led his own band of men towards Maelienydd, Owain Glyn Dŵr trusted that he would indeed meet his kinsmen again at Knighton, knowing full well that news of the Welsh incursion must have already reached Ludlow. Angered by such news Sir Edmund Mortimer might already be leaving Ludlow with all his power gathered around him, a force that would surely outnumber the scant thousand that now marched with Owain.

Sir Edmund had indeed left Ludlow, with fresh news of the pillaging and burning of towns and villages reaching him by the hour. Maelienydd Castle it appeared had fallen quickly to the Welsh as had Bleddfa, where the church had also been looted and burnt. Grim faced now, Sir Edmund pressed on as fast as his foot soldiers could trot, with his squire, bright-eyed de Lacey, riding beside him. As his men from Ludlow marched on they were joined by the knights he had arrayed from the Mortimer lands.

The first to join him was white haired Sir Robert Whitney of Wye, Knight Marshall to the king himself, who was shortly followed by the others: the elderly Thomas Clanvowe, Walter Devereux and Kinaird de la Bere all with their retinues, brought together no doubt not only from loyalty to their Earl, but perhaps from not wishing to incur the penalty for not meeting the array.

When Thomas Clanvowe joined with his retinue, he rode up to Sir Edmund and touched his helmet perfunctorily in salute. 'Greetings, Sir Knight,' he said, dour faced, his voice holding a suggestion of the sing song Welsh accent of his forebears. Then, glancing along the long column of foot soldiers and mounted men at arms, he shook his head as he added critically, 'This is no way to pursue the rebel, Sir Edmund! The Welshman has already fragmented his army, or more like his rabble of sheep minders. They've not come to face us in battle, but to burn and pillage, then scurry back whence they came taking what booty they can carry!'

Sir Edmund listened courteously to the older man for Sir Thomas, a former sheriff, was known to be an able soldier. Then, smiling, he agreed, 'Quite true, Sir Thomas! Skirmishers I sent ahead to Knighton tell of no house left standing 'twixt Llanidloes and Knighton, where all the men there are under arms ready to repel any such attempt upon their town. Yet we shall go together, Sir Thomas, 'til we gain further intelligence of the rebel's intent, for when at last I meet Glyn Dŵr I would'st have power enough around me to crush the rebel finally! We march beside the River Lugg, between Stapleton and Presteigne castles, where we should gain further intelligence of Glyn Dŵr's intent.'

Sir Thomas was clearly not convinced by Sir Edmund's argument, for there was more than a hint of stubbornness in his voice as he replied, 'I hold my men at your command, Sir Edmund, but will readily take them on to seek out Glyn Dŵr more speedily than this larger company allows!' With that he spurred his horse and rode off to join his retinue at the rear of the column.

Geoffrey de Lacey watched Sir Thomas ride off, then turned to Sir Edmund to say quietly, 'I trust him not, my lord! He is of the same stock as the rebels and comes from one who himself rebelled against King Edward, the second of that name!'

Sir Edmund laughed. 'You tilt at shadows again, Geoffrey! Sir Thomas is a loyal man who, like his father, is a proper soldier and holds his manors from the Earl. The Welsh have no great love for him or yet his kin.' He paused to give emphasis before adding, 'Nor he for them!'

There was no time to be lost if they were to reach Knighton before the Welsh rebels ravaged the town and Sir Edmund drove his men on with all haste sparing neither man nor horse. As they pressed on beside the languid River Lugg, steam rose from the horses like clouds in the June sunshine and the lancemen trotting alongside them ever wiped the sweat from their brows. Late that afternoon they passed Stapleton, with Presteigne on the far bank of the River Lugg.

The riders Sir Edmund had sent on to Stapleton though had little news when they came back to him at full gallop, for all they could tell him was that Glyn Dŵr was reported to be marching towards Knighton with a great band of rebels.

At the council of knights Sir Edmund called, the news was treated with disdain and Sir Thomas Clanvowe voiced everyone's thoughts: 'Such news is no news Sir Edmund! Were it not so then our long day's march had been but wasted effort! Yet I doubt Glyn Dŵr will assault the town this night, rather will he let the townsmen wait with apprehension for the morrow!'

From the nodding heads of the others it was clear that all accepted his assessment and Sir Edmund smiled as he said, 'As ever, Sir Thomas, your judgement is shrewd and one it seems we are all agreed upon. Let us therefore approach Knighton and set up camp close by the town tonight, so that we may meet tomorrow with the Welsh, fresh eyed and fit to do justice to our cause!'

As they made camp that evening close to the eastern edge of Knighton town, there were many who came from the town eager to see Sir Edmund's army, grateful they were too, for its presence there gave surety of their safety from the rapacious Welsh. Some men came armed, to add their sword to Sir Edmund's power, whilst some women it seemed came only to bring comfort to his soldiery.

There was a clear sky later that night when the solitary figure of an archer strolled from Knighton town in the moonlight towards the flickering fires of Sir Edmund's encampment. After pausing to seek directions from a group eating their meal by a fire, he walked on towards where the Welsh archers from Ludlow had settled for the night. There he was greeted with all the familiarity of an old companion, as indeed he was, for it was Idris the archer who, a few short months ago had completed his indenture with the Mortimers. Long into the night he talked with his fellow archers of battles they had fought and won and of what the morrow might bring, for it was soon agreed that when they marched to meet Owain Glyn Dŵr, Idris would be with them and would notch his arrows as cheerfully as they.

When the knights assembled early the next morning at Sir Edmund's tent to discuss the strategy for the battle they all felt the day would surely bring, he told them that he had already sent out skirmishers to bring back news of Glyn Dŵr. 'Whilst we await what they may learn of his intent,' he told them, 'we break camp now and march to the west of Knighton town to meet him there should he dare assault.'

'And if he dares not, my lord, what then?' asked the portly Sir Robert Whitney, who as the King's Knight Marshall was the most senior of the assembled knights.

'Why then, Sir Robert,' replied Sir Edmund. 'We march on and seek him out! No doubt we'll find him from the smell of sulphur the devil leaves from hovels he has burnt along his way!' He raised a finger in emphasis as he continued, 'But, when we march, each knight will keep his retinue well separate in our column for whilst I fear no combat with the rebel, I'll not have him ambush us without he pays high price for such audacity! When we march too, I desire that each of you has riders well out upon our flanks to guard 'gainst such eventuality.' There were one or two raised eyebrows at this order, but from their nodding heads it seemed that all there regarded it as a soldierly enough precaution.

Shortly afterwards, Sir Edmund's army was on the move, marching westwards in an extended column around the outskirts of Knighton town. Every man marching there was now alert and ever watchful, for all knew that soon they must meet the Welsh and that some there were who would not march back again.

They were barely to the west of Knighton when some of Sir Edmund's skirmishers came riding at full gallop towards them, to rein up hard alongside Sir Edmund. Breathlessly they told him that they had sighted a mounted band of fifty or so of Glyn Dŵr's men not far from Whitton town. Excited at the news, Sir Edmund turned to de Lacey. 'We have him now, Geoffrey! No more tilting at shadows for you my lad, ere the sun goes down you'll have earned your spurs!' He turned as the other knights came riding up towards him.

'What news, Sir Edmund?' asked Kinaird de la Bere curtly.

Sir Edmund grinned as he replied cheerfully, 'My skirmishers bring us news fit to lift our hearts, Sir Kinaird! They've sighted a band of rebels some fifty strong close by Whitton town. They must be a rearguard or perhaps a laggard group whose misfortune it will be to lead us on to greater prey!'

Sir Thomas Clanvowe frowned and shook his head. 'I smell ambush here, my lord! Glyn Dŵr's too old a soldier to whistle to his pursuer 'less it be to his advantage!'

Sir Edmund's face set stubbornly. 'Ambush I like as little as you, Sir Thomas,' he said sharply, 'and we shall not rush in blindly to such hazard. Yet from what we learned from the men of Knighton, Glyn Dŵr has a power no more than half the size of our army around him now, so we shall not shrink from such hazard like some maid frightened by a mouse.'

Sir Thomas flushed angrily and his hand went to his sword hilt as though to draw his weapon. 'I shrink not, Sir Edmund!' he snapped. 'Not from Glyn Dŵr or any man. I do but counsel caution, for this Welshman is a fox, who has given chase and been pursued a time or two 'fore this. We are all agreed that we march on and no man here shrinks from the clash of arms, nor from the sight of fresh spilt blood. Yet it would be but soldierly wisdom to send skirmishers ahead of our main force again to appraise us of Glyn Dŵr's intent.'

Sir Edmund smiled and nodded in agreement, as he said placatingly, 'Your sagacity is gained from long experience in the art of war Sir Thomas and you offer wise counsel on which we are all agreed! So we march on and ere the sun sinks this night a rebellion shall be quelled and we'll have gained our sovereign's gratitude!'

Sir Thomas gave a toss of his head and said dryly, ' 'Fore we gain either Sir Edmund, we must catch the devil by the tail and send his head to King Henry! I pray all here live to see the sun sink on that desired event!'

Southwards now they marched in all haste with none more eager to meet the rebels than de Lacey, still seeking honour on the field of battle. Across old Offa's Dyke they went, pausing hardly there to break their stride, then passed nearby Whitton town, the smoke still rising there as though Glyn Dŵr himself beckoned them on. It was there they saw a skirmisher ahead, urgently waving them on as he rode towards them. As he came up to them he cried out to Sir Edmund, 'They're still there my lord, by Pilleth Church!'

Sir Edmund turned to de Lacey, saying, 'Go back along the column, Geoffrey, and tell all that the enemy are close by the Church of my Lady of Pilleth and are not there for pilgrimage!' With that he spurred his horse and there was a ripple along the ranks of the column as all made haste to follow.

As the church came in view Sir Edmund could see a group of men mounted on small Welsh ponies gathered there and he turned to Sir Thomas, who had ridden up to the head of the column, saying, 'We have them now, I think, Sir Thomas!'

Even as he spoke the rebels were already spurring their agile little ponies up the hill behind the church. As he watched them go, Sir Thomas nodded. 'Aye, my lord, we have them, do we but get to the top of Bryn Glas Hill!'

Sir Edmund shook his head in exasperation. ' 'Twill only be the stiff and silent who do not reach the top, Sir Thomas, for now is the time our retainers must earn their pay! Have the column turn in line and advance uphill. Spread them thinly in the line, for I doubt not there'll be others atop the hill who even now are notching arrows.'

Minutes later the whole column had turned into line and had begun the ascent of Bryn Glas Hill. It was only minutes too before men were puffing and panting in their armour and chain mail, the sweat running down their cheeks as they climbed the hill in the summer sunshine. The group of rebels that had led them there were at the top of the hill now and were to be seen dismounting amongst the few trees atop the hill. Sir Edmund turned to de Lacey, who was beside him again now. 'It seems they intend to make their stand there, Geoffrey, if so those we followed will not be alone. Spread the word, that we must not hasten now, but conserve our breath for the final assault,' he grinned. 'I doubt not that we'll need it all when we reach the summit!'

As the young squire turned, the first arrows began to fall from the hill above them like a wintry shower. A shower that brought a chill to some of Sir Edmund's men from which they never would recover as here and there along the mountain's side men fell who would not rise again. Sir Edmund held a hand up towards de Lacey and said, 'Hold, Geoffrey! Better I think to be short of breath when we arrive than never to arrive at all! Urge them instead to press on, God and St. George will be our shield!'

As de Lacey raced along, a cry of 'St. George! St. George!' rose increasingly louder from the line as he progressed. Until, that is, he came to Sir Thomas Clanvowe's section of the line. When de Lacey passed his message and the first man raised the cry of 'St. George!' Sir Thomas glowered at de Lacey and, pointing towards the summit bellowed, 'Silence! Save your breath, you fools! You'll need all you have and more to wield your weapons when you reach those trees! Lest you do, 'twill take more than a Saint's blessing to save you there!'

Flushing at the implied rebuke, de Lacey went quickly back to Sir Edmund who grinned when told of Sir Thomas's action. 'Quite right too, Geoffrey. I meant it but as encouragement to our men. Such battle cry is wasted on Glyn Dŵr, who favours seers from the old religion more than he does the Holy Church!'

He glanced around him and added encouragingly, 'No need for battle cry now Geoffrey, for we are more than halfway, 'twill soon be hand to bloody hand!'

The steward seemed not to have heard him though, for he was glancing around behind them anxiously, pointing to their rearguard and crying out urgently, 'We are betrayed my lord, betrayed!'

All around them now men were falling to a rain of arrows, not from above but from their own archers, left to the rear for the men at arms and lancemen to make the first assault upon the enemy. The enemy, but who indeed, were the enemy now?

'Ambushed, by God!' cried Sir Edmund, and there was a look of anguish on his face as he added, 'Ambushed, by my own men!'

There was confusion for what seemed an eternity to Sir Edmund, with men falling all around them and the cries of the wounded piercing him to the very heart and echoing the cries of other men he seemed to remember crying out in another ambush. Then he was detaching men at arms and lancemen to go downhill to assail the traitors whilst urging all others onwards, uphill to make the final assault.

All along the line the same scene was being enacted as men already nearly exhausted from the ascent of the hill tried to cope with the enemy above and the enemy within. Decimated by the hail of arrows both from above and from their rear, it was at last only a remnant of Sir Edmund's original army which finally reached the summit, for the stiff and silent he had spoken of earlier and who now littered the mountainside, outnumbered those fit and able to wield their weapons.

The only battle cries that rang out now were in the alien Welsh tongue and they could be heard above the clash of steel upon steel. Amidst the exultant, wild Welsh cries, Sir Edmund's men were grimly silent as, outnumbered, they fought desperately atop Bryn Glas Hill. Silently they fought now not for St. George, not for King Henry, nor yet for Sir Edmund but for their very lives, for all knew they could expect no quarter from the Welsh.

The sun was still high in the western sky when Sir Edmund saw men from the remnants of his proud army begin to leave the field, at first in ones and twos they went, then in bands of a dozen or so seeking an elusive safety in their numbers. He and de Lacey were still fighting with some two or three score men about them when de Lacey suddenly turned to him and cried out above the noise of battle, 'I warned you my lord, those Welsh archers could not be trusted! I warned you!' Bitterly now he added, 'Lest there were conspiracy it could not have gone this far! The day is lost and I go to fight for the king with men that I can trust!'

Others about them had heard his angry words and, after wavering for a moment, the whole group turned and followed de Lacey as he fled downhill, pursued by as many Welshmen thirsting for their blood.

Suddenly the clamour of battle around him quietened and a man in full armour was riding up to him. This is Glyn Dŵr, he thought, for all around him men were leaning on their weapons respectfully, grinning and nudging one another expectantly. The man lifted his visor and Sir Edmund knew that he was right, and knew instinctively that the face behind the visor was one well used to command.

The piercing brown eyes gazed at him calmly as though they saw neither subordinate nor yet master. 'Lay down your sword, Sir Edmund,' Glyn Dŵr said quietly, 'there has been more than enough blood shed here this day, let there be no more of it!'

Whilst Sir Edmund could barely see the man's mouth above the lower part of the helmet, the man's eyes seemed to be smiling now, as he added, 'You have fought with honour this long day and though by far the younger you must be as weary of it as I am! 'Tis done and you have lost the day and now must be my guest for yet a little while!'

Dejectedly, Sir Edmund began to offer Glyn Dŵr his sword, but the Welshman waved it aside, saying with a laugh, 'No, Sir Edmund, you may have need of it to defend yourself, for I yet have some rebellious English in my Principality!'

With a wave of his hand he was about to lead Sir Edmund away from the battlefield when an archer came striding up the hill towards them. Dressed in a strong studded leather jerkin, he held his bow loosely in his right hand, his nigh on empty quiver slung over his left shoulder. At first Sir Edmund barely noticed the archer's approach, but as he drew near something about the man brought a flash of recognition to Sir Edmund. Looking at the archer, he recalled de Lacey saying something about one of the indentured Welsh archers leaving Ludlow some months ago. He shook his head, as if to clear his mind, for somehow he thought that it was not from Ludlow that he remembered the man: but if not Ludlow, where? Tired, confused, he could not think where it might be were it not Ludlow and turned to Owain Glyn Dŵr. 'This archer,' he said, pointing at the man, 'he served me once at Ludlow and today returned to seduce my archers to betray me!'

Nodding, Owain Glyn Dŵr smiled, before saying quietly, 'Served you once, I believe, Sir Edmund, but he is now my captain of archers and he seduced no man from his duty. Your Welsh archers notched their arrows today, not for Idris here, but for their country which they, like I, would have be free from English sovereignty!'

Chapter Thirteen

Sir Edmund Mortimer was on the march again but now it was to a place not of his choosing, for he was riding alongside his captor, the self-styled Prince Owain Glyn Dŵr. They were heading to the north-west now and had been for the last two days. At first there was a stiff formality in the relations between them but gradually Sir Edmund's tensions eased as he accepted the inevitability of his capture, secure in the knowledge that it was but a matter of time before his ransom would be negotiated. He smiled at the thought of regaining his freedom, of taking revenge for his defeat at Pilleth and taking this Welsh squire back to Ludlow in chains. He gave a toss of his head, thinking bitterly that there would be no Welsh archers at his back next time!

Eyebrows arched, Owain Glyn Dŵr looked sideways at him. 'It's good to see you smile, Sir Edmund,' he said quietly. 'I feared your setback at Pilleth had cast you into a gloom that would never be dispelled!'

Sir Edmund's lips tightened before he replied curtly, 'It was but my disgust at the betrayal that brought me to this state, Squire Glyn Dŵr, but 'tis a lesson that I learnt well albeit at great cost!'

'Come, Sir Edmund,' Prince Owain said with a laugh, 'that was no betrayal, 'twas but that your archers had a greater loyalty to Wales and that is the fortune of war.'

Sir Edmund turned his head to look back along the column and saw Sir Thomas Clanvowe riding helmetless between two watchful men at arms, his head swathed in bandages. He turned again to Owain Glyn Dŵr to say bitterly, 'I doubt Sir Thomas there sees ought but treachery in all of this!'

Prince Owain's eyes hardened as he said sharply, 'You and he, Sir Edmund are fortunate indeed, for by God's good grace you ride with me today and may yet ride safely back to your castles. Your fellow knights, Sir Robert and Sir Kinaird, who I have the grace to accord their proper titles, are left lying cold back there at Pilleth. Now, if you would have your stay with me befit your knighthood, then you will have the courtesy to accord me my proper title, for I am indeed no squire, but by all acclaim, Owain, Prince of Wales.'

Sir Edmund was silent for a moment before replying tersely, 'I know of but one by that title, Glyn Dŵr, and he is Henry, Prince of Wales!'

There was a sardonic smile on Owain Glyn Dŵr's lips now as he said ironically, 'Indeed, Sir Edmund! Is this Henry the son of the usurper who holds your nephew the Earl prisoner because he has a prior claim to England's throne?' His eyes hardened again as he continued, 'You dare talk to me of treachery by men who did but fight for their country's freedom when there is a greater betrayal amongst your own countrymen! If this Henry of whom you speak would indeed be Prince of Wales, let him come here and exercise his rule!' As he spurred his horse and began to ride towards the head of the column he turned his head to add, 'And would you wait for that day, Sir Edmund, long will you languish in my custody!'

Sir Edmund frowned as he watched Glyn Dŵr ride off, pondering now on the truth in the Welshman's words. His mouth twisted into a bitter grimace as he thought of the men he had left scattered on Bryn Glas hillside where they died fighting for a regicide, for he had no doubt now that Henry had had King Richard murdered. With Richard dead, how long would Earl Edmund remain alive as Henry's 'ward'? As a prisoner now himself, how could he protect his nephew and who else was there left who could do so?

He watched Glyn Dŵr talking cheerfully to some of the men at the head of the column and the thought suddenly crossed his mind, who else was there but this would-be prince with his dreams of Welsh sovereignty! As quickly as it came, he brushed the thought aside and he gave a thin smile, as he thought that his own ransom would soon be arranged and he would be free to protect Earl Edmund himself.

At the head of the column, Owain Glyn Dŵr's brother Tudor was saying heatedly, 'I still say we should have pressed on as agreed to South Wales, Owain. News of your victory at Pilleth would have gained us support there that we greatly need!'

Owain smiled as he nodded. 'Such support we shall always need, Tudor, but I would have Sir Edmund safely held in North Wales with Lord Grey. If this war 'gainst England is to succeed it yet has to be paid for and what better way can it be paid for than with English gold! I'll put a price on Lord Grey's head that will empty his coffers and have a pound of flesh on top o' that! Sir Edmund too will fetch a pretty price, for he is kin both to Hotspur and to my Lady Despenser.'

Deep in thought now, he was silent for a moment before adding quietly, 'E'en so, his bondage may yet be put to better use!'

Tudor frowned. 'What better use can it be put, Owain, than to fill your war chest with good red English gold?'

Owain smiled again as he tapped his nose with an index finger. ' 'Tis but a thought as yet, Tudor, and it may come to nought. I wonder though how reluctant King Henry might be to ransom Sir Edmund, who fought and lost and is guardian to Earl Edmund Mortimer, that other claimant to the English throne!' He tapped his nose again. 'So I must plan, Tudor, as to how we may make best use of the asset we have in Sir Edmund riding back there!' Then nodding thoughtfully, he added quietly, 'I almost hope that Henry may refuse Sir Edmund's ransoming!'

The Welsh army, together with its few English prisoners, made rapid progress northwards, avoiding the English held towns and castles on its way, for Owain Glyn Dŵr was anxious to ensure the prisoners' safe arrival in North Wales. A light rain was falling now and Sir Edmund pulled a cloak around him. All day they had been climbing steadily amongst bleak mountains and it was early evening with sunset not long away when Sir Thomas turned to him, scowling, to ask sullenly, 'How much further do we march today in this wild land, do you think, Sir Edmund?'

As Sir Edmund glanced at Sir Thomas he thought that the older man had aged considerably from the seasoned old warrior who had bravely assaulted the Welsh on Bryn Glas mountain just a few days before. The bloodstains on the bandages around his head were brown and crusted, his eyes were clouded as though with pain and the lines of age were etched deeper on his face. His shoulders sagged now as he added, 'I pray it will not be much longer ere we rest, or I'll fall off this horse of mine!' Then, he said bitterly, 'Though I suppose it is no longer mine, but belongs to these thieving Welsh!'

Sir Edmund smiled sympathetically. 'Patience, Sir Thomas. It cannot be far now, for I have no doubt that Glyn Dŵr will stop for rest before sunset, when we might rest as well and have a bite to eat.'

Sir Thomas snorted and gave a toss of his head then, wincing, put his hand to his head. Sir Edmund reached out to him and frowning asked, 'Are you all right, Sir Thomas?'

The older knight grimaced as he let his hand fall to his side. 'Aye, right enough, Sir Edmund, do I but remember not to shake my head! Nought wrong with me that a draught or two of wine and a meal would not improve.' He glanced around him at their captors, then added, 'All that and a few miles distance too from these bloody Welsh!'

Sir Edmund grinned, thinking that perhaps the knight's wounds were not all that serious after all!

They rode on in silence for a mile or so after that and were cresting a hill when Sir Edmund sighted a towering peak in the distance, its summit glowing pink in the setting sun. He turned to his fellow captive saying, 'There is no doubt where we are now, Sir Thomas, for that peak yonder can be nought else but Snowdon's tip.'

Sir Thomas snorted and said, 'I'd care little, Sir Edmund, were it the mount where Noah beached would it but give us respite from this march!' He frowned. 'Snowdon you say, but can Glyn Dŵr hold a manor hid in these hills?'

Sir Edmund shook his head. 'The king holds all Glyn Dŵr's manors confiscate, Sir Thomas, and has gifted them now to his bastard half brother the Earl of Somerset.' He grinned as he added, 'Who, I wager, will not be amused that young Prince Hal has put Sycharth Manor to the torch! But confiscate or not, I know of no manor that Glyn Dŵr held in these parts.'

As they began descending into a valley, shadowed from the sinking sun by the hill on its far side, they could see the dim outlines of what appeared to be a farm. There were a few sheep scattered in the surrounding fields and some cattle moving slowly towards a wooden barn.

Sir Thomas smiled for the first time that day as he gazed at the rural scene. 'I doubt not that we'll camp there for the night, Sir Edmund,' he said cheerfully, 'and we'll sleep soundly in that barn does the cowman but turn his cattle out!'

Sir Edmund smiled. 'Aye, though I'd relish some clean straw in the loft 'fore sleeping midst the dung!'

As they neared the farm nestling at the foot of a rocky outcrop, they saw the farmer leave the house and stride out into the yard to stand there hands on hips, waiting it seemed, for their approach. As Owain Glyn Dŵr and his brother Tudor rode into the farmyard and dismounted, the farmer walked over to them and touched his forehead in salute. Sir Edmund could hear the three men talking, but knew not what was said for they spoke not in English but in their own tongue. The farmer seemed not displeased at their arrival though for he was laughing and waving his arms towards the rocky outcrop behind the farm.

Glyn Dŵr nodded, then turning, began striding towards them. 'Come gentlemen,' he said as he approached, waving his hand in the general direction of the farm, 'if you dismount, these men at arms will lead you to your quarters for the night!'

There was almost a look of pleasure on Sir Thomas's face as he virtually leapt off his horse, saying as he did so, 'It's not the barn for us after all, Sir Edmund!'

Sir Edmund glanced from his fellow captive to Owain Glyn Dŵr and was surprised to see the look of amusement in the Welshman's eyes who, nodding, agreed, 'No, it's not in the barn you'll spend the night, Sir Thomas, but I shall have you kept safe and dry 'til with God and King Henry's grace you may return to Clusop.'

Sir Thomas raised an eyebrow at this and his nose twitched as he asked, 'You mean we stay in this godforsaken valley 'til we may be ransomed, Glyn Dŵr?'

There was irony in the Welshman's voice as he replied, 'Indeed, Sir Thomas. You'll share the pleasure of our Welsh land here 'til by your good grace I deem you fit to be released and then only on your given word you'll not take arms against me in the future!'

Sir Thomas retorted angrily, 'No word I give can release from my duty to take up arms at my lord's array or yet my king's command!'

Glyn Dŵr shook his head in apparent sorrow. 'Alas, Sir Thomas,' he said quietly, 'then I fear that you'll keep Lord Grey company for long days yet, for he said much the same!'

With that he nodded to the men at arms beside the two knights and smiling now, told them, 'Take these knights to join Lord Grey in his chamber!' Then, as the men at arms were about to march them away, he said to Sir Edmund, 'Reluctantly, Sir Edmund, I must relieve you of your weapon now, for you'll be safe enough where you shall stay!'

As Sir Edmund handed Glyn Dŵr his sword, the Welshman told him, 'Your apartment I fear is but bare and dry which is all I can offer here since Henry deprived me of my manors. You'll sleep well enough there though after this day's march and hot food I'll send to you within the hour. Now I must bid you Goodnight!' With that he turned away and followed his brother Tudor, who had been standing close by, into the farmhouse.

If there had been a touch of sympathy in Glyn Dŵr's voice, there was none in the eyes of the Welsh men at arms who, with drawn swords and much rough handling, led Sir Edmund and Sir Thomas towards the farmhouse. At first Sir Thomas had regained his cheerful mien, but his face fell as, after being led towards the farmhouse, they were then led around it towards its rear and he asked Sir Edmund almost petulantly, 'Where the devil are they taking us, Sir Edmund?'

No wiser than his companion in misfortune, Sir Edmund could only shake his head and their guards, even if they spoke English, did not seem anxious to enlighten them. As they got to the rear of the farmhouse, they found themselves facing the almost sheer wall of the rocky outcrop they had seen earlier. Mouths agape, they could only stare at it for a moment, before looking first at the men at arms with their drawn swords and then at each other in some dismay.

'Glyn Dŵr said that we'd sleep well enough, Sir Edmund, but this is no place to end a day's march!' Sir Thomas said quietly. 'Nor yet one's life.'

Sir Edmund looked around him in the gathering dusk, but there was no escape, hemmed in as they were with the farmhouse wall behind them, the sheer face of the outcrop in front of them and armed guards all around them. He turned to the other knight and, his voice a whisper, said, 'Bravely now, Sir Thomas! 'Twill be swift enough, though why he brought us all this way to die, I'll never know!'

He had barely spoken the words when the nearest guard raised his sword menacingly to prod Sir Edmund lightly in the arm before pointing towards a barely discernable pathway, such as a goat might use, that led up the face of the outcrop. As Sir Edmund hesitated, the guard motioned again towards the pathway, then led the way himself.

They were above the level of the farmhouse rooftop when they reached a shelf on the outcrop, no wider than a tall man might stand. There were some dark shadows on the face of the rock, shadows that might be openings, from one of which there appeared to be a glow of light, towards which the guard now led them. As they approached the glow, Sir Edmund could see that it came from the entrance to a cave alongside which a man at arms stood guard.

As they drew near the two men at arms said something to each other in Welsh at which the one standing guard at the cave laughed. Standing aside now, the one who had led them there grinned as he motioned Sir Edmund towards the cave, saying in English as he did so, 'There, Sir Knight, I've delivered you safely to your chamber as my prince instructed me to do. You'll find your bedding there,' then nodding to another of the men at arms he said, 'and Iestyn here will bring you food as soon as we may eat ourselves. He laughed now, saying, 'Though lest he find a goat to carry it, I doubt not that he might lose some along the way!'

As Sir Edmund walked towards the cave, the man at arms called after him, 'I bid you goodnight Sir Knight and wish you great pleasure of the company of your chamber mate!'

Even after the evening twilight outside the cavern, it took a few moments before the two knights' vision became accustomed to the dim interior of the cave and that despite the light from the small lantern at its far end. What they eventually saw was not such as to encourage them for their future captivity. The lichen covered rock walls glistened with moisture and there was a dank chill in the atmosphere that seemed to creep into their very bones. Beneath the lantern there appeared to be a recumbent figure asleep, huddled under a couple of sheepskins. Hesitantly now, they walked slowly towards the light, hoping it might reveal something more promising for their comfort there.

The figure stirred, as though awakened by their approach and sat up as they drew near. The light catching the figure's eyes seemed to make them blaze green like a wild animal's under the matted hair and a mouth opened like a black slash amidst the long grey beard. 'Who are you? What do you want of me?' he snarled, sitting upright now.

Stunned at the sight of this apparition, Sir Edmund could not answer for a moment, so horrified was he at the man's appearance. Gathering his wits together at last, he asked in disbelief, 'Are you Lord Grey, my lord?'

There was a manic look now in those wild green eyes and in the grin that distorted the mouth half hidden amidst the tousled grey beard. The strange figure gave an almost hysterical laugh. 'Who else do you think would seek Glyn Dŵr's generous hospitality in this commodious chamber?' he asked.

Sir Edmund gave a slight bow and frowning, replied, 'I am distressed my lord, to meet you in such circumstances, I am Sir Edmund Mortimer and this is Sir Thomas Clanvowe, both taken prisoner by Glyn Dŵr in battle.'

'Little use then are either of you to me! I would meet his victors here not his prisoners!' snarled Lord Grey. 'What incompetence led you to be his captives, Mortimer?'

Piqued at the implications of the question, Sir Edmund sniffed, before saying curtly, 'Incompetence such as yours, I have no doubt, my lord! Yet if we are to be companions in misfortune here I would that we could all make better company than you would have us believe!'

'Company?' asked Lord Grey petulantly. 'I seek no company here but rather the granting of my ransom by King Henry!' He waved a hand towards a few sheepskins on the floor by the nearby wall. 'Now for God's sake, sort out the bedding they have left you there and let me sleep in peace!'

Sir Edmund looked at Sir Thomas, who just shook his head in exasperation. Biting back the sharp retort that came to his tongue, he said quietly, 'If such be your wish, my lord, I bid you return to your slumber and dreams of early ransom, whilst we prepare ourselves for rest after our long day's march.'

'Had you fought more successfully, your march would have been the shorter, as would my imprisonment in this foul cave!' retorted Lord Grey angrily before pulling the sheepskins around him again and huddling down amongst them.

With sinking hearts the two knights went over to the heap of sheepskins and began sorting them into two equal bundles, looking as they did so at the hard rock floor of the cave. As he held up a sheepskin, Sir Thomas muttered irritably, 'Little enough are they, Sir Edmund, to keep out the chill of this dank cave, but 'tis not that I worry o'er so much as that hard rock floor. I'd give a mark or two, did I but have them, for a bale of straw to intercede 'twixt it and my old bones.'

Sir Edmund grinned ruefully. 'Nor will my younger bones fare better, Sir Thomas, but we shall speak with Glyn Dŵr the morrow and I trust that the promise of gold not withheld will alleviate our conditions here!'

Sir Thomas nodded towards the recumbent figure of Lord Grey, now noisily snoring. 'I fear no such promise has helped yon sleeping lord!' He shook his head. 'Yet perhaps their animus was too long held, too deep rooted, for there to be great hope of knightly courtesy between the two of them!' Then mustering a thin smile, he added, 'Nor, do I fear, have the Welsh much greater love for the Mortimers!'

They were still trying to find suitable places to lay their sheepskins when there was movement outside the cave, the silhouette of a man at arms at its entrance and the man called Iestyn came in followed by another: 'Here you are, my lords,' he exclaimed, 'I bring you sustenance after your march! Hot it is too, or was but a little while ago. Cawl it is, such as my mother used to make!'

'Cawl?' asked Sir Thomas. 'What gibberish name is that for food?'

Iestyn grinned. 'Why my lord, that is food such as you'll never see the like of in an English castle! 'Tis lamb, or likely mutton in this case, with vegetables and such, all simmered long together in a stew, 'twill sustain you well for your long march back to England,' he paused before adding with a grin, 'in but a little while, my lord!'

As they each took a bowl of the stew and a wooden spoon from the man at arms, he pointed with a thumb at the man behind him: 'My friend here has a pot of ale for you to share.'

As he eagerly reached out for the ale, Sir Thomas said in mock severity to Iestyn, 'Pray tell Glyn Dŵr that whilst this will do well enough for tonight, it is my custom to have a glass or two of wine with my evening meal, my good man!'

The man at arms was taken aback for a moment but soon rallied, to say with a grin, 'Aye, my lord, I'll tell him that. Yet I should warn you that your usual custom is no pattern for your future stay in these Welsh mountains and ale you'll find a better companion to your cawl than water from the mountain brook! Then turning, he touched his companion on the arm and led the way out of the cave, their chain mail rustling like a cold winter's wind as they went.

Sir Thomas grinned. 'No wine then, Sir Edmund!' he said dryly as he lifted the bowl of stew to his nose and sniffed at it. His face puckered in disgust and he looked at Sir Edmund in disbelief, as he asked, 'What devil's brew has Glyn Dŵr sent us? I would not give my hounds such food as this!'

There was movement in the far corner of the cave as Lord Grey sat up quickly, bright-eyed, saying, 'You have hot stew and don't want it? Favoured you are indeed to be offered such luxury, I've not had such food in all the months they've kept me here!'

Sir Thomas took one look at the emaciated face of the nobleman and, with a quick glance of resignation at Sir Edmund, went over and handed him the bowl. His hand trembling, Lord Grey grabbed it eagerly and began voraciously spooning the stew into his mouth, barely pausing for breath between mouthfuls.

Walking back to the sheepskins he had spread on the cave floor, Sir Thomas whispered to Sir Edmund, 'Foul as it smelled, I could have eaten it, but one look at Lord Grey there and I did believe his need to be the greater and that he has indeed not eaten as well in all the months that he has dwelt here!' He reached over for the earthenware pot of ale and took a deep draught, then wiped the froth off his lips with the back of his hand and picking up a chink of bread began munching at it, saying as he did so, 'There! That and an easy conscience will suffice for tonight, for who knows what the morrow will bring!'

Sir Edmund, already half way through his bowl of cawl, offered it to him, saying apologetically, 'Here, have this, Sir Thomas, I've had enough! All three of us are prisoners here and if we are to survive together must share our fortune as we share our misfortune!'

Sir Thomas patted his corpulent waist, to say with a laugh, 'No, Sir Edmund! The old and young have greater need than I, it will do me good to fast a little. Had I fasted more before I climbed Bryn Glas Mountain, I might have reached its summit faster!'

He paused for a moment before giving Sir Edmund a quizzical glance and asking, 'What was it that your young squire called to you about conspiracy before he fled the field back there at Pilleth?'

Tired after the long day and drowsy after the hot meal and a pot of ale, Sir Edmund yawned and leant back against the cave wall. He looked at Sir Thomas without understanding for a moment before asking, 'Conspiracy, Sir Thomas?'

'Aye, conspiracy!' Sir Thomas repeated. 'He called out something about having warned you and of our cause not having been lost were it not for conspiracy, before he fled the field with some two score or more of your men!'

Sir Edmund shook his head drowsily before replying, 'I recall it not Sir Thomas. I but remember that the day was already lost to the Welsh and whilst some were fleeing the field, the rest of us fought on in bloody hand to hand combat when de Lacey called out something then turned and ran whilst others followed him. When I am out of here and back in Ludlow, I'll have words to say to de Lacey that he'll not find pleasant to his ears!'

Sir Thomas rubbed his chin thoughtfully for a moment before saying quietly, 'I do but mention this, Sir Edmund, for that conspiracy has an ugly ring to it and 'tis not a sound that our new King Henry will find a harmonious one, should it reach his ears. Not all believe he wears his crown complete and without taint. Some few, I dare say, yet hold the view that your young nephew, the Earl, has prior claim. All this is fertile ground indeed for suspicion and cause enough for some to grasp at straws.' He sighed. 'Should your young squire go bruiting abroad words like conspiracy then all of us who led the march on Pilleth will be suspect 'til we prove the claim be false.'

Sir Edmund, roused now from his lethargy, looked at him in astonishment: 'What's all this talk of conspiracy, Sir Thomas? Think you I did conspire to place myself in captivity? Conspire perhaps to leave some thousand of my men lying cold on Bryn Glas Mountain?'

Sir Thomas shook his head, then winced as he had done before. 'None of these things do I accuse you of Sir Edmund, nor yet believe a grain of truth lies sheltered by those words.' He breathed a deep sigh before continuing, 'Nor is there any need for truth in such accusations for them to cause doubt in minds already conditioned to suspicion. In a usurper's mind, as some allege King Henry be, suspicion is ever present.' As Sir Edmund opened his mouth to respond, Sir Thomas held up his hand then continued again: 'If by God's good grace and ransom payment we are set free, Sir Edmund, I fear that we shall need to defend ourselves, for what de Lacey said before he ran he'll need to say again and louder to defend himself 'gainst a charge of cowardice. Think on these things is all I say for now, Sir Edmund, for we will have time enough to further debate this matter ere we are back in England once again.'

There was a rattle of chains and they both turned their heads quickly, to see Lord Grey standing by his heap of sheepskins, his legs in shackles. 'What's all this talk of conspiracy?' he asked querulously.

Sir Edmund looked at him wide-eyed. 'Conspiracy, my lord?' he asked innocently. 'I fear you must have misheard, my lord, there is no talk of conspiracy here, lest it be of one to set us free!'

Lord Grey snorted his disbelief, then offering the now empty bowl to Sir Thomas, he muttered, 'Here, you may have this, 'twas all cold!' With that he reached down and juggling with his shackles he rubbed his legs where they had been chafed by his chains, before saying irritably, 'I see they have not fitted you with shackles yet. No doubt they will tomorrow!' Then sitting down again and pulling the sheepskins around him, he laid down and it seemed was quickly asleep again.

Sir Thomas's eyes opened wide. 'Fitted with shackles tomorrow?' he asked of Sir Edmund incredulously. 'Where in God's name does Glyn Dŵr think we might get to, does he but leave us without shackles?'

Sir Edmund smiled. 'I do not know, Sir Thomas, nor for tonight do I care, for I would sleep so I might ponder that and all the questions you have left me with, in trust that dawn, should it ever come in these benighted mountains, may bring me answers.

Chapter Fourteen

Sleep did not come readily to Sir Edmund that night, nor was it the hard rock floor or the dank chillness of the cave that kept him wakeful, but rather was it the cause of his imprisonment there: the lost battle of Pilleth. In his nightmarish dreams he heard de Lacey scream again, 'I warned you, my lord, those archers could not be trusted,' but then the voice became distorted, the form blurred, as de Lacey turned away with his echoing voice calling repeatedly, 'Conspiracy! Conspiracy!'

Then it was Owain Glyn Dŵr, standing atop Bryn Glas Mountain, the hillside littered with the bodies of fallen English soldiers. He stood there shaking his head saying repeatedly, 'It was not treachery!' whilst the man called Idris, his captain of archers, stood grinning by his side.

It was that which made Sir Edmund wake with a start for he realised that he knew this archer from somewhere, knew it from the man's condescending smile. Awake now though, Sir Edmund knew not why he should feel so irritated, other than that in his dream he had just suffered again the shame of defeat at Pilleth. Wiping his brow, he sighed and gazed around him. The lantern had been snuffed, leaving the inside of the cavern dark, save that the full moon illuminated its entrance and that the patch of velvet blue sky within his sight was strewn with a handful of stars. His fellow prisoners were both sound asleep, with Lord Grey snoring noisily, so Sir Edmund stretched, then standing up, dropped his sheepskins where he had lain and walked quietly towards the cave's entrance.

Silently as he went, he had not stepped onto the ledge outside the cave before a sword's point was at his chest and the sentinel who barred his way came into view from alongside the entrance. Waving his sword menacingly the guard kept repeating, 'Nacoes' from between gritted teeth.

Ignorant as he was of the Welsh language, it was clear enough to Sir Edmund that this meant that he was not allowed out of the cave. He tried at first to explain that all he wanted to do was to stand out there in the open air, but the guard either did not, or would not, understand and, with that waving sword becoming ever more threatening, Sir Edmund was at last forced to back reluctantly into the cave.

He stood there, near the entrance but outside sword's reach, for a few minutes but though the air was fresher, there was little to see except a few stars that told him nothing, for he was no stargazer. The guard outside must have been standing there watching, waiting for him to step outside again, for there was no sound either save for the occasional hoot of an owl and, from behind him, the repetitive sound of Lord Grey's snoring. Shaking his head in exasperation, he turned and went back to where his blanket lay and sat there disconsolately, his back against the cave's wall, his mind going over and over again the battle at Pilleth.

Eventually he must have slept, for a cock's crow brought him to sudden wakefulness, to see the pale light of dawn filtering into the cave and hear the sound of voices outside. There was the sound of heavy footsteps approaching now, together with the metallic rustling of chain mail and the silhouette of a man at arms appeared at the entrance.

There was surprise in the voice that greeted him, 'Goodmorrow, my lord! Is it the chill mountain air or ill dreams that makes you thus welcome the dawn? I come but to see you still favour us with your company and that you spent a restful night!'

It was Iestyn, the not too unfriendly guard who had brought them food the previous night. Iestyn who, moreover, spoke English well enough.

Sir Edmund scowled as he muttered, 'I would have spent a more restful one, had my Lord Grey there not snored unmercifully.' Then with a nod towards the guard who now stood at the entrance watching all that went on, he said, 'And had your fellow there let me put a foot outside this dank hole to breathe the night air for but a moment!'

Grinning, Iestyn replied, 'Odd it is indeed Sir Edmund how neither man could, of his own self, help you to slumber! Lord Grey there has snored thus, with as little mercy as he would show us Welsh, for all of his captivity. Goronwy there, amiable as his nature ever is, knows that he would surely lose his head were he to let you venture outside this cave. I fear my lord, that you must therefore learn to endure the one and accept the other for as long as you may grace us with your presence!'

Sir Edmund sighed, then with a shake of his head, he said, 'The one,

Iestyn, I can accept, the other I fear is beyond all endurance! I must speak with Owain Glyn Dŵr, for I doubt that he would so torture men worth gold to him!'

Iestyn shook his head, before saying with a smile, 'Must is not a word that rests easily on Prince Owain's ears, Sir Edmund! Supplicants do not demand his attendance upon them but rather do they crave audience of the prince!'

Sir Edmund flushed and opened his mouth to speak, but drew breath instead and bit his tongue before saying calmly, 'I would meet with Owain Glyn Dŵr, Iestyn, that I might discuss the terms of my release with him. Since to resolve this matter must be his wish as well as mine, then neither of us is supplicant here. Be good enough then to convey my wish to your lord.'

Iestyn was silent for a moment as he strode over to the lantern and, with the aid of a flint, caused it to give its fitful light again at the far end of the cave.

Lord Grey turned over in his sleep and stopped snoring for a moment before settling down to continue with its irritating rumble. Sir Thomas brushed a hand across his face as though to brush away a fly, but neither man gave any other sign of wakefulness. Iestyn looked at them for a moment, as though to assure himself they were still asleep, then looked at Sir Edmund again and nodded. 'I will tell Prince Owain of your wish, Sir Edmund.' He shrugged. 'And will in time, no doubt, deliver his reply to you.'

He turned away then and began walking out of the cave, glancing over his shoulder as he reached the entrance to say, 'Some food will be sent to you anon, that you may break your fast.'

Sir Edmund called after him, 'Some water too, Iestyn, I pray, that we may wash the grime from yesterday's march away!' But Iestyn had disappeared and the guard who had been at the entrance just turned away showing no interest in what Sir Edmund might have said or wanted.

Sir Edmund called again, 'Iestyn!' but there was no reply and the guard outside showed as little interest as before. Evidently his duties only entailed ensuring that the captives stayed within the cave!

For Sir Edmund, an age seemed to pass before he heard footsteps outside the cave again only to be disappointed when he found that it was not Iestyn, but another guard bearing some food for them. It was only food he bore too, no water other than a pitcher with enough to wet their thirst but none sufficient to wash the grime of days away.

Lord Grey gave an ironical chuckle at Sir Edmund's complaint. 'We have food and water enough to wet our tongue, Mortimer, what else do you expect?' he croaked. 'These Welsh know nought of the need to wash, so in that they treat us no worse than they treat themselves.'

Seeing the manic light in the nobleman's eyes again, Sir Edmund ignored him, but turned instead to Sir Thomas and told him, 'I sent a message to Glyn Dŵr, saying that I would meet him to discuss my ransom, when we meet I will do ought I can to alleviate our captivity here.'

There was a cackle of laughter again from the far corner as Lord Grey mimicked in falsetto, ' "Alleviate our captivity here!" Think you he cares one jot about your condition in this den? The more evil the condition in which we are kept, the higher ransom he will exact. Ten thousand marks he expects ere he will set me free. Ten thousand marks! Why, 'tis more than all my estate will raise in many a year! Should King Henry yield to his demands, 'twill leave me in penury my whole life long!'

Sir Thomas glanced across at Lord Grey, to ask without apparent sympathy, 'Think you he'll take the common land at Croesau you filched from him in part payment of this ransom, my lord?'

Lord Grey snorted in disbelief. ' "Filched", you say?' he demanded. 'I filched no land from this Welsh squire, I did but repossess that which had been mine for generations, as both king and parliament agreed!'

'Indeed, my lord!' Sir Thomas replied without flinching. 'No less would I expect from Parliament, wherein you wear your baron's robes and our sovereign lord has debts enough to pay without incurring more!'

Lord Grey's lined old face flushed. 'I see now,' he retorted angrily, 'why Mortimer there lost at Pilleth, with such as you by his side! That must be why there was all that talk of conspiracy last night when you both thought I slept.' He tossed his head in emphasis. 'The king himself will know of this when my ransom has been paid!'

His threat struck a chord with Sir Thomas, who blanched at the very thought of being accused of conspiracy against the king. Sir Edmund though tried to bring the voice of reason into the acrimonious discussion by saying quietly, 'Sir Thomas did but try to seek a compromise to this costly business of ransom, my lord! You'd feel the pinch of the loss of a patch of common land far less than the marks by which your exchequer might be eased thereby!'

Lord Grey sneered as he replied, 'It is principle that I speak of when I say that this damned Welsh squire will have no land of mine, nor yet a blade of grass that grows on it! 'Tis mine, this common land of which you speak! 'Tis mine by right of conquest, as is a marcher's right!'

Ever pragmatic, Sir Thomas nodded in apparent agreement. 'Quite right, my lord,' he said firmly. ' 'Tis by such hold on honour that a marcher lord must live, for without his land he is but a common man.' He paused before adding quietly, 'Yet this Welsh squire, or prince, or what you will, seems to have like regard for that common land and, from the time that you have languished here, seems not over anxious to set you free!'

Lord Grey waved his hand dismissively. 'His negotiations with Harry Hotspur take overlong, I grant you, but each day that passes brings my release the nearer, of that I have no doubt, for King Henry has such regard for me!'

Thinking of the night he had spent listening to Lord Grey's reverberating snores, Sir Edmund nodded, to say fervently, 'We both pray for such a happy outcome, my lord!'

Each day that followed, Sir Edmund's hopes were raised with the changing of the guard at the cave's entrance, or as another brought food for them. Each time however his hopes were quickly dashed for no word came from Glyn Dŵr and the three prisoners continued to dwell in squalor in their cave. Nearly a month passed in this way and Sir Edmund had lost all hope of meeting his captor face to face. Then, one evening as dusk began to darken the patch of sky the prisoners glimpsed through the cave's entrance, Iestyn's stocky figure appeared there.

He stood at the entrance for a moment, a hand resting casually on his sword's hilt, the other twirling the end of his drooping moustache as if he were reluctant to enter the cave. Then, as if he had made some weighty decision, his hand dropped to his side and with a slight shrug of his shoulders, he stepped into the cave and unsmiling, walked over to where Sir Edmund sat on his crumpled blanket.

'You are to come with me, Sir Edmund,' he said gravely, 'for Prince Owain would have words with you!'

Sir Edmund sat there looking up at him without moving a muscle. 'I sought words with Squire Glyn Dŵr nigh on a month ago,' he replied bitterly, 'and heard nought from him! Now he speaks and I must rush to his heel like some hound grateful for his attention?'

Iestyn smiled now. 'Aye, grateful you should be indeed, my lord, that Prince Owain has not had you kept in chains in this place!' He waved a finger now, saying, 'If you would remain unchained, Sir Edmund, then it would be well that you remembered that Owain Glyn Dŵr is no squire but prince indeed.' He tapped the hilt of his sword. 'Now rise, Sir Edmund, or I must prompt you with my pricker here, for my prince is not a patient man!'

Sir Edmund glared up at the man at arms, but realising that he had no choice but to obey, rose reluctantly to his feet and began to follow Iestyn out of the cave. As he gained the entrance he turned his head, to see his fellow prisoners watching him. Smiling, Sir Thomas called after him, 'Good fortune, Sir Edmund!' but Lord Grey merely sat in his corner and asked with a sneer:

'Conspiring again, Mortimer?'

After his confinement in the cave, Sir Edmund found following Iestyn down the narrow path on the cliff face of the outcrop a precarious business and was glad enough when at last they reached ground level behind the farmhouse. Once there he was taken up a narrow flight of rickety stairs to a small chamber that was barely furnished with a narrow bed, a chair and a chest on which was set an earthenware bowl filled with water. Sir Edmund turned to Iestyn, who still stood in the doorway: 'What's this? I thought I came to see Glyn Dŵr!'

Iestyn grinned. 'And that you shall, my lord!' He waved a hand towards the bowl of water. 'Yet it is fitting that you should be cleansed and clothed according to your station before you meet!'

Sir Edmund snorted and said, 'What! Would your *prince* not wish to see the manner in which we have been kept, more fitting indeed for felons than for knights awaiting ransom!'

Iestyn smiled, saying quietly, 'Clothes you'll find in the cupboard there, Sir Edmund, and in but a little while I shall be back to take you to the prince, be you cleansed or not.' He withdrew and Sir Edmund heard the sound of a bolt being put across.

He looked out of the small window, but could see only the face of the rocky outcrop and the window too was barred. Going across to the chest he put a finger in the bowl of water, to find to his surprise that it was quite warm and that a large earthenware jug alongside was also full of warm water.

Opening the cupboard door now, he saw that Iestyn had spoken truly, for on hooks behind the door hung some clothes. Plain enough to be a clerk's, but they seemed clean enough he thought. He smiled at that. So Glyn Dŵr thinks a clerk's garb befits me! Then I must wear it regally and with that, casting his doubts aside, he began undressing.

There was a rattle of a bolt being withdrawn and the door opened to reveal Iestyn, who just stood there without entering as he asked, 'Are you ready, my lord?'

His eyebrows arched as Sir Edmund appeared from behind the cupboard door, his long fair hair no longer matted, his new beard brushed and his face at least now clean if pale from lack of sun, its paleness accentuated by the white ruffed shirt and black cloak.

'You've spent the minutes well, my lord!' he said with a smile. 'You are fit now indeed to meet my prince!'

Sir Edmund's eyes flashed and his lips tightened as he said angrily, 'I swear, Iestyn, you do but call him prince to spur me to anger.'

Iestyn shook his head. 'No, my lord,' he replied, 'I call him prince for that he has better title to it than does the usurper's son! Yet we have no time for debate of that matter now my lord, for be he prince or squire, my lord Owain Glyn Dŵr awaits you below.'

With a wave of his hand he prompted Sir Edmund to follow him and led the way along a narrow passageway to another staircase which they descended. At its foot, Sir Edmund was surprised to find himself in what might have been the great hall of a small manor, the centrepiece of which was a great oak table. In the middle of one wall was an open fire although now, in the middle of summer, only a few embers glowed amidst the grey ash. A man sat in a great wooden armed chair by the fireside, but Sir Edmund could not tell who he might be for his back was towards them and he stirred not even to turn his head.

Even when Iestyn led the way around the table to face the man by the fireside, Sir Edmund could not make out the man's features for the small windows let little light into the room at that time of day.

It was not until they were nearly upon him that the man looked up to say with a half smile, 'Ah, Sir Edmund!'

For a moment Sir Edmund was at a loss, reluctant to accord the man his self styled title, yet not wishing to irritate him unnecessarily by calling him Squire. After that moment's hesitation he compromised, after all the man had indeed been lord of a few manors and so, with a half bow, he replied, 'My lord Owain!'

Glyn Dŵr stood up, his presence seeming to lend stature to his stocky figure. Sir Edmund, his eyes accustomed now to the dim light of the hall could see Glyn Dŵr as he remembered him from their first meeting on Bryn Glas Mountain, clear brown eyes, unshadowed by any self doubt, a strong chinned face, brown hair, bearded, a prominent wart on his left cheek. The piercing eyes told of a man who would undoubtedly lead where others followed, but they also told of a man who would have his own way, at whatever cost.

Glyn Dŵr turned to Iestyn. 'Bring over a chair from the table for Sir Edmund, Iestyn, that we may talk awhile here by the fire.'

Sir Edmund's eyes half closed suspiciously. This was like no audience with a prince, nor yet like a lord meeting a prisoner from his dungeon to deliver judgement on him! Barely even like captor and prisoner held for ransom.

As Iestyn placed the chair across the fireside from Glyn Dŵr's, the rebel Welshman waved a hand towards it. 'Be seated, pray, Sir Edmund.'

Still viewing the Welshman suspiciously, Sir Edmund sat, determining as he did so that each word he uttered would be chewed twice before he spat it out!

Glyn Dŵr sat back in his chair, his hands lying relaxed upon his lap and both men sat for a moment eyeing each other, before at last Glyn Dŵr spoke, 'You will be concerned, Sir Edmund, that over a month has passed since you first asked that we might meet. I fear that my absence from this place has been the cause. An absence that has had perhaps more to do with my campaign 'gainst Henry than securing ransom for my guests here.'

He smiled a little complacently before continuing, 'But now, with no great threat to our security here, I can give greater thought to how they may be best turned to account.'

Sir Edmund's heart sank for, together with Sir Thomas Clanvowe, he had hoped that Glyn Dŵr's absence had signalled another assault on Wales by King Henry, which if successful may have ensured the hostages' early release from their captivity. Since that was evidently not so their only hope now lay in being ransomed, yet it looked doubtful if Lord Grey would survive long enough to be ransomed if they continued to be penned up in the cave.

Ignoring Glyn Dŵr's complacency, Sir Edmund snapped angrily, 'You call us guests, Glyn Dŵr, when you would not keep cattle in a pen like ours! If we would wash ourselves then we may not drink. Lord Grey and Sir Thomas are no longer young and if you would have ransom for them then you would do well to shift them to a drier shelter than that which they dwell in now, for they'll not survive there long!'

Glyn Dŵr listened courteously to Sir Edmund then, when the knight paused in the middle of his tirade to draw breath, said quietly, his hands still resting in his lap, 'Enough, Sir Edmund! The conditions you dwell in I know are not all that you might desire! Indeed did your King Henry but let me have my manors back, then I could offer better.' He spread his hand now in apology. 'But here, I fear I have little choice.' Smiling now, he added, 'But I have some good news that will alleviate much of which you complain!'

Sir Edmund's heart lifted, what good news might there be other than about their ransom, and whose but his, since it was he who had been called to Glyn Dŵr! He smiled. 'Good news, Glyn Dŵr?'

The Welshman nodded, his eyes sombre now. 'Aye, some good

news, Sir Edmund, though some that will not please, I fear.'

Sir Edmund shrugged philosophically and said, ' 'Twas ever thus!' Then continued eagerly, 'But what is this news you have for us?'

Glyn Dŵr looked at him thoughtfully for a moment during which Sir Edmund could have strangled the man, so anxious was he to hear the news. At last Glyn Dŵr said quietly, 'Over the last few weeks, Sir Edmund, I have spoken with your kinsman Henry Percy a number of times, for he has been charged to discuss the terms on which I might release Lord Grey.'

'You have discussed such things with Hotspur?' asked Sir Edmund eagerly.

Glyn Dŵr smiled as he nodded. 'Yes, we have met often enough for there to be regard between us for our integrity,' he waved a hand in dismissal, almost as though they were words he had not intended to utter. 'More to the point, we have now agreed on the sum I shall receive on Lord Grey's release,' he paused again, 'both on his and on Sir Thomas's!'

Sir Edmund waited, sure that Glyn Dŵr was holding something back, but the Welshman remained silent, just looking at Sir Edmund with something akin to sympathy in his eyes.

At last, unable to wait any longer, Sir Edmund asked, his voice husky with apprehension, 'And of my own release, Glyn Dŵr?'

'That I fear, Sir Edmund, has not been agreed.'

Wide-eyed now, Sir Edmund repeated, 'Not been agreed?'

Glyn Dŵr shook his head. 'No, Sir Edmund, it has not been agreed, nor can I offer promise of agreement being reached at some future date, for your King Henry accuses that you lost the day back there at Pilleth because of some conspiracy with me.' He gave a rueful smile, then said, 'I swear I know not to whom he offers the greater insult: to you, in that he calls you traitor, or to me in that he alleges I could but win the day by such conspiracy!'

Sir Edmund favoured him with a sour look. 'In that last at least Henry was right!' he said bitterly. 'For you won the day there, Glyn Dŵr, by treachery!'

Glyn Dŵr held up a hand and still smiling said in mild reproof, 'That is a battle fought and lost or won, nor can any talk here help pay the butcher's bill, Sir Edmund, so let us not fight it over once again! What will more profit us is to decide how we may resolve this matter of how you gain your freedom.'

Sir Edmund shrugged. 'That but depends, my lord, on how reasonable your demands might be! You say you spoke with Hotspur, I wager both he and Eleanor, lately the Countess of March, now the

Lady Despenser would assist me in my hour of need.'

Even as he was speaking, Glyn Dŵr was shaking his head as if in sorrow and he held up his hand now, to say quietly, 'I fear not, Sir Edmund! 'Tis true they would have, had Henry not forbidden them to pay the ransom price. Yet it seems that he was in such choler at this conspiracy of which he spoke, that he would in no way suffer them to do so.'

Chapter Fifteen

Owain Glyn Dŵr picked up a wooden stave from beside his chair and banged it against a copper bound wooden bucket on the hearth that held a few logs. It seemed to have been a recognised signal, for a serving man quickly appeared to ask of him, 'My lord?'

'Some wine, Trefor, red wine!'

The man nodded and left, only to reappear again quickly bearing an earthenware ewer and two goblets. With a sympathetic smile, Glyn Dŵr asked, 'A glass of wine, Sir Edmund?' Ashen faced, Sir Edmund just sat there for a moment staring at Glyn Dŵr, then nodded slowly and took the goblet of wine now offered him by the serving man.

He sat there in silence, head bowed, sipping the wine as Glyn Dŵr watched him thoughtfully. When he spoke at last his words were bitter as acid, his eyes wide in his disbelief: 'I conspired with no one, Glyn Dŵr, much less with you. Rather did I serve my liege lord the king against you at great cost to the Mortimers and with little hope of recompense! All this you knew! Did you not tell Hotspur the truth of this?'

Grave faced, Glyn Dŵr nodded. 'Aye, I told him and he was not loth to believe, for he had never believed the charge against you . . .'

Sir Edmund breathed a sigh of relief and interrupted Glyn Dŵr, saying, 'Thank God for that! Then all will be well when Hotspur tells the king of this! You'll get your ransom yet, Glyn Dŵr, and I my freedom!'

Glyn Dŵr shook his head. 'I fear not Sir Edmund, for the charge was made against you to the king's own person by one of your own household, a squire no less, who by all accounts fought bravely at Pilleth!'

Sir Edmund's face blanched as he muttered, 'de Lacey!'

Glyn Dŵr frowned and shook his head. 'I do not know, but it was some such Norman sounding name.'

His voice louder now in its bitterness, Sir Edmund replied, 'Oh yes, Glyn Dŵr, I doubt not that that is the traitor's name, nor that he wove this fabric to shield himself from the charge of cowardice on the field of battle!' As Glyn Dŵr's eyes widened in surprise, Sir Edmund nodded emphatically. 'Yes, Glyn Dŵr, this liar fled the field at Pilleth with the last remnants of my army, to leave me there not once, but twice betrayed!'

His shoulders sagging now, he put his goblet down on the table and looked up. 'What then, Glyn Dŵr?' he asked. 'I have not the wherewithal to purchase my freedom and all those who would purchase it for me are debarred from so doing! I fear that unless in charity you were to set me free, I must be your captive for some time yet!'

Glyn Dŵr shook his head disparagingly. 'Freedom, Sir Edmund,' he said quietly, 'is a transient thing. For were I to set you free and you returned to Ludlow, how long would you lodge there, ere Henry were to offer you more solitary lodging in his tower at London?' He sighed and there was a wolf-like glint in his eyes, a touch of menace in his voice, as he said thoughtfully, 'With Lord Grey and Sir Thomas departing soon, your presence does leave me with a problem . . .' he spread his hands, ' . . .an inconvenience, for as you know to some cost, we have little by way of comfort to offer prisoners, who thus become an encumbrance to me . . .' there was a glimpse of that lupine smile again, as he added quietly, 'and offer little hope of profit!'

Eyes blank now, his mouth dry, Sir Edmund replied in a voice he barely recognised as his own: 'You must deal with me as you must, Glyn Dŵr, for I am your prisoner fairly taken in combat. Yet I would tell you that by all the rules of war, since I am your prisoner you must either keep and feed me, or set me free e'en though you might demand my parole not to take up arms against you.'

Glyn Dŵr nodded his acquiescence. 'Quite true, Sir Edmund,' he replied just a little too smugly. 'Were this a war for Welsh Independence as I have claimed, then all you say might well obtain. Yet your own King Henry, who holds your nephew prisoner, tells all that I am but a rebel 'gainst his sovereignty. Had you won the day at Pilleth, how many of those 'rules of war' you speak of would have applied to me?' He snorted, then said, 'Short shrift would I have had 'fore I was shown a hempen collar with my four quarters being then disported for crows to peck!'

Glyn Dŵr snatched up his goblet of wine and took a deep draught before slamming the goblet down on the table again with such force that Sir Edmund expected to see it shatter. He could understand the Welshman's anger though, for he recognised the truth in Glyn Dŵr's assessment. He shrugged and sighing, looked Glyn Dŵr in the eye. 'As I have said, I am your prisoner and you are thus able to dispose of me as you will! Yet that regard which you said Hotspur holds you in and your own sense of honour will together be a restraint you'll not avoid!'

Glyn Dŵr returned his level gaze unflinchingly and took another draught of wine before looking into the goblet as though he would see into the future. Looking up at Sir Edmund again, he shook his head and sighed, saying, 'I fear for you, Sir Edmund, for you seem to live in an age of chivalry and honour on the field of battle and all such stuff of nonsense that never really was!

'What chivalry was there in King Richard's forced abdication? What honour did Henry gain in Richard's foul murder, or in holding young Earl Mortimer hostage for that he has greater claim to the English throne? We live in such real times, Sir Edmund, not in days of fantasy. We live in times when practical men must turn dreams into their own reality and my dream is that I would have Wales free from England's yoke as you would be free of mine!'

Sir Edmund listened spellbound by the vehemence of Glyn Dŵr's rhetoric yet wondering how any of this could lead to his own freedom. What was such freedom worth now anyway, if he could not return to England? From Glyn Dŵr's changed tone however, it seemed that at least his own execution was no longer imminent unless, of course, he was mistaken.

He opened his mouth and was not a little surprised to find his throat no longer dry and that when he spoke it was in a voice that was his own: 'If we must live in this practical world, Glyn Dŵr,' he said, mustering a smile, 'how do you intend to dispose of my inconvenient presence. All I can offer is my parole and since it seems I am not welcome in England, that may be of little worth to you.'

Glyn Dŵr looked at him thoughtfully for a moment then gave a thin smile as he nodded. 'True, Sir Edmund, for I doubt that you would have offered it to me yesterday!' He spread his hands again. 'Nor do I need it today. Instead, whilst we both allow our thoughts time to mature on what has passed between us today, we'll not talk of captive and captor but of you as my guest and me the host!'

Sir Edmund's eyebrows arched in surprise and, anxious now to break the news of their release to Lord Grey and Sir Thomas, he rose from his seat, saying as he did so, 'Then I must to my cave, Glyn Dŵr, and you to your evening fare!'

Glyn Dŵr shook his head. 'No, Sir Edmund, I fear I must now keep you separate from your erstwhile companions, for tomorrow they set out on their long journey to the marches. So no cave for you, you'll stay in that room you paused in on your way to me.'

Sir Edmund frowned. 'I must see Sir Thomas,' he expostulated. 'I must warn him that he may be in jeopardy of being charged with me of conspiracy!'

The Welshman shook his head again and said in a voice which brooked no denial, 'No, Sir Edmund! There has been no impediment placed on his ransom and Henry Percy, to whom I shall deliver the prisoners, knows the tale well enough to appraise him of any hazard he may face.'

Sir Edmund shrugged and said, 'As you wish, my lord, yet ere he departs, I would say farewell to Sir Thomas, for he fought valiantly by my side at Pilleth.'

Glyn Dŵr hesitated and then nodded, albeit reluctantly it seemed. 'Sobeit,' he agreed tersely, 'but you shall need be up betimes, for I leave at cock's crow! Now you must leave me, for I have much to think on, as no doubt you have yourself.' Then raising his voice to such as would raise the dead, he called, 'Iestyn!' and the man at arms, who must have been waiting behind an oaken door close by, instantly appeared. Glyn Dŵr called him over with a wave of a hand and told him, 'Show Sir Edmund to his . . . his chamber!'

Sir Edmund smiled to himself at Glyn Dŵr's hesitation over what to call the room to which he was being taken, evidently it would have been discourteous to have referred to a 'guest's' lodging as his cell! As he followed the man at arms up the staircase, he thought wryly that the room offered much improved accommodation and Lord Grey's snoring would not keep him awake this night. He sighed then as he thought at what great cost both to his pride and freedom this greater comfort had been achieved.

As he heard Iestyn shut the door of the room behind him and throw the bolt across he sat on the truckle bed and dropped his head into his hands, his mind whirling with all that he had been told in the few minutes that he had sat with Glyn Dŵr in the hall below. Charged falsely with conspiracy by the king, debarred from ransom and now, it seemed, Glyn Dŵr's prisoner without term or hope of release! The relative comfort of the room in which he now sat compared with the cave was small recompense indeed for his misfortune and his now still uncertain future.

* * * *

Owain Glyn Dŵr's brother Tudor, as alike his older brother as two peas in a pod, was smiling as he strode across the farmhouse hall. Standing with his back to the dying embers of the fire he looked at Owain, the quizzical smile still on his lips as he asked, 'What did friend Mortimer have to say at your news, Owain?'

'It pleased him little Tudor and he was much aggrieved both with the king's refusal to have him ransomed and with his young squire's treachery!'

Head on one side, Tudor, smiled. 'That can be little surprise, Owain!' His eyes narrowed now as he asked, 'Even as we marched north, you had some doubt whether, after his defeat at Pilleth, the king would ransom him! Why didst we bring him here, were it not for gold?'

'Can you not see, Tudor, that he is an asset worth more than gold? He can help create disunity amongst the English nobility, as a wedge can be used to split a giant oak! In but a few days now I meet his kinsman Hotspur, who together with his father the Earl of Northumberland, will not be enamoured with their king's refusal to allow Mortimer's ransoming.'

'That is why you did not send him back to the cave?' asked Tudor.

'Aye,' replied Owain with a nod, 'and for that separating him from the others now will serve to confirm to them this charge of conspiracy.' He gave that lupine smile again as he added, 'When he bids them farewell on the morrow, with your friendly hand upon his shoulder, they'll be convinced of the truth of it and there'll be no return to England for young Mortimer, not whilst Henry sits on England's throne!'

Tudor frowned as he shook his head doubtfully. 'I live not comfortably with such plot and counterplot, Owain,' he replied. 'If he is not worth gold to us, then he is but an encumbrance, let us be done with him! Send him back to Henry for him to hang, or save his steps and hang him here!'

Owain smiled at his brother's impetuosity. 'Patience brother!' he said pacifically. 'Time enough for that if all else fails! Tonight he'll sup with us, for I have plans for him in which I cannot serve him cold!'

The sound of the door being unbolted roused Sir Edmund from his slumber, for after returning to the room from his meeting with Glyn Dŵr, he had sought solace in sleep. Startled, he anxiously looked around the unfamiliar surroundings of the small room wondering for a moment where he might be. It all came back then though and he put a hand to his eyes, as though trying to brush away the memory of Glyn Dŵr telling him of the king's refusal to ransom him.

The door opened and the man at arms Iestyn stood there smiling. 'Prince Owain tells me I have no need to bolt your door!' he said and after a moment's pause, asked with raised eyebrows, 'Is't because he is now your prince as well as mine, my lord?'

Sir Edmund scowled up at him to say sullenly, 'I am his prisoner, so if it pleases him to call himself a prince, why not? If there is to be argument over that, let it be between him and that other Prince of Wales! Now, what is it that you want of me?'

'Nought my lord, except that Prince Owain would have you sup with him.'

Sir Edmund looked at him, eyes wide open in surprise. 'Sup with him?' he asked incredulously.

Iestyn nodded. 'Aye my lord, and were I you, I'd hasten at his command, for you'll fare better there than with my Lord Grey and Sir Thomas!'

The mention of his two fellow prisoners brought a frown to Sir Edmund's brow. 'They leave on the morrow, Iestyn,' he said quietly. 'Think you Lord Grey is fit to travel?'

Iestyn nodded firmly. 'There's nought wrong with him, my lord! He's feigned sickness, of the mind or of the bones, since he was first brought here, though but little good has it done him, for few here but Prince Owain care much whether he lives or dies.' Then, with a shrewd glance at Sir Edmund, he said, 'You stay with us then, my lord?'

Sir Edmund nodded. 'It seems perforce I must, Iestyn.'

'Well, with autumn at our doorstep, you'll be dryer here than in that cave, my lord, and 'twill save me a step or two! But now I'd best take you to Prince Owain or there'll be little left for me at my end of the table!'

When they got to the hall it was noisily full with barely a place left at the table which seemed to be occupied mainly with Glyn Dŵr's retainers. A fire blazed in the hearth, for the evening mountain air was chill now even though summer was not yet at an end. Despite the chatter and the bustle of serving maids rushing hither and thither with platters of food, Sir Edmund could hear the melodious sound of harp music. Looking around he saw a minstrel at the far end of the hall playing a harp and even as he looked the minstrel began to sing and the chatter ceased as if by common accord. The words seemed to pluck at his heartstrings, even though, or perhaps because, he could not understand them.

Iestyn led him towards Owain Glyn Dŵr and, as they drew near, Sir

Edmund was surprised to see that the men sitting at the top of the table with him were as though they were images of the same man at different stages of his life. Owain's brother, Tudor, he had already seen during the march to Snowdonia, but the other, much younger man could only be Owain's son, or perhaps nephew. Of a certainty, he was a kinsman.

Seeing Sir Edmund approach, Owain smiled in welcome. 'Come, Sir Edmund,' he said jovially as he patted the empty chair beside him, 'sit here, by my side.' And, turning to the younger image of himself he said, 'A goblet of wine, for our guest if you will, Gruffydd!'

Gruffydd, it seemed, did not share Owain's pleasure at Sir Edmund joining them at table, for he hesitated before at last with a shrug, pouring wine into a goblet from the ewer of wine on the table beside him.

There was a twitch of Owain's eye, that might have been mistaken for a wink as he said to Sir Edmund, whilst glancing at Gruffydd, 'My son is young enough, Sir Edmund, to see all as black or white and all men as friend or foe. Given time he may yet understand that those who were adversaries may indeed become friends through common interests and purpose.'

Gruffydd flushed at this and Sir Edmund's face set as he said stiffly, 'I share his problem, Glyn Dŵr, for whilst I believe that adversaries might treat civilly with one another their interests and purpose remain opposed.'

Owain Glyn Dŵr replied with a laugh, 'It seems you both need time to come to the same understanding! At least tonight, Sir Edmund, our interests are conjoint for we are all here to find common purpose in good Welsh lamb and shade harsh memories softly with a glass of wine.'

Sir Edmund's face softened into a smile as, with a half bow, he acknowledged, 'On that, Glyn Dŵr, we can agree!' Seating himself now, he raised his glass saying, 'Good health!' then grinned as he added, 'Although I never imagined I might drink to that!'

Owain Glyn Dŵr smiled knowingly. 'You see, Sir Edmund, you make progress already!' Then raising his glass he said, 'Iach i dda!'

Sir Edmund frowned, for the Welsh phrase suddenly seemed familiar to him and a vague memory came to his mind, of hearing those same words beside some water somewhere, but where or when he could not imagine.

As he sipped his wine in response to the toast he looked along the table and saw the archer who had once served as an indentured man at Ludlow. Their eyes met and Sir Edmund noticed a strong resemblance between the archer and Glyn Dŵr's son Gruffydd. There was the same arrogant look in the eyes and the thin smile held not welcome but condescension . . . and this from a mere archer! Sir Edmund turned to Owain Glyn Dŵr to ask, 'Your captain of archers there, he is kin of yours?'

Before Owain Glyn Dŵr could reply, Gruffydd snorted and said angrily, 'He is no kin of ours, Mortimer, he is but a peasant archer who plies his bow for whosoever pays, as you will know!'

Owain interrupted sharply: 'He plies it for me now Gruffydd and plies it well. Were he indeed a peasant, 'twould be but chance of birth, but he is captain of archers here and that of his own self's doing!'

Sir Edmund sensed that this was no new difference between father and son and, clearing his throat, he tried to change the subject, saying, 'You leave at dawn tomorrow, my lord Owain, will you be absent long?'

Owain glanced at his brother Tudor and then at Gruffydd, and grinned. 'We shall all be absent for a little while, Sir Edmund, for we have business to conduct along the marches! Yet I shall return the soonest, for my wife Marged and the older children of my brood will be arriving shortly to bring some civility to our rough ways!'

The banging on the door brought Sir Edmund to sudden wakefulness and he sat up to glance around his strange surroundings. A pale light filtered through the dirt and cobwebs of the small window and he realised that he was back in the room he had been taken to after his meeting with Owain Glyn Dŵr. His tongue clung to the roof of his mouth, his throat was rough and his mouth, for long unaccustomed to red wine, savoured of some foul bird's nest.

The door opened suddenly to reveal a grinning Iestyn. 'You supped well of the grape last night, my lord, but now 'tis dawn and time to pay for the night's jollity. If would you say farewell to your English friends, you must hasten to the yard where they are all but mounted and ready to depart.'

Blinking, Sir Edmund rose and stood there for a moment a little unsteadily, rubbing his eyes whilst he tried to collect his thoughts. He sighed as it all came back to him then, Sir Thomas and Lord Grey, their ransom paid, were being freed whilst he, with no ransom allowed was to remain here, a burden on his captor. For how long, he wondered! Then thrusting that bleak thought aside, he followed Iestyn down into the yard in front of the farmhouse.

As he reached the front door, he saw Tudor standing there, who greeted him as though he were a long lost friend and resting a hand on his shoulder, smiled as he said, 'You are up betimes this morning, Sir Edmund. After last night's carousing I wagered Iestyn there that you would be still abed!'

Sir Edmund glanced at Glyn Dŵr's brother in surprise, for last night they had said barely two words to one another. Taken aback by this sudden familiarity, he stepped aside to allow the Welshman's hand to drop away from his shoulder. As he did so, he looked around the courtyard to see Sir Thomas and Lord Grey already mounted on sturdy Welsh ponies, looking at him with evident astonishment. Lord Grey was the first to speak, although it was not before he turned his head and spat onto the dusty yard.

' 'Tis true then, Mortimer!' he said before adding contemptuously: 'You have indeed turned coat and joined these rebels! Even I had not thought that ill of you. Now is it clear why you lost at Pilleth! How many of your men paid with their life's blood that you might safely turn your coat, Mortimer? The king shall hear of this!'

Sir Edmund flinched as though struck by a mailed fist and looked at Sir Thomas for support, but there was a look of disgust on the elderly knight's face as he delivered the coup de grâce: 'I would never have thought it of you, Sir Edmund,' he said bitterly, 'that you, who cried 'twas treachery that lost us the day at Pilleth should have betrayed us, both then and now!'

Before he had a chance to reply, they spurred their ponies and followed as Glyn Dŵr led them out of the yard and on the road to their freedom.

Chapter Sixteen

Sir Edmund watched in dismay as his erstwhile companions rode off to freedom. He stood there watching them, his heart in his throat, until at last a bend in the track hid them from his view. He knew that, prisoner or no, he would never be able to follow them now. The tale they would have to tell the king about him would confirm the slander de Lacey had already spread and damn him forever.

He turned away disconsolately to see Tudor still standing there. 'Your friends seem ill pleased with you, Sir Edmund!' the Welshman said with an amused smile on his face.

'That should please you as little as it should my lord Owain,' said Sir Edmund bitterly, 'for it does but devalue my worth in terms of ransom!'

That knowing smile still on his face, Tudor replied, 'Why, there you have it wrong, Sir Edmund, for each friend my brother has amongst England's nobility is worth many a mark to him. He'd rather have such friends than the weight of gold that they might bring in ransom!'

'He has no friend in me,' Sir Edmund spat the words out fiercely, 'for each time he met with Hotspur, he could well have repudiated the calumny that de Lacey spread and which by your hand of false friendship you did so much to confirm!'

Eyebrows raised, Tudor's surprise was there in his voice as he replied, 'False friendship my lord? Never so! 'Twas but a hand of friendship I extended in your hour of need for since I saw you had no friends amongst the English, I knew you must be a friend of ours . . .' he paused before adding softly, malevolently, ' . . . and you would live!'

Sir Edmund looked at the Welshman blankly for a moment as the words sank into his consciousness, then his eyes widened as he recognised the truth in the malicious words. The slander that de Lacey had originated now ensnared him with bonds more sure than even those of his imprisonment. Not merely that but, since he was worthless to the Welsh rebels as a hostage, were he to survive then he must make his peace with them.

He gave a wry smile at that, as he realised that his very survival depended on him compounding the treason of which he stood accused now by not one but three men. He shook his head, knowing that as a baron of parliament, Lord Grey's word alone would be enough to hang him high. Even so, he knew that no action of his had brought him to this pass and stubbornly determined that neither would one of his lend truth to the calumny now.

His lips stretched thin in his bitterness, he spat his reply at the Welshman, 'It was no hand of friendship you reached out to me, but rather 'twas a Judas kiss you gave, that would have my friends unwittingly give false testimony against me! Indeed, I would as soon have Lucifer himself as my friend and would more likely turn my back on him than you, were you my friend or foe!'

Tudor stroked his beard, then tut tutted in mock sorrow before saying, his voice rich with irony, 'You are upset at losing your friends, Sir Edmund and so I forgive your harsh words knowing that your regret at speaking them will surely follow. How indeed can they be true friends when they have such little faith in you? Whilst we, once your adversaries, forgive so readily your past sins against us and would have you join us in our crusade against a usurping regicide.'

'You call this rebellion 'gainst your liege lord the king a crusade, a war of independence even, to grace it with a counterfeit legitimacy!' snapped sir Edmund angrily and, wagging a finger at him added, 'but I'll have none of it! You are in rebellion and I am no friend of yours, not even though I hang for it!'

Tudor grinned. 'Then 'twill be a race, my lord, whether you dance on air for Henry or my princely brother! Yet ere your neck is stretched for stretching loyalty too far, think well on these things: my brother seeks not to rule over England. Should he then succeed 'gainst Henry, would not your nephew, that other Edmund, be closer to the throne that some say is rightfully his? Were that to be so, this charge of conspiracy 'gainst you would mean little then, but rather would it be to your great credit!'

As Sir Edmund, his face flushed with anger, opened his mouth to reply, Tudor smiled and held up his hand saying, 'Enough of all this talk politic, Sir Edmund, ere we say things best left unsaid! Let us break our fast instead and, like wise old judges, meditate before we pronounce sentence.' With that he led the way into the farmhouse where the table was already laid for a meal.

Later that morning Sir Edmund was sitting by the fire in the hall, lost in thought as he gazed into the flickering flames as though hoping they might offer escape from his ensnarement. Gradually though he was roused from his daydream as he became increasingly aware of the bustle and noisy chatter in the yard outside.

Rising, he walked over to the window and peering out, saw that the yard was full of armed men, some mounted and many more afoot bearing lances or bows. As he stood there he heard heavy footsteps and a metallic chinking as someone came into the hall and turning saw that it was Tudor, clad in light armour.

The Welshman grinned, his dark beard making his teeth flash white, as he asked, 'Along with young Gruffydd I go to visit your friends along the marches, Sir Edmund, would you not ride with us?'

' No!' Sir Edmund snapped. 'Though I might wish I were there to greet you, for a warm welcome would I offer!'

Tudor, his grin even broader now nodded. 'Aye, my lord, 'twas such a welcome that you gave my brother that brought you to visit us here in the mountains.'

As Sir Edmund, with no answer to that riposte, remained silent, Tudor added more seriously, 'Along with Gruffydd I'll spend the rest of summer and into autumn reaping and harvesting an English crop along the marches, but Prince Owain will return soon, laden with ransom gold! Until he does, Iestyn will see to your needs and you may wander freely around the house and yard. Yet if you have a mind to go awandering further, the ever amiable Iestyn will fall upon you like an avenging angel, so stay close to home, my lord!'

With that Tudor turned and stomped out of the door and, as Sir Edmund watched from his vantage point, set off on his 'harvesting' of the marches with his villainous looking band of Welshmen.

The next two months passed slowly for Sir Edmund, left as he was to his own devices for much of the time. His meals he ate alone in the hall although on occasion one or two men, evidently armed retainers of Owain Glyn Dŵr, would partake of their meal at the far end of the table. Serving wenches flitted hither and thither about their chores, paying him but little regard, although now and again one or other of them would give him a sly glance then, giggling, chatter to another in her own tongue. Iestyn, burdened perhaps by his responsibility of care for Sir Edmund, had withdrawn into himself and seldom now entered into conversation with his charge, although he was civil enough when Sir Edmund spoke to him.

It was on occasions such as this that Sir Edmund gleaned what little news he might of the outside world, although this was in the main limited to news of Owain Glyn Dŵr's campaigning. It seemed that following his successes at Ruthin and Pilleth, he had now assaulted Cardiff and Abergavenny castles and put the towns there to the torch. Encouraged by his victories in Glamorgan and with his army growing daily, he went on to take Usk, Caerleon and Newport. Nor was it the English alone who suffered in Gwent, for the Welsh there favoured Glyn Dŵr as little as did the men of Pembrokeshire and had not rallied to his banner as had the men of Glamorgan.

His successes in South Wales however, only served to infuriate King Henry who sent out an array to all the sheriffs of the marches to marshall the forces at their command. By the end of August the forces they mustered were joined by men from Lancaster and Shropshire to begin a massive three pronged attack on Wales from Chester, Worcester and Hereford, designed to quell once and for all the 'Welsh wizard', Glyn Dŵr.

Iestyn could hardly contain himself as he told Sir Edmund how Glyn Dŵr had repelled the English assault. In lauding the success of Glyn Dŵr's generalship however, perhaps he failed to give sufficient credit to Glyn Dŵr's greatest ally in the campaign, the weather.

Such was the size of the English army that each prong of the attack was powerful enough on its own to meet and conquer all the power which Glyn Dŵr could muster. Therein perhaps was its downfall for it was an unwieldy force ill equipped to face the worst weather that Wales had known for a century or more. Battered by storms, rain, hail and even snow, the army had not penetrated far into Wales before its leaders, the Earls of Stafford and Warwick, Lord Codnor and Henry himself, had to withdraw and lead their bedraggled army ignominiously back to England, harassed as it went by the guerilla-like tactics of the Welsh.

Whilst all this was taking place, Sir Edmund was suffering the boredom of imprisonment in Snowdonia with growing resentment. Whilst he was no longer confined as he had been at first, his freedom was very much limited to the environs of the farm and his companions restricted to such as Iestyn who took the occasional pot of ale with him and the serving maids who brought him his food.

One day towards the end of October, when the time for military campaigning was drawing to an end, Sir Edmund was pacing aimlessly around the courtyard in front of the farm when Iestyn came to the farmhouse door and, raising a hand to attract his attention, walked over to him. Sir Edmund smiled and said dryly, 'You caught me just in time, Iestyn, I was about to break bounds and escape to England.'

Iestyn shook his head and, with a smile that held a hint of sympathy, replied, 'I fear not my lord, e'en in summer, these mountains are no place for a stranger to wander amongst alone and as autumn turns to winter, 'tis a place of hazard for such as you!'

Sir Edmund nodded his agreement, to say with a wry grin, 'I do not doubt the truth of that, Iestyn, although that is not the only reason I abide by the rules of your house. Is it news of the outside world then, that brings you hot foot to me?'

Iestyn smiled. 'Aye, good news indeed, my lord, for a messenger sent on by Prince Owain brought me word the prince himself will be here this night and that the Lady Marged will be here come the morrow!'

If he were expecting Sir Edmund to share his excitement at the news, he must indeed have been disappointed for, straight-faced, the knight merely replied, 'I wish them joy of their reunion, Iestyn!'

Iestyn's face set into a grim mask at the rebuff and, as he turned on his heel, he threw over his shoulder the words, 'Your meal's on the table and I wish you joy of that, my lord, for it's the last you'll eat in peace lest you wish to sulk up there in your attic room!'

If Owain Glyn Dŵr returned that night, then it must have been long after sundown, for Sir Edmund neither sighted nor heard sound of his captor before he sought solace from his own ills in sleep that night. As he stepped down from the staircase into the hall next morning though, a now familiar figure sat at the head of the long table. Glyn Dŵr welcomed him without a turn of the head in his rich, mellow tones, 'Goodmorrow, Sir Edmund, I trust our late return last night did not disturb your slumbers?'

Unsure whether to take the words as a rebuke for not being awake to welcome the return of Glyn Dŵr, he hesitated before replying, 'Your return last night must have been both late and soft footed, my lord Owain, for it was long after dark before I slept and then nought awakened me 'til Iestyn told me this morning that you had returned.'

With a dismissive wave of his hand, Owain Glyn Dŵr brushed aside his apology and smiled, saying, 'Long practice in the art of war has taught me, Sir Edmund, that one is ill advised to approach an encampment with great clamour in the night, lest that which you thought was yours is no longer so. If, in your silent approach you surprise your friends then after the first shock is over they will greet you with pleasure and will have learnt a thing or two. If they have long since gone and your enemy is at the gate, then surprise may lead to their confusion! Yet all that you will know well enough without my tutelage! I trust you fared well enough during my absence?'

Sir Edmund nodded and said with little enough enthusiasm, 'Aye, Glyn Dŵr, well enough.'

The Welshman's piercing eyes bored into him, as he said, with a shade of menace in his voice, 'No one did ought to harm you?'

Sir Edmund shook his head vigorously. 'No, of course not, no.' He smiled a little sadly, then said, ' 'Tis just I think they saw in me a turncoat and had as little taste for what they saw as Sir Thomas and Lord Grey liked the traitor they saw in me before they left!' Exasperated, he added vehemently with a toss of his head, 'Nor would I feel the pinch of either, were they not both untrue!'

Glyn Dŵr toyed with the food before him for a moment before, looking up, he said quietly, 'Would it then ease your troubled conscience if one or other were indeed true?'

Sir Edmund wrinkled his nose as if in disgust: 'Of course not!'

Glyn Dŵr looked at him with raised eyebrows, a half smile on his lips. 'How can you be possessed of such certainty, Sir Edmund,' he asked, 'when Henry Bolingbroke, the would-be king, stands in the way of your own kinsman's royalty?'

Sir Edmund's face set stubbornly. 'King Henry is my liege lord and whilst he lives will still be so, Glyn Dŵr!'

Owain Glyn Dŵr smiled, but there was exasperation in his voice as he said, 'You are ever a perverse man, Sir Edmund, who graces the usurper with his false title, whilst withholding mine from me! In another time, another place, such loyalty might be admirable Sir Edmund, but you give fidelity to he who has disowned you whilst denying one who offers friendship.'

Sir Edmund remaining silent, Glyn Dŵr shook his head and grinning now, said, 'For God's sake man, sit down and break your fast! Perverse and stubborn though you be, I'll not have you die on me for want of food whilst I break my fast!'

As Sir Edmund sat down across the table from Glyn Dŵr, a serving maid came to him bearing a platter of food and Glyn Dŵr gave her a smile and a wink as he said, 'There, you see, Sir Edmund, our lovely Megan is as anxious as I that you do not pine away like some lovesick swain!'

Blushing, the girl gave a little curtsy to Glyn Dŵr, then turned and fled back to the kitchen. Glyn Dŵr grinned as he asked, 'I seem to have struck a chord there, Sir Edmund, or is it rather that in my absence, you've played a tune or two?' Then, seeing the look if indignation on Sir Edmund's face, he said quickly, 'No, of course not, for you're a man who puts honour 'fore life itself . . .' He hesitated, and for a moment Sir Edmund imagined there was a calculating look in Glyn Dŵr's eyes as he continued, ' . . . and I am glad of that, for ere the sun sets today, my Lady Marged brings some of my brood here from Ynys Môn.'

That evening as he stepped into the hall from the staircase, Sir Edmund felt he was intruding upon a family gathering, for there was a festive air in the room. The log fire blazed in the hearth, the harpist strummed away at his harp in a corner, but seemed more intent upon gazing wistfully at one of the dark haired young girls there than upon his music. A sturdy young lad stood looking up at Owain Glyn Dŵr too, as if proudly allying himself with his father's cause.

Owain Glyn Dŵr saw him then and beckoned him over with a wave of his hand, saying as he did so, 'Come, Sir Edmund, join us! For I would have you meet my Lady Marged and these others here who plague me by their stubborn insistence that they are no longer children.' He gave a toss of his head in mock irritation. 'Their stubbornness reminds me of one I met the other day, Sir Edmund!'

As Sir Edmund approached the group a little diffidently, the Lady Marged held out her hand which, with a gallant bow, he took and touched lightly with his lips. As he looked at her he was surprised to see that she was totally unlike anything he might have imagined of the wife of a Welsh squire. As tall as Glyn Dŵr himself, she stood there almost regally in her long green silk dress, with her dark hair and blue eyes. There was amusement in those eyes now, as smiling, she asked of him, 'You seem surprised, Sir Edmund! Is it that we are so unlike the gentlefolk you meet in your English castles or is it that people so much alike can have so great a difference?'

He smiled as he gave that half bow again. 'Why no, my lady, it is but that I am amazed that your harsh Welsh mountains can harbour such gentility!'

Still smiling, the Lady Marged turned to the young girl standing beside her, who until now had been half hidden in the shadows of the candlelit room. 'There, Catrin,' she said. 'Did I not tell you to beware the gallantry of English noblemen?'

The girl moved now, so that her face was suddenly enveloped in the glow from a candelabra on the table and with one glance at her, he knew her. In that one glance he took in the dark hair, the blue eyes, that provocative, knowing smile. Wide-eyed in disbelief, he stepped back from her, as though from a signalled blow, to say in a hoarse whisper, 'Cathy!'

If he had indeed spoken aloud, then no one in the family group seemed to have heard him, for they were all still talking amongst themselves almost as though he were not there, all that is except the Lady Marged and Catrin, who were looking at him with amused smiles. The Lady Marged patted her daughter on the arm. 'There, cariad,' she said, seemingly holding back her laughter. 'No need for you to be afraid, Catrin, for English men are like all others, brave enough in battle yet they flinch before a woman's charms!' Then turning to Sir Edmund, she really did laugh as she said in mock reproof, 'Why shame, Sir Edmund, that you should be so frightened by a child of but seventeen summers and not a winter more!'

Trying to quickly recover from his shock at seeing Cathy there and sure now that the Lady Marged could not have heard his exclamation, he bowed again then muttered, 'I was but taken aback, my lady, that you could mirror so exactly her youthful charm!'

With arched eyebrows and disbelief evident in her voice, the Lady Marged asked, 'Were you indeed, Sir Edmund?' Evidently she did not expect a reply though, for she turned to Catrin to say firmly, 'There, Catrin. That is why I said beware the English noblemen, for by their mouths they say one thing whilst their eyes cry out another! One may never really know what their hearts might be telling. Come now, we must be seated or the meat will all be cold before ever it is served!' With that she turned away and touching Owain Glyn Dŵr on the arm, said something to him in Welsh and with a nod he led her to the table whilst the others followed, seemingly to some preordained seating plan.

Whilst the Lady Marged sat on Glyn Dŵr's left, Sir Edmund found himself sitting on his right as though he were the honoured guest. His heart gave a sudden leap then as, turning to his right he found himself looking into the surprisingly blue eyes of Catrin before she lowered them demurely.

He was still gazing at her, as if seeking her recognition when he heard Glyn Dŵr ask, 'Wine, Sir Edmund?' and turned quickly to see the amused look in Glyn Dŵr's eyes as he said, 'I thought I had lost you, Sir Edmund, or that you'd lost your taste for wine, for twice I had to ask!' Then, having filled Sir Edmund's goblet he poured wine into another and calling over a serving maid said with a smile, 'Take this to Iolo Goch, Megan, and tell him that when he has drunk deep, to play us a melody of hiraeth and homecoming.'

It was the same serving maid that had served Sir Edmund at breakfast and she blushed as she glanced at him on her way to take the wine to the harpist. It had not gone unnoticed for, as he raised his goblet of wine to his lips, Catrin smiled as she said to him quietly, 'It seems the serving wenches have greater need than I of my Lady mother's warning, my lord!'

Spluttering, he nearly choked on the mouthful of wine and heard her say, 'Here, my lord, let me help you!' Hand to mouth he turned towards her to see that knowing look in her eyes as, holding her napkin out to him she said again softly, 'Let me help you, my lord.'

His eyes clouded as he desperately tried to recall where he had heard those words said to him before this, yet could not imagine them ever having been said with such tenderness. The napkin was at his lips now as, with a light touch she dabbed the wine away, saying provocatively as she did so, 'There my lord, is that not better?'

As she took her hand away, he muttered his thanks and quickly turned his head, only to see the look of amusement on Glyn Dŵr's face. Flushing with embarrassment now, he looked across at the harpist, Iolo Goch, who putting down the now half empty goblet of wine glared at him before beginning to play his harp. After a few introductory notes the harpist began singing and, his eyes softer now, seemed to be singing to Catrin alone, for his eyes were upon her whilst he sang.

Whatever might have been the burden of the harpist's song, it claimed the attention of all around the table, for there was no chatter whilst he sang, other than that occasioned by the servants passing food or wine around the table. It meant little to Sir Edmund, however, for the minstrel sang in his own outlandish tongue and the sickly sweet melody seemed to match the soulful look in the man's eyes as he gazed at Catrin.

However little it might have pleased Sir Edmund, the others around the table seemed to like it well enough for there was loud applause when at last the minstrel was done and Sir Edmund noticed that Glyn Dŵr sent a gold coin across to Iolo Goch.

Smiling, he turned his head to say, 'You spend the ransom money readily, Lord Owain!'

Glyn Dŵr grinned. 'Aye, Sir Edmund, as readily as I'd spend yours, did I but get my hands upon it! Instead I have to watch whilst you spill good wine and glower at a lovesick minstrel lad!'

Sir Edmund frowned irritably. 'You are mistaken, my lord, for I did not glower, 'twas but that I am ill acquainted with your language and thus his lay meant little to me.'

'Just so!' replied Glyn Dŵr, the amusement there in his eyes again. 'Good reason therefore for you to learn a word or two of it, if your stay with us should be prolonged.' He put a hand on Sir Edmund's arm and, leaning towards him, winked as he said quietly, 'It seems my daughter Catrin there might be prepared to be of help to you in that!'

There it was again: Catrin of help to him! Unreasonably, the prospect irritated him and he turned on Glyn Dŵr to say irritably, 'And why, sir, should she be of help to me, a stranger?'

Eyebrows arched in surprise, Glyn Dŵr replied calmly, 'Why, for no reason, Sir Edmund, other than that you are her father's guest.'

Glyn Dŵr fell silent then as, no doubt prompted by that golden coin, Iolo Goch began to sing again, although from the triumphant rhythm of his lay, this time it seemed to be a song of victory and when he finished, the applause seemed to be louder than ever.

It only served to leave Sir Edmund gloomier than before for it seemed to emphasise to him that it was as a stranger he sat there amidst those who should be his enemies, yet who were, ironically, those he must rely upon for succour.

He was glad when eventually the meal was at an end and, as quickly as politeness would allow, he excused himself and climbed the staircase to his solitary little attic room. The day, with its succession of surprises, had left him exhausted mentally and that, together with a surfeit of Glyn Dŵr's red wine, resulted in him quickly falling into a deep sleep.

It was a deep but not restful slumber, for ever anon the fleeting image of the girl Cathy was there before him. Cathy, or was it Catrin? He tossed and turned, trying to fathom it out but she was always there ahead of him, always just out of reach and unattainable. Even in his sleep, he wondered why he had called her Cathy, why her provocative smile seemed so familiar.

He woke up with a start and struggled with a flint to light the lantern by the bedside. Succeeding at last he sat up in the bed and found that he was bathed in sweat and recalled the days at Ludlow when he had been just so afflicted. Remembered too de Lacey telling something of a girl called Cathy in Ludlow town, but try as he might he could not bring the substance of the tale to mind. Sitting there, his back against the bedhead, he tossed his head. Geoffrey de Lacey! Who could believe the half of what the traitor said!

As Sir Edmund sat there worrying over Glyn Dŵr's daughter Catrin, who he had only met a few hours previously; not far away, in the main bedroom of the farmhouse, the Lady Marged was talking with Glyn Dŵr about her. As she brushed her long fair hair, she said over her shoulder to Glyn Dŵr, 'Catherine seems quite taken with your Englishman, Owain!'

He smiled dismissively. 'Aye, but Catrin is of an age where she is 'quite taken' with ought that wears trousers, Marged.' He gave her an appraising glance, before adding, 'I am not displeased though, for Sir Edmund is comely enough and that in more ways than one!'

She stopped brushing her hair, holding the brush still in her hair and looked at him wide-eyed as she asked in some surprise, 'What mean you, Owain, "In more ways than one"?'

He pursed is lips and with a speculative look in his eyes now, replied, 'Well, Marged, whilst he has little wealth to call his own, he is kin to those who have. More importantly, can we but oust Henry from his English throne then, by all the odds, Sir Edmund would be uncle to their king and might then himself be Earl of March! That aside, he is kin to the Percies of Northumberland, who I would have as allies.' He grinned. 'Oh yes, my love, Sir Edmund is comely enough, indeed!'

Lady Marged gave a quick toss of her head and carried on brushing. 'Plot as you may, Owain,' she said, 'I doubt that Catrin will be compliant to your will in this, for she is much taken with that archer, Idris, and quite likes the attention that Iolo Goch pays to her!'

'Aye, no doubt,' said Glyn Dŵr with a smile, 'but were you to persuade her of the benefits of being aunt to the King of England and of being a Countess herself, do you not think she might succumb to the attentions of an English knight?'

Lady Marged laughed as she replied, 'Catrin will do as Catrin wills, I fear Owain . . .' She paused there and after a moment added pensively, '. . .and oft enough that is what I tell her she must not do!'

Chapter Seventeen

When Sir Edmund went down to the hall for breakfast the next morning, Glyn Dŵr was alone at table and, looking up, greeted him saying, 'You retired early last night, Sir Edmund, was the company not to your liking?'

Sir Edmund busied himself for a moment in pulling out a chair to cover his hesitation before replying, wondering as he did so whether Glyn Dŵr had noticed his reaction to meeting Catrin. Looking at Glyn Dŵr now though, it seemed to him that the question was innocent enough and he shook his head as he replied, 'No, my lord, 'twas but that I have not been used to such gentle company since I have been your guest and thought it would not mix well with too much wine! Nor did I wish to intrude myself too long upon your reunion with your family.'

'Such courtesy becomes you, Sir Edmund,' Glyn Dŵr replied with a smile, 'but it is misplaced, for all are family whilst under this one roof.'

The remark reminded Sir Edmund of something he had wondered about since his arrival at the farmhouse and he asked, 'Is then the farmer of your family too, my lord?'

Glyn Dŵr smiled as he shook his head. 'No! He dwells in his cottage nearby and farms the land around here for me.' He paused as the servant girl, Megan, came in with a platter of food and a pot of ale. With a little curtsy she placed it in front of Sir Edmund and, as he smiled his thanks, blushed furiously, then hurried away.

Glyn Dŵr grinned. 'You have indeed made a conquest there, Sir Edmund!' Amused it seemed at his own jest, he became unusually expansive and leaning back in his chair said with a smile, 'I've given thought to your stay here, Sir Edmund, and see little need now for you to be constrained as before. Henceforth therefore, you may come and go as you wish.' He laughed then as he added, 'Though should you wish to leave our company I'd ask you tell us, so I may gently break the news to Megan there!'

Surprised, Sir Edmund looked at him open mouthed for a moment, then laughed himself. 'That is kind of you indeed, Glyn Dŵr, though where I might wander to alone, afoot and with not a mark about me, I do not know.'

'Quite true, Sir Edmund, and all points that had not escaped my notice! However, there is a pony in the stables set aside for your use alone, whilst as to money, well you have little need of that here, for where would it be spent? All that is left for me to deal with then, is company, and there you have me at a loss . . .' he paused before, with an enquiring glance at Sir Edmund, adding, ' . . . except that my tomboy daughter Catrin said that she would ride with you for a little while today, if it be your wish?'

Completely taken aback, Sir Edmund looked at him speechless for a moment, before saying, 'That is most kind of your lady daughter, my lord, I would be greatly obliged. It will be a pleasure to ride again, the more so in such pleasant company.'

Glyn Dŵr burst out laughing. 'My lady daughter!' he exclaimed. 'Pleasant company! Why, if all that is so, her stay on Ynys Môn must have changed her indeed! More likely will she race you round the mountainsides!' Dabbing his lips with a napkin, he stood up saying, 'Now I have work to do Sir Edmund.' Then winked as he added, 'Affairs of state! My court here is ever busy with such things.' He was already at the door when he turned his head to say over his shoulder, 'You'll find your horse in the stable . . . and no doubt my daughter too!'

With that he was gone, leaving a somewhat bemused Sir Edmund sitting there alone, wondering why Catrin had volunteered to ride with him today. He picked up his pot of ale, but it was empty so, not wishing to bring a blushing Megan out of her kitchen, he rose to walk thoughtfully from the hall and out into the yard. He stood there for a moment looking around him and saw a young boy astride a horse over by the stables. As he started to walk towards the stables, he realised to his amazement that it was no young lad, but Catrin, attired as any boy might be. He smiled as he walked up to her saying, 'Your father said that I might find you here, my lady, and that you offered to ride with me this morning!'

She did not seem noticeably pleased to see him there, nor did she return his smile. Instead, with a toss of her head she told him, 'Your horse is ready saddled in the stable, my lord!'

Frowning now, he walked on into the stables to see that there was indeed a saddled horse in one of the stalls and leading it out, he mounted and walked it across to where she waited for him. Before he reached her though, she spurred her horse and was off at a fast canter across the yard and through the gate, leaving him to follow if he chose. Digging his spurs in, he caught up with her to say indignantly. 'Your father said you offered to ride with me, my lady, not have me follow in your dusty footsteps around these mountain sides!'

Pouting rebelliously, she snapped, 'Unlike you, my lord, I am no prisoner who must do as I am bidden, I ride with whom I choose, not with whosoever I am told!'

Perhaps it was seeing the hurt there in his eyes that made her relent and the brittle look her eyes had held softened now as she told him, 'Oh, very well, my lord, we shall ride together!' A moment later it was there again though as she added, 'But only for a little while, for Iolo Goch teaches me to play the harp and I must not miss my lesson!'

He still felt the hurt, though he did not know whether it was because he realised now that her father must have told her she should ride with him. Was it really that which hurt so much or was it her eagerness to get back to the farm for her lesson with the minstrel, the one with the pleading eyes and sickly sweet voice? It was only then that he realised to his surprise that this strange feeling of hurt was jealousy, something he had never thought to experience. How could that be, he wondered, how could he be jealous over someone who was hardly more than a child, someone he had met only hours before? Looking at her now he thought that she looked more like an arrogant young lad than a young girl as she sat there, head on one side, gazing at him with those blue eyes that would command rather than be bidden.

Nodding, he smiled his agreement saying, 'Let us ride together for a little while then, my lady.'

Wide-eyed, she looked at him for a moment before, laughing now, she replied, 'You may call my mother "my lady", but I am Catrin and I shall call you Edmund!'

Laughing, he agreed, 'That pleases me, Catrin, though somehow when we first met I thought of you as Cathy.'

For a fleeting moment he thought he saw an odd look in those blue eyes of hers but if so, then it was quickly gone and she glanced sideways at him to say firmly, 'No! my name is Catrin!' Then spurring her pony she added over her shoulder, 'Come, we must ride on or I shall be late for my lesson!'

Taken by surprise, he was left behind as her pony quickly gathered speed in its gallop along the valley. Giving chase now he was exhilarated by the rushing wind, the rhythmic movement of his mount and the impression of trees and fields flying past him. After racing along at this breakneck speed for some minutes, Catrin looked over her shoulder at him and he could see her flushed, happy face. Her pony's pace seemed to be slowing now and Sir Edmund was able to gain ground. As he came up alongside her he said laughingly, 'Had you not reined up, Catrin, my ride today would have been a solitary one, for I doubt my mount could match yours!'

She shook her head to say, 'It never would, for this is my favourite.' Leaning forward to stroke the pony's head she glanced up at him and smiling, added, 'She goes like the wind!' Dismounting, she began walking her horse towards where a nearby brook tumbled into the valley. Sir Edmund followed suit and a moment later watched as side by side both ponies drank from the brook.

Catrin took off the boyish cap that she had been wearing and shook her head so that her long black hair fell about her shoulders and, her face still flushed from the ride, said quietly, 'I love it here, Edmund! It reminds me so much of Afon Cynllaith!'

The name meant nothing to him and with raised eyebrows he asked, 'Afon Cynllaith?'

She tossed her head in exasperation. 'Of course!' she said. 'It's the river by my father's manor at Sycharth, where we used to live.' She was standing close to him now and he could see the tears welling in her eyes as she almost whispered, 'It was so lovely there, Edmund, before we had to leave there and go to Ynys Môn.'

He could see the tears brimming over as she looked up at him and knew instinctively what she was going to say. For the words came tumbling out then, how her idyllic life in the manor had been shattered by her father's rebellion. How they had had to flee for their lives from Sycharth and take refuge with their kin on Ynys Môn, whilst her father continued his campaign against King Henry. The tears really flowed though when Catrin told him of how after they had left, young Prince Henry sacked Sycharth and burnt it to the ground. She looked utterly forlorn as she looked up at him through her tears to say, 'We can never go back there now, Edmund! Never!'

He took her in his arms then and she clung to him as if he were her only hope of salvation and, her head nestling on his shoulder, she cried as though her heart would break. At last, when all her tears were shed, she looked up at him all puffy eyed and was still clinging to him as bending his head to hers, he kissed her and gradually lowered her to the ground.

* * * *

Later on, as she lay snuggled in his arms, her eyes no longer puffy and red, but soft and relaxed, Catrin said softly, 'I've missed my lesson with Iolo Goch!'

Edmund smiled as he stroked her hair. 'I'm sorry to have detained you, my lady!' Then as he looked towards the two ponies quietly grazing by the side of the brook he took his arm from around her, stretched and said, 'You've missed your lesson and do we not return soon, we both will have missed our midday meal and your father will think I have made my escape to England!'

With an artful look she asked teasingly, 'And do you want to escape to England now, Edmund?'

Looking at her lying there, he realised this was the question he had been asking himself ever since they set out that morning. Catrin or Cathy, Welsh squire's daughter or no, this was the elusive girl he had been seeking since longer than he could remember. Soft eyed, he said quietly, almost whispered, 'I shall never escape now, Catrin, for I am no longer your father's prisoner but yours, and your chains are stronger than his ever were!'

Even as he said it, he knew that in so doing he was renouncing his fealty to King Henry, all hopes of ransom and any hope he might have ever held of returning to England whilst King Henry reigned. He had bound himself to the fickle whim of this girl child. He held his hand out towards her, saying, 'Come, Cathy, we must go now.'

She looked up at him, pouting for a moment as she corrected him, 'Catrin!' then rising, slowly took his hand and stood up. Together now, they walked hand in hand over to their horses and mounting, trotted back at a gentle pace to the farmhouse.

For Sir Edmund the days that followed were no longer an imprisonment, for each day now he rode with Catrin and walked with her beside the brook or amongst the hills surrounding the farm. Nor was his mind engaged with thoughts of the turmoil into which Glyn Dŵr's rebellion had cast Wales and the marches but rather with the girl Catrin who was now his captor and who it seemed to him, he had known through all his years.

One evening at the end of August, he was drinking wine with Glyn Dŵr in the hall as they watched Iolo Goch teaching Catrin the art of harpistry when the Welshman turned to him, to say with a knowing smile, 'It seems you do not approve of my daughter's music lesson, Sir

Edmund, for your brow is as dark as a winter's cloud heavy burdened with snow!' Then said slyly, 'Or is it perhaps the tutor of whom you do not approve?'

With a sharp turn of his head, Sir Edmund said tight lipped, 'The man should watch his manners, my lord, for his hands are too familiar for a serving man.'

Owain Glyn Dŵr laughed. 'So! It is the tutor, not the harpistry, with whom you are aggrieved Sir Edmund! Yet he is no servant, for he is an artist who plies his trade with harp instead of brush, in song words are his palette and he lets our own mind present the images that we would see. Yet have no fear for Catrin, Sir Edmund, for she is not for a dreamer such as he!'

Sir Edmund shook his head and there was an urgency in his voice as he interrupted, 'I have no fear for Catrin, my lord, nor yet of her for I . . .'

Smiling, Glyn Dŵr held up his hand. 'I am no priest, Sir Edmund, confessions are not my trade nor do I sell my absolutions! Like Iolo over there I am a dreamer but my dreams are more tangible than his for I shape them into action. I dream of a sovereign Wales wherein we live in peace alongside our neighbour England. For that to become reality Henry Bolingbroke must go and there is justice enough in that, for he should never have sat on England's throne!'

He stabbed an index finger towards Sir Edmund now, to say passionately, 'When that is so, who shall reign in England other than your nephew, the Earl of March? Not I, for I have no such ambition. A prince am I and as such will rule by consent of my peers, here in Wales! Were that to happen and by God it will, how do I ensure the enduring peace between King and Prince that needs must be if our two lands may prosper?'

He stopped there, leaving the question hanging in the air as if expecting Sir Edmund to provide the answer. Having no answer though, Sir Edmund shook his head at last, saying with a frown, 'I know not, my lord!'

'You are an able enough soldier, Sir Edmund,' Glyn Dŵr said with a grin, 'and I have little doubt that experience will make you a better one! Of politics though, it seems you are as yet in infancy for I thought you'd shout the answer in my face as soon as asked!'

Seeing the perplexed look on Sir Edmund's face, he sighed and snapped, 'Why, the answer, Sir Edmund, is obvious to any child . . .' he paused, ' . . .at least, any child of mine! Were you to marry Catrin it would create a bond between the Mortimers and my family that would help ensure such peace between our two countries!'

Sir Edmund sat gazing at Glyn Dŵr open mouthed, before he was at last able to speak. He swallowed: 'Are you saying, my lord, that you would have me marry Catrin?'

There was an amused look in Glyn Dŵr's eyes as he nodded. 'Aye, that's the gist of it, Sir Edmund, and sharp as any blade you are to have picked it up!'

With disbelief in his voice now, Sir Edmund asked, 'It may be politic, my lord, but will she have me?'

Glyn Dŵr looked at him straight-faced. 'Oh, aye, I think she will, Sir Edmund, do you but ask her.'

Sir Edmund's lip curled. 'Just as she *chose* to ride with me me, my lord?'

Glyn Dŵr replied with some asperity, 'Catrin will ride with whom she chooses, Sir Edmund, as she will marry, for such is our way in Wales, yet that is not to say a good father may not advise where his child's best interests lie!'

Sir Edmund favoured him with a wary look. 'Then I will ask,' he replied, then raised a cautionary finger to say, 'but I'll have no unwilling bride beside me at the altar!'

Glyn Dŵr nodded. 'Nor I see my daughter there with an unwilling groom! Yet if she chooses to be your bride, she'll take with her a dowry fit for any countess and with it a writ that frees you, without ransom paid.' He paused and shook his head sadly before adding, 'I pray that none other of my daughters cost me so dearly in their matrimony!'

He stood up now and taking up his goblet, looked at Sir Edmund with raised eyebrows and asked, 'Shall we drink to that?'

Rising, Sir Edmund picked up his goblet, but he was thinking of Catrin as he replied, 'Aye, my lord, I'll drink to that!'

Sitting in her room Lady Marged looked up from her needlework to say to her daughter who stood gazing out of the window, 'You find Sir Edmund good company, Catrin?'

Catrin turned her head and shrugged. 'He is pleasant enough company Mam, who else is there in this outlandish place?'

Head on one side, Lady Marged smiled as she asked innocently, 'Iolo Goch with his harp perhaps, Catrin, dear?'

Catrin blushed. 'Oh, Iolo is nice Mam, but he's such a dreamer and his lays are either all about war and fighting or maidens in distress or something.'

Lady Marged laughed. 'Perhaps Iolo lives in a more real world than ours, dear, for men seem to be forever either in love or at war.' She gave a soft smile then as she added, 'And just sometimes they manage both!'

Catrin shrugged and turned to look out of the window again whilst Lady Marged worked quietly away at her needlework. After a few minutes she looked speculatively at Catrin's back and said quietly, 'I think Sir Edmund is quite taken with you my dear, for he speaks quite highly of you to your father.'

Catrin turned away quickly from the window, to say indignantly, 'He spoke to father about me?'

Lady Marged looked up at her from threading a needle and pursing her lips nodded. 'Well he had to, didn't he my dear, he wants to marry you!'

'Wants to marry me?' exploded Catrin. 'If he wants to marry me, why does he ask father, not me?'

Lady Marged smiled placatingly. 'Come now, my dear, you know your father must approve of who might ask.'

Catrin shrugged dismissively and face set, said firmly, 'I do not love him Mam and I will not marry him for I *love* Idris.'

Lady Marged smiled. 'Idris?' she asked. 'Is that the archer?'

Catrin shook her head, then said defiantly, 'No! He is father's captain of Archers!'

Her mother nodded. 'Yes, I know him. A nice young man for you to spend an hour with on a summer's afternoon at Sycharth, Catrin, as I know you oftentimes did, but he is no husband for a prince's daughter!'

Tears began welling in Catrin's eyes now as she pleaded, 'But Mam, I love Idris!'

'I know my dear,' her mother said sympathetically, 'and though your father holds him in high esteem as an archer, he cannot be for you. He is an archer my dear, who sells his bow wherever and to whom he must. He is but an archer, Catrin, who one day, when his fighting's done, will lie anonymously on some battlefield.'

With one horrified look at her mother and a hand to her mouth now, Catrin went dashing from the room to seek sympathy from her sister Alice, almost two years younger than herself. As she listened wide-eyed to Catrin's tale though, Alice seemed more excited than dismayed at her sister's predicament, interrupting only to ask when the wedding would be and whether she might attend upon Catrin on her wedding day and to say how nice it would be for Catrin to become Lady Mortimer.

For two days Catrin stayed close to her room but there being no peremptory calls for her, she eventually ventured to the stables and quietly walked her pony out of the yard. Mounting, she rode off to her favourite place: the small meadow with its brook that lay at the end of the valley. Once there, she dismounted and let the pony amble off to graze contentedly at the edge of the stream whilst she mused on all the things her mother had said.

She still did not really believe that Sir Edmund wanted to marry her, or that her father would wish her to do so. Yet should he do so, then what of Idris? She smiled to herself as she thought of all those days at Sycharth by Avon Cynllaith when she had watched Idris at his archery practice and of how they had walked hand in hand together along Afon Cynllaith's banks. She heard herself telling her mother *I love Idris*. and knew that it was true . . . but knew too that she had never really thought about the two of them actually being married! Her heart sank then as she realised that it was something neither of them had ever mentioned. Realised too that she could not really imagine herself following Idris from castle to castle, from one knight's retinue to another, like some camp follower.

She saw the rider then, coming towards her from around the small copse further down the stream and her heart missed a beat as she saw that it was Sir Edmund. She knew that he must have seen her too, though he gave no sign of having done so other than that he walked his horse purposefully towards her. He was only a few paces away from her when he reined up and with a quiet smile, dismounted.

Touching his whip to his soft feathered hat, he smiled, then said almost diffidently, 'I thought I might find you here if I came back this way, Lady Catrin.'

Catrin wasn't smiling though as she said abruptly, 'Only three days ago it was Catrin and Edmund between us two, is there now some constraint between us such that we are "Lady Catrin" and "Sir Knight"?'

Sir Edmund shook his head. 'None that I would have, nor yet would I impose myself upon you by too great a familiarity!'

Catrin sniffed, to say scathingly, 'Yet you are familiar enough to tell my father that you would'st marry me, Sir Edmund! Or is it that he would have you marry me?'

His eyes, which until now had held hers, looked down at the ground for a moment before, raising them again to hers, he said in a voice filled with emotion, 'I confess that I wish to marry you, Catrin, but not because any other would have me do so but for my own heart's sake.' He smiled now. 'I have often thought that I seem to have known you all my years, now I wish to know you for all the years to come! Will you marry me Catrin?'

She looked at him open mouthed for a moment, taken aback by the speech her scathing remark had brought upon her. She shook her head then and stammered, ‘I do not know, Sir Edmund . . . I do not know . . . I must think on this!’

He smiled at her, saying quietly, ‘I would not have it otherwise, Catrin! Think well on it for both our sakes.’ He turned then and mounting his horse, rode off in the direction of the farm.

Chapter Eighteen

As Sir Edmund rode into the farmyard, he saw Glyn Dŵr watching him from the front door of the house and waved a hand in acknowledgement. After stabling the horse however, he went into the house through the back door feeling that this was no time for talk of great politics. Climbing the bare wooden staircase to his room, he thought of the many times he had climbed the stone staircase of the Garderobe Tower at Ludlow and, his heart sinking, he faltered in his stride. Could he indeed exchange the comfort, the power, of being the Castellan of Ludlow and guardian of the young Earl of March for this he wondered? What, in all reality, could Glyn Dŵr offer but the fugitive existence of a rebel's ally? Though Glyn Dŵr might style himself Prince of Wales, to what boundaries of his principality did his writ really extend?

Thoughtfully, he walked on up the stairs to his little room and looked out of the window onto the rocky outcrop thinking that it was as bleak an outlook as his own future. Were he to marry Catrin, if indeed she would have him, what could he offer her other than his dependency on her father, his erstwhile captor? Were he to marry her, he would have short shrift indeed from King Henry were Glyn Dŵr to lose this war. All he would have to offer Catrin then would be an early widowhood.

He shook his head in despair as he realised there was little else that he might do. There was no way he might take Catrin safely back to Ludlow as his bride nor, if he could, was there some way in which he might persuade Glyn Dŵr to let them leave.

Whilst Sir Edmund sat unhappily in his little attic room, a forlorn Catrin was slowly walking her horse back to the farm thinking as she did so of Idris, now fighting for her father somewhere out there along the marches or at some castle's siege. Although she had never really contemplated marrying Idris, to marry someone else now seemed to be a betrayal. Somehow though, she knew she had never felt that being with Sir Edmund, being held and kissed by him, was any sort of faithlessness. She smiled now as she remembered that first day they had ridden out to the meadow together and how he had held her then, comforted her. Suddenly it seemed not like treachery at all. Spurring her horse, she raced back to the farm, to rein up as she saw her father standing in the doorway, smiling at her. 'A good ride Catrin?' he asked genially.

Face flushed from the short gallop, she nodded and reaching over, patted her horse on the neck. 'Yes Father, it has been a good ride, indeed!' Then with a wave of her hand, she walked her horse over to the stables.

The small church nestling amongst the foothills of Snowdon was an unlikely place for a royal wedding. Yet despite the supposed secrecy surrounding the marriage, it seemed that hundreds of people had flocked there from the surrounding countryside, all knowing that Owain Glyn Dŵr's daughter was to be wed there today. Some few had stayed away for that they had heard she was to wed an Englishman, but they were very few indeed.

As the small bell in its wooden tower rang out its peal, Sir Edmund stood inside nervously waiting for his bride, with Maredudd, Catrin's younger brother, at his side. Sir Edmund looked every inch the knight as he stood there, his rich blue apparel embroidered with silver thread, long fair hair glinting in the shafts of sunshine as it fell over the clear whiteness of his collar. Standing there, he remembered Iestyn coming to him in the attic room, to tell him that Glyn Dŵr wished to speak with him. He had found Glyn Dŵr standing with his back to the fire in the hall, hands crossed behind him.

Grinning broadly, Glyn Dŵr had walked over to the long oak table and filled two goblets with wine from a ewer on the table. Offering him one, Glyn Dŵr raised his own to his lips, saying as he did so 'Here's to the union of our two houses, Edmund!'

Sir Edmund looked into the glass he held in his hand, then doubtfully at Glyn Dŵr and asked incredulously, 'The union of our two houses, my lord?'

There was a fleeting look of irritation on Glyn Dŵr's face as he asked, 'Do I always have to repeat myself to you, man?' The look faded and he smiled again now as he said, 'Catrin has agreed to marry you!'

Sir Edmund looked at him suspiciously for a moment before saying dryly, 'Then I would hear it from her myself and know she says it from the heart, my lord!'

Glyn Dŵr replied, 'And that you shall, never fear, but at least meanwhile drink to the *hope* that our two houses may be united, ere I die of thirst!'

He had drunk to the amended toast and later when he sought out Catrin she had told him that she would indeed marry him. Thrice he had asked her, until at last with some exasperation she had replied, 'I fear my lord you do not want to marry me at all and thus ask me over again, in hope that I will at last say no! Do you ask me only because my father wills it, my lord?' A soft look in his eyes, he shook his head and took her in his arms to kiss her lightly on the lips, but she clung to him as she had that first day by the meadow before, breathless at last, she had pulled her head away and, laughing, had said, 'I think perhaps I will marry you, Edmund!'

Even now standing there in the church, Sir Edmund still could not believe that it was all really happening, that he was actually cutting his ties with England, denying his fealty to King Henry and more importantly was about to marry Catrin. He glanced around him, at Maredudd, at Lady Marged sitting in the pew behind him then at Hywel Cyffin, the Dean of St. Asaph standing there in his rich robes waiting to marry them, and knew that it was so indeed.

There were gasps from the congregation and Sir Edmund turned his head to see Catrin walking up the aisle with her father at her side and her sister Alice following her. Gazing at her, a lump rose in his throat as he thought how beautiful she looked. Jewels glinted in her dark hair turning her blue eyes to amethysts and the blush on her cheeks told all of her happiness. If she was beautiful in his eyes, then Owain Glyn Dŵr's stocky figure was regal in his purple robe, a princely coronet atop his thick dark hair, a gold medallion hanging from the heavy gold chain around his neck.

It all seemed unreal to Sir Edmund as he listened to the Dean of St. Asaph recite the Latin words of the marriage ceremony in sonorous inflections and he gave his own responses as though they were words uttered by another. Then he was walking along the aisle with Catrin at his side towards the door, with shafts of sunlight illuminating specks of dust as though jewels were being strewn along their pathway.

Although the church was isolated, with only the odd farm or cottage scattered around the nearby hillsides, it seemed that it might have been market day at Ludlow for all the people that were gathered there. All dressed in their best attire they were too, to celebrate the wedding of their prince's daughter.

As Sir Edmund and Catrin stepped outside into the late summer sunshine, there was much laughter, cheering and throwing of flowers, with young girls trying to touch the bride's dress for luck, before the couple could break through the crowd. There was no gilded coach waiting for them though, but rather a simple carriage for the journey back to the farm. As they climbed into the carriage there were shouted good wishes from the crowd, or what Sir Edmund hoped might be good wishes, for they were called in the alien Welsh tongue. Then, after a short delay, the couple were finally sent on their way.

As they set off, Sir Edmund was about to put his arm around Catrin when he was surprised to hear the clatter of many hooves, far more than that occasioned by the pair of horses that drew the carriage, even were they accompanied by a couple of outriders. Looking out now, he could see that they had a sizable escort of mounted men at arms with more than a score or so of lancemen and archers trotting alongside on foot. He saw too that, both grinning, Owain Glyn Dŵr and Maredudd accompanied them, one on either side of the carriage. Feeling a little guilty he surreptitiously began to take his arm from around Catrin but laughing now she stayed his hand and reached up to put a hand around his neck and, gently pulling his head down to hers, kissed him whilst the carriage lurched and swayed on the rough track as their escort laughed and cheered them on.

Theirs was a triumphant arrival at the farmhouse. Men at arms saluted their prince with their drawn swords and greeted his daughter and her new husband with loud cheers. All around the house itself banners, emblazoned with Prince Owain's device of four lions rampant, fluttered in the breeze, giving it a festive air. Trestle tables, laden with meats and ale, were set out in the freshly swept yard and, as Sir Edmund led his bride into the hall, a profusion of flowers and greenery added to the festive atmosphere. Here too, the long oak table was laden with rich foods and wine there was in plenty.

Barely had they entered the hall before a blushing Megan was offering Sir Edmund a goblet of wine, whilst other smiling serving maids attended to the wants of all the wedding guests. Glasses were filled and refilled before at last Glyn Dŵr and Marged, his wife, went to their seats at the head of the table with Sir Edmund and Lady Catrin beside them. As they sat down, Sir Edmund heard the first few notes of a harp being played above the chatter of people settling at the table.

Gradually the chatter quietened as the wistful tones of the harpist's melody stilled every voice in the room.

To Sir Edmund, however, it seemed to be more a dirge than melody and at last he turned to Glyn Dŵr to say, 'This is a doleful tune your harpist plays, my lord, can he not play something more befitting this happy occasion?'

Glyn Dŵr looked across to where the harpist Iolo Goch nestled his harp in his corner of the room and laughed. 'I fear he does but put his heart into his melody Sir Edmund and did he put words to it, I doubt not that he would sing to us of unrequited love!' Turning his head, he called across to the harpist, 'Come Iolo, play us a more lively air, there are more glum faces here than I would have around me on my daughter's wedding day!'

Iolo Goch nodded in acknowledgement and though his face remained dolorous enough, his music took on a livelier pace and after a minute or so he began to sing. The words were Welsh, but even to Sir Edmund's untutored ears, the minstrel sang to Catrin, for she lowered her eyes and there was a flush on her cheeks that was nought to do with the wine, much of which yet remained in her glass.

Sir Edmund smiled as he raised his glass to his lips, sing on minstrel, he thought, sing of love as you might, it will not be in your arms that Catrin will lie this night! The smile still lingering on his lips, he turned to Glyn Dŵr with the wine glass in his hand. 'Well, my lord,' he asked, 'now that I am family indeed, what work will you have for me to do, for I must earn my keep?'

There was a wary look in Glyn Dŵr's eyes but he replied affably enough, 'Surely, no talk of work today, Edmund, today is a holiday for us and all the kin around us!'

Sir Edmund smiled. 'True, my lord, but Henry will take no holiday today, nor yet upon the morrow and I have been rested these past few months by your hospitality.'

With arched eyebrows, Glyn Dŵr asked, 'With Dean Cyffin's blessing upon you both yet barely cold, would you leave my Catrin so readily and take up the sword on my behalf?'

'Our wedding,' Sir Edmund replied, 'united both our houses in peace or war and I would have this war ended speedily that, with Catrin, I might enjoy the peace the more.'

'Truly said, Edmund,' Glyn Dŵr agreed. 'Yet many a man at arms have I to wield a sword for me whose loss I would feel none so great as yours. Your time mayhap will come for that but for yet a little while I must keep you from the risky business of cut and thrust, for there are greater purposes that you may serve.'

Though the festivities went on long into the night, Sir Edmund was still trying to persuade Glyn Dŵr that he should now take an active role in the rebellion as the Lady Marged and Alice quietly led Catrin away from the table.

At last Glyn Dŵr turned to him and, with a wave of his hand that seemed to encompass the whole room, said firmly, 'You have duties less military to attend to tonight, Sir Edmund, and 'tis time you paid them regard!'

Looking around him Sir Edmund saw that there were but few now remaining around the table and of those few some were slumped in their seats from either a surfeit of wine or food. The harpist, it seemed too, had long since gone, taking with him not only his harp but his personal loss.

Glyn Dŵr touched Sir Edmund on the arm. 'Your bride will surely think you have gone off to fight my war already, Edmund!' Then with a malicious glint in his eyes added, 'Lest you hurry to her chamber, I fear you'll find a harp holding the door tight shut!'

Sir Edmund glowered as he rose, saying as he did so, 'An' were it so, my lord, I fear your minstrel will reach a higher note when next he sings for you than he has ever reached before!'

Then Maredudd was escorting him to his chamber and led him not to the narrow staircase that led to the back of the house, but to the main staircase and to a large bedchamber in the front of the house.

As they paused outside the chamber, Maredudd, a sturdy young lad now just sixteen, drew himself up to his full five foot seven and held out his hand. 'I hold not with Catrin's marriage to you, Sir Edmund,' he said quietly, 'for I trust not he who turns his coat, but you and I are brothers of sorts now, so I offer you my hand.' Then as they clasped hands he looked up at the taller Englishman and added tight lipped, 'But you treat my sister well, or this same hand will slit your gullet as readily as it shakes your hand tonight!' With that, he withdrew his hand and turning on his heel, strode back along the corridor the way he had come.

Sir Edmund watched him go, wondering how many of Glyn Dŵr's household thought the same, and he shook his head thinking a little sadly that there were now few indeed either side of the Welsh marches that he could truly call friends, with the English thinking he had conspired against them and the Welsh as suspicious of him as they were of all Englishmen.

He was still somewhat thoughtful as he gently turned the door handle and carefully opened the door, thinking that Catrin might be asleep. There was a soft glow in the room from a candle still alight in its holder by the bedside. By it he could see that Catrin was not asleep, but sitting up in the bed, her long dark hair cascading over a dusky pink nightdress that emphasised the blush on her cheeks.

She looked at him from under those long lashes of hers and asked softly, 'What were you and Maredudd arguing over, Edmund?'

He smiled at her. 'We were not arguing, my love, Maredudd was just bidding me welcome to the family ere he bade me goodnight. Even as he said it, he smiled ruefully to himself, thinking that he had but spoken the truth, for it had been a sort of welcome. As good a one as any turncoat might expect, either side of the march!

A few days after the wedding, Glyn Dŵr turned to Sir Edmund as they sat at table to say, 'I depart tomorrow, Edmund, for I must tend to my soldiery, who now besiege Henry's castles at Harlech and Aberystwyth, both key to his hold on West Wales!'

Sir Edmund's eyes brightened. 'And do I accompany you, my lord?'

His face fell though as Glyn Dŵr shook his head and said with a frown, 'No, I think not, Edmund! Are you so tired of wedded bliss already that you would embark on such a venture? Sight of you at those castle's walls would of a certainty have Henry condemn you as traitor!' He smiled. 'Marriage to my daughter he might see as human frailty, but to have you storming Harlech at my side would be too great a pill for him to swallow whole!'

Sir Edmund snorted, before he replied bitterly, 'Think Henry what he will, my lord, for I see now that in crossing the Teme in pursuit of you, I crossed my own Rubicon. There was no turning back for me then nor is there now, and Henry of his own self ensured that when he rejected your offer to ransom me.' Frowning now, he shook his head. 'Though why he thus renounced me, I'll never know!'

Glyn Dŵr smiled as he looked sideways at Sir Edmund. 'Perhaps he heard you were enamoured of my Catrin and feared your wrath were he to come between you two?' He shook his head as though denying his own hypothesis before, his eyes narrowed now, he added, 'More like, he welcomed a division 'twixt his house and yours for that he sees the Earl of March, your nephew, as a threat to his continuance on England's throne!'

Sir Edmund shook his head. 'That cannot be, my lord, did I not take up arms against you on his behalf at great cost to me and my tenantry?'

Glyn Dŵr nodded. 'True enough, Edmund, and in such a battle that Henry could not lose, but only gain, for had you won at Pilleth, 'twould be his gain over me and did you lose then he could say that 'twas but by your own treachery that I overcame you!' He waved a finger at Sir Edmund. 'Which belittles the Mortimer name and thus weakens your nephew's claim to kingship!'

He leaned back in his chair, hands crossed on his stomach and looked down at his platter thoughtfully, as though considering whether to divulge a secret. At last he looked up at Sir Edmund and pursed his lips, as if he had reluctantly made a decision: ' 'Tis a game he's played again, Edmund,' he said confidentially and, as Sir Edmund raised his eyebrows in surprise, Glyn Dŵr nodded. 'Aye, he has played it again, Edmund, and against kin of yours.'

He did not wait for Sir Edmund to question him this time, but continued, like a river in full spate: ' 'Tis the Percies this time, who guard the northern march for him, Edmund! Just two months gone, Hotspur and his father the Earl won a great victory against the Scots at some bleak hilltop called Homildon Hill and took many prisoners of note, a score of whom were French knights and gentilhommes. For most of these, together with the Scots of note, ransoms were agreed and paid and that you would say is that, with honour duly satisfied. 'Twould indeed be so, except for one prisoner, the Scots Earl of Douglas whose ransom Henry, through greed or malice, would have for himself. It seems that the Earl and Hotspur are disaffected by Henry's avarice, for they say their campaign against the Scots on his behalf cost them dearly in men and gold and therefore the Earl's ransom would be their just recompense.'

Sir Edmund looked at him in disbelief as he asked, 'Hotspur and his father disaffected you say, my lord, how can this be when they helped put the crown on Henry's head? Have they not fought for Henry against you here in Wales and, as your words show, in Scotland too?' He shook his head. 'The man is mad, for he would make enemies of his friends even as he breathes.'

Nodding his head in agreement, Glyn Dŵr smiled. 'Just so, Edmund and I would that he had more such friends, for I would have them all as allies, that I might topple him from his perch the quicker! It pleases me though, that his quarrel with the Percies may have echoes across the sea in France, for the French were ever friendly to the Scots and will not welcome their defeat at Homildon. I too have hopes of a French alliance and have proposed a common purpose with the French King Charles 'gainst Henry for they relish his hold on Calais and Aquitaine as little as I do his claim on Wales.'

Sir Edmund glanced at him and there was exasperation in his voice now as he said, 'You talk of your need for allies, my lord, and yet have one at your side you will not use!'

He winced though as Glyn Dŵr asked cuttingly, 'And what army do you bring to fight under my banner, Edmund? Would I have you to fight afoot as any lancemen, I could have a thousand such men readily enough!' He grinned. 'Aye and a thousand such that had not cost me as dearly in daughters and in gold! My senses tell me that the time will come, quite soon now, to talk with the Percies of an alliance that will spell the end of Henry's reign and in such talk you will play a greater part than any lanceman could. No, I cannot spare you to have your blood spilt by some careless arrow 'neath Harlech or Aber's walls and were I to do so, Catrin would not readily forgive me!' He reached across and patted Sir Edmund's arm. 'So, when I depart tomorrow, I leave you in command here and give you my family in trust to safeguard well!'

Sir Edmund glowered at him. 'Does not my command extend to the cattle, sheep and hens as well, my lord?' he asked scathingly.

Glyn Dŵr grinned as he shook his head. 'Oh no, Edmund,' he replied confidentially, 'the farmer will look after those, for they require a greater skill than I might expect of you!'

In London Sir Geoffrey de Lacey who, as a king's knight, now had the king's ear, was not displeased that there were problems over the ransoming of the Scots Earl of Douglas. For reasons of his own self interest he had no wish to see Sir Edmund return to England and had been assiduous in undermining the Earl of Northumberland's efforts to have Mortimer returned to the king's favour. Nor when Hotspur sought to have Sir Edmund ransomed had de Lacey hesitated to draw the king's attention to the fact that they were brothers-in-law.

News of Sir Edmund's marriage to Glyn Dŵr's daughter in November had served to ensure that Sir Edmund would not be returning to raise charges against him. The Earl of Northumberland's disagreement with the king over the Earl of Douglas ransom affair now not only cast doubt on the Percies' loyalty but equally cast doubt on the reasons for their support for Sir Edmund. All of this was good news for Geoffrey de Lacey, for every question that cast doubt over the loyalty or motives of Sir Edmund and his supporters could only strengthen his own position with the king. If such great houses as the Percies and the Mortimers were to fall, who knew what prizes might be plucked from the debris? As he sat in the Royal palace overlooking the Thames thinking of the Mortimers, he recalled seeing the young Earl of March riding from Ludlow with his mother to Berkhamsted. Now, with Sir

Edmund dishonoured, he is the key, thought de Lacey, for without the young Earl and his brother Roger, the whole house of Mortimer would fail. If that were so, an earldom would be there for he who had the stomach to grasp it . . . did he but have the king's favour.

In the Royal chambers, not far from where de Lacey dreamed of advancement, the sixteen year old Prince Henry looked in some trepidation at the stocky figure of his father the king. His father was obviously angry and whilst, fortunately for the prince, it was not at him the king's anger was directed, it was not unusual for it to spill over onto those not directly connected with its cause.

'Avarice, that's all it is!' the king stormed, thumping the arm of his chair with his fist. 'Aye, greed and impudence combined to show the true nature of the Percies who yet profess their loyalty!'

The prince suppressed a sigh, thinking of Hotspur, the Earl of Northumberland's son, at whom the king's anger was directed. Prince Henry rather liked the impetuous Hotspur and indeed had sympathy with the young nobleman's request, even though the repeated request had come to sound more like a demand. It was all over the ransoming of the Scots Earl of Douglas, captured by the Percies at the battle of Homildon Hill. King Henry saw the ransom as a royal perquisite, whilst the Percies saw it as a prize of war and theirs by right.

The prince bit his lip, then asked hesitantly, 'Might not they be satisfied with a share of the ransom money, Father?'

The king looked at him in disbelief for a moment then, his face reddening as his anger rose again, he demanded incredulously, 'Share? Are you mad? Have you no idea of the demands upon my exchequer? Or thought of how much this damned Welsh rebellion costs, or how it deprives my purse of income from our holdings there? Were that not enough, the French refresh our Scottish enemies with men and arms to prolong our struggle there whilst themselves harrying our southern shores. Nor is that all, for lords in Ireland resist our lawful rule while scant revenue comes from Aquitaine where the French ever probe our borders, held secure at no small cost! With all this, you'd have me share what little gain there is from Scotland? The Percies had their *share* from all the lesser fry caught in their net at Homildon and more of that than I wot of, I wager!'

His tirade over he scowled as he sipped his wine and relapsed into sullen silence. Prince Henry, taken aback by his father's fury, prudently held his tongue, tempted though he was to mention the fact that the Percies had borne the brunt of the cost of protecting the northern marches.

It was the king who at last broke the silence that hung heavily in the chamber. He was thoughtful now and Prince Henry found the quiet voice in which he spoke more menacing even than his anger. 'The Percies are kin by marriage to the Mortimers, Harry, and the Mortimers kin by marriage now to that Welsh rebel Glendower! Would you have me give them the Douglas ransom to fund this Welsh rebellion? No! I'm damned if they shall have one mark!'

Looking at the prince through narrowed eyes, he sipped his wine again then continued, his voice still low, menacing, 'The Mortimers conspired with Glendower for their own defeat on the western march you know, Harry! I doubted de Lacey when he first warned me of this, but testimony by Lord Grey and Sir Thomas Clanvowe of what they saw with their own eyes puts Sir Edmund's perfidy beyond all doubt.'

Wagging a warning finger at the prince now, he asked, 'Aye, and where does such perfidy end when there is such interwoven kinship. If Sir Edmund is so tainted, what of his sister's husband, Hotspur, who presses me with such impertinence for that which is mine by right?' Looking sideways at the prince, King Henry's face darkened as he whispered, as though putting his most secret thoughts into words, 'Indeed, if such perfidy runs in the blood, what of that other Edmund, the Earl of March, in his soft nest at Berkhamsted? Should I have a care as to what cuckoo is reared there?'

Surprised, Prince Henry's eyes widened as he exclaimed, 'He is but a child, father!'

The king smiled a little sadly. 'Aye and it seems but yesterday that you were so, yet you have commanded on the field of battle and long since earned your spurs. The Mortimers have ambitions beyond their Earlship and Sir Edmund is not the first of their line to have rebelled against their king and I would have him be the last.'

A cold chill ran up the young prince's spine as he looked at his father and wondered for a moment whether there was any truth in the palace rumours that he had had King Richard murdered. If that were indeed so, were his words now an implicit threat to the young Earl?

He shook his head and looking his father in the eye, reiterated firmly, 'The Earl is but a child Father! He is your ward and is no threat to you whilst held secure at Berkhamsted.' He paused before adding, 'He is a cousin of sorts to me and I would beg he be treated so!'

The king gazed at him thoughtfully for a moment then nodded. 'Aye, kin he is to you and though in our trade kin can oft represent the greatest threat, he'll rest safe enough in Berkhamsted, though I trust that neither you nor I have cause to regret that bond of kinship!'

Chapter Nineteen

Whilst Sir Edmund, the object of King Henry's wrath, was living a quiet and somewhat bucolic life with his new young bride in the foothills of Snowdonia, Owain Glyn Dŵr was, not without some success, actively pursuing his dream of ousting the English from Wales. At the beginning of July 1403 the constable of Carmarthen Castle surrendered that imposing pile to Owain Glyn Dŵr, who, whilst no doubt pleased with his accomplishment, seemed unaware of dramatic events to the north-west of his Principality. Unaware, too, that a powerful potential ally desperately needed his support there, support that could well bring about the downfall of the usurper, Henry Bolingbroke.

Whilst Glyn Dŵr was accepting the surrender of the Carmarthen Castle from its constable Robert Wigmore, King Henry was marching to Scotland to aid the elderly Earl of Northumberland against the Scots, still unsubdued after their defeat at Homildon Hill. The king had only got as far as Nottingham however, before news of yet another rebellion reached his ears. Hotspur, it seemed, had had enough prevarication from the king over the ransoming of the Earl of Douglas and, unswayed by the king's financial problems, had raised the banner of rebellion at Chester early in July.

The army Hotspur had raised was mainly loyalists of the late King Richard from Cheshire and North Wales. This fresh rebellion, however, cast further doubt in Henry's mind as to how far the Earl of Northumbria himself might be trusted: had his call for the king's aid in Scotland been merely to lure Henry away from the south whilst Hotspur raised rebellion? Had Hotspur chosen to rise in rebellion in Chester, because of his kinship with Sir Edmund Mortimer and thus now with Glendower?

Whatever King Henry's thoughts on these matters might have been, his actions were, for him, unusually decisive. Leaving the Earl of Northumberland to his fate at the hands of the Scots, he turned abruptly to commence a forced march to Cheshire, anxious to arrive there before there was any possibility of Hotspur gaining support from Glendower and the traitor Sir Edmund Mortimer.

Sadly for Hotspur, the king reached the outskirts of Shrewsbury before him and the field of the ensuing battle was of the king's choosing. If Hotspur had hoped to join forces with Glyn Dŵr he was disappointed in that also, for he was forced to face the king's anger with only the forces he had managed to muster from the King Richard loyalists.

With King Henry already having the advantage of dominating the field of battle and also outnumbering Hotspur, the outcome was an inevitable and bloody defeat for the Northumbrian. The Earl of Worcester and other leaders of the rebellion whose support Hotspur had gained were executed before the dust had settled on the battlefield, but such dignified passing was not accorded to Hotspur. He, having been hanged, drawn and quartered was displayed piecemeal in London, Bristol, Chester and Newcastle as a dreadful warning to all those who might be tempted to rise in rebellion against Henry.

Henry was well pleased with the result of his decisive response to this fresh rising. Not only had the outcome been disastrous for Hotspur, it had also succeeded in robbing Glyn Dŵr of a powerful potential ally, for there was no doubt in Henry's mind that it had been Hotspur's intention to join forces with the Welsh rebel. The battle had not been one-sided however, for although Hotspur had been caught wrong footed, the butcher's bill was a heavy one on both sides. Nor was the king personally absolved from such cost, for young Prince Henry received an arrow wound to the face. Such was the severity of the wound that the king was forced to appoint a group of nobles led by the Earl of Arundel to govern Wales and the marches whilst the prince was disabled from attending to his Lieutenancy in Wales.

A few fleecy white clouds were scattered across the blue sky one July afternoon as Edmund and Catrin walked arm in arm beside the placid stream in the meadow where he had first asked her to marry him. Remembering that other day, he smiled as he turned to look at her, thinking as he did so that Ludlow and the king's favour were well lost for her. Thinking too that it was as if he had always known her, always loved her and that his life at Ludlow had been but a dream and this reality.

Catrin glanced sideways at him, a smile on her lips and in those blue eyes too as she asked, 'What are you laughing at, cariad?'

Cariad: lover. It was still one of the few words of Welsh that he understood, one that warmed him to her every time she used it to address him. He shook his head. 'I wasn't laughing, my love, just smiling, happy!'

A shadow crossed her eyes and she frowned anxiously now as she asked, 'Are you truly happy, Edmund? Do you not sometimes yearn to be back in your great castle with all the ladies in their fine clothes and all the power you had there?'

Looking at her standing there in her plain green dress, her dark hair ruffled by the breeze, he reached out and, touching her cheek, shook his head. 'No, cariad, never!' He grinned then as he thought of the imperious Countess Eleanor as she had been then. 'I knew an old battleaxe but there were few "fine ladies" there!' The fleeting memory came to him then of seeing a Welsh farm girl in Ludlow Market but, frowning now, he drew back from telling her about the girl, that other Cathy, and just repeated, 'No there were no fine ladies there!'

Drawing closer to him, Catrin looked up into his eyes as she asked softly, 'Was there truly no fine lady that you cared for there, Edmund?'

Putting his arms around her he shook his head again and drew her to him, saying, 'No, my love, there was just a poor little Welsh girl I always wanted to know!'

They were still kissing, when they heard the sound of hooves coming towards them at a gallop and with a hand on his chest now, Catrin gently pushed him away. Still holding her to him, Edmund turned his head to see Iestyn, the man at arms from the farm, riding hard towards them and giving no sign of reining up until he was nigh on upon them.

Slightly irritated at the interruption, Sir Edmund asked the man at arms curtly as he drew up alongside them, the horse still snorting and breathing heavily, 'What news do you bring, Iestyn, that is so urgent it could not wait upon our return?'

One look at Iestyn's face though was enough to tell Sir Edmund that it was not good news and both he and Catrin were frowning now as they waited anxiously for Iestyn's reply.

'There's been a great battle at Shrewsbury, my lord!' Iestyn said at last and their frowns relaxed, for they both knew that Owain Glyn Dŵr was campaigning in the west and far enough away from Shrewsbury.

Perplexed now, Sir Edmund asked, 'Save us your riddles then Iestyn and tell us who fought this battle?'

'Why, it was the English king himself my lord, who fought and vanquished Henry Percy there.'

Sir Edmund, his arm still around Catrin, now clutched her tightly as he asked, wide-eyed, 'Hotspur and the king in battle, Iestyn? How fared Hotspur?'

Although he had been told by the Lady Marged to hurry to Sir Edmund with the news, Iestyn was unaware of its significance to the knight and so, nodding now, he replied straight-faced, 'Aye, 'twas as I said, my lord. Hotspur raised his banner in Chester but was vanquished when he faced the king's power at Shrewsbury and paid in full the penalty for treason, as we must too an' Prince Owain an' our cause fails!'

Sir Edmund blanched as the full impact of Iestyn's words registered and he visualised the penalty that Hotspur had paid. The energetic and impulsive Hotspur, dead, dismembered! Sir Edmund closed his eyes, thinking of his sister Elizabeth, alone now in some bleak castle in Northumbria with no one but the elderly Earl to protect her and her children from Henry's wrath.

Suddenly he was aware of the silence, broken only by Iestyn's horse as it snorted and pawed the ground. He looked up at Iestyn, still sitting there on the horse, waiting for a response from him and he nodded slowly before, totally subdued, he said quietly, 'Thank you, Iestyn, we shall be back at the farm shortly.'

The man at arms looked at him for a moment as if unsure what to do, then touching a finger to his helmet said, 'Aye, my lord!' and spurring his horse, galloped off in the direction of the farm.

Clutching Edmund's arm, Catrin looked up at him anxiously, as she said softly, 'Oh, cariad! Your poor sister!'

The air was suddenly chill, for the sun had slipped below the mountains on the far side of the valley to leave it in shade. With it had gone too, the warm glow he had felt before an unwitting Iestyn had dealt his blow. Blank eyed he looked at Catrin now as he said dully, 'Aye, poor Elizabeth!' As he stood there looking at her, he wondered how long it might be before someone else might be saying, poor Catrin!

In silence now, they walked over to where their horses were cropping the meadow grass then mounted and walked their horses back to the farm. It was a little while before Catrin plucked up courage to break the silence and ask, 'What are you thinking, Edmund?'

Lost in thought, he seemed not to hear her, so she asked again. Startled, he turned towards her as though wakened from a dream. 'Thinking?' he asked. 'Oh, I was just wondering why Hotspur chose to do battle with the king at Shrewsbury! 'Twas over the Douglas ransom he rebelled, that I see. But why raise his banner in Chester, not Northumbria, where all his power lies? 'Tis true King Richard, God rest his soul, had men enough in Cheshire to support his cause who now would join with any lord to avenge his death, but why should Hotspur choose to rise in rebellion there?'

His brow suddenly clearing, he turned on Catrin to say, almost shout, 'Why, he chose Chester so he could join his power with that of your father's, Catrin! That's why he met the king at Shrewsbury, he was trying to come to Wales . . .' Frowning again now, he paused there before asking rhetorically, 'but why did not your father race to meet and support him there?'

Catrin, her horse close to his, reached out to touch his arm. 'I know not Edmund, but I know that father liked Hotspur, for he often said as much. He has need of allies too and has even written to the King of France, so he would not readily desert one so close to home.'

Looking at her as she sat there so close to him, so trusting of her father, his heart melted even in the midst of his sorrow at Hotspur's horrific death and he shook his head. 'No,' he agreed. 'your father could not have known that Hotspur was in such great need of aid.'

Whilst in Snowdonia Sir Edmund pondered over the lost opportunity of an alliance between Glyn Dŵr and Hotspur, his father-in-law had more immediate problems to worry over as did his captains. Idris, his captain of archers stood with his friend Dafydd the captain of men at arms, looking out over Carmarthen town from the castle ramparts. 'We should not be lingering here, Dafydd,' Idris was saying. 'We should have marched northwards ere Hotspur's messenger dismounted from his weary nag!'

Dafydd grinned. 'Aye and marched straightways into my Lord Carew's arms! You and I know well that Prince Owain seeks not to engage in battle such forces as Carew commands to our north and thus the reason for their negotiations. Fortunate we are indeed, Idris, that our prince peruses well the butcher's bill before the battle is engaged rather than counting bodies on the field when it is done! 'Tis why before this morning's dawn he sent out men to seek a path that we may safely take to the north.'

Idris snorted. 'Aye, full seven hundred went, whose footfall Carew could well have heard as they marched along those streets below! 'Tis now nigh on noon and listen as I might I hear no sound of their return!'

The reconnaissance party had still had not returned by nightfall, nor had they seen the sun set that day for all seven hundred had met with Lord Carew and had fallen. There was no path open to the north for Glyn Dŵr now and the next morning Prince Owain, together with Idris and Dafydd, led his men out of Carmarthen to commence a long march to the east.

Eastwards they marched, but Prince Owain, ever cautious, ensured they marched well north of Gower, for had not the seer Thomas ap Hopkins from Gower warned him that he would be captured there by a knight under a black banner? Whether it was indeed prophecy or merely the self interest of Thomas the seer, Prince Owain gave no hostage to fortune and hurried on past the Gower peninsula. Nor was he alone in his eagerness to put Gower behind him, for word of the seer's prophecy had spread amongst his men and there were many amongst them who breathed a sigh of relief as they marched on, east of Swansea now and on towards the Black Mountains.

Ever since Idris had been told of Catrin's marriage to the turncoat Edmund Mortimer, he had been in a dark mood, which nothing that Dafydd said could dispel. Nor had the pleasure that Gruffydd, Prince Owain's eldest son, taken in the telling of the news done much to take away the sting, for there had been little but enmity between Gruffydd and the archer since Idris first joined Prince Owain's retinue at Sycharth.

Having left Abergavenny behind them now, they were marching on to Hereford when Idris saw the glint of a man in chain mail skulking in the undergrowth. Leaping off his horse he was upon the man, a dagger at his throat and had not Dafydd stayed Idris's hand the man would have died there and then without a cry. 'Steady, Idris bach!' said Dafydd quietly. 'Do not take out your wrath with Mortimer on this poor wretch and still his tongue, for he may have that to tell us which might save a life or two!'

Kneeling astride the man, Idris glared up at Dafydd. 'Tell us?' he snarled. 'All he will tell us will be English lies!'

Dafydd's massive hand still held Idris's in an iron grip and looking the fear crazed Englishman in the eyes, he shook his head. 'No, Idris,' he said softly in English, 'an' you let him live, I do believe he'll tell us what we need to know!'

The Englishman's chin quivered as he tried to nod his head without cutting his throat on Idris's dagger. Reluctantly, Idris eased his hold on the weapon, allowing Dafydd to take the hand holding it from the man's throat. As they both rose to their feet, Dafydd drew his sword and waved it at the prostrate Englishman.

'On your feet, soldier and thank your God that whilst neither of us two do love the English overmuch, I forgive them their sins more readily than does my comrade here!'

The Englishman rose slowly to his feet, edging away from Idris as he did so, his fingers all thumbs as he unbuckled his sword belt at Dafydd's command. As Dafydd had predicted the man talked readily enough later, albeit in English, but had little to tell other than that his lord, William Beauchamp, Lord Abergavenny had sent for urgent aid from the king because of Prince Owain's depredations throughout South Wales, especially in Pembrokeshire where Beauchamp had responsibility for several castles.

That snippet of information was good enough reward for Dafydd having had the man's life spared, for it gave Prince Owain early warning of a hazard he now faced from the east. Whilst King Henry had reacted decisively enough to the threat of Hotspur's rebellion, he appeared less willing to react swiftly to calls for help from his lords in Wales, perhaps because of the demands on his exchequer. So, whilst the king pondered on Lord Abergavenny's urgent plea, Prince Owain marched on eastwards, causing that somewhat biased historian, Adam of Usk, to record that:

> ' . . .Owain and his manikins marched through Wales with great power as far as Severn sea and brought all who offered resistance into subjection . . . then with vast spoil retired for safety to North Wales whence are spread all the ills of Wales . . . amidst smothered curses on his open adulteries.'

Dafydd was not displeased when at last they turned northwards from their eastward progress for, like Prince Owain, he was too old a soldier to seek confrontation with a superior force. Unlike him, Idris, still bitter over Catrin's marriage to Sir Edmund, grew more withdrawn and sullen the further north they went.

The day's march over, they were encamped one night in mid Wales and were talking together over their pots of ale, though mostly it was Dafydd talking whilst Idris sat in silence, his nose deep in his pot as he sought to reach its bottom. At last Dafydd slammed his pot of ale on the stump of a tree that made shift as table. 'When will you ever see that Catrin was not for such as you?' he demanded angrily. 'Were you betrothed, that you now moon around like some calf bereft of its mother's milk? No! Nor could you have ever been, you an archer and she a princess!'

As Idris opened his mouth to protest, Dafydd raised a hand like a ham to silence him. 'I know! You walked with her beside Afon

Cynllaith, a tryst or two by the old dovecote at Sycharth, a stolen kiss or perhaps e'en three! All this when she was but a maid, aye, a maid who knew no better.' He nodded now to give his words emphasis. 'Aye, Idris, knew no better then than to catch an archer's eye, when such as she are born to wed a knight, perhaps a lord, or help form alliance with families of power!'

There was hurt now in Idris's eyes instead of the sullen look they had held before and with a sigh, Dafydd continued, his voice pleading now, 'Can you not see it, Idris, Catrin is married to her own kind, a knight, who by his marriage to her brings hope of a powerful alliance for our prince.'

It seemed as though Dafydd's words fell on deaf ears, for Idris just sat there looking into his ale, devastated. Looking up at last he whispered, 'All that I know, Dafydd, and yet I loved her . . . we loved together!'

Dafydd looked at him for a moment without understanding then, wide-eyed, he whispered, 'Then do you value your head upon your shoulder, Idris, tell no other soul what I misheard then and pray that all Catrin's babes be fair haired Mortimers!'

Picking up his pot of ale he drained it before slamming it down on the tree stump again. Then, shaking his head as if in despair, he said tersely, 'I'm off to my sack of straw! Til now I thought that all we had to fear was capture by the English king, but you my friend will find his justice mild indeed compared to that of Owain's if you are indeed discovered.

Summer was still with them as they marched on towards the safety of North Wales, the long baggage train that trailed behind them laden with the booty from their long summer's campaign. They felt secure now in their march north, for news had reached them that King Henry had sent out a widespread array from Worcester calling upon all those who had any form of benefit from the Crown to muster there for yet another incursion into Wales. Dafydd turned to Idris, as they rode beside each other to say, grinning, 'A poor stableman is Henry, Idris, shutting the door on an empty stable!'

Idris just nodded despondently and Dafydd, exasperated at his moodiness, said with a toss of his head, 'Oh, come on Idris bach! Perhaps you left an empty stable behind, too!' Then, as Idris just glared at him, he shook his head and spurring his horse, rode off to rejoin his men at arms.

Henry's incursion into Wales in that summer of 1403 began at least more auspiciously than his previous attempts, for he met with fair weather as he entered Wales by way of Brecon and the Usk valley. His safe arrival in Carmarthen in late September was perhaps the most successful part of the campaign however, for Glyn Dŵr's rebel supporters there prudently disappeared into the hills to the north. Having recovered Carmarthen Castle and satisfied that order had been restored to that part of his realm, Henry withdrew to the east again congratulating himself no doubt that at least this time he left Wales dry-shod. Even before his army reached the English borders however, the rebels were already streaming down from the hills to resume their domination of the West Wales countryside.

Calling for Iestyn, Sir Edmund hurriedly buckled on his sword belt as he saw a small group of armed men approach the farm: Secure as they all felt here in the foothills of Snowdon, it was as well to take nought for granted. As he did so, Catrin came hurrying into the hall accompanied by Iestyn, whose chain mail gave a metallic whisper with every step he took.

'Are your men ready then, Iestyn?' asked Sir Edmund, still settling his sword belt comfortably around his waist.

'Aye, my lord, ready enough,' replied Iestyn with a grin, 'though I wager few of them would readily face Captain Dafydd over there with that weapon of his he calls a claymore!'

Sir Edmund knew well enough what a claymore was, but did not even know Captain Dafydd and could not have known that he had campaigned with Glyn Dŵr in Scotland for King Richard. Stern faced, he turned on Iestyn saying sharply, 'Like you and I, they'll earn their pay and face whosoe'er they must! Get them out in the yard, arrayed along its walls, 'til we are sure who it is comes calling!'

Still grinning, Iestyn replied, 'Aye, my lord, they'll face the devil an it pleases you, for that pony over there that buckles at the knees bears our good Captain Dafydd and he'd not be best pleased with me did we slumber when he arrived.'

Ten minutes later Glyn Dŵr was leading a group of some forty men into the farmyard. There was much laughter and loud talk as weary and grimed with the dust of their long march that day, they dismounted. Whilst some took their mounts to water, others were relieving theirs of the personal booty they had borne. As Sir Edmund strode towards Glyn Dŵr to greet him formally, Lady Marged and Catrin stood smiling in the doorway, though Lady Marged touched a kerchief to her eyes, perhaps at her husband's safe return.

Whilst all around him women held their men again, back from warring with the English, Idris stood alone, for there was no woman there to greet him now. Then, with a last glance at Catrin standing there in the doorway, Idris led his horse away to the stables. Touching his helmet as he passed Prince Owain, Idris heard Sir Edmund saying, 'I am pleased indeed to see you safely here, my lord, for there has been ill news enough since you departed, with Hotspur's untimely death and Henry's . . .' Idris was past them now though, out of earshot and, his heart in his throat, he turned his head again to glance at Catrin and saw her looking at him. Even though she quickly lowered her eyes and blushing, turned away, it was with a quicker step and a lighter heart that Idris led his horse to the stables.

Chapter Twenty

Catrin and Edmund were down by the meadow, where the pale sunshine touched the few leaves left on the trees with gold to announce that summer was over. They had gone there at least in part to escape the bustle and clamour of the farm, which had become more like a military encampment since Glyn Dŵr's return. It was likely to remain so too, for the campaigning season was over until the spring. At least unless King Henry forced Glyn Dŵr's hand thought Edmund.

Frowning, Catrin looked up at him to ask, 'Will they be here all winter long, Edmund?'

Smiling, he countered, 'Why do you frown my love, would you have your father gone again so soon, or is it that you'd have me march away with him?'

She clutched his arm the tighter as she shook her head. 'Oh, no! You'll not leave me, will you Edmund?'

With a toss of his head he said sourly, 'An' we would have this war end, then I should indeed march alongside your father when he leaves,' then, sighing, he continued, 'yet I fear he'll keep me here for sake of some plot he has in mind.'

Still frowning, she asked, 'Plot? What plot could Father have in mind that touches you, Edmund?'

He grimaced, then shrugged as he replied quietly, almost as though he were thinking aloud, 'I know not Catrin! Whate'er it is, he keeps it secret e'en from me. I once thought 'twas over some alliance with Hotspur with which he would have me involved but that it cannot be, for poor Hotspur's dead! I only know I'd sooner take my place in your father's campaigns than in his intrigues!'

He smiled then and changed the subject abruptly by saying, 'You have been strangely quiet since your father brought his men back to the farm, Catrin dear, is there ought wrong or that concerns you?'

For a moment he thought he sensed fear in her eyes, but realised it could only have been his imagination, for shaking her head she said quickly, almost urgently, 'No, cariad, there is nought wrong,' and smiling now, said again, 'there is nought wrong at all.'

He held her close to him and looked in her eyes to ask, 'Are you sure, my love?'

Still smiling, her eyes all innocent and with the breeze ruffling her hair, she replied, 'Of course I'm sure, Edmund! What could be wrong? I have you here and Father's home from his campaigning.' Her eyes clouded then though as she added, 'If only we were at Sycharth and this stream was Afon Cynllaith.'

He smiled sympathetically, Sycharth! That's what it had all been about. His arm still around her, they walked slowly back to the horses and made their way along the valley at a gentle pace back to the farm.

As they approached the house though, Sir Edmund frowned, the morning's peace was suddenly dispelled, for there were all the signs of frantic activity about the place. Tents that had been erected near to the house by the soldiery were being hurriedly dismantled, horses were being led from stables and barns and there was all the bustle of soldiers preparing to break camp. As an archer hurried past them, Sir Edmund stopped him to ask curtly, 'What's amiss, archer?'

Perhaps because the question was in English, the archer glowered at him. 'Nought amiss!' he replied abruptly. 'We go to aid the siege of Castle Harlech!' Then he hurried on his way.

As he looked at Catrin now, Edmund was surprised to see her look so crestfallen, for he knew not why the news should affect her so, lest it be the departure of her father so soon after his return.

Hurriedly dismounting, Edmund handed his reins to Catrin, saying as he did so, 'I must see your father, Catrin, perchance I march with him to Harlech!' She nodded absently as she took the reins, her mind obviously elsewhere, for she was anxiously looking around the yard as though looking for someone. Shrugging, he hurried into the house to find Glyn Dŵr. A winter siege of the remote castle perched on a cliff high above the sea was enough to chill the soul of any man, but it would be better than sitting listening to the campaign tales of Glyn Dŵr's retainers all winter long!

He found Glyn Dŵr beside the fire in the hall, a sheep dog at his feet basking in the warmth of the fire already lit, for there was an autumn chill about the house. 'I learn you go to the siege on Harlech my lord!' he blurted out. 'May I not accompany you and lend my sword in this affair?'

Glyn Dŵr glanced up at him with shrouded eyes then, with a sigh, put a nearly empty goblet back on the table at his side. Still silent, he shook his head, then said, 'I do not go, Edmund! The siege will last all winter long and will do well enough without me there! It just needs patience, for ere the winter's through we'll starve those English buggers out.' Seeing the look of disapprobation on Sir Edmund's face, he laughed before adding, 'I mean you no offence Edmund, for I do mean those other English buggers!'

Unsure whether that was meant as apology or insult, Sir Edmund's face was grim as he asked tersely, 'You intend no assault then, my lord?'

Glyn Dŵr picked up the goblet and took a sip of wine then said, with raised eyebrows, 'If by assault you mean shall I storm its lofty walls or burrow 'mongst its foundations, why no, Edmund! The one is expensive in the men I'd likely lose and the other is work fit more for moles than men and little would it achieve on Harlech's rocky perch! No, better that with patience I starve them out. At sea my good French friend Jean d'Espagne interdicts the castles on the western shore and stops the . . . er . . . your compatriots, replenishing them with victuals and with arms. The men I send today do but relieve the guard on Harlech's front door and come the spring they'll guard the battlements as surely as they will its gate!'

Still straight faced, Sir Edmund asked, 'May I not go with them and help them keep the guard, my lord?'

Glyn Dŵr grinned, as he replied, 'What, tired of the bonds of matrimony already, Edmund?'

Sir Edmund shook his head, then said curtly, 'Never that my lord! 'Tis just that I never happily brook idleness when there's work to be done.'

'Well come the spring there'll be work enough for all of us!' replied Prince Owain and smiling now added, 'If patience is rewarded 'fore then and Harlech falls to our hands, we'll move to its more spacious lodgings. 'Til then we'll stay snug here, for I've work enough to last me the winter through that calls for my pen more than my sword.' He glanced at the empty goblet in his hand then with a shrug, rose to his feet, saying, 'Come, Edmund, I must give my men a word of cheer 'fore they embark upon their winter's watch.'

When they got out into the yard, Sir Edmund could see that there were some two or three score men at arms and archers, some mounted, all ready it seemed to begin their long march to Harlech, with a few pack horses bringing up the rear of the small column. At the approach of Glyn Dŵr and Sir Edmund, Dafydd, the big captain of men at arms, wheeled his horse towards them and touched his helmet in salute.

Smiling, Glyn Dŵr asked him, 'All ready for the winter watch then, Dafydd Mawr?'

Dafydd grinned. 'Ready as ever, my lord!' Then with a nod towards the captain of archers beside him now, added, 'though some there are who'd rather spend it watching sheep in yonder meadow than at Harlech's windy gate!'

Looking at Idris the archer, Sir Edmund thought that there was more than a grain of truth in the man at arms' words for the archer, sitting there unsmiling on his horse, grimaced before saying, 'I'll watch Harlech's gate as well as any, my lord and ably wield my sword as well as any of Dafydd's men!' Then shaking his head he said, 'Yet though the winds 'round Harlech's walls this winter will not favour my shafts, they'll reach its battlements before ever Dafydd with his great weight sets foot upon them!'

Grinning at the friendly rivalry of the two captains, Glyn Dŵr nodded. 'I never doubted it Idris and would I were there to watch your shafts fell the enemy, but I fear affairs of state detain me here!'

Perhaps it was only Sir Edmund's imagination, but he could have sworn that Idris gave him a quick glance before replying, 'Oh, be assured they will, my lord, wherever your enemies may stand!'

Wheeling their mounts now, the two captains walked them to the head of the column and with a wave of his arm, Captain Dafydd led the small column off along the track that led westwards, the foot soldiers trotting on either flank of the mounted men. As they moved off, the two captains turned their heads and raised a hand as if in farewell salute to Glyn Dŵr, but to Sir Edmund it seemed as if Idris was looking not at Glyn Dŵr, but beyond him, at the farm. Turning his head he saw that Lady Marged and Catrin were standing in the doorway and Catrin was waving her kerchief. He smiled, thinking that it was, as ever, kind of Catrin to bid farewell to her father's soldiery as they went off to war.

As Catrin stood on the doorstep waving farewell to the departing soldiery she had eyes only for one and, as Idris caught her eye, she remembered the times that he had walked with her in the meadows beside Afon Cynllaith. She blushed now too as she remembered the time when he had lain with her in the minstrels' gallery above Sycharth's great hall. Tears welled in her eyes now as she thought of him going off to war again, perhaps never to return. A gust of wind made her shiver as she stood there in her silken gown and she put the kerchief she had waved to her eyes as she imagined the many cold days he'd spend this coming winter beside Harlech's walls. Suddenly she saw Edmund smiling at her from where he stood beside her father and felt guilty now as she wondered whether he would still smile at her, did he but know of all that had passed between Idris and her.

She saw Edmund say something to her father and then, still smiling, he was striding towards her. For a moment it seemed to her that it would always be this way, with Idris riding away from her as he went off to war and Edmund, considerate and ever loving, being with her constantly. The conflicting emotions suddenly overcoming her, she rushed indoors and up the stairs to her chamber where she flung herself onto her bed and, her head buried in the pillow, she burst into tears.

In the courtyard, Sir Edmund stopped in his tracks as he saw Catrin rush into the house, then walked on quickly towards the doorway where Lady Marged stood watching him. Then, as he drew near, she glanced over her shoulder before, smiling, she said almost apologetically, 'Leave her, Edmund, she will be herself again in a little while! Catrin could never bear to see her father's soldiers going off to war without a tear shed!'

He stood there hesitantly for a moment before saying, 'I must go to her, my Lady!'

Standing there blocking the doorway now, she shook her head, saying firmly, 'No, Edmund! 'Twas ever women's work to comfort the others when the menfolk go off to war!' She stood there for a moment then waving him away with her hand, she turned and went indoors.

Uncertain what he should do now, Sir Edmund rubbed his chin thoughtfully, surprised that Catrin should take on so when she must have seen her father's men march off often enough. Then, shrugging his shoulders, he turned and walked back towards Glyn Dŵr.

The prince grinned at his approach. 'What ails you Edmund?' he asked. 'Surprised at a young girl's tears when my men march off? Think of the flood there'd have been had you gone too! Worry not, there was never any understanding of womenfolk, for 'twas ever thus: tears when you go, tears when you come back and scolding in between!'

Frowning, Sir Edmund nodded. 'Aye, I suppose so, my lord,' he agreed. The frown was still there though, for he wondered what might be the reason for Catrin's tears, when he still stood there in the yard.

Winter came early to Snowdonia in 1403 and Sir Edmund thought at first that it was the cause of Catrin's deepening melancholia. Despite his solicitude, nothing he could say or do seemed to rouse her from the

j

lassitude which accompanied her constant state of depression. Nor did the weather help to heal her ills, for by the end of September the isolated farm was a bleak place indeed, lashed as it was by gales and heavy rain.

Whatever it might be that was wrong with her, he could not bring her to confide in him what ailed her. Nor could Lady Marged offer him any comfort when one day he sought her advice, saying only that Catrin was but young and found it difficult being confined to the farm. He looked at Lady Marged doubtfully, wondering if that were so, why Catrin could not share his happiness at being there together, away from the bloodshed and turmoil of her father's rebellion.

The doubts came then as he thought of her waving farewell as Glyn Dŵr's men departed to join in the siege of Harlech. Picturing her standing on the doorstep waving to them as they rode off, the doubts came flooding back, despite the reassuring words Lady Marged had offered in explanation. He shook his head, doubting now that she had waved in encouragement to them all as the dutiful daughter of the prince, fearing rather, that she had been waving a more personal farewell to that damned archer fellow.

It was not until early in October, when he went to Catrin in her chamber as she was preparing for the evening meal, that he was to learn the reason for her melancholia. As he entered the room Catrin paused in brushing her hair and pale-faced, turned towards him then hesitantly put down the hairbrush beside the mirror. Suddenly concerned, he halted in mid stride and with an apprehensive smile asked quietly, 'Is all well, my love?'

She frowned, his own apprehension mirrored in her blue eyes, then nodded slowly to say, 'Yes, I think all is well, Edmund.'

He smiled again. 'If you only *think* all is well, Catrin, then I think something must be amiss, cariad! Pray tell me what it might be.'

She told him then, hesitantly at first, then blurting it all out, that she was afraid and so young to be with child.

Walking over to her he gently put a hand on her shoulder and tried to calm her fears, telling her that she was young and strong, that her mother would be there to help her, take care of her. Told her too of his love for her and how proud he would be for her to bear his son, his heir.

It seemed though that Catrin did not share his excitement at that prospect for she just looked at him dull eyed as she replied, 'It is bad luck to talk of such things so early, Edmund!' She shrugged. 'When the time comes, my lord, it may be a girl child, not a boy that I bear for you.' Then, with a touch of bitterness, she said, 'Would that distress you?'

Smiling, he shook his head, to say confidently, 'You would never distress me, my love, and one day we shall indeed have a son to bless our marriage and be my heir!' The smile faded then and sighing, he added, 'Though what he shall inherit, I know not!'

She smiled for the first time now as she reached out and held his hand, to say softly, 'It is enough, Edmund, that he shall inherit his father's name!' Then, as she held out her arms to him, he went to her and all thoughts of the archer fled from his mind as he held her close to him and they kissed as though there could be no other for either of them.

It was no feast but a frugal meal they partook of in the hall that night as it would be in the weeks that followed. With the prospect of a harsh winter and the tracks to the farm already nigh on impassable, their resources had to be husbanded carefully so that they might, if needs be, last 'til spring. Sir Edmund though needed no banqueting or false jollity to bring him cheer, for despite the coming of winter he looked forward eagerly to all that the new year might bring.

The edge of his excitement however, was blunted no little by the fact that it did not seem to be something he shared with Catrin, who seemed now to have fallen again into her previous moody despondency. Such was the depth of her melancholia that Catrin finally withdrew from him to share her chamber with her maid whilst Sir Edmund, perforce, reluctantly retreated to his old attic room at the rear of the farmhouse.

Because of the harsh winter, news from Prince Owain's forces laying siege to the English castles on the western shores was sporadic. This caused no great concern, because it seemed that there was little progress by Glyn Dŵr's forces there. His men, despite the harsh winter conditions, stoically maintained the sieges whilst the garrisons of the castles still stubbornly resisted all assaults or inducements to surrender.

One day, at the end of February when Sir Edmund was more concerned about Catrin than any siege, Prince Owain rushed into the hall where Sir Edmund was morosely supping a pot of ale.

' 'Twill not be long now, Edmund,' he said in a state of great excitement. 'Harlech cannot hold out much longer, its garrison is reduced to but two score and the Welshmen amongst them fight on knowing that I'll stretch their traitorous necks when Harlech falls.' Eyes gleaming, nostrils flaring as though scenting victory, he nodded. 'Aye, I have no doubt that soon now, Harlech will fall. Jean d'Espagne maintains his blockade by sea and our siege bars relief reaching them by land, so fall they must! From harsh experience Henry dares not attempt another sortie into Wales while winter holds and ere spring tempts him to such adventure, the western castles will surely be mine!'

Sir Edmund looked at him thoughtfully for a moment before saying, 'If Henry cannot offer them relief by land, surely my lord his fleet will break Jean d'Espagne's seaward hold?'

Glyn Dŵr shook his head. 'Unkind as the weather is to him ashore, it favours him no better at sea, for the southwesterly winds ever favour the French ships more than they do Henry's! Why, 'tis but a week since that five French vessels landed wine, provender and machines of war here in the north to our great aid. In the south of my Principality too, they brought men and ordnance to aid my good friend Harry Dwnn in his assault on Kidwelly Castle.' Smiling confidently now, he added, 'Come summer, Edmund, the castles will be mine and my writ shall run over all of Wales, when Henry would do well to talk of peace rather than adventure into Wales again!'

It was only two weeks later that, when Sir Edmund went into the hall, he found Glyn Dŵr standing with his back to the fire, his hands crossed behind him. Glancing at Sir Edmund, the prince frowned, his face black as thunder as he said irritably, 'Despite pestilence and starvation, Harlech yet holds out, Edmund, nor do the other western castles show promise of early surrender to our power. Needs must I go to see what inducement might lure them to concede defeat or what fearful threat may weaken their stubborn resolve.'

This change from Glyn Dŵr's optimism of only a few weeks earlier surprised Sir Edmund and with arched eyebrows he asked, 'Surely my lord, they cannot last the winter through, so promise of safe passage should suffice to open their gates and see them come trooping out?'

Glyn Dŵr grimaced and shook his head. 'This they have been offered together with reward for their quiet submission but I fear they trust us not, Edmund, and the Welshmen within the walls are notably reluctant to submit, fearing it seems, for their very lives.'

Sir Edmund could well understand that reluctance, remembering that only a few weeks before Glyn Dŵr was promising to 'stretch their necks' when the castles were taken. Smiling at the thought, he replied, 'Perchance they feel the reward they have been offered will only serve to pay for a hempen collar, my lord!'

With a quick glance at him, Glyn Dŵr said sharply, ' 'Tis but their traitorous nature that doubts our given word!' Then with a dismissive wave of his hand he told Sir Edmund, 'I am resolved that the western castles shall proudly bear my banner ere spring brings hope of relief to their garrisons. To that end I ride to Harlech tomorrow, for Harlech's submission will signal the end for all the others!' He paused as if to give emphasis to that positive note, then said, 'You shall ride with me, Edmund, for you shall be my emissary to the castles' constables.'

Sir Edmund's eyes widened in surprise. 'I am to be your emissary, my lord?'

With a quick nod of his head, Glyn Dŵr replied firmly, 'Yes! Oft enough you've offered to serve me with your sword, now you may serve me with your tongue! Perhaps the constables of these English castles will take your given word where they've rejected mine. Over all else, what I would have from you is that you leave Harlech's gate ajar when you walk out!'

Sir Edmund hesitated, trying to fathom the real meaning of Glyn Dŵr's remark then, as the prince asked impatiently of him, 'Well?' he nodded his agreement, saying:

'Yes I'll speak with them but I'll have no part in treachery, Glyn Dŵr!'

Shaking his head Glyn Dŵr smiled as he replied, 'Perish the thought, Sir Edmund, only Henry Bolingbroke could accuse you of that!'

Sir Edmund's hand went involuntarily to his sword hilt and glaring at Glyn Dŵr he said angrily, 'Aye, he did and unjustly accused me as you well know, when I could defend myself with neither word nor sword!'

Still smiling, Glyn Dŵr raised a restraining hand. 'No need to clap your hand to your sword hilt here, Edmund, for I know better than most the charge was false! Nor would I have you open Harlech's gate other than by the silver tongue that won my Catrin's heart!'

Sir Edmund glanced at him and sighed, wondering how much Glyn Dŵr knew of their present relationship. If Glyn Dŵr noticed at all, however, he made no comment and, his angry flush fading, said more conversationally, 'We ride tomorrow then, Edmund! 'Twill do your spirit good to breach the confines of the farm, even though we do but go to parley with your English countrymen!'

Sir Edmund looked at him, open-mouthed and frowning now, asked, 'I ride with you on the morrow, my lord?'

With an ironic smile, Glyn Dŵr responded by asking, 'What great business have you here, Edmund, that should detain you, who 'til now have been so eager to join the fray?'

Sir Edmund scowled. 'Aye, eager enough have I been and steadfastly have you denied me! Yet now is not the best of times for me to be away, with Catrin with child and deep in melancholia. Must you have me away from here to do nought but talk with those who, I fear, would scorn my very presence there?'

As they stood there facing each other in front of the fire, Glyn Dŵr grinned. 'Aye, I would indeed have you away from here and I would have you talk! The one to have you out from under the women's feet when you can be of little use. The other to have you talk where it may better serve my cause than lengthy siege.' He shrugged. 'If all fails and the castle's garrisons yet resist, despite our reasoned plea, then I'll assault them with such power that shall not be denied nor any hope of clemency shall they then find!'

When he finished speaking, Glyn Dŵr's mouth was set firm, his beard bristling aggressively, his piercing brown eyes glinting fiercely in the light of the fire. Looking at Glyn Dŵr, Sir Edmund shivered, knowing that if he failed to persuade the commanders of the castles to submit, Glyn Dŵr would show little mercy when finally the castles fell.

Suddenly, as though he had shrugged off a dark surcoat, Glyn Dŵr's mood lightened and he slapped Sir Edmund on the shoulder. 'Enough of all this,' he said cheerfully. 'We ride tomorrow and if fortune favours us, I shall hold court in a castle befitting a prince before the first green shoots of spring appear! Now you must make your farewells to Catrin and doubtless dry a tear or two before we leave!'

Catrin was alone in her chamber, sitting in front of a mirror, brushing her long dark hair. Sitting there with her back to him, her head tilted as she looked at his image in the mirror and said listlessly, 'You were talking long with my father, Edmund.'

He felt a pang of hurt, for she had not smiled and he sighed, thinking almost with resignation that she seldom seemed to smile these days. He smiled himself though as he asked, 'How did you know I was with the prince, my love?'

She shrugged dismissively, as though it were a silly question, then said tersely, 'Megan told me!' Megan the serving girl had been given a step up in the world and was now Catrin's maid.

He gave a rueful smile, realising that there were few secrets that could be kept in the farmhouse. As he opened his mouth to tell her that he was going to Harlech with Glyn Dŵr, Catrin half turned her head and, still brushing her hair, asked, 'When do you leave, Edmund?'

Nonplussed by the fact that she already knew of his departure and the matter of fact tone of her question, he gaped before gathering his wits and asking, 'How did you know that I must leave, my love?'

Turning to face him now she gazed at him for a moment sober faced then, shaking her head, said in a low voice, 'I knew my father strained at the leash to be at Harlech when it fell to his men. When Megan told me that you were long closeted with my father I knew that it was of the western castles that you spoke and that he would have you with him when he left. She was frowning now, the tears welling in her eyes as, her voice pleading, she asked, 'Must you go, Edmund, I am so frightened!'

Looking at her he could see that she was indeed frightened and going over to her, he took her in is arms and held her close, his fingers brushing the tears away as he murmured, 'I must indeed go when your father bids, my love, but 'twill all be well and I shall soon be back with you.'

A cold rain was falling the next morning as Sir Edmund and a small escort of men at arms waited for Prince Owain in the dark courtyard. There was a glow from lanterns in a few of the farm's windows, but the window of Catrin's chamber showed no light. Earlier, when he had gone to bid her farewell, only Megan her maid had stirred, to ask sleepily, 'Who's there?' Quietly closing the door again he had left then without answering, stepping softly down the stairway to the hall and out into the cheerless courtyard. Over by the stables a lantern danced in the gloom now, touching the falling rain with silver and then an ostler was leading Prince Owain's mount across to where they waited.

The farmhouse door opened and Prince Owain stood there silhouetted against the warm glow of the interior. He held a hand up to his eyes, as though peering out into the darkness of the courtyard, his eyes as yet unaccustomed to the gloom of the early morning. Then the door shut behind him, cutting off the shaft of light that had given the illusion of warmth and he was striding purposefully over to where the ostler stood waiting with his horse.

Mounting, Glyn Dŵr turned to Sir Edmund, his teeth gleaming white in the glow of light from a window, as he said with a grin, 'No kerchiefs waving us farewell this murky morn, Edmund, perhaps 'tis saved for our return!'

Sir Edmund wiped the rain off his mouth with the back of his hand, thinking despondently as he did so, aye, or perhaps saved for the likes of that archer fellow! Then Sir Edmund spurred his mount and followed as Glyn Dŵr led the small group out of the courtyard and began the long march to Harlech Castle.

Chapter Twenty-one

Daybreak came grey and cheerless, with Snowdon cloaked in cloud and rain as, heads bent, Sir Edmund rode with Glyn Dŵr to the south-west with their escort. Each man was left to his own thoughts for much of the time, for with the wind and rain in their face and the cold grey day enshrouding them, there was little to encourage idle chatter. Nor were Sir Edmund's thoughts such as to lift his spirits or make him relish the prospect of being rebuffed by Harlech's constable who would no doubt view him as a renegade. Rather he was thinking that probably his time would be better spent with Catrin. He was brought back to the present with a sudden jerk as his horse stumbled.

Glyn Dŵr turned to him to say with a grin, 'This is no place to dream of soft beds and idle days, Edmund, though how you may doze in your saddle on such a day I cannot tell!'

Irritated, Sir Edmund glanced at him to say with a toss of his head, 'Would that I could, my lord, and that you roused me not here but in Harlech's hall, the siege long over!' He brushed a hand across his mouth: 'Do we pause along the way, my lord? Were there sky enough to see, the sun would surely be at its zenith now.'

Glyn Dŵr nodded. 'Aye, soon enough now. A mile or two ahead a cottage lies close by our track where we shall pause and rest the nags awhile and then press on, for I would be at Tudor's camp ere the sun goes down on this dismal day.'

Lord Tudor was in command of Glyn Dŵr's men laying siege to Harlech and although there was no great love lost between them, Sir Edmund nodded, pleased at the prospect of arriving at Harlech before dark. It would be as well for them that there would still be light enough to be identified by Tudor's men, for an arrow notched by a friend could be just as deadly as one loosed by an enemy!

Nor was he the only one who gratefully dismounted when they arrived at the small cottage a few minutes later. Clearly it had not been lived in for some time and though the door swung to and fro at the wind's behest, inside it was dry, for the roof seemed sound though the room was dark, for a shutter closed the only window.

'No cottager lives here then?' asked Sir Edmund of Glyn Dŵr.

The prince shook his head, saying tersely, 'No, long since gone!' Then, in answer to the unspoken question of Sir Edmund's raised eyebrows, continued, 'War's casualties lie not only on the battlefield, Edmund, for some die starving from the famine it leaves behind!'

They were crowding into the one room of the cottage now, out of the rain, with a few seeking shelter in the roomy but malodorous cowshed alongside the house. As he went into the surprisingly large single room of the cottage, Sir Edmund fleetingly imagined that he saw Cathy, or was it Catrin, sitting there on a sort of mattress against the far wall. Smiling at him seductively, she held her hand out towards him in invitation and he took a pace towards her. Then, as quickly as it came, the image was gone and there was only Glyn Dŵr and the men at arms beside him in the dank room of the deserted cottage.

Standing alongside him, Glyn Dŵr gave him an odd sideways glance to ask, 'Are you all right, Edmund? I'd swear you'd seen a ghost, so ashen is your cheek!'

Sir Edmund shook his head, to say with a confidence he did not feel, 'There are no phantoms here, my lord, only the more substantial presence of ourselves, although the clanking of our armour would indeed suffice to wake the dead!'

From the unbelieving look that lingered in Glyn Dŵr's eyes it was evident that he still doubted the brave words but he waited for a moment before saying, a touch of sympathy in his voice now, 'I know it is not a good time for you to make your first foray against our common enemy, Edmund, but I must take these English castles in the west ere spring gives Henry opportunity to bring them succour. In but a little while we shall accomplish that and you shall dwell in Castle Harlech with Catrin and the child. Meantimes Catrin shall be safe enough with Lady Marged to look after her.'

Sir Edmund nodded as he replied, 'I never doubted it, my lord!' Even as he spoke though, the old doubt returned and he frowned as he recalled seeing Catrin waving to the two captains, Dafydd and Idris, when they had departed to relieve Glyn Dŵr's men besieging Harlech. Was it really to the two captains she had waved though, he wondered, or had it been just to the archer, Idris?

For a few minutes they all stood or squatted around the bare room eating their chunks of bread and cheese, drinking water from their flasks and talking amongst themselves of what they might find at Harlech, or of other sieges they had fought and won or lost. Sir Edmund though only listened to the chatter half-heartedly, thinking of Catrin . . . and of the archer Idris. As he did so, he remembered Gruffydd's angry retort when he had asked Glyn Dŵr whether the archer was of his family. Turning to Glyn Dŵr, he asked casually, 'That archer, Idris, with Lord Tudor at Harlech now, my lord, looks as alike your son as two peas in a pod, yet Gruffydd said they are not kin?'

Laughing, Glyn Dŵr replied, 'Trace kinship back far enough, Edmund and we Welsh are all related. 'Tis why you English can never tell us apart, one from another, thinking that we all do look alike!' Smiling now, he waved a hand dismissively, saying as he did so, 'Come, we have loitered here long enough, 'tis time we set off!' Then, in a voice loud enough for all to hear, called out, 'Mount up!'

As he went out of the door of the cottage, Sir Edmund turned his head, to catch his breath as he saw Catrin, or was it Cathy, sitting on that mattress over by the far wall again. The wraith was smiling at him now, waving to him and he broke out into a cold sweat at the sight of the strange apparition. Hurriedly he turned away to mount his horse. As he did so, Glyn Dŵr turned to him and frowning now, said sharply, 'Is all well with you, Edmund? It seems you've seen that ghost again, 'tis as well we stay not in this cottage overnight!'

Sir Edmund glanced at him, to say curtly, 'As fit as any man here, my lord. I am just glad enough to leave this hovel!' Then, turning away quickly to avoid Glyn Dŵr's penetrating gaze, he dug in his spurs and set off again on the road to Harlech.

He was indeed glad to get away from the cottage for his mind was in a turmoil now as he wondered what could have made him imagine he had seen Catrin, or was it Cathy, sitting there in that deserted hovel. Even so he was unable to resist turning for one last look and a clammy sweat came to his brow again as, for a moment, he imagined he saw her standing there at the doorway, an ironic smile now on her lips as she waved a kerchief to him.

Quickly he turned away again, knowing, despite his momentary fear, that it was all but an illusion. Whilst they had sheltered in the cottage, the rain and the wind had abated a little. Now though he was grateful to feel the wind in his face again; it cooled his brow and blew away the ghosts that seemed to haunt him. The soft drizzle that fell was no discomfort now but rather a balm that soothed the turmoil of his mind.

As they rode on, Sir Edmund, preoccupied with his doubts about Catrin's relationship with Glyn Dŵr's captain of archers, was silent for much of the journey, responding only in monosyllables when Glyn Dŵr tried to engage him in conversation. After a while, Glyn Dŵr gave up these attempts and left him in peace to endure his imaginary pain in silence.

It was late afternoon before Glyn Dŵr roused him from his melancholy by saying, 'There it is at last, Edmund, Harlech! As dark a picture as your own face!'

It was too, for he could see Castle Harlech now, looking impregnable as it stood there on its rocky pinnacle, darkly silhouetted against the lowering sky. Below it lay the town of Harlech with Owain Glyn Dŵr's banners fluttering defiantly in the early evening's offshore wind from a small encampment below the castle itself.

Sir Edmund turned to Glyn Dŵr, to say with a look of astonishment on his face, 'With such a small force laying siege, it is no wonder the defenders have held out so long, my lord!'

Glyn Dŵr looked at him with raised eyebrows. 'Small force?' he asked incredulously. 'Why, the castle has no more than some two score left in its garrison! That is the reason their provender has lasted thus long, but they cannot hold out much longer. I would hasten their departure now by calling on their good sense, for they shall leave now with safe conduct to an English town of their choice or have their bones bleach on yonder turrets whilst my banner waves above them!'

Looking at the prince sitting there glowering on his mount, Sir Edmund doubted not his words for a moment. The glowering changed suddenly to a knowing smile and Glyn Dŵr said softly, 'And that, Edmund, is the reason for your visit here! Mayhap your countrymen will listen to your English words more than they have to the language of the bards!' He paused and there was iron in his voice now as he added, 'But mark my words, Edmund, and mark them well, when I tell you that leave they shall, be it on foot or to dance on air!'

Seeing the stern visage of the prince, Sir Edmund marked and believed every word he said. Often enough in these troubled days, a garrison's refusal to surrender led only to their massacre if defeat eventually followed, for such were the unwritten rules of war.

'I hear you well, my lord,' he said curtly, 'though such alternative tends to stiffen the sinews of the weak rather than bring defiant men to their knees. I will speak to them, but rather to persuade them that their cause is lost and that they will find magnanimity in honourable surrender to force majeure.'

Glyn Dŵr sniffed. 'As you will, Edmund,' he said deprecatingly, 'so be it they follow you out of yonder castle disarmed and afoot!'

Stubbornly, Sir Edmund persisted: 'I'll bring them out of there, my lord, so be it they are accorded safe conduct and all the honours of war!'

Glyn Dŵr scowled. ' "Honours of war" indeed,' he said disdainfully. 'I've told you before, Edmund, that you live in some fairy world of make believe. There is no honour in war and fewer courtesies in this battle for independence that Henry calls rebellion!' He gazed at Sir Edmund for a moment before at last saying grudgingly with a wave of his hand, 'Oh, very well! If they march out within twelve hours of your entrance there, they can march out with their tattered banners and their side arms. They bear any more than that and they forfeit my indulgence of your whim and I shall fall upon them like an avenging angel! Make sure they understand that well, for in their default no man amongst them shall be spared my wrath!'

Shocked by the venom of Glyn Dŵr's words, Sir Edmund could only nod his agreement, less enamoured than ever of venturing into Castle Harlech and even more doubtful of the success of his mission. Shortly after this exchange they were approaching the encampment of Glyn Dŵr's besieging force with Glyn Dŵr's brother Tudor and the two captains, Dafydd and Idris, standing there waiting to greet them.

As Glyn Dŵr dismounted, Tudor strode over to him, hand held out, whilst the two captains touched their helmets in salute. Smiling now, Tudor greeted the prince: 'Did you not trust me to take Harlech on my own, brother, that you come to aid me in its downfall?'

As he grasped the offered hand, Glyn Dŵr grinned and replied, 'I never doubted that you would take it sometime, Tudor, 'tis but that life is too short for me to wait upon your laggard ways. I come therefore that we may take it quickly and by guile, where your forceful ways have not gained us entry!'

Tudor frowned as he queried, 'By guile, Owain?'

Still smiling, Glyn Dŵr replied, 'Aye, by guile, Tudor! Tomorrow, whilst the sun is still low in the east, Sir Edmund here will enter the castle under a flag of truce to call upon them to surrender.'

Scowling at Sir Edmund, Tudor sniffed before saying haughtily, 'Think you the turncoat will succeed my lord, when oft enough we have parleyed with them without success?'

Glyn Dŵr frowned. 'Sir Edmund is no turncoat, Tudor,' he said calmly, 'but valued ally and kin to you through my daughter's marriage, which you would do well to remember! Reason enough too, he has to rebel against the usurper, Henry.'

He turned towards the two captains standing there, grinning now at the exchange between their prince and his brother, to say sharply, 'And you two jackanapes can cease your foolish smirking, for you'll need to be up betimes on the morrow, for you shall be Sir Edmund's escort.'

Suddenly serious, the man at arms, Dafydd Mawr, touched his helmet, saying as he did so, 'Aye, my lord, and with us beside him, he'll need no other! Why, an' we gain entrance there the garrison will come trooping out like so many sheep with dogs at their tails.'

Glyn Dŵr stared at him for a moment, uncertain it seemed as to whether the man at arms' words were a heartfelt promise or mere irony. 'Aye,' he said at last, 'well, make it so, or you'll bear a lance beside your own sheep instead of leading them into the fray!'

Subdued now, Dafydd Mawr bent his head in acknowledgment to say quietly, 'It shall be so, my lord.'

Meanwhile, Idris the archer just stood there silently, head unbowed, staring at Sir Edmund with what the knight felt could only be a look of contempt. The uncomfortable silence that followed this exchange was broken by Glyn Dŵr saying with a smile, 'Well, do you not have a bite to eat and a draught of ale to cheer us after our journey here, Tudor?'

Tudor waved a hand in the direction of one of the larger tents. 'Of course, my lord,' he said with a just suggestion of mock obsequiousness, 'I have a table laid ready in my tent there!'

In good humour again now, Glyn Dŵr smiled. 'Well, why do we stand here then, Tudor? Lead on!' As they walked towards the tent, Sir Edmund noticed that Dafydd Mawr held back, obviously giving instructions to one of his men to take care of the escort which had accompanied Glyn Dŵr on the journey.

The tent was gloomy and cramped when the five men got inside, it was cold too, but they were out of the wind and Idris quickly set about lighting a lantern which soon gave an illusion of warmth. A table was already laid as Tudor had promised, spread with ewers of ale along with platters of meat and bread. Barely were they seated, bunched close together, before a man was bringing steaming bowls of cawl into the tent for them. The sharpness of the words that had been exchanged on the arrival of Glyn Dŵr were quickly forgotten as they all hungrily set about their meal. Toast after toast was drunk in ale to Castle Harlech's fall to Glyn Dŵr and to the success of their war of independence. Gradually the chill left their bones too as the tent became warmer with so many bodies cramped into its confined area.

If the tent became warmer, Sir Edmund sensed veiled hostility each time he met the glance of Idris the archer and thought that he could well do without such escort when he approached the castle the next day.

Long into the night they sat there drinking, exchanging tales of the siege with news of the progress of the rebellion. Eventually though, when the last ewer of ale had been emptied, Tudor showed his brother to a tent erected next to his own and Dafydd Mawr led Sir Edmund to a smaller tent nearby in which a lantern was already lit. 'Sleep well, Sir Edmund,' he said with a crooked smile as he stood just outside the open flap of the tent, 'and God grant you success on the morrow, for this is a cheerless rock we sit upon out here and I'd sooner gaze down on it from yonder ramparts!'

Sir Edmund was huddled under a few blankets on a straw mattress the next morning when the sudden call roused him, but it took a second call to bring him to wakefulness and to stare at the perpetrator with eyes still only half open. ' 'Tis dawn,' he heard the man remind him curtly.

Dawn, he suddenly realised! The dawn of the day when he must meet the constable of Castle Harlech. He looked up, to take little comfort in the fact that it was the archer Idris, who had so rudely awakened him. With a sarcastic, 'Breakfast, my lord!' Idris placed a pot of ale and a hunk of bread roughly on the small trestle table that was the only piece of furniture in the small tent.

Sir Edmund looked up at him, thinking that Idris seemed to find as little pleasure in his duty as he found himself in the archer's presence. Biting his tongue however, he mustered up enough civility to say, 'Thank you, Idris.'

If it were meant as a gesture of amity, it met with little response, for with a toss of his head, the archer responded with a curt, 'We set out for the castle within the hour, my lord!'

Sir Edmund felt the words held contempt rather than respect, but disregarding the archer's manner said pleasantly enough, 'I shall be ready, never fear Idris! I should be grateful though if someone would bring me a bucket of water that I might cleanse myself before we embark upon our mission.'

With a toss of his head, Idris muttered, 'There's a small brook below the encampment that we all use for such things,' then, as an afterthought, an even more reluctant, 'my lord.'

Thinking of the probably icy water of the brook, Sir Edmund mustered up the courage to nod and reply, 'Thank you, Idris, that should indeed wake me nicely for our parleying!' He was talking to deaf ears though, for the archer had already gone, leaving a cold wind blowing through the open tent flap.

Sighing, Sir Edmund flung the blankets aside and rose, grateful immediately that he had slept fully clothed, for the cutting wind was onshore now and keen enough to penetrate the warmest clothing let alone bare flesh. Peering out of the tent he saw that the ground fell away sharply and, venturing out, made his way downhill in the direction he hoped the brook might lie.

When at last he found the stream its waters were as icy as he had imagined, but after the first shock he found splashing it on his face both invigorated and dispelled the irritation of his early morning encounter with the archer for whom he had a growing feeling of resentment. As he stood there on the side of the rocky pinnacle, the wind stinging his wet face, he wondered for a moment why the archer had such obvious hostility to him. Could it really be, he asked himself, that there had indeed been some sort of relationship between the archer and Catrin? He shook his head, that could never have been the case he thought; a mere archer and a lord's daughter, surely not!

He was still shaking his head as he walked back up to his tent to prepare himself for the morning's forthcoming mission to Castle Harlech. It was not without some trepidation that he did so. Not because of the mission itself, for he had no fears for his person in such a situation. Even in these outlandish parts meeting an enemy under a flag of truce should be safe enough. No such flag, however, could preserve a turncoat from the looks of scorn and verbal abuse of one's compatriots. Even the thought of that concerned him less than the possibility, indeed the probability of the failure of his mission. Could he indeed persuade the constable of Harlech to surrender now, with spring and the hope of succour only a matter of weeks away, when he had already held out for long months against Glyn Dŵr?

Buckling on his sword belt, Sir Edmund sighed as he imagined what his own response might have been only a short while ago had a rebel come to Ludlow Castle under a flag of truce in an attempt to persuade him to surrender the castle to Glyn Dŵr. Knowing the answer to his own question, it was with a heavy heart he stepped out of the tent a moment later, feeling as he did so that his previous optimism as to the result of his mission had been misplaced. Once outside the tent he saw the two captains waiting for him nearby, with Dafydd Mawr holding a stave around which was furled a white cloth.

Touching his helmet the man at arms favoured him with a sardonic smile, as though he had been on such missions more than once before and had little hope for this fresh venture. 'A fine day for it, my lord,' he said evenly. His voice held no trace though of the resentment that was evident in the archer's eyes, but then, Sir Edmund knew that the veteran man at arms had fought for more lords than one and would have fought as dispassionately for each one as for the next.

After the rain and wind of his march to Harlech, he found that it was indeed a fine day, with the castle etched sharp against clear skies that had left the grass underfoot crisp with frost. 'Aye Dafydd,' Sir Edmund agreed with a nod, 'a fine day indeed, perchance it will bring the garrison to see the reason of our demands!'

Idris, a hand clasping the bowstring of the bow slung loosely over his right shoulder snorted. 'They have not done so yet, nor do I think a change of the weather will make them change their minds!'

Sir Edmund took a sharp intake of breath, then smiled to say calmly, ' 'Twill be the message, not the weather, that will change their stubborn hearts, Idris!'

Idris smiled thinly. 'Aye? Then 'twill be the message not the messenger I fear!'

'Enough!' snapped Sir Edmund, 'or that bowstring you clasp will etch your back!' Then turning to Dafydd Mawr, he said firmly, 'Well Dafydd, unfurl your banner and let us be about it!'

With that they set off up the hill, with Dafydd's white flag fluttering in the chilly breeze. They were silent as they climbed, at least in part because of Sir Edmund's brief altercation with Idris, but perhaps more on his part because he was thinking of what he had to say to the constable, of what he had to achieve and the dreaded consequences of failure.

They were nearing the castle now and Sir Edmund could see a sprinkling of figures watching their progress from the ramparts. There was a movement there and suddenly he saw an arrow in flight, winging its way towards them. He held up a hand and all three stood stock still watching it, until at last it fell quivering in the earth a few yards in front of them. Dafydd grinned. 'I think that's meant to tell us we've advanced far enough, my lord!'

Smiling, Sir Edmund nodded. 'Aye, 'twould seem so, Dafydd! Since we are within arrow range then I do believe your bellow should reach them well enough from here, so call upon them to parley!'

The stave of his banner now held out at arm's length, its foot resting firmly on the ground, Dafydd cupped a hand like a ham around his mouth to call out in a voice fit to raise the dead, 'Ahoy the castle! Sir Edmund Mortimer comes to treat with your constable!'

There was no immediate reply from the castle, but they could see the few heads that appeared above the ramparts drawing together in a knot as though conferring amongst themselves. Minutes passed and there still being no reply, Sir Edmund was about to order Dafydd to hail the castle again, when one head separated from the knot on the ramparts to call out, 'Let Sir Edmund Mortimer and only he, approach the drawbridge and wait there!'

Dafydd Mawr turned to Sir Edmund and shaking his head, said, 'No, my lord! Prince Owain said we all three go, or not at all!'

Sir Edmund grinned. 'Think you I go to bring succour to the garrison, Dafydd, and that once in, I'll not come out? If it is their wish, I'll go alone or not at all, which would give little pleasure to the prince nor, I fear, to you!'

Dafydd Mawr stood there hesitantly for a moment before, nodding, he said with obvious reluctance, 'I fear only for your safety, my lord! If you must, then go and may God go with you, for this siege has lasted long enough!'

Idris, it seemed, was not so easily satisfied, for as Sir Edmund began walking towards the castle's drawbridge he heard the archer say to Dafydd, 'You should not have let him go on alone Dafydd, if he's turned his coat once, shall he not turn it again?'

He did not hear the old retainer's reply, but there was no word to halt his progress and he smiled to himself now at the thought of the rebuff that Idris had obviously received. Head up, he walked on towards the drawbridge, not daring to glance at the ramparts lest he were to see yet another archer notching an arrow to his bow. Were that to be, so, he could not find it in his heart to blame them, remembering the tale of a one time constable of Castle Harlech, captured by one of Glyn Dŵr's men, Robin Holland, when he had ventured out to parley with the Welsh.

Though his heart was in his throat, he came to the outer end of the drawbridge with no misadventure and stood there waiting for whatever might now befall him. All was silent though and he stared at the great gate of the castle feeling more vulnerable and alone than he had ever felt before. He knew full well that if ought went wrong now, Idris the archer, standing there behind him, would not hesitate to send an arrow into his back as readily as those above would send one into his chest.

It was with some relief he heard bolts being withdrawn and a creaking of hinges then saw a small door in the great gate of Castle Harlech being opened. A figure appeared there now and slowly, reluctantly it seemed, stepped out onto the inner end of the drawbridge.

Sir Edmund frowned, for this was no knight, but the emaciated figure of a grizzled man at arms attired in chain-mail, his grey hair straggling from beneath a rusty helmet. Sir Edmund took a step back in surprise. Surely this was no person with whom to negotiate the surrender of the almost impregnable Castle Harlech!

'Sir Edmund Mortimer?' the apparition enquired.

'Aye and I came to parley with Sir William Hunt, King Henry's constable of Harlech Castle.' Sir Edmund replied curtly.

'He sent me to do his business with you!' croaked the apparition. 'What is it that you would have of him?'

Sir Edmund paused, nonplussed. What constable would allow a feeble and obviously aged retainer to do his parleying for him? Drawing a breath however, he replied courteously enough, 'My business is with him, sir, and is of great import for the safety of the garrison here!'

Apparently the English man at arms had never heard of Sir Edmund for, frowning now, he asked, 'Why would Glendower send an Englishman to offer safety to my men?'

Why 'my men' not 'Sir William's men', wondered Sir Edmund, but stalling now, he merely smiled and replied, 'I come as Prince Owain's envoy to assure your constable that does he but surrender now both he and all here shall receive all the courtesies of war!'

The man at arms seemed unmoved for he merely sniffed. 'The constable died of fever,' he replied, before adding bluntly, 'I command here now Sir Knight. Scant courtesy I've found in war, wherever I've fought and less than most from Glendower!' He frowned now in obvious wonderment, before asking almost incredulously, 'But you, my lord, are English! How is it an English knight comes to plead Glendower's cause?'

Sir Edmund laughed. 'Perhaps because you and I speak the same tongue and I do yet love my countrymen so would see them safe again on English soil rather than spill their blood needlessly here in Wales!'

The man at arms stared at him for a moment and Sir Edmund, remembering his ambitious squire, de Lacey, imagined the man at arms balancing the prospect of a knighthood for holding Harlech for his king against the prospect of safety.

'Come man,' he said after a moment's pause. 'How much longer can your men hold out before starvation or the fever that perhaps killed your constable, brings them to their knees? Certainly not till spring or summer might bring them aid! You can walk out now, with no disgrace, for you shall have yielded to force majeure. Those sick amongst you will be cared for by the townsfolk and all others may safely go to where they will, with Prince Owain's safe conduct tucked in their belt. He shook his head in apparent sorrow as he added, 'This offer shall not be made again . . .' he paused there before adding softly, ' . . .should you refuse to surrender now, I need not tell you what shall befall all those you now command when Harlech finally falls, as fall it must, to Glyn Dŵr.'

Looking at the stricken face of the man at arms now risen to the command of Castle Harlech, he turned away. Then, almost sickened by his own words, he turned back to say, almost in a whisper, 'Surrender now, man, whilst there is still time, there are no knighthoods beyond the grave!' He turned away and leaving the man at arms, hand on chin, staring after him, walked slowly downhill to rejoin Dafydd Mawr and Idris.

Chapter Twenty-two

As Sir Edmund approached the two captains, Idris the archer, barely hiding his contempt now, was the first to speak: 'You return alone then, my lord?'

Sir Edmund stared at him to reply evenly, 'Why, did you think they would let me bring back the castle cat as promise of their submission?' Looking at Dafydd Mawr now, he added with more confidence than he felt, 'They have much to ponder over and I doubt not that ere the sun sets we shall have their reply, for hunger and fever have already so wasted them they'll not see the winter out!'

With that he turned and began walking downhill towards their encampment, with Idris and Dafydd following, the man at arms still bearing the white flag fluttering in the breeze. Prince Owain was waiting for them by his tent when they arrived and, his face dark and brooding, asked imperiously, 'You return alone then, Sir Edmund? Then needs must we use the iron fist where silken words have failed!'

Sir Edmund shook his head, to say calmly, 'That time has not yet come, my lord, for we shall have their reply before night falls and I do not fear what it might be. Their constable is dead of fever, a half starved man at arms is in command there now and I doubt not that the rest of the garrison is in like state. Ere spring comes you could knock upon the door and find none therein to answer you!'

Glyn Dŵr looked at him doubtfully for a moment then, reluctantly it seemed, nodded. 'Very well, Edmund. Yet the sun shall not set this day without they yield or they shall rue the day they barred their door to Owain Glyn Dŵr!' Then, with his anger evident in the thrust of his bearded chin, he turned and stomped into his tent.

Watching him, Sir Edmund felt his spine tingle as he prayed silently that the man at arms up there in the castle was even now preparing to surrender, for he had no wish to participate in the massacre that he knew would ultimately but surely, follow rejection.

Subdued now, he turned to Dafydd to say quietly, 'Watch the castle well, Dafydd, and tell me of any movement there!'

Nodding, Dafydd replied with a terse, 'Aye, my lord!'

As Sir Edmund glanced at the archer though, Idris was just smiling knowingly, as if taking pleasure in Prince Owain's displeasure.

The morning passed slowly for Sir Edmund who, his mind racing with conflicting emotions, was unable to sit quietly in his tent. Instead, with no obviously friendly face to join him, he paced along the outskirts of the encampment, the while keeping an anxious eye for movement around the castle. It was nigh on noon when the prince's brother, Lord Tudor, approached him, to say with a hint of a sneer, 'No sign of surrender yet then, Sir Edmund?'

Sir Edmund glared at him to snap, 'Not yet! Nor does it seem that any other than the prince and I would take great pleasure in their submission!'

With a sardonic smile, Tudor replied easily, 'Oh there you are in error, Mortimer, for we would all take great pleasure in that. 'Tis just that we take equal pleasure in your discomfiture and hope that my brother might see you as the turncoat that you are!' So saying he turned away abruptly and swaggered off, leaving Sir Edmund wondering why he should fight for either English or Welsh when both it seemed resented him!

The day wore on, with Sir Edmund becoming increasingly anxious for sight or sound of movement on the castle's walls but noontime came and went without such sign. Nor did he join the others for the midday meal, reluctant now to face the contempt or derision of such as Tudor or Idris. Some two hours past noon, tired of impatiently pacing the perimeter of the encampment, he was glumly sitting on his haunches in his tent, chin in hand, when the flap was drawn aside to reveal Dafydd.

'Their captain is at the castle's gate bearing a flag of truce, my lord,' the man at arms said without a flicker of emotion.

Sir Edmund jumped up bright-eyed now and asked, 'At the gate, you say Dafydd, how long has he been there?'

'Not more than a minute or two,' Dafydd replied in that same cool voice. 'I came as soon as I set eyes upon him,'

Sir Edmund though, was already outside the tent now, waving a hand to Dafydd and saying impatiently, 'Come on man! We must hear what he has to say!'

Dafydd though was unmoved by his plea for haste, saying stolidly,

'No need for haste, my lord, he'll not be going anywhere 'til we arrive at his gate.' He paused, then added with a touch of malice, 'Aside of which, he has kept us waiting on this cold rock all winter through, 'twill do his soul good to chill his bones at his own front door whilst he waits upon us!'

Sir Edmund smiled, then said, 'No doubt it shall, Dafydd!' And with raised eyebrows asked, 'Have you had Prince Owain told?'

Dafydd nodded. 'Aye, my lord, and he said that me and Idris should escort you to the gate.'

Sir Edmund sighed, feeling that he could well do without Idris at his side if the English man at arms' response were to be rejection of the offer. Nodding though, he merely echoed the words he had used that morning: 'Well then Dafydd, let us be about our business . . . oh, and bring your banner with you, lest those inside the castle think we come to take their captain, as their one time constable was taken!'

Dafydd gave a grim smile and, slapping the scabbard of his great sword, said in a sibilant whisper, 'Have no fear there, my lord, I am not in the trade of taking prisoners here!'

Sir Edmund looked at him for a moment, a shudder running down his spine as he wondered whether that was some hidden message from Glyn Dŵr. He stood there for a moment wondering too what assurances of safety he could truly give the castle's commander when they met. Tight lipped now, he ignored Dafydd's reply, just saying, 'Come on then, let's get on with it.'

Minutes later, he was walking up the hill again with Dafydd and Idris either side of him. It seemed though that he went too fast for Dafydd, who cautioned, 'There's no need for haste, my lord, we are not the supplicants here! The slower we go the more they'll think we are reluctant to offer clemency to them in their plight!'

Sir Edmund glanced at him, about to make a sharp retort, then realised that there was a grain of truth in Dafydd's comment and eased his pace. Despite that it took them only a little time to reach the outer end of the drawbridge, there to face the grizzled man at arms Sir Edmund had met that morning. He stood there staring at them, head unbowed, thin shoulders drawn back, chin out aggressively as though he were on parade.

Sir Edmund took a sharp intake of breath thinking that from the man at arms' appearance he was not there to surrender! Glancing sideways, he saw Idris grinning, obviously thinking much the same and taking no little pleasure in the thought. Bracing himself and looking the English man at arms straight in the eye, Sir Edmund spoke now, his voice harsh with the inner tension he felt, 'This morning I gave you your final chance to surrender with honour. All day you've been allowed to consider this at your pleasure whilst we waited peacefully in our camp for your response. 'Tis time now that we have your answer that you submit or else Prince Owain will unleash his dogs of war, whose fury shall not abate until your bones bleach on those ramparts above.'

The man at arms' eyes remained impassive but he seemed less stiff backed than he had been and when he spoke his voice had a quaver that might have been due to age alone. 'Yes we spoke,' he said with a nod, 'but you offered little in the way of terms.'

Dafydd took a step forward, his hand on his sword hilt, to say angrily, 'You speak of terms when twice or even thrice, you've been offered . . .'

Sir Edmund held out a hand towards him to say with a sting in his voice, 'One man speaks for either side here, Dafydd!' Then to the English captain he said, 'The terms are as I offered: the sick to be cared for in the town, all others may leave with Prince Owain's safe conduct and carrying side arms for their own protection, I add now that when your men march out of the castle you may bear your banner, but for your own safety should dispense with it once out of sight of Harlech. Those are the terms and there shall be no other. Do I have your answer?'

The old man at arms flinched a little under Sir Edmund's stare, yet though his eyes were duller now, his chin still stuck out stubbornly and he replied, 'You speak of safe conduct for my men, but what of their journey to safe shelter, how might they exist with nought to buy food or drink along the way?'

It was not an unreasonable question, since there was little likelihood that any of them had been paid since their constable had died, even if they had before that. It was one too that he was prepared for. 'You shall be given three hundred marks,' he replied, 'to see your people to safe shelter and for their pay along the way.' He smiled as he added, 'No doubt King Henry will see you all recompensed for the time you have held Harlech without being paid your dues!'

Evidently not entirely convinced of that, the man at arms sniffed, to say with a touch of irony, 'Aye, no doubt my lord.'

Sir Edmund smiled, satisfied now that he had Harlech's surrender in his hand, but it seemed the old man at arms had not yet finished, for he asked, 'You spoke of safe conduct for my men Sir Knight, but what of the womenfolk, the children too?'

Sir Edmund sighed, but he nodded. 'They too shall go unmolested, Captain.'

Stubbornly, the man persisted: 'But with safe conduct too?'

Another nod from Sir Edmund as he said, 'Aye, safe conduct too.'

Looking at him with eyes half closed, hand scratching his thin beard, the man at arms asked again, 'But how can we be sure of all this, Sir Edmund?'

Out of the corner of his eye, Sir Edmund saw Dafydd's hand go to his sword again, and he said hurriedly, 'Why, you have my word on it, man!'

Eyes still half closed, head on one side, the captain of Harlech Castle said innocently enough, 'Aye, there's the rub, Sir Knight, for I hear Edmund Mortimer's word is not what it was!'

There was a snigger from Idris on Sir Edmund's left and he flushed angrily to snap back, 'I have given you your terms, which were not gained easily after your stubborn refusals ere this. You have my given word and that on behalf of Prince Owain Glyn Dŵr. Now give me your answer or be damned, for damned you'll surely be if you refuse Prince Owain's magnanimity!'

The captain sighed and there was a hiss of breath as, shoulders drooping, he nodded slowly. Then reluctantly he said, 'You have my answer, Sir Edmund, we yield and may you be damned if you do not keep your word.'

Sir Edmund's face paled as he nodded in affirmation, saying, 'You have my word, Captain!'

The words were barely out of his mouth before Dafydd was stepping forward and pointing at the captain's sword, to say harshly, 'Right you, I'll have that!'

Sir Edmund put a restraining hand on Dafydd's arm, to say quickly, 'No Dafydd, I told him they may keep their side arms!'

Dafydd turned to him to protest, 'Why, my lord, 'tis the rules of war! Does he surrender, then he offers you his sword in token that he yields!'

Sir Edmund shook his head, then smiled as he said firmly, 'From all that I've been told Dafydd, there are few such rules in this rebellion and I've told him he keeps his sword.' He glanced at the English captain, who stood there irresolutely now, then added, 'Instead we'll have three men at arms and three archers from the garrison as hostages now in token of his surrender and in surety that he keeps his word! Then one hour after dawn tomorrow, he shall lead the garrison across this drawbridge.'

Frowning, Dafydd Mawr stepped back as if about to argue but Sir Edmund continued calmly, 'Should our friend here reject my offer, he shall accompany us to continue this discussion with Prince Owain who might generously offer him a hempen collar for his trouble!'

Evidently the captain saw this as a real possibility, for his grizzled face blanched beneath its tan and, with a sigh, he nodded his agreement. Minutes later a small group came trooping out of the castle to stand outside its gate glaring at their captain. A quick look served to satisfy Sir Edmund that his demand had been met and calmly, in a voice that belied the tension he felt, he told the captain, 'Tell them to drop their weapons here, 'twill only bring them grief should they carry them where they now go.'

There was a rebellious muttering amongst the group, its hostility directed now at Sir Edmund, with murmurings of 'Traitor, turncoat!' A sharp word though from their captain and one by one they began divesting themselves of their weapons to stand there looking beaten, dejected.

Breathing a silent sigh of relief, Sir Edmund glanced at his companions. It seemed that they too had been uncertain of the outcome of his strategy which had left them so outnumbered, for grim faced, they stood there with swords drawn, ready to do battle.

Smiling, he told them, 'Come, put up your swords, for these gentlemen of Harlech will come peacefully with us, to rejoin their comrades when the frost is still on the ground tomorrow.'

With a nod, Dafydd turned to the English captain to say with iron in his voice, 'Aye, they'll join their comrades outside these castle walls tomorrow or dance on air for their entertainment!'

Ashen faced now, the English captain ignored Dafydd, and speaking instead to Sir Edmund, he pleaded, 'Keep them safe, my lord, for we'll be out betimes!'

Sir Edmund nodded. 'Fear not Captain, our war with them is over! Do you but keep your word then I'll keep mine. Send them across now.'

A word from their captain and the hostages came trooping dejectedly across the drawbridge in single file with Dafydd and Idris, their swords still drawn, guarding either side of the bridge. As one of the hostages passed Sir Edmund he spat at him defiantly, muttering 'Traitor!' as he did so.

Barely had he taken another pace forward though before Sir Edmund was amazed to see Idris strike the man viciously across the shoulder with the back of his sword, snarling as he did so, 'Yes, but he's our bloody traitor, you English pig!'

Smiling to himself as he followed the file of hostages downhill, Sir Edmund wondered whether the archer's remark hid some strange sort of compliment.

A few minutes later they were trooping into Prince Owain's encampment with all of the besieging force gathered there to greet them. Nor from their cheering did it seem that there was one amongst them who doubted what their arrival meant. Prince Owain with an unsmiling Tudor standing beside him, was at their fore and unlike his brother was smiling broadly as he said, 'I take it that with these guests you bring good news, Edmund?'

Sir Edmund nodded to say quietly, 'Indeed my lord, for these men are here as surety that the garrison march out one hour after dawn tomorrow.'

Glyn Dŵr's smile faded. 'Tomorrow?' he asked harshly. 'Why not now?'

Sir Edmund controlled his rising irritation to reply calmly, 'Their captain has surrendered, my lord. 'Twill do no harm that they spend the night gathering together their few possessions in readiness for their travel rather than embark upon it this winter's night!'

Tudor's lip curled and, piqued perhaps at his own failure to obtain the garrison's surrender, he broke into the conversation to ask, 'What other concessions have you offered to get them to yield, Sir Edmund?'

'Nought but that which is in within reason, Tudor,' he replied calmly.

Prince Owain stared at him for a moment, then queried warily, 'And what might that be, Edmund?'

Hesitating for a moment, Sir Edmund then replied, 'Why, as we agreed, my lord: that they may wear their side arms and bear their banners whilst yet within sight of Harlech,' he paused there, before adding quietly, 'and that their captain shall receive three hundred marks for their subsistence along the way.'

Prince Owain frowned saying sternly now, 'I did not agree to that, Edmund!' Then, as Sir Edmund waited in some trepidation for the prince to break into an angry outburst, Glyn Dŵr slowly smiled and instead said, 'Well, I suppose we may grant them that from Lord Grey's generous donation to our cause.' He turned to his brother to ask, 'Might we not, Tudor?'

Magnanimity seemed not to be in Tudor's nature however, for scowling he replied, 'Marks, my lord? The only marks I'd give them would be across their stubborn backs, or better yet, the ones a hempen collar might leave around their necks!'

Glyn Dŵr smiled good-naturedly as he commented to Sir Edmund, 'Generous to a fault is my brother Tudor, a trait that runs in the family, Edmund, for like you, he would heap gifts upon his captives rather than punish them for their stubborn ways!' Then turning to Dafydd

Mawr he said, his voice harsh, 'Take them away, Dafydd, and mind you guard them well, for I would have them to display to our English friends up there should tomorrow bring no exodus from Castle Harlech!'

Sir Edmund watched apprehensively as Dafydd Mawr herded the dejected prisoners away to shouts of derision from the assembled besiegers. Remembering now the humiliation of his own long march into captivity from Pilleth, he turned to Glyn Dŵr to ask quietly, 'You'll have these scarecrows fed and watered, my lord? From the way their clothes hang loose about them they've not fed well these many days.'

He flinched though at Glyn Dŵr's reply, for with a sardonic glance at him, the prince nodded. 'Oh, aye, Edmund,' he said, 'they'll be fed and watered well enough tomorrow, when their friends up there come out of their lair. Till then I fear they must yet fast, for it would not do to hang them on full stomachs!'

Silenced by that reply and the bile rising to his throat, Sir Edmund turned quickly away, praying as he walked over to his tent that tomorrow, whilst the sun was yet low in the east, the garrison would indeed walk out of the castle.

Sitting in the cold tent, the flap tight shut to give him the illusion of peace and solitude, he pondered yet again over how he had become involved in Glyn Dŵr's rebellion. Of how it had brought him loss of honour too amongst his countrymen in return for which he had found only an obvious contempt from most of those to whom he was now allied.

Was it merely the rejection by the usurper Henry that had made him rebel, he wondered? Sitting there dejectedly, he shook his head, knowing that it was not that, but his love for Catrin that had really made him deny his king, his country.

The thought brought him little comfort as he sat there alone in the darkening tent. Instead it only brought to his mind again how she had waved to Idris, for somehow he felt sure that it was to him she had waved when the archer had left for Harlech that day. When he tried to conjure up her face too, he found it was not her face that he pictured in his mind but that of the Welsh girl he had seen back in Ludlow market. Confused now he frowned, unsure whether it was there or somewhere else he had first seen her. Sitting there alone in the dark, his mind going around in circles, he seemed to see Cathy clearly now, hear her saying, softly, seductively, 'I can help you.' Head nodding, he drowsily pulled a blanket around his shoulders, wondering how it was that Catrin, or was it Cathy, could help him now?

He was cold when he awoke, cold and disorientated, knowing neither the time nor the place where he might be. Clutching the blanket which had fallen off his shoulders, he pulled it around him, then still half asleep, he peered around in the darkness. He could see nothing though, not even his hand in front of his face and he sat there for a moment, trying to collect himself. Gradually as he became fully awake, he remembered too, how he came to be there. Fumbling around in the dark, he at last found the tent's flap and made his way outside.

He stood there for a moment, looking around, trying to find his bearings. Clouds scudded past a sliver of moon that shed little light and in amongst the broken cloud he glimpsed a few pale stars. Still looking up he saw the dark mass of Castle Harlech above him, brooding, it seemed to him, over what the morning might bring. A few lanterns still burned around the camp and in the yellow light cast by one he saw a man standing beside a tent, a lance or pike across his shoulder.

Unsure in the dark of the lay of the ground, he stepped, slowly, warily towards the man, his careful steps making his approach almost silent. He was still outside the pool of light cast by the lantern when suddenly he found an arm around his neck, the point of a knife at his throat. A harsh voice said something in Welsh and, understanding only the menace of the words, he froze, praying that his silence would convey his submission to his assailant. Whatever had been said was, it seemed, repeated now in English and he heard Dafydd Mawr say in a voice heavy with deadly threat, 'Gently now, or I'll slit your throat! Who are you that comes creeping round the camp at night?'

His throat constricted by Dafydd's arm, Sir Edmund found he could hardly speak and only managed to croak, 'Mortimer.'

That brought no relief though, for with the dagger still at Sir Edmund's throat, Dafydd's only response was, 'Then slow and careful, step forward into the light!'

The dagger pricking his throat as he stepped over the uneven ground, Sir Edmund did as he was told. Slowly it was too, of necessity, because of Dafydd's restraining arm, but it was only a few steps and they were soon bathed in the lantern's light. With the sentry's lance prodding his chest menacingly now, Sir Edmund felt Dafydd relax the hold on his neck and take the dagger from his throat. Dafydd came around into the light, but it was no friendly face that Sir Edmund saw, for the man at arms looked grim indeed as, waving his dagger threateningly and with menace conveyed with every word, he asked, 'What are you doing, approaching the prison tent silently in these small hours, Sir Edmund? This is no time to be asking after the health of your English friends.'

With a hand massaging his neck, Sir Edmund replied irritably, 'They are no friends of mine, Dafydd! I woke and seeing the light shed by this lantern, came over to speak with the sentry here who, I hoped, might have a friendly face!'

Awed not by his rank it seemed nor yet satisfied by his answer, Dafydd still menaced him with the dagger, asking now, 'Would that friendly face be indeed outside or rather within the prison tent? If it be within I can readily usher you inside!'

'For God's sake, Dafydd,' retorted Sir Edmund angrily. 'Do you, who looked on as I gained the surrender of the castle to Prince Owain, believe I came here to release the hostages I took in surety of that surrender?'

Unmoved, Dafydd replied, 'I am no believer, Sir Edmund! Some say there is a man who lives in that moon up there, yet I do not believe it to be so, I only think that, just perhaps, there might be. It is for others to prove that point. Now, as to you, I think much the same. I do not believe you came to set the prisoners free, I only think that it might be so and that it is for others to prove the rights or wrongs of that.

'If they find it is not so, then you'll walk free. If not, why then, I'll become a believer, in that I do believe you'll hang along with the hostages!' He paused after his peroration and stroked his drooping moustache reflectively then, as though coming to a decision, said quietly, 'But we must not hasten that decision, for one given in haste may be repented later, so I'll not rouse our prince now, but escort you back to your tent where you may safely rest to see what the morning brings!'

Turning to the guard, he ordered, 'Call your relief, Maldwyn, and send him to Sir Edmund's tent to see our knight's sleep remains undisturbed for the remainder of the night!'

With a nod, the guard raised his lance and, sloping it over his shoulder, ambled off into the night to return a few minutes later to say something to Dafydd in Welsh. Dafydd in turn said to Sir Edmund, 'Well, let us get you back to your tent, Sir Edmund, to tuck you up safely in your bed, where I would advise you rest quietly till morning comes and Prince Owain, advised of this night's adventure, may decide thereon!'

With a wave of the dagger still held in his hand, he ushered Sir Edmund off in the direction of his tent, outside of which a sleepy man at arms stood scowling at him, a lit lantern in one hand, a drawn sword in the other.

Raising the tent's flap, Dafydd gave Sir Edmund a sharp push that hastened his entry, saying as he did so, 'And you value your life do not venture out again, Sir Edmund, 'til dawn comes, when I doubt not that Prince Owain will have words with you!'

Chapter Twenty-three

Whether it was the hour of his rising or the tale that Dafydd had told him of the night's happenings, Glyn Dŵr was evidently not in the best of humours. Guards on either side, Sir Edmund stood before him in his tent in some trepidation now. Blinded as he was by the lantern hanging behind Glyn Dŵr, he could barely make out the prince's features. Perhaps it was as well the prince was a mere silhouette though, for when he spoke his voice was harsh and unforgiving as he asked, 'Are Dafydd's words indeed true, that you crept up on the prisoners' tent in the silent hours Edmund, when all but sentinels should be in their bed?'

Head up but mouth dry, Sir Edmund looked directly at the prince's shadowed face to reply with no echo in his voice of the concern he now felt, 'No! I did not creep, my lord; with the moon on the wane it was dark and I, unsure of my footing, did but walk with care towards the light!'

If Glyn Dŵr's face, with his back to the lantern, was shadowed, the sneering face of Tudor, standing to the right of his brother, was plain enough for all to see. So was the disbelief in his voice plain for all to hear as he interjected, 'Walked with care indeed! Why walk abroad at all at that hour and with what intent? If walk you must, why did you not hail the sentinel and warn him of your approach, or identify yourself to him?' He snorted, then added, ' 'Tis clear you went with no honest intent but rather to free the hostages and have them fall upon us in our sleep!'

Glyn Dŵr held up a hand to say peremptorily, 'Silence, Tudor! Justice is ill served if judgement is arrived at hastily. 'Tis on evidence and facts alone that judgement should be made and whilst rank or kinship should not weigh in the balance, neither should prejudice or bias determine what we should find. We'll hear what Edmund has to say and hear him fairly for, so far, we've heard but one side of things from Dafydd!' Then turning to Sir Edmund, he said quietly, 'Now, explain yourself, Edmund, and tell us what brought you to last night's misadventure.'

Reassured somewhat by Glyn Dŵr's response to Tudor's accusation, Sir Edmund cleared his throat and began with more confidence than he inwardly felt, 'There was no purpose to my walk in the night, my lord, nor yet great reason that I might offer . . .' Tudor's sneer was as much of an exclamation as if he had shouted his disbelief and Sir Edmund glanced at him before continuing, ' . . . I was wakeful, for my mind was active with the day's events and I was concerned that the castle's captain should hold to his word and bring the garrison out this morning as he had promised. Restless, I left my tent to take the air and seeing the lantern, walked towards it to seek company, speak to someone and nought else.'

Pausing, he glanced at Tudor before continuing, ' 'Twas for that reason and that alone, I left my tent my lord! What other reason might I have, when 'twas I who had the hostages brought out from the castle and I who gained the promised surrender of the castle for you. Married as I am to your daughter Catrin, could you believe I would jeopardise all for the forlorn gesture Tudor there suggests? The forlorn gesture too, he would have you believe, that I would make for those whose king has rejected me?'

Evidently it was dawn now for in the pale light that filtered into the tent through a gap in the loosely tied flap, Sir Edmund could now see Glyn Dŵr's face, warts and all. The prince was sitting there leaning forward, an elbow on the table in front of him, chin in hand, listening intently. As Sir Edmund came to the end of his tale, Glyn Dŵr nodded and smiling, turned to his brother to say, 'There, Tudor, you see? I knew there must be some reasonable explanation for all this!'

Breathing a sigh of relief at Glyn Dŵr's acceptance of his explanation and smiling now at Tudor's evident discomfiture, Sir Edmund relaxed for the first time since he had entered the tent. Only for a moment though, for Glyn Dŵr's judgement was evidently not without its qualification, for he turned back to Sir Edmund to add, 'All we need now Edmund, is for the garrison to march out and that will clear up this little misunderstanding!' Leaning back in his chair, he waved his hand in dismissal and they all trooped out of his tent, with Tudor glowering as Sir Edmund was taken back to his tent by his two guards.

As he waited there in his tent, anxiously awaiting the call he now expected, he heard sounds of people working nearby, with grunts of effort and hammering keeping him from the sleep he yearned for but did not now dare seek. At last the flap of the tent was pulled aside and his guards ushered him out to lead him towards a level piece of ground in clear view of the castle's gate. There he saw a wooden structure had been erected, in front of which the six hostages were standing apprehensively in their shackles. Saw too, the seven nooses hanging suspended from a sturdy beam that stretched across from the trestles at each end of the structure.

It took only a moment for the significance of the seven nooses to register by which time his guards were roughly knotting a rope around his wrists. Helpless now, he watched as Glyn Dŵr left his tent to walk up to him. There was a quaver in Sir Edmund's voice now, the threatened rope already seeming to constrict his throat, as he asked the prince. 'Do you then yet disbelieve me, my lord?'

Glyn Dŵr shook his head and, smiling affably said, 'Why, no, Edmund!' Then with nod towards Tudor, standing beside him he said, ' 'Tis but that I would have Tudor here confounded by fact rather than by my belief in your affirmation.'

Sir Edmund favoured him with a sour look, to say bitterly, 'I would, my lord, that your belief were sounder based than to have me stand shackled here with a noose before my nose!'

Still smiling, Glyn Dŵr, said apologetically, 'Patience, Sir Edmund, 'tis but to show the rabble that only true loyalty, not kinship or rank, brings any favours in this world. Why, when your friend up there, the captain of Castle Harlech, brings his men out of its gate, you will be free again and bring confusion to those who doubted you!'

Sighing, Sir Edmund said glumly, 'Why then, my lord, I trust he be a truer friend to me than any I have here!'

With a nod and a wink, Glyn Dŵr replied, 'We'll find the answer to all that in but a little while now, Edmund, and I pray for both our sakes that your friend the captain walks out of there, for does he not, I fear neither Catrin nor Lady Marged will forgive me for what then takes place!'

With a heartfelt sigh Sir Edmund replied quietly, 'Nor I, my lord!'

Glyn Dŵr walked away out of sight and, for Sir Edmund, hours rather than minutes seemed to pass without any sign of movement around the castle as he stood there pinioned. Each minute that he spent standing there anxiously staring at the castle gate, he seemed to spend counting the seconds of his life away, with hope lessening by each one as the castle gate remained firmly shut. There was movement at last, but not that which he awaited impatiently, for it was only the hostages' guards leading them forward and placing the nooses around their necks. They saved him until last though, before finally leading him towards the centre one of the seven nooses. Helpless, he stood there waiting for the noose to be placed around his neck as, eyes closed, he prayed for he knew not what: the garrison to march out of the castle perhaps? King Henry and Glyn Dŵr to meet in hell and that right soon? Or perhaps Dafydd Mawr wiping off Tudor's sneering smile with one swipe of his great claymore? He thought of Catrin then and of the mysterious Cathy who always kept on saying somehow that she could help him. God! How he wished she could indeed help him now, for if anyone needed such help it was he . . . and that right soon, before it was too late for help at all!

He heard cheering then, loud and prolonged. His eyes still firmly closed he found himself thinking that it was too loud, too prolonged, for it to be just over the hanging of the first of the hostages. Slowly, fearfully, he opened his eyes and looking straight ahead he saw the castle gate was open, men streaming out of it, a ragged banner fluttering above them in the breeze. There was a raggle taggle group following them too, women and children bearing bundles, dogs yelping around them, as they all came walking, jostling, tumbling across the drawbridge as though eager now to leave the stronghold that had become a prison for them.

He was still staring at the castle in disbelief as he stood there, rubbing his neck imagining the noose that had so nearly been placed there. Suddenly Glyn Dŵr was there in front of him, grinning, saying cordially, as though he had never doubted, 'Well done, Edmund my boy! Harlech is ours!' He turned now to Tudor, who stood there like a disappointed shadow at his heels, to say admonishingly, 'There, d'you see Tudor? It never pays to rush into judgement!' Then he was off, with Dafydd Mawr at his side now, no doubt to see the castle's garrison safely away from Harlech and its environs. Remembering his promise to the English captain, Sir Edmund called after Glyn Dŵr, 'Don't forget their three hundred marks, my lord!'

There was only a wave of the hand though from Glyn Dŵr, which seemed to be more in dismissal than acknowledgement and Sir Edmund thought he heard, or perhaps merely imagined, the prince calling back to him, 'Marks, Edmund? What marks?'

Minutes after he was freed from the threat of the scaffold it seemed that he was in the midst of a great bustle of activity as men scurried around breaking camp, eager now to occupy the castle at whose gates they had so long been knocking without avail. Nor was it long before, with banners flying and a victorious song on their lips, they were marching up the hill, across the drawbridge then through the gate now hanging open and into the castle that had seemed so impregnable from their camp at its base. Minutes later, Glyn Dŵr's banner was flying from the great inner gate towers to tell all that King Henry had been ousted from one of the most important of his castles in West Wales.

Nor was it long before foraging parties were out, scouring the surrounding countryside for provender and supplies to stock the castle so that they would be secure should they in turn be besieged. The night however, was given over to feasting to celebrate their victory and there was no one there happier or with more to celebrate than Sir Edmund. Toast after toast was called for to Prince Owain's victory and to the defeat of King Henry which, in the absence of wine were all drunk in ale. At last, when there seemed nought left to which they might all drink, Tudor rose to his feet to raise his glass and, his voice slurred by copious draughts of ale, called out, 'Confusion to the English!'

Across the table, Idris sniggered and raising his glass replied, 'I'll drink to that my lord!' Sitting beside Idris, Dafydd Mawr put a steadying hand on his arm and whispered something to him in Welsh, but Idris brushed it aside and raising his glass again, repeated the toast.

Rising, and with his hand on his sword hilt now, Sir Edmund glared at Lord Tudor to say pointedly, 'I'll drink to the confusion of Prince Owain's enemies as long and deep as any man here, for there are both Welsh and English who love him not. Yet I'll not drink to the confusion of the English more than that of the Welsh, for did not Hotspur, who was my kin, die for his rebellion 'gainst Henry Bolingbroke and does not the one eyed Dafydd Gam fight alongside Henry?' He paused then and there was silence as he gazed at Lord Tudor before saying in a voice that seemed to echo around the great hall of the castle, 'No, I'll not drink to your toast, Lord Tudor, and if you like that not, then we can meet in combat with any weapon of your choice and may the devil take the loser to his bosom!'

Glyn Dŵr had been sitting at the head of the table, stroking his beard meditatively as he listened to the heated exchange but he rose now with his hand raised as though to silence all. Looking first at Lord Tudor and then at Sir Edmund, he said in a voice like thunder, 'What's this? Are we to fall to squabbling like children amongst ourselves in our hour of victory and that over words said whilst in our cups?

If there is to be jousting at all then let it be with my enemies and that to deadly purpose, not amongst my kin. My quarrel is not that a man be English or Welsh, Scots or Irish, but that a usurping English king would have domination over us Welsh. For centuries now, Welsh blood has intermingled with that of the English so that many amongst us here have that rich and heady mixture and who can tell with whom that might be so! Have done, therefore and be at peace with one another to save your vitriol for our real enemy!' He paused a moment, then raised his glass before saying, 'Drink now to the damnation of our enemies wherever they may be and that there may be an honourable peace between us and our English neighbours!'

There was silence now as all raised their glasses to drink to the prince's toast, but Sir Edmund, looking around over the top of his glass, noticed that Idris the archer barely sipped his ale before slapping his glass back down on the table as though in disgust. There was a somewhat uncomfortable silence in the great hall of Castle Harlech after that and it was not long before men were slipping away to their beds in ones and twos to rest after the excitement of the day.

Glyn Dŵr turned reassuringly to Sir Edmund to say, 'Pay little heed to Tudor, Edmund, it was but that, in his cups, he felt diminished that after all his efforts here, it was you to whom Castle Harlech fell!'

Sir Edmund shook his head. 'He has no need, my lord, for mine were but the words that secured the victory he won over long months of siege.'

Glyn Dŵr smiled. 'That is gracious of you after tonight's fracas, Edmund! Why do you not tell him so? It might cool the heat that is evident between you two.'

Sir Edmund shook his head. 'I think not my lord, for I fear it would take more than that to cool Lord Tudor's suspicion of my motives for being here. Only my actions rather than any words of mine are likely to change his mind and little enough action have I seen to make it so!'

Glyn Dŵr seemed to be mulling that over, for he stayed silent for a moment before, nodding, he replied thoughtfully, 'You may be right, Edmund, for Tudor was ever a stubborn man! 'Tis why I think your work is well done here and that you must now return to the farmhouse and your Catrin . . .'

Frowning, Sir Edmund interjected quickly, 'My work done, my lord? Why it has but started! You said that Harlech taken, we'd go on to Aberystwyth and see your banner fly o'er its battlements there as well!'

His hand raised to silence Sir Edmund, Glyn Dŵr nodded. 'Aye and so we shall Edmund, but with Harlech now in our hands, I have no doubt the garrison at Aber will see the folly of their stubbornness and that they too will yield to less subtle persuasion! No, you have done your work here well and now must go to comfort Catrin, for I have other, greater, parts for you to play in this great enterprise!'

Sir Edmund looked at him in some surprise as he asked, 'What greater part could I play, my lord, than help have your banner fly over these western castles?'

Glyn Dŵr though only favoured him with a secretive smile as he answered, 'That is yet to unfold Edmund, and that when the time is ripe. It will be soon now, of that I have little doubt. 'Til then, you must have patience to await my call and in the meantime, care for Catrin.'

At that he rose, saying, 'Now it is high time we were both abed for, come the morning, you shall set out for the farmhouse, for soon I would have you bring Catrin and her mother back here to Harlech where I shall now hold court!'

With that it seemed that the discussion was at an end, for Glyn Dŵr abruptly turned and walked off across the hall to his chamber above the gate-house leaving a somewhat bemused Sir Edmund standing there, wondering what 'greater part' it was that Glyn Dŵr now had in mind for him to play!

With his mind in a whirl thinking of all that had happened during the day, culminating in the surrender of the castle, the confrontation with Tudor and with what Glyn Dŵr had just told him, he was in no mood for sleep. So, following Glyn Dŵr out of the hall he did not go to the chamber he had been allocated but instead crossed the inner ward and climbed the narrow stone staircase that led up to the battlements of the south western tower. The long day, the night's feasting and the exertion of climbing the steps left him breathless by the time he reached the battlements and he shivered as he stood there for a minute, catching his breath in the cold wind, wishing that he had a cloak around him. He folded his arms around his chest, the cold night air clearing his mind of the drowsiness and confusion left by all the day's events.

Standing there looking over the dark sea, the breaking waves flecked white by the pale moonlight, he felt relaxed for the first time that day and smiled, for despite all, he had indeed gained the surrender of Castle Harlech, to the chagrin of those who doubted him and now it seemed too that he had regained Glyn Dŵr's confidence.

The smile faded and he sniffed, the cold air stinging his nostrils as he thought, not without a little bitterness, that he had regained the trust he never should have lost, having been nigh on hanged into the bargain! The thought sobered him as he realised afresh that his new kinsman's trust was held in place only by a tenuous thread and that not even bonds of matrimony would keep him safe if ought went wrong!

Strangely it seemed that the sea's very restlessness contributed to his mood now as he thought how different a scene it was from the tranquil one he had so often viewed from the Garderobe tower of Ludlow Castle. From there, at this time of night, it would have been a dark but peaceful scene that he would have looked out upon, with the dim glow from the few cottages scattered across the river plain below hanging there in the darkness like so many glow-worms.

Shrugging his shoulders, he thought that at Ludlow the threat from the east had been every bit as real, for Henry had menaced him then with his hold over the young Earl Edmund whilst, towards the end, there had been the equally threatening rumbles of the Welsh rebellion. Little had changed since those early days of Glyn Dŵr's rebellion, for King Henry loved the Mortimers no more now than then, concerned as he ever was, only with his own tenuous hold on his stolen throne. As for himself, it seemed that the Welsh did not love him any more now as an ally than they had then. Love him or not, it was clear they did not trust him, for even his own father-in-law, Glyn Dŵr, was cheerfully prepared to have him hanged should it suit his purpose!

Thinking of Glyn Dŵr made his thoughts turn as they ever did, to Catrin, whose fickle moods seemed to him to change with the wind. Catrin, one moment lively, loving, even flirtatious and the next waving her kerchief at some soldier below her station before lapsing into despondency. Over what, he asked himself miserably. Of a certainty over nothing of which she would speak nor yet for any reason that he could imagine!

As he recalled leaving the isolated farmhouse in Snowdonia to come here to Harlech, he sighed, thinking with not a little resentment, that there had been no waving of her kerchief for his own departure that bleak morning! Shaking his head, he wondered what he had gained from allying himself with Glyn Dŵr. Assuredly a wife he knew and loved, but a wife over whose love for him he still had lingering doubts. Certainly he had gained a powerful ally in Glyn Dŵr, but one it seemed who viewed him as a doubtful asset and one to be readily sacrificed should the need arise. As for the prince's cohorts, there was not one amongst them whom he could call a friend, nor yet any who even liked or trusted him.

Perhaps de Lacey was right after all, he thought. Perhaps he should indeed have gained King Henry's favour by offering him support more patently. Had he indeed gained his favour, then surely his ransom would have been paid after Pilleth and he'd be standing now on Ludlow's Garderobe tower.

As he stood there shivering, he recalled that other rebellion when Henry Bolingbroke had wrested the throne from Richard, but try as he might he found it difficult to reach back in his memory to the time before Henry's return from France. He recalled though that de Lacey had come to him in his sick chamber in Ludlow. Remembered too, the squire's remarks about some woman he had supposedly hailed before being struck down by a wagon outside the goldsmith's. He smiled now at the memory of having sought that Welsh girl after seeing her in Ludlow market, wondering now what was the reason for the urgency of his search, but he could not bring it to mind. He shrugged, thinking that it must all have been but part of the sickness which had ailed him then. The smile faded though as he realised that try as he might, the events before Henry had landed in England to begin his challenge for the throne were all shadowy as though they were events related to him by someone else.

He shook his head as if to shed himself of the mists that enshrouded his past, but they lingered still as if to keep a corner of his mind behind a veil that he could not penetrate. At last, sure that it was all the result of that accident in Ludlow, he surrendered to the night's chill and his thoughts returned to the present. Thinking now of the journey he had to make to Snowdonia on the morrow, he turned to step out of the wind and into the shelter of the stone staircase that led down to the inner ward and sought his chamber.

It was a cold crisp day with a dusting of frost on the ground that glistened in the morning's sun when Sir Edmund set out from Harlech the next morning with Maldwyn the man at arms and two others as escort.

They were still in the inner ward when Glyn Dŵr strode over to him to hand him a letter for the Lady Marged, saying as he did so, 'I shall send for you soon Edmund! So have the womenfolk prepare themselves for the journey here bringing what trinkets they most desire, for it is here that I shall hold my court. Warn them though that I may not be here to greet them on their arrival, for there is yet much to be done to make the western coast secure so they may safely dwell here.'

Still resenting the fact that he was not to be allowed at the taking of Aberystwyth Castle, Sir Edmund touched his helmet in acknowledgement, then with a terse, 'Aye, my lord!' spurred his horse and with a wave of his hand led his escort out of the bailey and across the drawbridge their horses' hooves echoing loudly as they rode over the wooden bridge.

Once clear of the castle, Sir Edmund set a fast pace, eager now, despite all his doubts, to see Catrin. Hoping too that after their short time apart she would be as eager to have him return. He thought too of Glyn Dŵr's comment about the need to make the western coast secure and of his optimism that the great castles at Caernarvon and Aberystwyth would be taken now that Harlech had fallen. He pursed his lips thoughtfully; perhaps Castle Harlech's surrender would indeed shake their resolve and the freeing of Harlech's garrison might encourage them in the belief that similar magnanimity would be shown to them were they to yield.

Maldwyn interrupted his thoughts, saying in his hoarse voice, ' 'Tis good to get away from Harlech my lord!' Pausing, he added with a grin, 'I never was smitten with sieges, for there's neither honour nor yet booty to be gained in them!'

Sir Edmund glanced at him to ask with a wry smile, 'Do you follow your trade for the honour of it then, Maldwyn?'

Expressionless now, Maldwyn nodded. 'Oh aye my lord, for it is honour which enriches a poor soldier's life, sobeit's flavoured with a pinch of booty!'

Sir Edmund nodded as he replied quietly, 'Oh, aye, Maldwyn, and to go with booty's salt, no doubt one needs must add a generous sprinkling of some poor wretch's blood!'

Maldwyn seemed taken aback for a moment before saying reproachfully, 'Why, my lord, that is but the burden of my trade: to bring peace through pain to those who would deny my prince!'

Exasperated at the man of war's mock air of piety now, Sir Edmund sighed, saying, 'If you would bring them peace, a priest you should have been, Maldwyn! A pardoner perhaps, to give them absolution in return for their silver!'

Maldwyn looked at him wide eyed, as though finally reaching understanding and nodding now, replied, 'Why my lord, that is indeed what I am . . . a pardoner! For in giving them peace I also pardon them their sins and take their silver!' His face clouded then though, and he frowned as he added doubtfully, 'That I can only do though if they follow the true Pope, the pope of Rome, for my prince does not acknowledge the false one who dwells in Avignon!'

Thinking of the schism in the church which had lasted for nearly a hundred years now and left two popes each claiming they were the true successor to Saint Peter, Sir Edmund's eyebrows arched in surprise. Then, giving the man of war a sideways glance, he said with a touch of irony in his voice, 'As we do but fight 'gainst Henry Bolingbroke you have no problem there, Maldwyn, for 'tis only the French who acknowledge Benedict, the Pope of Avignon!'

Maldwyn smiled. 'You had me worried there, my lord, but now all is clear again and I can give my absolutions freely for we fight not against the French who some say will soon be our allies!'

Tired of this strange conversation, Sir Edmund snapped, 'You are no pardoner, Maldwyn, for their absolutions are never given freely!'

It seemed that at last Maldwyn had no answer for Sir Edmund who was grateful that they could now ride on in silence; he had much to think about, most of which was the cause of his irritability. He had been looking forward to the prospect of at last being involved in some action directed against King Henry, feeling as he did that only in the usurper's defeat lay security both for himself and his nephew, the young Earl Edmund.

Up to now, however, Glyn Dŵr had seemed intent upon excluding him from playing any real part in the war and now, when at last it seemed that he was to be involved, he had been sent elsewhere for no apparent reason. He was becoming increasingly resentful of being told that there was some great part for him to play, never now but always in the future and always cloaked in a great air of secrecy.

He sighed, thinking with no great conviction, that perhaps when he returned to Harlech with Catrin and the Lady Marged, something might come from Glyn Dŵr's plotting and there might indeed be some role for him to play.

Maldwyn turned towards him with something of an anxious look on his face. 'It should not be long now, my lord, that old cottage is but a few miles further on, where we can pause and have a bite to eat!'

Eyebrows raised questioningly, Sir Edmund glanced at him, wondering at the man at arms' concern, then suddenly realised that that sigh must have been the cause. Bending forward he patted his horse's neck and looking up at the burly man at arms, said with a smile, 'Our mounts have the greater need for rest, Maldwyn . . . and yours the most of all!' Then, seeing the burly Maldwyn about to reply and fearing a lengthy discourse on the subject of weight, he hurriedly fended it off by adding, ' 'Twill be good indeed to pause, if but to stretch our legs!'

Remembering though how his own imagination had run riot when they had rested in the cottage on the way to Harlech, he felt that he would rather stop anywhere than there. There being no logical reason he could offer for not doing so however, he just nodded and, as if to reassure himself, said again, 'Yes, it will be good indeed!'

If nothing else his remarks succeeded in silencing Maldwyn who only favoured him with a quizzical glance then, with a word in Welsh to his companions, spurred his horse, seemingly anxious now, to hasten their progress. Even so it must have been past noon by the time they sighted the cottage though it was difficult to tell the hour, for the clear skies of earlier that morning were now overcast with lowering cloud threatening rain. The cottage, with its lean-to cowshed alongside, its shuttered window and the door they had wedged shut on their way to Harlech, was not a welcoming prospect, but at least it offered shelter from those menacing clouds.

As they drew near though, Sir Edmund hung back and when they dismounted, let Maldwyn lead the way into the cottage. When at last he followed the others inside, he looked around the room apprehensively, to breath a silent sigh of relief at seeing they were its only occupants. He smiled then, thinking that the noisy behaviour of Maldwyn and his companions was enough to ensure there would be no interruptions as they ate their bread and cheese.

Gradually the tension that he had felt when entering the cottage eased and, relaxed after their rest, he turned to the others and ordered them to mount up. As he rose, Maldwyn said with a wry grin, ' 'Tis as well, my lord, for my saddle offers more comfort than this earthen floor and I would as soon reach the farm whilst Iestyn is yet sober and has the light to see we come in friendship!'

With a grin and a wave of his hand, Sir Edmund ushered him out of the door and, bringing up the rear, took one last look around the room. Then, feeling more than a little relieved that there had been no reappearance of the wraith he had witnessed there on his last visit, he slammed the door shut behind him.

As they rode away at a gentle trot, Sir Edmund turned to look back at the desolate little cottage and wide-eyed, took a sharp intake of breath, for there standing in the open doorway smiling at him was the woman Cathy. Nor was there any doubt in his mind that it was the girl of Ludlow market place, for he seemed to recognise the green dress that she had worn then as she did now. Pulling on his reins, he halted his horse in its tracks and Maldwyn also reining up, turned towards him to ask, 'Is all well, my lord?'

Sir Edmund was about to ask him if he too saw the woman, when he realised that she had gone as suddenly as she had appeared and where she had stood, the door was now shut fast.

Chapter Twenty-four

Sir Edmund stood looking open-mouthed at the man at arms for a moment before he heard the question. Even then, he didn't answer but turned to look at the cottage again before, nodding thoughtfully, he replied, 'Aye Maldwyn, all is well, but I think I left the letter for Lady Marged there.' With that he walked his horse back towards the cottage and, dismounting, took a deep breath before opening the door that he found as firmly shut as it had been left by him. So convinced was he that the girl had been standing there and that at last he would be able to confront her, that he felt a sharp pang of disappointment now as he gazed at the empty room. It was utterly empty, just as he had left it, nor was there anywhere in that bare room that even a field-mouse might hide.

His hand to his forehead, he closed his eyes in disbelief, wondering what ailed him that made his mind play such tricks upon his sight. Or if it were no trick, how it was that people who looked so vital could yet be so insubstantial. He stood there for a moment, almost hoping that she would reappear, but there was nothing, no sight nor even sound other than the rattle of the shutter in the wind and the pawing of the horses outside, impatient it seemed to be away from this place. He shuddered, as if the room's dankness had seeped into his very bones and with a last look around the room, hurried outside, fumbling with the pouch at his waist as he did so.

Patting the pouch now, he smiled at Maldwyn, saying, 'Aye, 'twas there! As well that I turned back, for Lady Marged would not have forgiven me!'

Maldwyn looked at him askance, before saying in apparent agreement, 'Nor would Prince Owain, my lord, for he forgives less readily!'

With a crooked smile, Sir Edmund nodded. 'So I've learned,' he muttered. Then louder said, 'Now let us make haste, those clouds get darker by the minute!'

With that he spurred his horse and soon the wind was in his face and blowing away the illusions that the bleak hillside seemed to encourage.

They approached the farm late that afternoon, when the evening shadows were beginning to soften the harsh outlines of Snowdonia and they were soaked from the deluge that those dark clouds had presaged. They were met by a sharp challenge from Iestyn, nor was he alone, for the few men at arms and archers Glyn Dŵr had left at the farm were all evident as, in response to the challenge, Maldwyn bellowed, 'A Mortimer! A Mortimer!' Barely were his words echoing back from the stone walled farmhouse, than there was a flash of colour as someone came hurrying out of the farmhouse, skirts held prudently high out of the yard's mud. Sir Edmund's heart rose, for this was no illusion, it was Catrin, walking as quickly as her condition might allow, to meet him, a hand on her stomach, a smile on her lips! Behind her too came Lady Marged, walking sedately as well became a prince's consort with Megan following a step or two behind.

Then Sir Edmund and his escort were dismounting amidst all the excited chattering exchange of news, there were cheers too from Iestyn's men as they learned that Harlech had fallen at last. Catrin was beside him now though and Sir Edmund took her tenderly in his arms and, as she looked up at him, bent his head to kiss her on the lips only to desist as he heard the cheering renewed.

As the cheering died it was suddenly quiet, for in answer to a question Maldwyn was recounting the names of friends and comrades they had lost during the siege.

With Catrin's arm in his now Sir Edmund was leading her and Lady Marged into the house, when Catrin paused as they reached the door, saying, 'I will follow my lord, but I would hear what Maldwyn has to say of those who fell at Harlech!'

He glanced at her as her arm fell away from his to say a little sourly, 'There are few of those who went to Harlech with Dafydd Mawr who do not now man its battlements, although I so nearly fell, I find it hard to swallow!'

Catrin, however, did not seem to have heard him for she had taken a few steps back into the yard and was listening anxiously to Maldwyn's recital. Sir Edmund turned to the Lady Marged, to say, 'Your daughter yet shows great concern for her father's soldiery, madam!'

She glanced at him and with a lift of her eyebrows replied, 'Indeed she does, Sir Edmund, and would you have it otherwise, when they are all we have between us and King Henry's wrath?'

He was about to reply when he heard hurried footsteps behind him and turned to see Catrin, her face all smiles now, coming towards him. Turning back to the Lady Marged he said with a wry smile, 'Catrin hides her sorrow well, my lady, in the face of such peril!'

She gazed at him for a moment then, with an imperceptible sigh said, 'Catrin is too young to let sorrow lay heavily for long, yet this war brings enough of it to keep her downcast for longer than I would wish.'

They had reached the open doorway to the hall where the table was laid ready for the evening meal and the fire blazed its welcome in the hearth. Looking at Lady Marged's greying hair Sir Edmund nodded, thinking that with her sons, Gruffydd besieging Aberystwyth and even sixteen-year-old Maredudd at Caernarvon for their father, she would have more than her share of anxiety.

'Soon now my lady,' he said quietly, 'Prince Owain will send word for us to go to Harlech, although first he must ensure the western coast is secure for you to safely dwell therein.' With that he pulled the letter from within his pouch and handed it to her, saying, 'No doubt, my lady, this will confirm much that I have already said.'

With a brief smile she took the letter. 'No doubt, Edmund,' she replied and smiling, waved a hand towards Catrin as she added; 'Now I must read what my husband has to tell me and you must go and care for our Catrin.'

Whilst at the farm Sir Edmund was plagued with his doubts and uncertainties over his young bride, back at Harlech, Prince Owain had even weightier problems of strategy to resolve. Sitting at the head of the table in the great hall of Harlech Castle, he gazed steadily at his brother. 'No Tudor,' he said at last, 'you must wait here! Then, whilst I march on Caernarvon to strengthen the siege there, you will deliver Harlech to Sir Edmund and then go south to Aberystwyth . . .' Tudor looked at him in astonishment, to ask in disbelief, 'Me, deliver Harlech to that English turncoat?'

Glyn Dŵr sighed and said, 'Yes Tudor! I would have Sir Edmund, my son-in-law, here as my constable, whilst you go on to take Aber and I, Caernarvon. Who better, Tudor, to hold Harlech for me? Nothing else could show Edmund more firmly opposed to Henry than this.

Married to Catrin, holding Castle Harlech under my banner, what could divorce not only Edmund, but all the Mortimers, from Henry Bolingbroke and the English crown more clearly than that? Were Henry to come knocking on his door, think you that Edmund could surrender him the keys with any hope of gratitude? No Tudor, fear not, for Edmund must hold Harlech for me more dearly than any other and he would live! Why else do you think I would leave both Catrin and my Lady Marged here in his care?' He shook his head. 'No, Tudor,' he said, 'with Edmund holding Castle Harlech it shall be bruited abroad that Hotspur's kin holds this castle for the Welsh 'gainst the English king! Who knows what other English gentry may turn against Henry because of that!'

Tudor did not seem convinced however, for he merely sniffed as he replied, 'For every one of them, no doubt there'll be another Dafydd Gam to curse us with his blind eye!'

Glyn Dŵr shook his head in mock despair. 'Whilst I have you to cheer me, Tudor, what need have I to carry the cross of such traitors as Dafydd Gam?' He tossed his head. 'He is but the legacy of our divisive past, for whilst we quarrelled and fought amongst ourselves it made us easy prey for the English. 'Tis why, when we have cast off the English yoke, we must forgive much of the past quarrels amongst our different factions to achieve that unity once gained when Prince Llewellyn held sovereignty over Wales. To this end, Tudor, I shall soon call upon a Parliament to meet . . . a Parliament that shall herald a new and just governance for Wales!'

Tudor sniffed dismissively. 'A parliament!' he snorted. 'Men drawn from the uchelwyr, no doubt, who will deliberate for days over that which you have already decided upon and each one mindful only of his own best interest! No Owain, you must have men of like minds with you in this Parliament of yours. Men who will see reason from the same ground you stand upon, have the same values, the same belief in that which is right for Wales!'

Glyn Dŵr smiled. 'Closer they would be then brother, than you and I, for have we not often disagreed? Closer too than my sons Gruffydd and Maredudd . . .' He grinned. ' . . .and other sons who know me not!' He shook his head. 'No, Tudor, it is in this Parliament that we must resolve the differences that have riven Wales in the past. Resolve them by debate and reasoned argument and through such reason arrive at a governance for Wales that offers justice for all,' he paused as though recalling something, 'without favour to his rank or penalty for the prejudice that might be held against him!'

Tudor coloured. 'I held no prejudice 'gainst Mortimer,' he protested a little too quickly, then added a little doubtfully: 'Leastways, no more than I would 'gainst any other English turncoat!'

Glyn Dŵr grinned, then and shook his head. ' 'Tis there you err Tudor! For if he, being English, rebels against Henry Bolingbroke, then he has common cause with us.'

Tudor, always better at wielding a sword than bandying words, flushed again and slammed his pot of ale down on the table. 'As ever, Owain, you twist my words,' he protested, ' 'tis a trick you learned when you studied law! Better had you stuck to soldiering, for that's an honest trade!'

Glyn Dŵr laughed now, saying, 'There you have it, Tudor! That's the nub of my argument, for I would have the uchelwyr, the gentry of Wales, argue their case in parliament, a Welsh parliament, rather than we should resort to warring amongst ourselves!' He sighed, then added quietly, 'All that apart, Tudor, I fear that those of us who shall survive this conflict with Henry shall all have had enough of war to last our lifetime!'

Tudor had no response to that and smiling at him now, Glyn Dŵr rose, saying, 'Now I must to my bed, for I make an early start tomorrow for Caernarvon to join young Maredudd at the castle there.'

Whilst Lord Tudor impatiently held Castle Harlech and Prince Owain equally impatiently besieged Castle Caernarvon with his son Maredudd, life at the farm had resumed its quiet, even humdrum routine. As the weeks passed, this became increasingly centred around the eagerly awaited birth of the new young Mortimer, which Lady Marged assured everyone would be any day now. Despite her assurances however, it was not until one morning in early April that Sir Edmund went to Catrin's chamber to be ushered away by a flustered Lady Marged who quickly made it clear that his presence was neither welcomed nor appreciated.

If his presence was not wanted, it seemed that young Megan, Catrin's maid, was in great demand, for she was scurrying hither and thither with bowls mysteriously covered in fresh white towels, none of which it seemed was what Lady Marged really required, for minutes later Megan was hurrying off on some other errand.

However much Megan hurried though, it seemed to hasten the great event not one jot, for all morning Sir Edmund wandered aimlessly around the farmhouse feeling that he was as little needed there as he was on Glyn Dŵr's campaigns. He was sitting in the hall, desultorily toying with his midday meal, a glass of wine raised to his lips, when

Megan, her face flushed from scurrying around, or perhaps from the importance of her mission, came rushing into the room. As she stood there before him now though she seemed lost for words, or perhaps out of breath.

'Yes, Megan,' he asked at last, 'do you have some news for me?'

Still out of breath, she nodded importantly, then minding her manners, gave a little curtsy before saying, 'Yes, my lord, my Lady Marged says that you may come up now!'

Smiling, he took another sip of wine before asking quietly, hopefully, 'Is my Lady Catrin well, Megan?'

The maid took a deep breath then nodded, to say, her face glowing with the excitement of it all, 'Oh yes, my lord, she's lovely and the baby . . .'

He held up a hand to stop her there, saying with a smile, 'I think you'd better let my Lady Catrin tell me the rest, Megan, don't you think?'

Taking a deep breath, Megan nodded and with a bob of her head, said, 'Yes, my lord.' Then, her important mission completed, went hurrying off upstairs.

He sat there for a moment sipping his wine before rising and walking thoughtfully across the hall to the stairway, wondering as he did so whether he had an heir to his dubious fortunes or a baby daughter.

When he entered Catrin's chamber she was lying in bed, her arms resting on the bedcover looking defenceless, vulnerable. As he walked over to the bedside, she gave him a wan smile, then looked anxiously at the cot beside the bed. Glancing up at him then, she said quietly, 'I'm sorry, Edmund!'

There was a sudden wail from the cot and he looked around anxiously at the wide open mouth of the new born baby lying there crying heartily, before he gave a concerned glance at Lady Marged standing at the other side of the bed.

With a glance at Catrin, she snorted. 'Don't be foolish, child,' she said sternly. Then, with a glance at Sir Edmund, she sniffed before saying, 'She's worried that you'll not be pleased that it's a girl child!' Then with another sniff she said, 'I've told her the pain's the same, boy or girl! Fortunate you are indeed that they're both alive and well!'

The baby echoed her sentiments with another burst of crying and, walking around the bed, she bent over to pick up the baby with what Sir Edmund thought was a surprising tenderness. He went over to her, to peer at the baby now held in her arms, wrapped in a soft white woollen shawl. All he could see though, was a small head covered in a fuzz of dark hair and a remarkably red little face that puckered up in apparent anguish at his sudden appearance and broke out into renewed complaint.

Lady Marged smiled at Sir Edmund as she said softly, 'A lovely baby, isn't she? Looks just like her father, too!'

Running his hand through his long fair hair, Sir Edmund nodded, then said dutifully, 'Yes . . . yes indeed.' Then, with a wry smile, continued, 'Though I doubt that that will do her many favours!' Turning now to Catrin, he smiled at her to say, 'We have a lovely daughter, Catrin, and we shall call her Alice after your sister, just as you wished.' Then he was at the bedside and, bending down he kissed her on her forehead.

She looked up at him drowsily as Lady Marged, touching him on the elbow, said quietly, 'You must let her rest now, Edmund. You shall see her again later.' With unusual warmth for her, she added then, 'I'm glad that you are happy with my granddaughter, Edmund.' Before he could reply though she was fussing and ushering him from the room as though she regretted her lapse into sentimentality.

The weeks passed uneventfully for Sir Edmund and whilst the main focus of his thoughts were now centred on Catrin and his daughter, Alice, they strayed increasingly to wondering when Glyn Dŵr would send for them to go to Harlech.

At first he spent much of his time in Catrin's chamber, having his meals there with her rather than in the hall, so intent was he in watching the daily changes in their young offspring. Then as Catrin regained her strength he often spent hours sitting in the small garden outside the farmhouse with them, amused at Alice's apparent surprise at the few chickens scratching around. Sometimes they were even joined by Lady Marged who often remarked, as she gazed lovingly at little Alice, how much like her father she was.

On his part, Sir Edmund as often thought that adorable as she might be, the dark haired little bundle looked not like him at all! As Lady Marged repeated her comment yet again one day, Sir Edmund felt forced to respond: 'Why, my lady, Alice looks not at all like me: dark haired, blue eyed, she takes after Catrin, as is appropriate for my lovely daughter!'

Lady Marged had not lived with Owain Glyn Dŵr and borne his many children without being adept in the art of flattery and responded tartly, 'How like a man, Sir Edmund, to see the superficial looks and not the character that lies behind! Do you not see that nose, that firm young chin that denotes that she was born to command?'

Sir Edmund had noticed neither, having seen only a chubby little face with bright blue eyes and a little head topped with an ever increasing thatch of dark hair. At Lady Marged's comment however, he unconsciously braced his shoulders and smiled before asking deprecatingly, 'Command, my lady? Pray what might it be that Alice here is ever likely to command?'

Lady Marged gave him a withering glance that held both derision and superior wisdom. 'You seem to think, as all men do, Edmund,' she replied, 'that the power to command pertains only to the battlefield. Think instead of command being the power to control and therein lies your answer!'

As she got up and stalked away, Sir Edmund looked at the baby held in its mother's arms in a new light and nodded thoughtfully.

As the April days passed and the farm took on a more cheerful aspect so to did Catrin regain her strength to slowly become the happy young girl that Sir Edmund knew and loved. She seemed more content with their isolated life at the farm now as well, even venturing occasionally to take gentle rides with Sir Edmund along the bank of the stream to the meadow where he had first asked her to marry him. If she yearned at all now for her life at Sycharth or dreamed of the days she had spent walking by the placid Afon Cynllaith, she never mentioned it now, happy enough it seemed with her life at the farm with Sir Edmund and Alice.

Her happiness was shared by Sir Edmund, who seldom looked back with longing to his days at Ludlow, or yearned for the more active life of campaigning with Glyn Dŵr. His happiness was only clouded by the ever present concern he felt for his sister Elizabeth, so young to have been left a widow. That, of course, and the guilt he felt at being unable to help his young nephew, Earl Edmund. Isolated as he was at the farm, he knew not even whether the Earl was still alive and safe at Berkhamsted, or whether King Henry had ceased all pretence of the Earl being his ward and had him incarcerated in the grim Tower of London. He consoled himself though that surely Lady Despenser, the Earl's mother, yet had enough influence and friends at court to ensure no harm came to the lad.

Sir Edmund knew that such innocent, peaceful days, marred only by his concerns for his close kin, could not last forever and with every new day, he expected to see a messenger arrive at the farm to order them to leave for Harlech. It was not a journey that he relished now, not with Alice being still so young. Knowing it was something they would have to face when the time came, however, he began to make what preparations he might, whilst hoping that the call might not come. Not yet!

Idris the archer looked up at the massive battlements of Caernarvon Castle, then turned to Dafydd Mawr standing alongside him. 'It will take more than soft words to lower that English banner, Dafydd!'

Nodding in agreement, the man at arms grinned: 'True enough, Idris,' he replied, 'nor will a blast of trumpets bring down those walls!' He pursed his lips, then added, 'Even though it seems the garrison are few indeed to man those battlements, they hold them stubbornly enough, so we must either talk them out or starve them out.'

'Then starvation it must be for them!' said Idris. 'For Prince Owain himself has not persuaded them to yield.'

Dafydd shrugged. 'Nor would I, were I ensconced within those walls. I'd hold out 'til all hope of relief had gone, aye, and the last crust too! One thing is certain, they are more comfortable within than we are encamped out here, whilst they from their vantage points whittle away at any flesh that shows itself to them! What we need . . .'

What that might be was left unsaid, for whilst they were engrossed in the problem of capturing the castle, Prince Owain's son, Maredudd, had walked up to them. Smiling, he interrupted them to say, 'What the prince needs, Captain Idris, is for you to attend upon him!'

With a toss of his head, Idris replied, 'As well I attend upon something, or someone, other than these stone walls, my lord, for 'tis little good that I do here!'

Maredudd grinned. 'And less you have to moan about than those of us who've knocked at those gates all winter through!'

Idris, scowled. 'Nor were me and Dafydd here, standing idle my lord, for have we not trudged all through Wales with barely a pause to interrupt our marching? Laying siege would have been a rest that we would oft enough have welcomed!'

Maredudd grinned. 'Aye, no doubt, though marching it seems has not stilled your tongue! Rather than standing here holding discourse with me, though, I would advise that you hasten to my father's bidding, for he is not a patient man!'

Touching his helmet in salute but obviously still unrepentant, Idris nodded, then hurried off in the direction of Prince Owain's tent.

Watching him go, Maredudd turned to Dafydd Mawr. 'Though Idris is of an age with my brother, Dafydd,' he said with a sigh, 'he has not learned to curb his tongue when talking with his betters!'

Dafydd Mawr nodded. 'Aye, that's his trouble right enough, my lord,' he acquiesced, 'and though it may cause others pain, 'tis what makes him a good soldier, for he sees no man his better!'

Young Maredudd frowned as though unsure whether or not Dafydd had been agreeing with him. 'Have words with him, Dafydd,' he asked now, 'counsel him for his own sake, to speak more courteously.'

Dafydd touched his helmet and grinning now replied, 'Oh, I will, my lord, be sure of it! The trouble I find in doing so is that whilst some say he is an archer's bastard others would aver he is but a bastard. Wherever the truth may lie in that, he is as cocksure of himself as though he were a prince himself and so he is most difficult to advise humility!'

It seemed that Maredudd felt he was getting into deeper water than he had intended, for he snapped at Dafydd, 'He is no prince but an archer, so just tell him to keep a civil tongue in his head, Dafydd! I cannot forever suffer such arrogance!'

With that he strode off leaving a grinning Dafydd standing there, stroking his moustache as he wondered whether it would indeed be a waste of time to speak to Idris about his lack of respect for his superiors.

With a last glance up at the battlements he began walking back to the tent he shared with Idris when he saw the archer striding towards him, his face black as thunder. Wondering now whether Idris had suffered a rebuke from the prince, he paused there, waiting for Idris to come up to him. He was about to speak as they met, when Idris blurted out angrily, 'I'm being sent as escort now, Dafydd, a bloody nursemaid for that turncoat Mortimer!'

Nonplussed, Dafydd frowned as he asked, 'Escort Sir Edmund, Idris? Where would the prince have you escort him?'

Idris almost spat out his reply, 'To Harlech! He is to command at Harlech and sit there safely with my Lady Marged whilst others do the fighting!'

Dafydd gave him a sideways glance, to ask with raised eyebrows, 'With my Lady Marged and Catrin too?'

Scowling, Idris snorted. 'Aye, and Catrin too!'

Dafydd grinned. 'I would have thought being given leave from this siege would be a cause for thanks rather than be such as to rouse you to anger, Idris.'

Still scowling, Idris said resentfully, 'I am no man at arms, Dafydd, to escort such as he! Iestyn is back there at the farm and Maldwyn too, what other escort does Mortimer need?'

Dafydd sighed his exasperation, as he replied, 'God save us from a soldier who ever questions where his duty lies! Do you not see, Idris, you do not only escort Sir Edmund, but the prince's consort and his daughter too. Their rank and station demands a captain's escort!'

Belligerently, Idris demanded, 'So why then me, not you?'

Dafydd, clearly irritated now, snapped, 'Reason enough lies in the fact the prince so orders, Idris! Perhaps too, that when we next storm those castle walls, 'twill be the likes o' me will lead the assault, whilst archers such as you ply your weapons from a safe distance!' He glared at Idris for a moment then shook his head before saying more quietly, 'Nought of this is about men at arms or archers, nor yet who should escort whom, Idris, but 'tis about you and Catrin! Nor do you resent Sir Edmund for that he turned 'gainst his own king, but rather that he married Catrin! If you would live out this war then 'tis time you accept that it is so and that Catrin is wed to her own sort, of her own choice.'

Idris had been listening, mouth agape, to this tirade but as soon as Dafydd finished speaking he asked somewhat petulantly, 'Is your sermon finished now, Father Dafydd?'

Face set stubbornly, Dafydd nodded, then said, 'Aye and you would do well to take heed, my friend! For his few pence a day a soldier does his duty though it be to the death,' he paused, then grinned as he added, 'though I do not see you dying from a ride to the farm nor yet from being at Sir Edmund's beck and call, for you were indentured to him long enough!'

'Aye, long enough,' replied Idris, 'but I sought service with Prince Owain of my own free will, not for that he held me prisoner!'

'No?' asked Dafydd. 'Why! I could have sworn I recall putting you in Sycharth's dungeon myself after you threatened Lord Gruffydd with an arrow aimed at his heart!'

Idris flushed, then quickly said, 'Twas just to cool my heels that night, Prince Owain had no thought to keep me there!'

'No, perhaps not,' Dafydd conceded, 'but you'd do well to guard your tongue with such as Lord Maredudd and Sir Edmund or else you might find harsher judgements prevail!' He smiled and with a shake of his head added, 'Come, if time allows, let's share a jug of ale 'fore you depart!'

It was with mixed emotions that Idris rode up to the farm a couple of days later for it had been a long wet ride with a light rain falling during most of his journey. He had sheltered overnight at a cottage along the way, but it had been a hard winter and the old cottager and his wife had nought to offer by way of food, nor other than water from the nearby brook to drink. Rather had they been glad enough to share the bread and bit of mutton he had brought with him for the journey. Still, he thought, it would be good to meet old friends like Iestyn and Maldwyn, shed his soggy leather jerkin and have a pot of ale with them before a log fire. If only he could have all that without having to meet Mortimer . . . or see Catrin . . . or even see one without the other!

His thoughts were interrupted by a challenge from behind the stone wall surrounding the farm and he called back at the top of his voice, anxious to ensure there would be no misunderstanding as to who he was: 'Idris the Archer, with word from Prince Owain!'

He could see that the bodies scurrying around the yard were mostly womenfolk for their figures were splashed with colour and the men wore drab that better blended with the hills and fields, or would were it not for the wet glint of mail about them here and there.

Then he was in the yard, with Iestyn and Maldwyn all smiles as they greeted him, asking him what news he brought. They fell silent though as an unsmiling Sir Edmund Mortimer, his sword scabbard slapping his thigh, came striding across the yard. As he neared, he asked peremptorily, 'What news of Prince Owain, archer?'

Idris hardly heard him though, for he was looking beyond the Englishman to where Lady Marged stood in the doorway with a smiling Catrin beside her. He seemed to feel, rather than hear, Sir Edmund's question hanging in the air and tearing his eyes away from Catrin, said huskily, 'The prince would have you go to Harlech, my lord, taking with you the ladies there and all the men under arms you have around you here!'

There was a broad smile on Sir Edmund's face now as he replied, 'You bring us welcome news. I shall ensure the ladies and their servants are ready for the journey. Meanwhile, you will have the soldiery ready to march by dawn tomorrow . . . and have them warned they shall not return!' With that, he turned on his heel and hurried across to Catrin and the Lady Marged.

Idris, his face flushed with anger stood there for a moment, biting his tongue as he remembered Dafydd's cautionary words. Then, touching his helmet in acknowledgement of the order, he turned to Iestyn and Maldwyn to say, 'What? Would you have me freeze and die of thirst? A glass of ale and a bite to eat, for God's sake!'

Maldwyn grinned. 'That you shall have, Captain, for you've brought the best news I've heard since I left Harlech! I weary of thinking of booty as a scraggy capon stolen from the farmer's flock!'

Chapter Twenty-five

Idris turned his head as the farmhouse door opened and Sir Edmund appeared, accoutred in light armour. He stood there for a moment looking around the yard at the score or so of soldiers assembled there before asking Idris, already mounted, 'All ready, Captain?'

With a cursory salute, Idris replied straight faced, 'Ready as ever, my lord!'

Sir Edmund had already turned away though, his hand held out now to help Lady Marged and Catrin, both attired in warm riding cloaks, out into the yard. Stable-hands were hurrying forward now and soon the ladies were mounted on their palfreys. Sir Edmund though still stood there as if waiting for someone. There was the sound of heavy footsteps and to Idris's obvious surprise two men servants bearing a blanketed litter appeared with Megan, muffled in a cloak, fussing alongside as they made their way to the baggage train.

Wide-eyed, Idris turned to Sir Edmund as the knight was mounting his horse to ask, 'The litter bearers come with us, my lord?'

With a curl of his lip, Sir Edmund retorted, 'Why, would you have me leave my baby daughter behind, Captain? She comes with us even though it slows our pace a mite!' As Idris hesitated he snapped, 'Well, don't just sit there man! Lead on.' He paused, then added by way of explanation, 'We go by way of Beddgelert.'

Touching a finger to his helmet, Idris walked his horse towards the head of the small company. Perhaps it was only his imagination that as he rode past Catrin he saw her look at him with that provocative smile on her lips, her blue eyes shining mischievously. Imagination or not, he quickly averted his eyes and set off at a trot.

Even so, the escort had to hasten its pace to keep closed up and there was an indignant hail from Sir Edmund, 'Hold up there, Captain, there is no need for such haste! The ladies and my daughter are not used to your rough warlike ways!'

Beneath his breath, Idris muttered, 'Nor I to playing nursemaid, Englishman!' He grinned then at the thought of what Lord Maredudd might have said about that but raising his hand in acknowledgement, he glanced behind to see whether the pace he set now was to the knight's liking. It seemed so, for there was no further comment, other than a broad grin on Catrin's face and an amused smile from Lady Marged.

Sir Edmund had dropped back along the column to ride alongside Catrin and Lady Marged near the baggage train and even more importantly to ensure that Alice was handled gently by the litter bearers. Wanting to satisfy his curiosity as to why they went by way of Beddgelert, he turned to Lady Marged to ask, 'Why do we visit Squire ap Roberts at Beddgelert, my lady?'

She smiled at his persistence for he had asked the same question of her before they had set out. Then she had merely replied that it was Prince Owain's wish. She relented now though, to say evenly, 'Prince Owain is concerned that Squire ap Roberts is somewhat lukewarm towards this war with King Henry, Edmund!'

He looked at her for a moment, waiting for her to continue and when she did not, asked with raised eyebrows, 'So, we visit him to persuade him to the cause?'

With an amused smile, she replied, 'Persuade, Edmund? Our very presence there so soon after Harlech's surrender will commit him to the cause more than any words that he might utter!' She laughed then and leaning over towards him added confidentially, ' 'Tis called guilt by association, Edmund!'

It was late afternoon when they came to Beddgelert's few cottages huddled around a crossroads, and shortly afterwards Sir Edmund was gratefully dismounting in the courtyard of ap Robert's small manor. As he waited to greet the lord of the manor, he saw that Idris and Maldwyn, the man at arms, were standing nearby and called over to them, 'You there! Where are your manners? Assist the ladies!'

Maldwyn hurried over to Lady Marged, but Idris still stood there hesitating until Catrin, smiling demurely, asked, 'Will you not help me, Captain?'

Walking over to her now, Idris held his hands up to her. As she slipped from her horse, the archer seemed to step back as though reluctant to touch her and she almost fell into his arms.

Sir Edmund snapped anxiously, 'Have a care Captain! Would you have my lady fall?'

The lord and lady of the manor were at the doorway now though, to greet their guests and with a dismissive glare at Idris, Sir Edmund turned to meet their hosts. As he looked at ap Roberts, Sir Edmund wondered again about their reasons for being there. Face breaking into a gap toothed smile, the lord of the manor welcomed him in the falsetto voice of age, 'Welcome to our simple home, Sir Edmund,' he said, obsequiously. 'Owain Glyn Dŵr's kin are ever welcome here!'

Sir Edmund glanced at Lady Marged who was beside him now, but she seemed not to notice as she chattered away in Welsh to their hostess. Out of the corner of his eye, he noticed a serving man talking to the archer then lead him off to a barn. Together with Catrin and Lady Marged though he was being ushered into the manor now and being shown to the chambers where they would spend the night. 'I fear we cannot seat all your retinue in our hall, Sir Edmund,' ap Roberts was saying, 'but we have a table laid for them in the barn which is warm and dry and where they may bed down for the night.

Later, when they had cleansed themselves after the day's journey, they were seated around a laden table in the great hall, whilst ap Roberts professed at length his support for this most righteous of wars. As the meal came to an end, he turned to Sir Edmund with his head on one side and, looking more scraggy cockerel than squire, proclaimed, 'Yes, Sir Edmund, it's young men like you that must wield freedom's sword, whilst we old men can offer only counsel and our prayers for victory!' He gazed pensively into his goblet of wine for a moment before raising his eyes to say softly, 'There's strange it is though, Sir Edmund, that you fight for Prince Owain,' he gave an apologetic cough, 'I mean . . . you being an Englishman!'

Perhaps it was the wine, the warm room, the sly innuendo, but Sir Edmund found his choler rising and he rose suddenly to slam his goblet down on the table and glaring at ap Roberts now he snapped, 'Perhaps, *my lord*, because I have quarrel enough of my own with Henry Bolingbroke, as did my kinsman, Hotspur! Perhaps too because there are too many amongst the Welsh gentry who wait to see which way the wind of battle blows ere they buckle on their sword!' Then with a bow to his hostess and a nod to ap Roberts he added, 'Pray excuse me, the war you spoke of continues tomorrow, when we shall face an early start!'

As he walked away from the table, ap Roberts sniggered before saying in his high pitched voice, 'I fear your lady wife has already retired with the vapours, Sir Edmund!'

If it were meant as a jibe, it was lost on Sir Edmund as he stalked stiff backed out of the room. As he went into the entrance hall he noticed the door was ajar and thought he heard Catrin's voice coming from outside. There was a patch of light outside the door now as he opened it wider, but there was no sign of Catrin, so he called out, 'Is that you, Catrin?'

As if by magic, she was there in front of him, her face lit by the light from the hall. Her head on one side, she smiled as she asked him, 'Is ought wrong, Edmund?'

Still irritated from his exchange with ap Roberts, he snapped, 'Why do you stand out here in the dark, Catrin? Who were you talking with?'

Still smiling innocently, she countered, 'Why so cross, Edmund? The heat, the noise in there and the constant chatter of our hostess made me yearn for fresh air and a moment's peace before I retired!' She paused and stepping forward now, put a hand on his arm to ask innocently, 'Why, do you think you had lost me, my lord?'

Before he could answer, he heard the sound of running feet and looking over her shoulder, he saw the man at arms, Maldwyn, running towards him with one or two others. Concerned now, he called out, 'What's amiss, Maldwyn?'

All out of breath, Maldwyn replied, 'A false alarm, I think my lord. Cap'n Idris thought he heard someone creeping 'round the manor and called out the guard!'

Relaxing now, Sir Edmund replied, ' 'Tis good to know he is so watchful. Where is he now?'

Maldwyn shuffled his feet and coughed before answering, 'He skirmishes around the manor my lord, to make sure all is secure!'

Sir Edmund smiled. 'Good! 'Twill do no harm!' Then with a casual wave of his hand to Maldwyn, he turned to go inside, saying to Catrin as he did so, 'Come, my dear, I fear I must make my apology to our host for some over-hasty words of mine!'

Maldwyn breathed a sigh of relief as the manor door shut behind Sir Edmund then shook his head as he looked at Idris, pressed flat against the manor wall by the side of the door. His voice a sibilant whisper now, he said, 'By god, you play a dangerous game, Captain!' The archer shrugged as he eased himself away from the wall, to say coolly, 'I did but pause in my rounds to bid goodnight to Lady Catrin, Maldwyn!'

Pouting his lips, Maldwyn nodded, then said doubtfully, 'Aye, no doubt, Captain, yet 'twas as well I stargazed as I supped my ale, for we'd not want the Englishman to get the wrong drift on things, would we?'

Grinning now, Idris replied, 'Of course not Maldwyn, which is why I'll continue with that skirmishing you spoke of . . . over a pot of ale, if you've left me any to sup!'

As Idris sat astride his horse in the courtyard the next morning he felt as if all eyes were upon him, perhaps not all though, for it seemed as though Lady Catrin was studiously avoiding his eye as Sir Edmund silently helped her mount her palfrey. With a glance to satisfy himself that Lady Marged was also safely mounted, Sir Edmund turned to give a half bow to the lady of the manor before touching his riding whip to his helmet in casual salute to Squire ap Roberts.

The lord of the manor favoured him with that gap toothed smile before saying in a querulous treble, 'My compliments to Prince Owain, Sir Edmund, when next you see him!'

Sir Edmund gave him a thin smile. 'Oh, be assured I will, my lord and I will add that he should visit here, to see for himself your loyalty to his cause!'

From the look on ap Robert's face it seemed he did not take it as a compliment, for his face blanched behind that scraggy ginger beard. The look he gave registered with Sir Edmund too, for there was the momentary flash of a complacent smile on the knight's face as he mounted.

Sir Edmund was in good humour though, as he turned to Lady Marged and a subdued Catrin to ask courteously, 'Are you ready, ladies?' As they both nodded, he turned to Idris and his voice sharper now said, 'What are you waiting for then, man? A long ride and a short day brooks no laggard escort!'

His face expressionless, Idris just touched a finger to his helmet and led off with Maldwyn by his side, leaving Iestyn to follow with the rearguard. There were no litter bearers with them now though, for the tracks to Harlech being more suitable, young Megan rode in a cart, with little Alice borne in her arms.

As they journeyed on, it seemed to Sir Edmund that Catrin became more and more withdrawn, for his attempts at conversation were met with little response. Eventually he gave up trying and relapsed into a gloomy silence that cast a cloud over the whole group. It seemed that his mood was one shared by the weather for the drizzle of mid morning became heavy rain by the time they reached Penmorfa, forcing them to seek shelter in the cottages by the roadside there.

*   *   *   *

With Sir Edmund and the ladies going into one of the cottages, Idris and the van of the escort took shelter in the byre alongside to be near their wards. Its foetid atmosphere though soon drove Idris to stand in the doorway.

Standing there watching the track become a muddy rivulet, he remembered all that had happened the previous night. Remembered how he had stood in front of the manor, imagining Catrin up there behind one of the lighted upstairs windows, lying in Sir Edmund's arms! It was then that he had heard a whisper, had known that it was Catrin whispering his name! He smiled now as he remembered holding her, as they had once held each other at Sycharth. She had leaned back from him then and opened her mouth to speak but before she did the door had opened and he had heard Sir Edmund calling her, a shaft of light almost illuminating them as they huddled against the wall. He wondered now what Catrin had been about to say and his heart sank, for he knew that nothing she might have said then could alter anything!

He sensed Maldwyn hovering at his elbow now and heard him ask, 'The rain is easing, Captain, shall I have the men mounted?'

He hesitated a moment, reluctant to be drawn away from his memories and Maldwyn, as if realising the cause, muttered, 'Best leave well alone, Captain, there's nought but trouble there!'

Idris turned to him, to say sharply, 'Trouble is what we're paid for, Maldwyn! Pray mine are the only troubles we have to fret over on our way to Harlech!'

He stood up from the doorpost he had been leaning against then and strode over to knock on the cottage door. Hearing Sir Edmund's curt 'Enter!' he went in, to see what might well have been a tableaux fixed in time. Lady Marged and Catrin were sitting hands folded on the table before which they sat. Sir Edmund was sitting at the head of the table, his helmet on the table in front of him, his blond hair hanging untidily around his ears, whilst Megan sat over in a corner, nursing the infant.

No one moved as he entered and Catrin did not even look up, but sat there, head bowed, staring at her white clenched knuckles.

Idris hesitated for a moment, reluctant somehow to break the spell in which they all seemed embraced. It was broken at last by Sir Edmund who looked up at him to say quietly, 'Well man, what is it?'

Taken somewhat aback by the knight's subdued manner, Idris replied equally quietly, 'The rain has eased, my lord. I thought you might wish to press on!'

Sir Edmund did not reply for a moment, just sat there looking at

Idris, as though his cold blue eyes would reach into Idris's very soul. Then, as Idris began shuffling his feet, Sir Edmund said almost with an air of resignation, 'Very well then Captain, mount up and let us be on our way!'

Idris hesitated, taken aback by the knight's mood swing from his earlier hostility to this present air of resignation, and it was only when Sir Edmund said again, 'Well, mount up then Captain!' that he roused himself to see Catrin looking at him now, an unspoken plea in her eyes.

Perhaps it was the weather brightening, but there was a more cheerful air about the company as they made their way south that afternoon with even Sir Edmund joining in the chatter from time to time. Even so it was late afternoon before the imposing towers and keep of Castle Harlech came into view.

It was an emotional moment for Sir Edmund, thinking now of his last visit there and wondering what hope of action it might offer him. When he turned to Catrin though, she did not seem stimulated at the prospect of their arrival, for there was an air of resignation rather than excitement about her. In an effort to cheer her, he said with an enthusiasm he found difficult to muster, 'There, cariad, your new home! Rather better than the farmhouse, is it not?'

There was only sadness in her eyes now though as she replied quietly, 'It does not seem a happy place, Edmund, not like Sycharth!'

He smiled. 'Oh, it will be a happy place for us my love and a safe one in which we might nurture little Alice!'

She did not seem entirely convinced though, for she just replied, 'I hope so, Edmund.'

They were approaching the ramp to the castle now though, and there was a hail from the inner gate-house tower. Maldwyn, bearing Owain Glyn Dŵr's banner, bawled the reply, 'A Mortimer! A Mortimer!'

There was no reply to that but slowly and with much creaking, the drawbridge was lowered and the portcullis raised to allow their company to enter.

Flanked by Idris and Maldwyn, Sir Edmund led the way into the castle's inner ward where Lord Tudor stood waiting to greet them. Looking at him, Sir Edmund thought that it might be the prince himself who stood there, so much alike were they.

'Marged! It is good to see you safely here!' Tudor was saying now as he helped her down from her palfrey. Then turning to Catrin he said, 'And you, cariad fach! Prettier than ever you are!' He looked at the bundle Megan carried, then glanced at Lady Marged to ask, 'And who is this, can it be that you are a grandmother now? Surely not, for you are still the girl that I remember!' As Lady Marged blushed and replied that it was indeed her granddaughter, Lord Tudor turned a cool gaze on Sir Edmund to say formally, 'You are welcome here, Sir Edmund.'

There was no offered handshake though, and Sir Edmund's hand fell to his side. Stung by the apparent lack of courtesy, Sir Edmund said somewhat waspishly, 'It seems you are all secure here, Lord Tudor, for there was little challenge when we arrived!'

Lord Tudor grinned. 'Challenge enough you would have found, Sir Edmund, had you not had the ladies there to see you safely in!'

Bridling at the taunt Sir Edmund, hand on sword, replied, curtly, 'Challenges I am well used to Lord Tudor and I hide behind no woman's skirt!'

Tudor smiled and said softly, 'Unhand your sword, *nephew*, for you may have better use of it should Henry Bolingbroke come here to see you keep a tidy house!' Then as Sir Edmund frowned he added, 'I leave on the morrow for Aberystwyth, when you shall hold Harlech for my brother!'

Unwilling to confess his ignorance of Glyn Dŵr's intention, Sir Edmund merely inclined his head to say calmly, 'Prince Owain honours me indeed! Be assured I'll not readily give up that which was so hard won by you!'

It seemed that the brief confrontation was over, for with a half smile and a nod of his head, Lord Tudor replied, 'I never doubted it, Sir Edmund!' With that he turned to Lady Marged to say, 'I am remiss, Marged, to keep you standing here when you must be weary after your journey. Come, let us seek some refreshment for you!' Then with a wave of his hand he led the way towards the great chamber.

That night Idris sat with Maldwyn and Iestyn towards the foot of the table in the great chamber of Castle Harlech, sipping their ale and gazing around them at the lavish spread, whilst away at the head of the table Lord Tudor sat in some state. Beside him sat Lady Marged and to his right, Sir Edmund and Lady Catrin.

Idris turned to Maldwyn. 'I knew that Prince Owain would have his court here when Harlech was taken,' he said quietly, 'but it seems his brother has outdone him, for with them all in their silks and satins, it seems Tudor holds court here already!'

Maldwyn grinned. 'Silks and satins!' he said scornfully. 'Why, that be women's garb. I would have more manly clothes!'

Idris looked at him with raised eyebrows and sniffed. 'Aye, and I would too, did you but change them every year or so, for I still savour the smell of the byre we paused at on our journey here!'

Maldwyn grinned. 'Nay, Captain, 'tis but that I wet myself when I saw you there at the manor's door!'

Idris was not listening though, but looking at Catrin, up there at the head of the table. With a whispered word to Sir Edmund, she had risen and, her face pale, was walking away from the table now towards the doorway that led to the courtyard or perhaps to her chamber.

Idris knew only that wherever it might be, he must follow and he rose, only to find Maldwyn's hand on his arm. He turned on the man at arms to say angrily, 'Hold off, Maldwyn, this is no affair of yours!'

Maldwyn raised his pot of ale to Idris and slurped at it before saying with a grin, 'Oh, but it is, Idris, for it's a man's duty to protect his captain and there's great hazard in what you think of doing now!'

As Idris hesitated, Maldwyn said quietly, 'Come, Captain, sit down and drink your ale, for all eyes are upon you. Should you leave, then others will surely follow! Have thought for the Lady Catrin, who needs must dwell here with Sir Edmund when you and I follow where Prince Owain's banner leads.'

Reluctantly, Idris sat down and reaching for his ale, drank deep until, as the night wore on, his mind was as hazy as the cloudy liquid he drank.

The next morning a bleary eyed Idris was at the stables saddling his horse ready for the journey back to Caernarvon, when she came to him. So soft footed did she come that it was not until she was at his elbow that he was aware of her presence and then only from the heady smell of her perfume.

He turned quickly and with an eager cry of 'Catrin!' reached out to her, wanting, needing, to hold her in his arms again. Her eyes moist though, she shook her head and stepped back from him to say in a faltering whisper, 'No, Idris, I cannot, must not! I did but come to bid farewell, for I fear we shall not meet again!'

He reached out to her again, but she was already turning away from him and, head bent now, was hurrying back towards the keep, clutching her shawl tightly across her slender shoulders.

His hand lying loosely on the saddle as if waiting there ready to tighten the cinches, he watched her go but she did not turn again until she reached the doorway to the keep. She paused there, but only to glance over her shoulder before, with a quick wave of her hand, she went quickly into the keep and out of his sight.

He stood there for a moment, the impression of her standing in the keep's doorway still imprinted on his eyes, when there was a movement in the neighbouring stall and Maldwyn rose to his full height.

Eyes blazing, Idris snapped, 'Have you been sitting there spying on me Maldwyn?'

Maldwyn grinned. 'Me spy, Captain? I doubt I ever had the form to be so furtive! I was but here seeing that my horse was well shod before we set out for Caernarvon's siege again. Not that there was much to be a'spying of, was there? A farewell word from my Lady Catrin as none could take exception to, except perhaps that it was said at all! Still, 'tis better that's all said and done, if you know my meaning, Captain. A good hard ride on this cold day will clear away the cobwebs and all the imaginings of things that cannot be!'

Idris nodded, to say a little bitterly, 'Aye, Maldwyn a cold day and a good hard ride is all we need!'

Maldwyn smiled almost as if he had won a little victory and said consolingly, 'Aye, and with no lords or ladies to hold us back we could even reach Prince Owain's camp tonight!'

Idris though, was looking at the keep's doorway again as he said softly, 'No doubt Maldwyn, but to what purpose, eh?'

Sir Edmund watched from the inner gate-house tower of Castle Harlech as the archer took his few men across the drawbridge and onto the track that led north. The thought still rankled in Sir Edmund's mind that Catrin had been talking to the archer the other night, when he had found her outside the manor's doorway. Of a certainty she had been talking to someone and to whom other than the archer could it have been?

He bit his lip, reason telling him that it must have been his imagination: the wind in the trees perhaps or the echo of people talking in the hall of the manor. Yet he could not persuade himself that it was so.

Despite himself he gave a reluctant smile as he acknowledged that perhaps it was his own envy of the archer that caused such doubts, such fears. For he knew that he did indeed envy the archer his relative freedom, his certainty of being actively involved in Glyn Dŵr's campaigns rather than being like himself, Castle Harlech's housekeeper, however important that might be in Glyn Dŵr's great scheme of things.

Watching Idris the archer leading his troop of men out of sight now around a bend in the track, Sir Edmund gave a toss of his head and smiled, thinking that the archer's trade was such as to ensure his footsteps were not likely to be retraced.

Turning to go down to the inner ward he paused to give a final glance towards the track below the castle's walls but it was empty now that the archer and his troop were out of sight. He stayed there for a moment looking at the empty track and thinking, aye and after Caernarvon, there'll be yet another siege, another battle for Idris. He may well have paid his due and gone the way of all such men before ever he might return.

Standing there thinking of the sturdy captain of archers he found himself wondering, almost aloud, what would become of them if Idris the archer and he were indeed still there at the ending of it all. Just as there was no one there to hear the question there was no one to offer response and the only sound he heard was that of his own footsteps on the stone staircase as he descended to the inner ward.

Later that morning Sir Edmund was standing in the inner ward of the castle with Catrin and the Lady Marged, to bid a more formal farewell to Lord Tudor as he set out with his escort to join Prince Owain's son Gruffydd at the siege of Aberystwyth Castle. Despite the fact that there had been no repetition of the veiled hostility there had been between them at their meeting the previous day, Sir Edmund was not sorry to see the prince's brother leave.

He was straight-faced though as he offered his hand to Tudor to say, 'God grant you the success at Aber, my lord, that I pray the prince gains at Caernarvon.' Then he added with a thin smile, 'With those two citadels taken, Prince Owain's hold on all West Wales will be secure, I do but wish I came with you to lend my arm in the assault.'

'Never fear, Sir Edmund,' replied Tudor with a grin, 'arms enough I'll have with me to take it stone by stone if needs be, but should all else fail, I'll call for you to talk the English out!'

Catrin glanced anxiously at her husband but, perhaps because he was glad enough to see Tudor's back, Sir Edmund maintained his composure, merely replying, 'And gladly will I come, my lord, for the English are a stubborn race who respond better to courtesy than to rough handling!'

As Lord Tudor mounted, he looked over his shoulder at Sir Edmund to reply with a grin, 'And it is courtesy they want, Sir Edmund, then I fear I shall have to send for you, for rough handling is more my trade!'

So saying he dug his spurs in and with a forward wave of his arm to his retinue, set off confidently through the gate-house and across the drawbridge to conquer Aberystwyth for Glyn Dŵr.

As the portcullis clanged shut again after Lord Tudor's exit, Sir Edmund, hand on hips, looked around him at Castle Harlech and smiled at he thought that he was lord of this castle now, as he had been of Ludlow. It was not all that he might have hoped for had things gone differently at Pilleth, but it was a far cry from that prison cave in Snowdonia. He looked at Catrin and smiled, thinking that he was secure enough here and with a pretty young bride to keep him warm of nights to boot. With Glyn Dŵr's star in the ascendancy as it was, who could tell what fortune it might bring to those who followed in his train!

Catrin came over to him and taking his hand in hers, said shyly, 'It is good to be together here, my lord, I feared that you might be leaving me here alone, whilst you went off to fight my father's war!'

He wondered for a moment whether she had looked up that way at Idris the archer back there at the manor but brushed the thought aside and gave a wry grin. 'No chance have I of that, Catrin, my love, I think at times your father fears I bruise too easily to be exposed to such hazard!'

She laughed now and pulled him closer to her. 'Then I am glad he thinks so, Edmund, for I would have you here with me, where I might be of help to you!'

Wide-eyed, he looked at her but her face was a blur now and around him lay, not Castle Harlech, but an ancient ruin and another's voice was echoing in his ears, 'I can help you . . .'

Lady Marged's voice penetrated the mists that seemed to be enveloping him then and he heard her say, as if from a distance, 'Come Catrin, there is much for us to do if we are to make this bleak castle fit for a prince's court!'

Her head on one side Catrin was looking at him now, her forehead etched with a slight frown as she asked, 'Are you all right, my lord? You are so pale . . !'

He nodded and gave her a wan smile. 'Of course, my love! Go with your lady mother now, for I too have much to do to make this castle safe for when your father comes to stay!'

There still seemed to be a shadow of concern there in her eyes but, nodding, she turned and began following her mother who was already bustling away towards the great chamber as though she had not a moment to spare.

Sir Edmund watched them go, wondering for a moment what

shadow had crossed over him just then that had brought that other Catrin, the Cathy woman, to his mind. He shrugged, thinking, a relic of that illness that struck me down at Ludlow, no doubt! He looked at the gate-house then and thought of Tudor leaving through those portals for Aberystwyth and his lips tightened. Glyn Dŵr should have sent me to take Aber, he thought bitterly, does he not trust me yet, that he keeps me penned up here out of harm's way? He gave a toss of his head and sniffed, it's that great plan he has for me he thought cynically, 'tis a pity it is not one that he shares with me!

Chapter Twenty-six

Arriving at Prince Owain's encampment below the lofty walls of Caernarvon Castle, Idris found the prince looking out over the Menai Strait watching a few men o' war making sail. Turning, the prince smiled. 'Ah, Idris,' he exclaimed, 'I trust you left Sir Edmund and the ladies safe and well at Harlech?'

Idris touched his helmet with a knuckle. 'Indeed, my lord, and as I left, Lord Tudor prepared to march to Aberystwyth.'

Prince Owain gave a satisfied smile. 'Good! Then he shall be there to greet those French men o' war who sail to blockade Aber's seaward lanes! With no replenishment by land or sea Aber's constable must perforce yield ere long!' He glanced at the French squadron again before turning back to Idris to say, 'Go now to Maredudd, for he has news for you, some of which will be to your liking and some I fear, not!'

Frowning, Idris opened his mouth to speak, but Prince Owain was gazing seawards again, watching with apparent interest the manoeuvring of the French ships. Touching a finger to his helmet, Idris turned and went off to seek the young Lord Maredudd.

He wondered what the bad news was but thought that such as there might be he would as soon hear it from young Maredudd as any, and smiled as he thought of the times that the young lord had stood between him and Lord Gruffydd's wrath over his dalliance with Catrin. Perhaps too, that was why his dislike of Sir Edmund was no great secret from Maredudd! When at last he found Maredudd, the prince's young son gave him a cheeky grin as he asked, 'You suffered no mischance on your holiday with Sir Edmund then, Idris?'

Idris sniffed. 'It was no holiday that took me to Harlech, my lord, but duty!'

Maredudd pursed his lips and gave a sympathetic nod: 'Aye, I sorrow for you Idris, suffering that long journey and missing all the excitement of gazing at these walls!' He smiled then to ask cheerfully, 'And my sister Catrin, you left her well, I trust?'

Stony-faced now Idris replied, 'Aye I left her, my lord!'

Maredudd grinned again to say, 'That you left her is well indeed Idris, for had you not, then there would be little hope for you in this life nor yet, perchance, much in the next!'

Still stony-faced, Idris ignored the comment to ask, 'Prince Owain said you had news for me, my lord?'

All serious now, Maredudd nodded, saying, 'Though I asked Prince Owain that you might yet stay with me to invest the castle here, at first light tomorrow, Idris, you march with him for Shropshire and there cry havoc along the marches!'

Pursing his lips Idris nodded thoughtfully, then asked, 'Is that the bad news you have for me, my lord?'

Maredudd glanced at him and gave a thin smile. 'I thank you, Idris, that you might think that leaving me here to maintain the siege alone is the bad news, but I fear that it is not so.' Maredudd took a deep breath, then touched him on the arm, to say quietly, 'Come with me, Idris!'

Leading the way to one of the nearby tents, he turned to Idris and, finger to lips said, 'Quietly, now!' Then pulling the flap aside, he ushered Idris inside.

Looking into the tent's dim interior Idris saw a figure lying recumbent on a straw palliasse, a leg swathed in bandages. As Idris peered down, trying to see who it was that lay there, the man's head turned to look up at him and, with a wry grin beneath that familiar drooping moustache, Dafydd said in his gruff voice, 'A friend I thought I had in you, Idris bach, but when I needed you, you were off on some jaunt!'

Idris knelt by the palliasse to clasp hands with the old man at arms. Moist eyed now, he said despairingly, 'I only leave you alone for a few days, Dafydd and come back to find you lying here! What have you done to your leg, man?'

Shamefaced now Dafydd gave a toss of his head. 'Taken by the English I was, Idris, in an assault that failed. Up there on the battlements I stood alone, the scaling ladders all pushed back from the walls.' He grinned as he added, 'I thought I'd take a few of the English with me before I fell, but a spear in the leg put paid to that!'

Mystified, Idris asked, 'What happened then? How did you escape?'

'Escape, lad, with but one leg of use?' asked Dafydd incredulously. 'No, 'twas an exchange of prisoners that got me here!' Proudly now he added, 'A knight's son I was worth to Prince Owain and, when he saw me lying here, he told me he'd had the best o' the bargain!'

Maldwyn's head was poking in through the open flap now and he said with a broad grin, 'However you got here Captain, 'tis good to see you and that's no error!' Then still grinning, he added, 'Though 'tis an ill wind that brings no good, for I hankered after a captaincy myself!'

Dafydd grinned. 'Aye, that I always knew, which is why you ever marched in front o' me and never behind!'

He tried to sit up now but ashen faced, he fell back in obvious pain and Idris said quietly, 'Rest easy, old friend, I'll leave you in quiet now . . . but I'll be back, never fear!'

Eyes clouded, Dafydd nodded. 'Aye, come back in a little while, Idris, and as you love me, bring a pot of ale!'

The next morning Idris set off with Prince Owain across North Wales on the long march toward Shropshire. Dafydd went with them but as it would be many a long day before he marched again, he went with the baggage train, telling all those who would listen how a baggage train should go!

Even though the castles at Caernarvon and Aberystwyth were still held by the English, Sir Edmund Mortimer felt secure enough at Harlech that spring. Well provisioned and with an adequate garrison, he felt in no immediate danger of attack from land by the English. Nor, with the French squadron still blockading Aberystwyth, could any king's ship approach Harlech from seaward without early word of its approach reaching him.

As he stood atop the inner gate house tower looking over the green countryside to the east, there was little for him to see nor yet much for him to hope for other than the arrival of a messenger with news of Prince Owain's progress along the marches or of the sieges at Aber or Caernarvon.

He sighed, as much from boredom as depression. It was peaceful enough there, keeping watch over Castle Harlech, but he yearned for action, such as there would be were he with Glyn Dŵr in his foray along the Welsh marches, or even the more stolid watching game at the castle sieges to north and south of Harlech.

Catrin, seemed to have fallen into a deep melancholia again and had withdrawn to her own chamber. Inevitably, as so often happened these days, a wave of nostalgia swept over him at the memory of standing on one of Ludlow's lofty towers. He smiled almost with affection at the memory of bandying words with the ambitious de Lacey, wondering as he did so what had become of him. He sighed, thinking all that he and de Lacey had in common now was that both their hopes and aspirations depended largely on whether Glyn Dŵr's rebellion, his war of independence, prospered or failed.

It was then he saw a lone rider approaching the castle and, after watching the man's swift approach for a moment or two, turned to make his way down the tower to the gate-house. Reaching ground level, he heard the echoing sound of hooves on the lowered drawbridge and watched the horseman come through the entrance into the inner ward.

Horse and man alike were panting as the horse stood there, the breath from its nostrils hanging like plumes of spectral feathers in the cool spring air.

Walking up to the rider, still sitting there on his mount and breathing heavily, Sir Edmund said with a smile, 'Your haste betrays you bring news of some import, rider! What is it that you would tell me?'

His face mud-spattered, the rider wiped a hand across his lips and grim faced, said as he began to dismount, 'I bring news from the marches of Prince Owain, my lord, both good and ill!'

Frowning, Sir Edmund gazed silently at the messenger for a moment and, seeing the man's drawn face, turned to a man at arms close by to say, 'Fetch this man a pot of ale, and quickly!' Turning back to the messenger now he said impatiently, 'Tell me the nub of your errand man, I do not hang the bearer of ill news, which most often I've heard before!'

Holding onto his stirrup strap as though for support, the man gulped. 'The ill news, my lord, is that Prince Owain on his march south was brought to battle by the Earl of Warwick at Campstone Hill nigh to Grosmont Castle.'

A hand to his brow, Sir Edmund snapped impatiently, 'The nub of it man, the nub!'

Pale faced, the man continued, 'The Earl, with his great army o'erwhelmed the prince, my lord, and a thousand Welsh were lost that day.'

Sir Edmund blanched, but, hearing light footsteps behind him, glanced around to see Lady Marged hurrying towards him. His voice low now, he whispered urgently, 'And Prince Owain lives?'

Tight lipped the messenger nodded. 'Aye, my lord, the prince lives, though he was nigh on captured and Ellis ap Richard lost his banner there!'

Sir Edmund breathed a sigh of relief, as much that he was spared the task of telling Lady Marged her prince was dead as that there was still hope for the rebellion. Hope for both the rebellion and his own future! The loss of the prince's standard and indeed his standard bearer Ellis ap Richard, was a small price to pay for that!'

Lady Marged was beside him now, hands clenched tight, knuckles white. 'The messenger, Sir Edmund,' she asked anxiously, 'he comes from Prince Owain?'

'Aye and he has good news for us!' replied Sir Edmund with a nod, glancing hopefully at the messenger now.

The messenger was taking great gulps of ale from the pot given him by the man at arms, but thirsty and weary though he might be, he was not slow witted, for nodding, he smiled to say cheerfully, 'Indeed my lord, for after the battle at Campstone Hill, Prince Owain pursued the Earl towards Monmouth and brought him to battle again at Craig y Dorth and there avenged himself upon the Earl and left the field the victor.'

Sir Edmund took a deep breath, thinking as he did so, Aye, the victor of a Pyrrhic victory, for he could ill afford such losses as he suffered at Campstone Hill. It was with a cheerful face though that he turned to the Lady Marged to say, 'There! Good news indeed, my Lady, for the prince has won a notable victory over the Earl of Warwick!'

Lady Marged was not deceived however, for clearly having heard at least some of the earlier part of the message, she shook her head and replied with a sad smile, 'You men, Sir Edmund! You see victory in a field strewn with the bodies of husbands, fathers, who'll not go home again. Tell their wives, their children, of the victory they so dearly bought, but linger not to listen if you hope to hear their laughter at the news!'

Sir Edmund watched her go, thinking with a wry smile as he did so, be grateful your husband lost only his banner there, my lady! He still stood there for a moment then, after giving instructions for the messenger to be taken care of, walked over to the entrance to the south eastern tower wherein lay his chamber. Climbing the stone staircase he hesitated at the door to Catrin's chamber, then with a sigh opened the door.

She was sitting sewing by the log fire in the hearth and looked up apathetically as he entered. Holding back another sigh, Sir Edmund smiled, to say in a voice brimming with enthusiasm, 'A messenger has arrived, my love, bringing news of your father's victory over the Earl of Warwick, not far from Monmouth!'

Her hands holding the needlework resting on her lap, she looked up at him and, her eyes brightened for a moment, as she asked hopefully, 'Does that mean this war will now end, my lord?'

With a rueful smile he shook his head, saying, 'I fear not, cariad, but mayhap this victory will bring its end the nearer.'

Catrin's face fell and her eyes clouded again as she asked quietly, 'Will it ever end, Edmund?'

He walked over to her and his hand rested on her shoulder as he said quietly, 'Oh, aye, it will end my love and we must pray it ends in your father's victory over the usurper Henry!' Smiling confidently at her, he nodded. 'Aye we must pray for that Catrin dear, so that Alice and the brother she may have one day shall live in a peaceful world!' Even as he said it, the thought crossed his mind that with many more victories such as that at Campstone Hill there would be few enough men left to celebrate the war's end when it came!

Catrin was frowning now as she looked up at him, to say with a hint of reproof, 'I may bear you a daughter again, not a son, my lord!'

Feeling that he was on safer ground now than the retailing of pyrrhic victories, he smiled confidently again as he replied, 'No, my love. One day you'll bear a son and heir for me!' The smile faded though, as he added quietly, 'Though heir to what I do not know, unless it be to your father's charity!'

Catrin smiled though as, dropping her sewing, she put her hand in his and said softly, 'He will be rich indeed for 'twill be enough, my lord, that he bears his father's name!'

There was little enough rejoicing in Castle Harlech that night over the news of the battles at Campstone Hill and Craig Y Dorth. But the tides of war soon brought more encouraging news to the garrison, dependent as it was upon others for hope of a final victory over King Henry. This time the messenger had not had to travel all across Wales to bring his news, but only from Aberystwyth along the coast to the south of Harlech. Having been warned of his approach, Sir Edmund was waiting somewhat apprehensively in the inner ward to meet the messenger as he rode in through the raised portcullis.

Dismounting he turned towards Sir Edmund, grinning, to say, 'Lord Tudor sends me, my lord, to tell you that he has taken Castle Aberystwyth for Prince Owain!'

Sir Edmund smiled. 'Then that is good news indeed and you shall join us at table to tell us more of what brought about this happy chance!' Then, calling over a man at arms, he told him, 'Have this good man's horse stabled and himself refreshed then bring him to me in my chamber!'

He turned away, to see Lady Marged and Catrin both standing there smiling, evidently having already heard the news. Smiling too, he was about to speak to them when a rousing cheer went up within the castle, echoing and re-echoing around its enclosing wall. Then men were rushing forward, eager to clap the grinning messenger on the back as if to share in some small physical measure the news of good fortune that he brought.

Grinning himself now, Sir Edmund raised both arms: 'Peace!' he cried out. 'Peace! Let the man rest after his journey! It is enough for now that Aberystwyth has fallen to Prince Owain's arms!'

Turning he walked over to the smiling ladies to say quietly, 'We sleep safer in our beds this night, ladies! With Aber fallen, soon we'll hear of Caernarvon yielding to Maredudd!'

The capture of Castle Aberystwyth, heartening though it was to the garrison at Harlech, was not the only cheering news they learnt that spring. Every messenger that arrived at the castle brought word either of Glyn Dŵr's victorious progress along the Welsh marches, or of Lord Tudor, freed from Aber's siege, making a triumphant march through South Wales. News from North Wales was less encouraging to Sir Edmund though, for the English still stubbornly held most of the northern castles even though Glyn Dŵr's supporters there, led by his cousins, the Tudurs of Ynys Môn, dominated the surrounding countryside.

Whilst the news gave Sir Edmund some cause for optimism it also left him increasingly frustrated at his role, which he saw almost as that of an interested spectator rather than active participant. It was of some comfort to him though that Catrin appeared happier now, content it seemed in caring for young Alice. That was something that she seemed to share willingly enough with Lady Marged who seemed to take great pleasure in her role of grandmother.

There seemed to be a constant toing and froing of messengers now bringing word by letter from Prince Owain to the Lady Marged or by word of mouth, either from the prince, or Lord Tudor on his march through South Wales, of a castle taken here, a town laid waste there.

Lady Marged, who did not share Prince Owain's distaste for the clergy other than the Friars Minor, was distressed at the news that he had sacked both Buildwas Abbey and the nunnery at Aconbury, convinced as she was that such sacrilege would bring the wrath of God upon him.

If it were indeed to fall upon him, then it was not to be yet, for all the news that reached Sir Edmund at Harlech was of the prince's continuing success as he marched south along the marches, wreaking havoc amongst the English inhabitants there. Reaching Severn's shore he marched on through Newport to Cardiff to lay siege to the castles there.

Some two weeks after Glyn Dŵr laid siege to Castle Caerdydd, Sir Edmund gave a sigh of exasperation on being warned that a rider was approaching the drawbridge. He was exasperated because these messengers always seemed to arrive when he was about to have a meal, one of the few events at Harlech to which he now looked forward with some degree of pleasure. Reluctantly, he rose from the table in the great chamber to walk across the inner ward towards the main gateway thinking as he did so that were he to tarry at the table the messenger would surely have King Henry close on his tail with a great army!

He had barely reached the main gateway when there was the creaking of the drawbridge being lowered followed by the harsh grating of metal on metal as the portcullis was raised. The inner gates were opening now and the rider rode into the inner ward. Whatever his mission, he had evidently ridden hard, for his horse was all lathered and slavering at the mouth. As the horse stood there just inside the gate, chest heaving, spittle flying from its tossing head, the rider spoke to the guard before walking his horse over towards Sir Edmund.

Frowning, Sir Edmund wondered what it might be that had brought the messenger to Harlech with such obvious haste. He contained his impatience however, and waited whilst the rider dismounted, bracing himself meanwhile for ill news. The man stood before Sir Edmund now, holding the horse's reins and touched his helmet in salute as Sir Edmund asked with as much patience as he could muster, 'Well, what urgent news do you bring to Harlech that you treat your poor horse so?'

Inevitably the news of the messenger's arrival had spread around the castle and men and women alike were hurrying towards them to hear what he might have to say and then purvey it around the castle to all those who chose to listen. Sir Edmund though, aware that in such a closed community as the castle garrison there would be enough buyers of their wares, touched the messenger on the arm and led him away to the entrance of the great hall, then asked again, 'Now what news have you for me?'

The messenger took a deep breath, then his eyes lit up as he replied,

'It is good news I bring, my lord, for Prince Owain bade me ride here in all haste to tell you that Castle Caerdydd has fallen to his arms and that he now marches west to join you here!'

Sir Edmund smiled as he slapped him on the shoulder. 'Then that is good news indeed! So why such a glum face?'

The messenger favoured him with a wry glance before saying with evident reluctance, 'For that I must not linger here my lord, but ride on to Caernarvon to give Lord Maredudd the news there!'

Sir Edmund nodded. 'Quite so, 'tis only right that Lord Maredudd should share the good news, so he may tell Caernarvon's stubborn constable in hopes it might weaken his resolve!' He paused there, thinking that it was unlikely that knowledge of Cardiff Castle's surrender would induce the constable to follow suit. Then looking at the weary messenger he smiled as he added, 'But I think you must make haste slowly to Caernarvon and rest here tonight, for do you ride on, I fear your nag will drop beneath you!'

The man stood there uncertainly for a moment before, frowning, he began to say, 'But my Lord Owain . . .'

With his hand held up to silence the man, Sir Edmund interrupted the messenger, saying, 'You stay here tonight to rest! At table later you can share with Lady Marged more fully how her husband fares on his campaign.' Turning, he called over a man at arms who had been standing as close by as he dared, ears flapping. With a nod towards the messenger, Sir Edmund told him, 'Take care of him, for he has ridden hard to bring us good news from Prince Owain and I doubt not that he would relish a pot of ale and a bite to eat!'

Glancing around he saw Catrin entering the inner ward through a doorway from the outer ward and smiling walked over to her. As they met, he said cheerfully, 'Good news from Cardiff, cariad, your father's campaign in the south progresses well and he has taken the castle there!'

With a glance at Megan standing beside her, Catrin said firmly, 'Take Alice to the chamber now, Megan, she has been out in this chill air long enough!'

Sir Edmund laughed. 'Chill air my dear? Why 'tis summer and 'twill do her nought but good to share the day out here with us!'

As the nurse hesitated, Catrin said sharply to her, 'Megan!' and flushing now, Megan hurried away.

Smiling sweetly, Catrin turned to him now to say with calm authority, 'I grant you, Edmund, that in the governance of all things martial you may know better than I, but in matters domestic perhaps I may be the judge!'

He looked at her in surprise for a moment thinking that whilst summer might have dispelled her melancholia, Catrin was more matron now than the light-hearted girl he had first met in Snowdonia. Grinning though, he merely replied, 'Oh, I would your father agreed with you on that Catrin my dear, so that I might better aid him than to be a sentinel at a safe held fortress!'

It was Catrin's turn to be taken aback now as she asked wide-eyed, 'Why, would you leave me alone here at Harlech, Edmund, whilst you go off to fight your compatriots?'

He gave a wry smile at the thought that even Catrin still saw him as an Englishman rather than her father's ally. Holding back a sigh though, he nodded. 'Aye, my compatriots, Catrin, but your father's enemies and mine as well!' He paused before adding with a grin, 'Nor would I be leaving you alone, for you have little Alice to care for now and your lady mother is here to stand guard over you both!'

She flushed at that, but deftly changed the subject to ask innocently, 'Did the messenger confide when father would bring his men back to Harlech, Edmund?'

As she stood there her blue eyes guileless, he felt guilty at the sudden pang of jealousy he had had as it crossed his mind to wonder whether her question was truly about her 'father's men', or but one of them: the archer Idris. He shook his head and remorseful now at the suspicious thought, said quietly, 'No, my dear, the messenger said nought of that, but he shall be at table with us tonight, when he may tell us more of your father's intentions.'

Between them Catrin and Lady Marged ensured that there was a festive air at table in the great hall that night. Food and ale there was in plenty and wine enough at the head of the table. It was there that Sir Edmund sat in state as befitted the custodian of Castle Harlech and the consort of Prince Owain's daughter. Catrin and the messenger sat on either side of him whilst Lady Marged, of her own choice sat beside the messenger, so that she might glean from him all tidings of her husband. Iolo Goch was there too, with his harp, not in the minstrel's gallery, but there near the head of the table.

The harp's soft sweet notes were clear enough too as Iolo came to the end of his lay in which he had sung of Prince Owain's righteous sword bringing the English to their knees. Fortunately, Iolo had sung in his native Welsh tongue, which saved Sir Edmund from some embarrassment, although from the titters at the lower end of the table each time the minstrel had used the word 'Saesneg' – stranger – he had realised there had been some derogatory comment about the English.

Straight-faced now, Sir Edmund watched Catrin rise gracefully from her chair to walk over to the minstrel and, with her hand resting gently on his shoulder, offer him a glass of wine. The hand rested there too long for Sir Edmund's liking, but Catrin's glance as she walked back to the table was innocent enough and he smiled at her before turning back to the messenger.

'Aye, my lord,' the man was saying. 'Fair put out the Friars Minor were at Caerdydd!' After we took the castle there, we put the town to the torch, save that the prince directed that we spare the street wherein dwelt the Friars.'

Bewildered, Sir Edmund looked at the man with a puzzled frown: 'So why should the Friars be distressed when Prince Owain spared their friary though he burned all Cardiff down?'

With a crafty grin, the man replied, 'Why, my lord, for that as we marched on Cardiff the friars put all their books and silver in the castle for safekeeping!' Still grinning, he added, 'So upset they were when they came to the prince in the castle and he asked them, "Why do you seek them here? If you had kept your goods at home they would have been safe enough there!" '

Sir Edmund smiled. 'Yes, I can see why they may have been upset! Did they get their books back?'

The man shook his head. 'I know not my lord, but with the town burnt to the ground, there was little but the castle for our men to scour for booty, so whilst the friars might have found their books, I doubt they saw ought of their silver again!'

Sir Edmund looked at him thoughtfully, wondering how much of the silver might have found its way to Glyn Dŵr's war chest. Then, sharing the messenger's pessimism, he nodded saying, 'Nor I and if they regained their books that should be benison enough for them!'

After the meal was finished and the great hall empty, save for a few men at arms who seemed intent upon supping all the ale that was left, Sir Edmund, with a word to Catrin, left to do his nightly rounds of the castle. Later, having ensured that all was secure and the night guard alert, he was crossing the inner ward and walking quietly towards the south-east tower when, in the shadows left by a light from a wall cresset, he saw two figures standing there as if in converse that they would have be private.

His curiosity aroused he walked as softly towards them as he might, anxious to find out what it might be they would talk about so secretively. Softly as he went though, the objects of his curiosity must have been alerted by his footfall for there was sudden movement amongst the shadows and Catrin came walking towards him, the messenger following.

Catrin smiled at him in the light shed by the cresset and asked innocently enough, 'Have you finished your rounds, my lord?'

Sir Edmund stopped in his tracks, surprised at Catrin's presence there when he had thought her safely in her chamber. Finding his tongue at last, he replied curtly, 'Aye, I have, but what brings you out here to hold such secret discourse, when you should long since be abed?'

Chin up, eyes flashing in the cresset's light, Catrin asked imperiously, 'Secret, my lord? This is my father's castle, wherein I go wheresoever I choose by right! Nor is there ought secret in my request that the messenger gives my sisterly love to my brother Maredudd!'

Sir Edmund bit his lip to stem an angry response, for he felt humiliated that Catrin had spoken to him so in front of the messenger, who would no doubt retail it with embellishment amongst the garrison. Not only humiliated, he was angry with himself that he had allowed his jealousy to give rise to suspicion of Catrin's presence there. With a stiff smile he replied calmly, 'I was surprised to find you here at this hour with the night so chill madam, but would share in your felicitations to Lord Maredudd!'

With a nod to the messenger, who appeared to be looking at the battlements with great interest, he said, 'I bid you a speedy journey to Caernarvon on the morrow.' Then with a touch of acid in his voice, added, 'Pray give my compliments to Lord Maredudd on his tenacity in maintaining the siege so long!' Whether it was the thought of the journey, or of offering Maredudd the double edged compliment, the messenger did not appear to be enthused with his mission, but touched his helmet in acknowledgement before walking off towards the garrison's quarters.

Offering Catrin his arm, Sir Edmund smiled, 'Let us to our chambers now, Catrin dear.' He paused as he stood there, her arm in his, before saying quietly, 'Should you wish to send messages to your many siblings my dear, I would prefer it that you would have the messenger come to you by day than have you whisper them here in the night's dark shadows!'

Catrin opened her mouth to reply but he placed a forefinger gently on her lips and said softly, 'No, Catrin. I would not have more words put cold distance between us two. Leave it until the morrow, when the same words, more gently said, may heal the wound that I trust was never intended.'

* * * *

The sun was still low in the eastern sky as hearing the clatter of hooves on the drawbridge, Sir Edmund looked down from the window of his chamber to see the messenger crossing the ditch then set off at a canter along the track that led to the north. He stood watching the man go for a few minutes, envying him his freedom, constrained though it might be by his errand. Just a man at arms he thought, yet a freer man than he, tied as he was to the castle by bonds of fealty and marriage.

As the rider disappeared from view Sir Edmund wondered what message he might be carrying to Maredudd from Catrin. He smiled to himself, a sister's love of course, what else? He pondered that for a moment, thinking that it was natural enough that Catrin should send such a message to her brother and, shaking his head in annoyance at the way he had treated Catrin the previous night, he walked down from the tower to breakfast in the great hall.

Whilst Sir Edmund breakfasted, Lady Catrin was roused from her sleep in her chamber by the sound of movement in the antechamber and thought sleepily that it must be Megan attending to Alice. Turning over she snuggled down under the blankets again, smiling happily to herself at the thought of the message from Idris she had been given the previous night. As she repeated the message to herself now she thought, no harm in that, is there? Just sent his felicitations he had, that's all! It left her with a warm feeling though, and she was still smiling as she dropped off to sleep again.

Chapter Twenty-seven

Sir Edmund soon found that any apprehension that the sharp words he had exchanged with Catrin might have caused a rift between them was unfounded, for she seemed happier than she had been for some time. Sir Edmund watched her now from Harlech's south-western tower as, laughing, she and Megan played with little Alice down there in the outer ward.

Her happiness would have been enough to lift his own spirits, but at the end of July in that year of 1404 news had come to Harlech that gave him greater hope for the future than he had held for some time. Glyn Dŵr's envoys had at last signed the long awaited treaty of alliance with France and had gained the promise that a French army under the Count of la Marche would be sent to Prince Owain's aid.

He wondered whether that meant that Glyn Dŵr would now change his religious allegiance from Rome to Benedict, the Pope of Avignon. With a wry smile, he thought that Glyn Dŵr would care little as to which Pope gained ascendancy in the Great Schism which had divided the Church for the last seventy years or more. He chuckled then as the thought crossed his mind that Glyn Dŵr would as readily acknowledge the old seer, Crach Ffynant, as the only true Pope, were it to mean gaining France as an ally!

Far below him a fisherman's boat tossed unsteadily close inshore, but he hardly noticed it as his thoughts ranged over the last two years. His face clouded as he fought the battle of Pilleth all over again, then cleared at the memory of the hours he had spent at the farm in Snowdonia, racing along the meadow there with Catrin. Saw her in his mind's eye now as she rode, her body crouched low over her horse, her hair streaming in the wind, then turning her head towards him, laughing at his attempts to gain on her fleeing horse.

He sighed, thinking that those were the carefree days. Now he was a virtual prisoner again, bound to this isolated castle, penned in with those who saw him as a stranger yet, except little Alice of course, her and Cathy. He pulled himself up with a start. Not Cathy, Catrin! Cathy was that Welsh girl with the mocking blue eyes he had seen in Ludlow's market place. The elusive Cathy who kept flitting through his thoughts like a will o' the wisp on a summer's day. Shaken that this vestige of the malady he had suffered at Ludlow should reappear, he frowned thinking that the wraith, if such she was, had such blue eyes as might have been a match for Catrin's!

He brushed the thought aside, remembering instead how peaceful it had been at Harlech that summer, with Glyn Dŵr away campaigning again along the borders. Only the occasional messenger from the prince had served to remind Sir Edmund that the bloody conflict with England continued. Despite yearning to be more actively involved, he realised now that watching young Alice grow day by day had brought him a contentment that he had not known since Henry Bolingbroke had returned from France to seize the throne.

Catrin too seemed more relaxed and less worried about the future. As Sir Edmund looked down at her now from the tower, she seemed to say something to Megan, then passed her the child to hold. Touching Megan on the arm, she pointed seawards to where the small boat lay almost motionless in the lea of the land, its brown sail hanging limp. Megan seemed to say something to her and, in apparent response, Catrin looked up to wave to him. Even though the distance made her face appear only as a small white patch, he was sure she was smiling up at him, so waving back, he turned and went down the tower to go to her.

He met Catrin as, together with Megan still holding Alice in her arms, she was entering the inner ward. Walking over to them he greeted Catrin cheerfully: 'Alice seemed happy enough in the outer ward, my dear, I was just coming down to join you!'

Smiling, Catrin replied, 'Too late, I fear my lord, for Alice must have her rest now.' Then seeing his disappointment, she added with a laugh, 'She shared the day out here with Megan and I, Edmund, whilst your thoughts up there on the tower were on matters more martial! She is tired now and must rest awhile.' Then, with raised eyebrows, she said, 'Perhaps tomorrow we shall take the air together!'

Remembering their last such discussion, Sir Edmund grinned. 'Indeed we shall, my dear, I shall look forward to it!'

*   *   *   *

The fresh days of autumn were upon them when the news came to them that at last the constable of Caernarvon had surrendered the castle to Glyn Dŵr's son Maredudd. Sir Edmund smiled when he heard the news, thinking how galling it must have been for the constable to hand over his sword to young Maredudd, still barely eighteen.

It was not long after that news reached Harlech though, that alarms were sounding throughout the castle and men were rushing to their battle stations. An armed band had been seen approaching the castle. Whilst that of itself did not seem to pose a threat to the security of Harlech, nought could be taken for granted in these uncertain times and it was as well to be prepared.

Soon it was apparent from the banners the approaching company bore that Glyn Dŵr was at its head. Tensions eased as they all cheerfully made ready to welcome him, looking forward as they did so to the news he might bring of the world outside the castle. Whilst others proclaimed loudly that they had known all along that it was Glyn Dŵr who approached, Lady Marged kept her counsel and made sure that the prince's chamber was warm and fit for his arrival.

Catrin though, seemed to be excited and Sir Edmund looked on amazed as she flitted from one room to another, trying on this dress or that. Laughing, Sir Edmund told her that her father would care little which dress she wore, sobeit that it was tidy, but changing now from a blue gown to a green one, she seemed to hear him not and, shaking his head in amusement, he left her to her toilet.

He was standing in the inner ward when Prince Owain rode slowly, regally, through the gate, followed only by his bannerman and his two captains, Dafydd and the archer Idris. Soldiers of the guard, already mustered there, raised their swords to their lips to kiss the cross, then swept the blades across their bodies with a flourish, to point their swords harmlessly at the ground.

Having dismounted, the prince stepped forward to greet Sir Edmund who, after a handclasp with Glyn Dŵr said, with a wave of his hand to where the Lady Marged waited with Catherine, 'My lord, the ladies are all anxious to greet you on your return and wait to lead you to the hall where food and wine are ready in celebration of your return.'

Even as he did so though, he could see that Catrin's gaze seemed to be directed beyond Glyn Dŵr and turned his head to see a grinning Idris quickly avert his eyes to glance nonchalantly around the inner ward. Sir Edmund gave a sharp intake of breath, but Glyn Dŵr was already walking towards the ladies and all Sir Edmund could do was follow.

Later that night, when they were all seated around the table in the great hall, there was only happy chatter around the table as Glyn Dŵr entertained those around him with tales of his victorious campaign. He was in confident mood too, talking as though the end of the conflict was in sight, now that King Charles of France was sending an army to his aid.

Sitting there toying with his food and with Iolo Goch's triumphant lays in the background, Sir Edmund morosely hoped that Glyn Dŵr's optimism would prove to be justified. He wondered too, how long it might be before he could take Catrin away from this isolated fortress on its crag above the sea to more gentle Ludlow. Suddenly looking down the table, he saw Idris talking to Captain Dafydd, but all the while watching Catrin with a soft look in his eye. Aye, Sir Edmund thought, I'd take her away to Ludlow and away from such as you, archer! Turning to Glyn Dŵr, he asked innocently, 'How long are we to be graced with your presence here, my lord?'

Glyn Dŵr grinned. 'Longer than you would have me, I have little doubt, Edmund, yet not as long as I would wish! Two or three days is all the leisure I can afford here, for then I must go to the north, where I am to meet with Gruffydd Young to discuss matters of state which have come to his notice.'

Sir Edmund smiled as he asked quietly, 'Should not the servant come to his master, my lord?'

With a sharp glance at Sir Edmund, Glyn Dŵr snapped, 'Aye, were there not others he would have me meet who cannot come this far!'

Mystified, Sir Edmund opened his mouth to seek an explanation of that cryptic remark, but evidently Glyn Dŵr was not about to elucidate it for him, for he said tersely, 'Tonight though is not for such matters of state, but for good food and wine.' He glanced at Lady Marged and rising added, 'But there's been enough of that for now and I must get me to the first soft bed I've slept in for many a night!'

Lady Marged was rising now too and offering her his arm; Prince Owain swept her regally out of the great hall, leaving Sir Edmund alone at the head of the table with Catrin. She turned to him to say cheerfully, 'My father's homecoming has been a happy occasion, has it not, Edmund?'

He looked at her straight-faced for a moment, then nodded in agreement. 'Indeed it has, Catrin,' he replied, 'and I see you found much to entertain you below the salt!'

Head on one side now, she pouted, to say with raised eyebrows, 'Why, my lord, I did but smile at my father's captains!'

Straight-faced, he replied curtly, 'Indeed, I saw you smile, Catrin!

Once would have been a courtesy, but too often becomes a familiarity that does not become the constable's lady!'

Catrin flushed and tight-lipped now, she rose, to say scornfully, 'It pleases me that you yet see me as your lady, but now I must go to see your daughter, Alice, settled for the night, my lord!' Then she rose and flinging a shawl around her shoulders flounced out of the hall, her head held up imperiously.

The chatter around the table seemed to quieten for a moment, as eyes other than Sir Edmund's watched her make her exit, but as he glanced around the table, no man even dared to smile at his discomfiture and soon the chatter resumed whilst he was left alone at the head of a cluttered table, moodily drinking his wine.

Soon it seemed that the few others remaining around the table found reason to depart and he was left there in solitary state pondering over the events of the evening. Mostly he thought of Catrin and wondered whether his jealousy had been misplaced. Wondered too whether it had all been in his imagination. Perhaps he should have spoken differently, to keep her by his side instead of rushing off like that.

At last, the wine offering no solace for his ills, he sent the goblet crashing against the wall. Then frowning, he seemed to remember that, beyond the veils of memory, there had been something, somewhere, that had healed all his ills. He could not bring to mind what it might have been though and so, rising unsteadily to his feet, he staggered out of the hall and into the inner ward.

As he weaved his way across the ward, he imagined he saw two figures skulking in the shadows, whispering to each other, but, intent now only on getting to his chamber, he paid them no heed and left them undisturbed to their fumblings.

Catrin stiffened in Idris's arms as she saw Sir Edmund come out of the great hall and stand swaying in the doorway for a moment before lurching off across the ward towards the south-eastern tower.

'There, my love, he'll not bother you tonight,' said Idris with a smile, his teeth white in the flickering light from a wall cresset.

Catrin was looking towards Sir Edmund but turning now to Idris, whispered, 'I must go to him, Idris, for he is not well! He may fall and hurt himself on those stone stairs!'

Idris only pulled her the closer, saying, 'Not well? Why, the man is drunk, Catrin, and no man so drunk ever hurt himself by falling!'

As he bent his head to kiss her again though, she put a hand firmly on his chest to push him away. 'No, Idris,' she said sharply, 'I must go to him, we shall speak again tomorrow!'

He still held her though, and laughed now as he replied, 'Speak, my love? Such speaking does but tease, the more so when you plead to run after your Mortimer!'

She struggled to release herself, pleading now, saying, 'No Idris! Tomorrow, I promise!'

Releasing his hold on her, he grinned. 'But briefly shall we speak then Catrin, my love, for on the morrow, I ride for Caernarvon.'

Ceasing her struggles, she whispered, 'You leave tomorrow? I thought . . .'

Pulling her to him again he said softly, seducingly, 'Aye and so did I my love, but your princely father thought otherwise I fear!' Then, as he bent his head to kiss her again, she did not resist, but with all thought of Edmund's safety quickly fading, yielded to her own desire.

Head throbbing, Sir Edmund stood in his chamber watching from the window as the soldiers who were leaving with Dafydd and Idris mustered outside the castle in preparation for their long march to Caernarvon. As he left his chamber, he gave a wry smile, thinking that for once he did not envy them, not relishing even the walk down to the inner ward.

It was not just the effort he would have to make to do so, but the thought of seeing the knowing looks or hearing the whispered comments of the folk within the castle. Worse would come later he knew though, for then he would have to apologise to Catrin for having abused her for but a smile. He grimaced, not so much at that prospect but at the foul taste in his mouth, sure in his mind now that the wine at table last night must have been sour, even though he knew that he had partaken of a trifle more than prudency dictated.

'Good morning to you, Edmund!' Glyn Dŵr greeted him breezily when he arrived at the gate-house. The prince paused, then added drily, 'You do not look yourself this morning, do you sicken for something?'

Sir Edmund scowled, then replied bitterly, 'Aye, my lord, I sicken for this famous role I am to play for you, which as ever lies in the distant future!'

Glyn Dŵr grinned. 'Aye? Then do you go on sickening, your Maker shall have a greater role for you than I!' He turned his head away then and smiled as the two captains, Dafydd and Idris, marched up to him and touched their helmets in salute. 'Ready for your journey then Dafydd? he asked amiably.

'Ready as ever, my lord,' Dafydd replied, adding with a grin: 'Why,

I'd march there on my knees were I sure to meet the lanceman who pricked my leg on Caernarvon's battlements!'

Glyn Dŵr shook his head as if in sorrow. 'I fear that young Maredudd has robbed you of the pleasure,' he rejoined, 'for I hear he gave safe conduct to those of the garrison who survived the siege!' Suddenly serious, he continued, 'When you meet Lord Maredudd, charge him to march with all his power to Conwy. King Henry has held it for too long and I would have it mine! Tell him too that should the constable there ponder overlong over his submission, he should be offered neither clemency nor safe conduct but pay instead with blood for his stubbornness!'

If Sir Edmund flinched at the import of the message, Dafydd seemed to see nought wrong with it, for he responded straight-faced, 'Aye, my lord!'

A smiling Glyn Dŵr turned to the archer. 'Look after him Idris, and do not let him go storming battlements at his great age!'

As Idris grinned and nodded in acknowledgement, Dafydd snapped, 'One legged, I'd yet climb a scaling ladder 'fore a stripling such as he could lay a hand on my good peg, my lord!' He grinned as he added, 'Why my lord, he'd not lay a hand on me for he knows full well it would bring him as much trouble as does that over-used other peg of his!'

Idris flushed, but before he could respond, Glyn Dŵr said with an exasperated wave of his hand, 'Get off with you both!' He relented then though to add quietly, 'And God go with you.'

Following Glyn Dŵr onto the drawbridge, Sir Edmund saw them mount up and walk their horses to the head of the column. Then at Dafydd's command, the column began its march to Caernarvon. As they set off, Idris the archer turned and waved a hand as if in farewell, but though Sir Edmund turned his head quickly towards the battlements, he saw no one there. He shrugged dismissively, thinking that the archer was arrogant enough to believe that all those in Harlech grieved at his departure!

He turned to Glyn Dŵr to say, 'I thought you might be leaving with that company, my lord.'

With raised eyebrows and a sardonic smile Glyn Dŵr asked, 'Why, was the wish father to the thought, Edmund?'

Sir Edmund flushed in embarrassment. 'Why, no, of course not, my lord! 'Twas but that I thought . . .'

Glyn Dŵr laughed. 'Fear not, Edmund, I leave tomorrow and where I go I do not need such a large escort. They shall serve me better with young Maredudd at Conwy! Now though, I must break my fast, will you not join me?'

His stomach churning, Sir Edmund hesitated, thinking that he needed nothing less than to break his fast at that moment. Glyn Dŵr seemed to read his thoughts though, for he touched Sir Edmund on the arm and said with a knowing smile, 'Come Edmund, a good breakfast will settle the stomach!'

Early the next morning Glyn Dŵr set out for his mysterious destination without great ceremony. Only Lady Marged and Sir Edmund were there to bid him farewell and success to his mission, Catrin having sent word to Sir Edmund that she was not feeling well enough to attend the prince's departure. Sir Edmund stood at the outer end of the drawbridge and saluted as the prince with his escort of a few men at arms rode off, then turned to go to Catrin's chamber, intent now only on discovering what it might be that ailed her.

Entering her chamber, he found her sitting on her bed, her hair not pinned up, but hanging loose about her shoulders. She turned her head as he entered and he could see from her red rimmed eyes that she had been crying. Concerned now for her rather than for his own troubles, he asked anxiously, 'Catrin, my love, what ails you?'

She sat there for a moment, just looking at him before saying, with what he felt was a note of reproof in her voice, 'Nought ails me, Edmund.' She paused, but as she sat there gazing at him with solemn eyes she added wistfully, ' 'Twas just that with Caernarvon and all those other castles taken, I thought that this war would end!'

Seeing the concern in her eyes, he reached out to caress her face and as he did so, she frowned and whispered, 'I am so frightened, Edmund!'

He smiled reassuringly and, trying to comfort her, said softly, 'There is no need for you to be so fearful, my love, for each castle taken, each battle won by your father, brings the end a little nearer. France sending an army here next spring to aid your father will surely signal the end which we so desire.'

He rested a hand on her shoulder and she put her own hand over his to say with a note of resignation, ' 'Tis just that with this war going on for so long, I worry for little Alice . . .' she touched her stomach then with her other hand and added, 'for her and this new child of ours, Edmund!'

He took a deep intake of breath and wide-eyed now, asked, 'You mean that you are with child, Catrin dear?' As she nodded, he smiled and said softly, 'Then have no fear for them cariad, the two of them shall be safe enough here at Harlech.' His smile even broader now, he added, 'Aye, the two of them, Alice and her little brother!'

Her eyes were still clouded though, as she replied quietly, 'I may bear you another daughter, Edmund.'

Caressing her cheek he shook his head. 'No, my love. I'm sure that this time it will be a son you bear for me, and then we shall be doubly blessed!'

Chapter Twenty-eight

Sir Edmund's growing frustration at being restricted to the daily routine of his duties at Harlech was exacerbated by the fact that he felt excluded from the conduct of the war against King Henry and knew no more than any other in the garrison of Glyn Dŵr's plans. His irritation was lost upon Catrin though, for she had lapsed into despondency again, something for which he could discover no cause, other than that she was with child.

There was a coolness between them now too, which at first he saw as a reaction to his own low spirits. He soon realised however, that the edge of her indifference was honed with resentment. Sometimes despairing of overcoming the barrier that now seemed to exist between them, he strove to maintain a cheerful face, for Catrin was the only person with whom he had any great human contact other than on the affairs of the castle. Without that, his office as constable of Harlech would be little better than a prison sentence.

Shortly before Christmas, however, Catrin's despondency seemed to dissipate with the unexpected return of her father to Harlech. He came accompanied only by a small retinue and his Chancellor, Gruffydd Young. Smiling, he greeted a surprised Lady Marged only with the words, 'I came, so that I may celebrate Christmas mass here with you and my family, my dear!'

Sir Edmund looked askance at Prince Owain, thinking that it was more likely the furtherance of some new plot that brought him back to Harlech. Such thoughts were far from his mind though as, when sitting with Catrin at Christmas mass in the small oratory between the east towers, she gently placed her hand on his. Glancing at her, he saw that there was a warmth in her eyes that had not been there for some time and for him, the bleak winter was already over.

After Christmas he became less despondent and was even able to view with some equanimity the comings and goings of messengers on their secretive errands for Glyn Dŵr. It was following the arrival of such a messenger that, one morning at the end of January, he was called to attend upon Glyn Dŵr in the audience chamber. With a toss of his head he sniffed as he walked across the inner ward wondering what scheme Glyn Dŵr now had in mind.

Entering the chamber, he found Prince Owain sitting at the head of the table, silhouetted against the light from the mullioned window. With a curt, 'Good morrow, Edmund!' he waved Sir Edmund to a seat by his side. Sitting beside the prince, grey haired Gruffydd Young nodded to Sir Edmund and gave a slow smile. Barely was Edmund settled in his chair before Glyn Dŵr slapped a hand on the table and said abruptly, 'Well, Edmund, the time has come!' Startled at the exclamation, Sir Edmund could not imagine to what Glyn Dŵr referred and, somewhat bemused replied, 'The time has come, my lord?'

Smiling sardonically, Glyn Dŵr nodded. 'Aye, the time you have long awaited Edmund, the time for you to play your part!'

With a marked lack of enthusiasm, Sir Edmund replied with raised eyebrows, 'Indeed my lord, pray what might that be?'

Exasperated, Glyn Dŵr snapped, 'Why, your part in Henry Bolingbroke's overthrow, of course! Tomorrow we ride to Bangor, where we shall meet Hotspur's father, the Earl of Northumberland.'

Amazed, Sir Edmund looked at him open-mouthed to ask, 'We meet Northumberland at Bangor, my lord?'

Glyn Dŵr smiled complacently and nodded. 'Aye, Northumberland and others such as he.'

Frowning, Sir Edmund looked at him without comprehension as he asked, 'To what purpose do we meet him, my lord, for does he not yet guard the northern march for King Henry?'

Smiling, Glyn Dŵr replied, 'He does so with ill grace I fear, Edmund, for that business over the ransoming of the Earl of Douglas rankles with him yet. Though himself pardoned by Henry, he grieves e'en more that after his battle with Henry at Shrewsbury, Hotspur was executed as a traitor.'

Tight lipped, Sir Edmund nodded, then said curtly, 'I grieve too, my lord, for whilst the Earl lost a son, my sister lost a husband!'

Glyn Dŵr brushed the comment aside with a terse, 'Indeed!' Then added, 'Now, as to the purpose of our meeting, that map on the table before the Chancellor displays better than words that which might be gained from such a meeting.'

Glancing at the map, Sir Edmund saw now that it purported to be a map of England and Wales, yet not one that he recognised. Whilst Wales was shown as being from west of the Severn to the heads of the rivers Trent and Mersey, England was clearly divided by a line marked boldly across its middle, separating the north of the country from the south.

Running a finger along the line representing the eastern border of Wales he looked up at Glyn Dŵr with a puzzled frown on his forehead to ask, 'Are you so confident of victory over Henry, my lord, that you would have him increase your Principality?' Then tapping his finger on the line dividing England said, 'And what pray, does this represent?'

With a superior smile, Glyn Dŵr nodded. 'Confident enough am I, Edmund, that Wales shall be so separated from England and that there shall be not one England but two, as that map clearly shows!'

Sir Edmund laughed. 'I grant, my lord, that do you but gain victory over Henry he might concede a stretching of the ancient border 'twixt our two countries, but carve up England so? He will never agree to that, my lord!'

Complacent now, Glyn Dŵr shook his head as if in sorrow, saying, 'You do not see it yet, do you Edmund? This has nought to do with Henry . . .' he gave a derisive snort, ' . . .except perhaps in absentia! For this is the subject of our debate with Northumbria and the other English nobles.

'This map shows three sovereign countries.' His finger rapped the map of Wales as he continued: 'This, my Principality,' then waving his hand over the rest of the map, 'and a divided England reigned over by two kings, the Earl of Northumberland in the north and your nephew the Earl of March in the south.'

As Sir Edmund looked at him in amazed silence, Glyn Dŵr asked, 'Do you not see, Edmund, this will bring a lasting peace, not only to these three countries, but to Scotland also, for no one country alone could with impunity threaten its neighbour, yet together they could well defend our island shores?'

Sir Edmund gazed at him pensively for a moment, then shook his head as he replied firmly, 'Is this the important role you have long promised me, my lord? That I should deny my nephew his rightful claim to England's throne? No! I can never be a party to that!'

Glyn Dŵr glared at him to say tersely, 'Half a kingdom is better than none at all, Edmund! Where your nephew now dwells it is likely he'll wear a noose before ever he wears a crown. Come man! Can I but persuade Northumberland and the others to agree on this, then Henry's days as King of England will be numbered and your nephew shall be freed and wear a crown to boot!'

With pursed lips, Sir Edmund pondered Glyn Dŵr's remark before at last asking him, 'Would not Northumberland and these others of whom you speak agree upon a sovereign Wales as you propose, yet accept a united England under my nephew's kingship?'

As if sensing victory, Glyn Dŵr smiled. 'What great incentive is there for the Earl to change one king for another, for whose rule he might, with time, care as little?' He paused, then said, 'What surety have I for peace along my borders with a powerful England as my neighbour, resentful of my new won sovereignty?' He shook his head. 'No, Edmund, such division would gain approval not only in England but in Scotland too, where Robert, King of Scots, would feel his own borders the more secure.'

As Sir Edmund still hesitated, Glyn Dŵr said brusquely, 'Come, Edmund, your nephew has nought to lose in this and much to gain.' Seductively then, he added, 'And with him crowned, surely he would reward you with the earldom that he vacates?'

Sir Edmund sat there for a moment, tempted by the proposition despite himself. At last he sighed, then rising slowly, he glanced at Glyn Dŵr, to say quietly, 'I shall think on these things, Glyn Dŵr, and give you my answer when I have slept upon them!'

As Sir Edmund broke his fast next morning after a restless night, Glyn Dŵr came into the hall and sat at the head of the table. His meal served, he glanced at Sir Edmund to ask gruffly, 'Did you sleep well, Edmund, having given thought to the matters we discussed last night?'

Sir Edmund gave him a sour glance, to answer with a short, 'Not a lot, my lord, for you gave me much to think upon!'

Glyn Dŵr sighed at his prevarication. 'Well,' he asked, 'what is the result of your deliberations. Do you ride with me to Bangor?'

Sir Edmund looked down at his plate before glancing again at Glyn Dŵr. Then shaking his head slowly, he replied quietly, 'I fear not my lord. I wish you well and if you succeed in gaining approval for your proposals, then sobeit.' He sighed as he added with evident regret, 'For my part though, I cannot lend my hand to that which denies my nephew his rightful heritage. He is, by Richard's given word, the heir general to the throne of all of England, not just part of a divided one.'

Clearly exasperated now, Glyn Dŵr snapped, 'Aye, heir general he surely is and that to a prison cell if I know ought of Henry! When I have Henry on his knees, your nephew will be a pawn for Henry to bargain with and should I fail, he'll be a sacrificial lamb, his blood spilt to secure Henry's crown! What hopes for his kingship then, Edmund, or you an earldom?'

Sir Edmund replied disdainfully, 'I have no hopes there, my lord, and were I to do so, I'd not relish to achieve them from betraying my own kin!'

Glyn Dŵr scowled. 'You will not ride with me then, Edmund?'

Subdued, Sir Edmund shook his head to say firmly, 'I cannot, my lord!'

Glyn Dŵr sighed. 'Then, I fear for you Edmund, with your notions of the 'courtesies of war' and misplaced loyalty. In this war the only courtesy is to win; the only duty, to share the spoils as equitably as may be. Ah well, I must be away, to gain for Wales and for your nephew, the best price I may for the blood already spilt. I sorrow that you cannot share the burden that it places upon my shoulder, so blame me not if my haggling gains you not the earldom you yet covet!'

Sir Edmund rose to the jibe. 'I covet nought, my lord,' he said angrily, 'except my nephew's freedom . . . and my own.'

Rising from the table, Glyn Dŵr grinned and there was irony now in his voice as he replied, 'Oh, you are free already, Edmund, as your refusal to accompany me on this mission proves. Would that I were so free, for there is nought that I may refuse that leads to a Wales free of English governance!' With that he turned away and Sir Edmund watched as, stiff-backed and spurs jingling, he left the great hall.

Sitting there morosely now, Sir Edmund gazed at his plate for a moment, then, no longer hungry, pushed it from him in disgust. So this was the great role that Glyn Dŵr had in mind for him, he thought, the betrayal of his nephew! A sudden thought crossed his mind and he frowned as he wondered how Glyn Dŵr might react to his refusal to accompany him on the mission.

That was a problem over which Sir Edmund was to ponder upon alone for the next few days as he waited with some apprehension for Glyn Dŵr's return. It was not one he was able to share with Catrin, for her sole concern now appeared to be shielding Alice from the hazards of the childish ailments she faced through the winter. That and preparing herself for the forthcoming birth of their second child.

With Glyn Dŵr's return imminent, Sir Edmund was sitting in his chamber, fearing that he had made the wrong decision in not going to Bangor with Glyn Dŵr. He sighed at the thought that perhaps it would indeed be better for his nephew to be king of half a country than be Henry's hostage. He wondered too whether now, as at Ludlow when he had refused to join Henry's rebellion out of loyalty to King Richard, his loyalty to his nephew was misplaced. He gave a wry smile at the thought that if that were so, then only he would suffer, for Glyn Dŵr needed young Earl Edmund for the plot to succeed.

There were no fanfares of trumpets the next day when Glyn Dŵr led his small escort into the castle's inner ward where, in some trepidation, Sir Edmund waited to greet him. As Prince Owain dismounted, Sir Edmund walked over to him to say with a smile, 'I trust you fared well at Bangor, my lord?'

If the look Glyn Dŵr gave him was cool enough, the response sent a chill down Sir Edmund's spine. Without offering his hand, the prince replied tersely, 'Indeed Sir Edmund? I thought you stayed at home for that you did not approve of my mission there! 'Tis late now for you to hope that it went well and if it did or not, then I wouldst not discuss it here!'

With that he turned away abruptly and strode off towards the great hall to leave a frowning Sir Edmund even more convinced now that he should have gone to Bangor with the prince.

His misgivings were to prove unfounded, however, for at table that night, Glyn Dŵr's frosty mien had gone and he even smiled at Sir Edmund now as he said amiably enough, 'You asked how it went at Bangor, Edmund. It went well enough but I gained no agreement there. It seemed the pill I offered them was too big for them to take it at one gulp, so they sought time to ponder 'pon it, but we are to meet again in February.' Then with a glance at Sir Edmund, he added, 'Yet I sense they favoured it more than you!'

Sir Edmund breathed a quiet sigh of relief, feeling now that Glyn Dŵr's wrath had, at least, receded. 'Perhaps I was too hasty, my lord,' he replied, 'for I see now there is indeed some merit in your proposal.' He hesitated, then said diffidently, 'Perhaps though, the English lords shared my view as to Earl Edmund's legitimate claim to England's throne.'

Glyn Dŵr shook his head. 'Were that indeed so, Edmund, it would not satisfy my concern over the security of my borders with England. No! I must have England's power divided so that, so weakened, it offers no threat to Wales!'

Clearly he had no room for further debate on the matter, for he turned abruptly to speak to Lady Marged, leaving Sir Edmund wondering whether this was yet another occasion when he should have offered his support more patently.

It was something he was to reflect upon again in February when Glyn Dŵr rode off once more to Bangor, this time without asking Sir Edmund to accompany him. He returned more quickly on this occasion and was in ebullient mood as Sir Edmund greeted him. Evidently he remembered the last occasion clearly, for before Sir Edmund could say a word, he said cheerfully, 'Oh yes, I fared well, Edmund, for I have the 'Tripartite Indenture' agreed! They all put their hand to it: Northumbria, Mowbray and Bardolf. With them and France as allies Henry's fate is now surely sealed!'

Sir Edmund slowly nodded his agreement, saying, 'Indeed, my lord, with you having such powerful allies, Henry will have cause to wonder what future England holds for him.'

Glyn Dŵr glanced at him and asked, 'And you, Edmund? Are you now with me in this new venture?'

Sir Edmund nodded. 'I am indeed, my lord!'

Over the next few days, Sir Edmund fretted over his change of heart, consoling himself that when he had wavered over allying himself with Henry, events had proved him wrong. His confidence in having now made the right decision was shattered however, when only a few days later he was again called to Prince Owain's chamber where, as before, Gruffydd Young sat beside the prince. The prince greeted him bluntly. 'Your sister-in-law, the Lady Despenser, has put the fox amongst the hens, Edmund!' Then, without waiting for a reply asked, 'Did you know ought of this?'

Bemused, Sir Edmund gazed at him blankly, to ask, 'Know ought of what, my lord?'

Glyn Dŵr sighed. 'Ought of her abduction of your nephew, the Earl!'

'She has taken Earl Edmund from the king's care?' asked Sir Edmund incredulously.

'I take it then, you knew not of this affair!' Glyn Dŵr replied with a toss of his head. 'Aye, it seems she has indeed abducted him,' he paused, then continued, 'aided it is said by her brother Edward, Duke of York, she has taken young Edmund with his brother Roger and is now on her way to Chepstow, where she would have me take them under my protection!'

Frowning, Sir Edmund asked anxiously, 'And will you not, my lord?'

With an exasperated snort, Glyn Dŵr asked rhetorically, 'How can I not? It will strengthen my position with Northumbria and his friends if I have the Earl in my care. I ride within the hour for Chepstow and you ride with me . . .' he paused before adding peremptorily, 'and this time I'll have no buts or maybes!'

Sir Edmund nodded to say emphatically, 'Nor shall you have, my lord! I shall prepare this instant for the journey!'

Glyn Dŵr grinned. 'Good!' he said. 'Come well armed if you would join me now, for I fear that Henry will not lose his chicks from their nest without a struggle!'

Within the hour, Sir Edmund was alongside Glyn Dŵr as they rode over Harlech's drawbridge with a hastily gathered company of men at arms, intent upon taking Earl Edmund and his brother Roger from under Henry's nose.

It was not to be, however, for before the Lady Despenser and her brother Edward reached Chepstow, Henry intercepted them and took the two young lads once more into his doubtful care.

After the exhilarating ride to Chepstow it was a deflated Sir Edmund who rode wearily back to Harlech with Glyn Dŵr, for he had been looking forward to being reunited with his nephew. He had been looking forward also, to having a companion, be it howsoever young, whom he could trust in that somewhat friendless place.

Perhaps it was that disappointment which committed him fully now to Glyn Dŵr's Tripartite Indenture. Why should Henry, he asked himself, deny Lady Despenser's right to control the destiny of her own sons, what right had he to keep the lads confined? Thinking of his own children, he tried to imagine how Catrin might feel were she in Lady Despenser's position and resolved that, whatever the cost might be, he was now more than ever, committed to Henry's overthrow.

Their return to Harlech empty handed left Glyn Dŵr ill tempered, as the next day he muttered to Sir Edmund that Lady Despenser's plan was ill conceived. 'Had she left it to me,' he complained bitterly, 'her lads would have been freed in but a few months. Now with her ill timed intervention, Henry will be on his guard and who knows in what peril they might be placed when he is ousted from his throne?' It was a question to which Sir Edmund had no answer.

Despite this setback, 1405 began well for Glyn Dŵr, for he now held all the west coast castles and his cousins, the Tudurs of Ynys Môn held Anglesey, together with its powerful castle, Beaumaris. In the south, his brother Tudor and son Gruffydd had confirmed Glyn Dŵr's hold on Glamorgan and were now marching eastwards. With his alliances with France and the English rebel lords, Glyn Dŵr was now confident of victory over Henry and of regaining Wales its sovereignty. Sir Edmund shared his confidence and looked forward to seeing his nephew king, at least of southern England.

There is no certainty in war, however. In their drive eastwards through South Wales, Lord Tudor and Gruffydd assaulted Usk Castle, only to be stoutly repelled by Lord Grey of Condor and Sir John Greyndor. Lord Grey then boldly sallied out with the garrison and pursued Lord Tudor across the river Usk to inflict a bloody defeat upon the Welsh at Pwll Melyn. Nor did he then offer any mercy to the vanquished, for there, before the very gates of Pontfold Castle, the noble lord had some three hundred prisoners cut down like so many cattle at the shambles. Neither Lord Tudor nor Gruffydd were amongst those slaughtered, for Lord Tudor fell honourably in battle and Gruffydd was sent, trussed like a farmyard fowl, to the king's tower in London, there to meditate upon the sins of rebellion whilst he awaited the king's pleasure.

The man at arms who brought the news to Harlech was himself a survivor of the massacre at Pwll Melyn. Sir Edmund immediately hurried to Catrin's chamber, anxious that it should be he who told her of her brother's incarceration, rather than she gleaned it from the castle gossip. When he reached her chamber in the south-east tower though, Megan was with her, comforting her it seemed, in her hour of distress.

Red-eyed, Catrin turned quickly towards him, to ask, 'Is it true, Edmund?'

There was little he could say to that, so he nodded, saying with a sigh, 'Aye, I fear so, my love.' Nor, despite the fact that there had been little love lost between Gruffydd and himself, was it a false note of regret with which he agreed with her. As much as any, Sir Edmund knew well the fate which faced rebels taken by King Henry. Nor did he welcome that fate which awaited him too, should he also be captured by the king.

Her voice low, pleading now, Catrin asked, 'Will King Henry not ransom Gruffydd to my father, Edmund?'

Knowing well from personal experience that magnanimity was not one of King Henry's strengths, he shook his head, saying sadly, 'I fear not, Catrin, my love.'

He regretted having told her the truth as soon as he said it, for she burst into tears and he went over to hold her in his arms, to comfort her as best he could in her distress. She looked up at him then to ask, to plead, 'He won't hang Gruffydd will he, Edmund?'

He lied to her then: 'No, cariad, he won't hang Gruffydd. He'll wait until your father captures someone of noble birth for whom he might be exchanged.' He knew he lied to her though, for he believed in his heart that it was more likely that Henry would display Gruffydd's head and quarters from the towns and castles that Henry yet held in Wales

n

and the marches as a dreadful warning to all those who yet wavered on the brink of joining the rebellion.

Looking at Catrin, all puffy eyed from crying, he smiled at her to say reassuringly, 'Never fear, cariad, for soon now Prince Owain will prevail and Gruffydd shall be freed.' Bending down he kissed her on the forehead and added, 'Then, stone by stone, I'll rebuild Sycharth for you and we shall dwell there with our children!' He paused, wishing there was some way that he might comfort her, ease her pain, yet knew that there was nothing that he might say in truth that would do so. Bending now, he kissed her on the cheek, then said quietly, 'I must go, my love, for I would speak with your father and hear what plans he might have to secure Gruffydd's release.'

Turning, he walked quickly towards the door, which opened even as he reached it, to reveal an anxious looking Lady Marged. He stepped aside to allow Lady Marged to enter. With a glance at Catrin, she whispered to him, 'Catrin knows of Gruffydd and of her uncle Tudor?'

Whispering too, he nodded. 'Of Gruffydd, yes, my lady.'

Raising her eyebrows she confided, 'They sparked often enough, but she loved her brother, Edmund, and she is so young yet to learn the grief that war brings to us womenfolk.

He nodded, to say a little bitterly, 'We are all ever too young to learn what war brings us in its train, my lady!' Then, with a glance at Catrin, he gently closed the door behind him.

Chapter Twenty-nine

If Glyn Dŵr grieved over his brother's death and the incarceration of his son Gruffydd after their defeat at Pwll Melyn, he showed little sign of it to Sir Edmund. Indeed, when Sir Edmund offered his condolences at their fate, the prince brushed them aside with a brusque, ' 'Tis the nature of war, Edmund, and the cost we must suffer to gain our independence!'

Sir Edmund nodded his agreement, thinking that there was indeed a cost to war and one which he knew only too well. He sighed then, thinking that at least young Earl Edmund still lived and with little likelihood at present, it seemed, of sharing Gruffydd's fate.

Some three weeks after the news of Pwll Melyn reached Harlech, a further blow was struck at Glyn Dŵr's optimism over the outcome of his rebellion.

It was towards the end of May when the Earl of Northumberland, deserting his role of guarding the northern marches for Henry, was on the march south to implement his part of the Tripartite Indenture. King Henry, however, was at Derby, on his way to the northern marches when he heard the news. He acted promptly to quell that which he correctly interpreted as another rebellion by the Percies. He soon brought Northumberland and his fellow conspirators to battle and, on their defeat, the Earl together with Bardolf and the Welsh bishops, Byford and Trefor, fled to Scotland, leaving Archbishop Richard Scrope and Lord Mowbray to be executed at the field of battle by Henry.

It was not merely the news of their defeat which cast Glyn Dŵr into despondency though, but the fact that it effectively ended the hopes he had entertained of the Tripartite Indenture. With it vanished any hope he might have had of gaining further alliances or support from the

English nobility.

Sir Edmund shared his concern, for his own future and that of his nephew, the Earl of March, was tied to the success or failure of Glyn Dŵr's war of independence. Of more immediate concern to him was the fact that whilst Glyn Dŵr's residence at Harlech when he was in the ascendancy was bearable if not entirely welcome, his presence there when suffering adversity was nigh on unendurable. Now he seemed to find fault with everything that Sir Edmund essayed.

Worse was to follow, for a few months later in early summer, news came to Harlech of yet another disaster for Glyn Dŵr's cause. Anglesey and the great castle of Beaumaris had been taken from Glyn Dŵr's cousins, the Tudurs, by Henry's deputy lieutenant of Ireland, one Stephen Scrope, kin to the Archbishop Scrope who had been executed at Bramham Moor.

It was not merely the loss of the island and Beaumaris that concerned Glyn Dŵr but, as he was to tell Sir Edmund, the fact that it gave Henry a foothold from which to threaten the whole of North Wales.

These setbacks cast a shadow over all those at Harlech over the next few weeks, including Catrin. Already grieving over Gruffydd's imprisonment and worrying as to what his fate might be, she was now more than ever fearful for the safety of Alice and her unborn child, fears that Sir Edmund found difficult to dispel.

Finding her sobbing in her chamber one day in July, he went over to her, to hold her in his arms and comfort her. As she looked up at him, the tears welling in her eyes, he said quietly, 'Come, my dear, why the tears? Your father's cause is not lost, this is but a setback for him and there are many such in any war. It is the final battle that matters and that he shall surely win! Why, even now the French are preparing to send an army to our aid and will soon join with us. We shall have such power then the very thought of which will make King Henry quake in his shoes and sue for peace!'

Megan came into the room then with Alice and, taking his arms from around Catrin's shoulder, he smiled, to say to the nurse, 'Your entrance is as ever well timed, Megan, for I was telling Lady Catrin that on such a sunny day we should take Alice to the outer ward for her to take the air.'

The look on Megan's face told him that she was not entirely deceived, but with a quick glance at Catrin, she nodded, saying in her lilting accent, 'I'm sure 'twill do her good, my lord.' Then, frowning, she glanced at Catrin with concern in her eyes and asked, 'Are you well enough, my lady?'

Catrin gave her a wan smile. 'Of course, Megan, I am indeed well.' Then walking over to her, took Alice's little hand in hers and started walking out of the room with short, slow steps.

With a couple of strides, Sir Edmund caught up with her to say cheerfully, 'Come, let me carry Alice down the stairs my dear!' He stooped to pick up Alice and, as he straightened, Catrin smiled at him for the first time since he had entered the room.

A few days later, Glyn Dŵr rode out of Harlech to meet his French allies, who he expected to land at Milford Haven any day now. Rejecting Sir Edmund's request to march with him though, he said bluntly, 'Your place is here Edmund, to protect your family and mine!'

If Sir Edmund was disappointed at the order, Catrin seemed well pleased as she stood beside him smiling, as together with Lady Marged they bade godspeed to Glyn Dŵr. Sir Edmund smiled too now as he saw that there was no waving of kerchiefs by Catrin on this occasion. The smile faded though, as he realised that Glyn Dŵr's two captains, the burly Dafydd Mawr and Idris were not in the prince's company, for they were to join up with him later on his march south to Milford Haven.

If Sir Edmund waited impatiently at Harlech for news of Glyn Dŵr's campaign in the south with his new allies, down there in Milford Haven, Glyn Dŵr was even more frustrated at the late arrival of the French. His frustration was heightened when they finally arrived, for they had no horses for their hommes d'elite, knights and gentlemen, whose effectiveness as heavy cavalry was therefore somewhat limited!

That led to further delay whilst the countryside was scoured for mounts for the French cavalry. Glyn Dŵr and his allies meanwhile treated Pembrokeshire as enemy territory before at last marching westward for their fateful confrontation with King Henry.

When news of the allied incursion into England eventually reached Sir Edmund however, it appeared that its conclusion was hardly more successful than its beginning. Apparently, the allies having ensconced themselves amongst the old earthworks on Woodbury Hill, some eight miles north-west of Worcester, they were soon faced from across the valley by King Henry's more powerful army.

After eight days of stalemate, with the allies not having dared to meet his challenge, King Henry broke camp and marched off, leaving the dispirited allies to march back to Milford Haven, where the French embarked again for France.

If Glyn Dŵr was disappointed at this result of the long awaited French support, Sir Edmund was even more dismayed. His dreams of this being the final battle, the one in which Henry was finally defeated, had proved to be but an illusion. If Glyn Dŵr was not prepared to meet Henry in battle when supported by his French allies, what hope was there now, when he fought on alone?

Despite this disastrous news, that year of 1405 was to be a year of grace for Sir Edmund, for two months later Catrin was delivered of a healthy baby. Like the debacle of Woodbury Hill, however, it was another event from which he was excluded until it was all over. Even then he was only allowed to enter Catrin's chamber briefly by Lady Marged, now, more than ever, protective of her daughter.

As Megan showed him the baby, Sir Edmund stood there for a moment looking at the little pink face, wondering what he should say. Before he could say anything though, Catrin looked up at him from where she lay, pale faced, on the bed to say proudly, 'It is a boy child, Edmund!'

Soft eyed, he looking down at her to say with a smile, 'It is a blessing upon us cariad, as is our daughter Alice, and we shall call him Lionel after my grandsire, for he was a Prince of England!' Lady Marged touched him on the arm then though, to usher him out of the room, and he was still smiling as he went, thinking, all he needed now is time: time to provide him with an inheritance fit for a Mortimer.

Despite his pleasure at the birth of his son and heir, the seriousness of Glyn Dŵr's setbacks over the Tripartite Agreement and Woodbury Hill, soon brought Sir Edmund to the harsh reality that he was now Glyn Dŵr's only ally and a powerless one at that. It was on that alliance that Sir Edmund reflected somewhat despondently as he stood on the battlements braving the blustery January winds. He shivered and pulled his cloak more tightly around him as he thought bitterly that the French would be unlikely to send another army to Wales after so ignominiously scuttling back to France. Nor would Lady Despenser, much as she hated Henry, risk his wrath with another attempt to free the young Earl of March, the only legitimate challenger to Henry's throne.

The only glimmer of hope the last year had left him with was Henry's failed attempt to invade Wales after the disaster at Woodbury Hill. Even then, he thought, it had been the weather, not the Welsh, that had driven a bedraggled Henry back into England. He gave a wry smile, thinking that if it was unlikely that the French would be back, perhaps Henry might be equally unenthusiastic about another such venture!

In a somewhat happier frame of mind, he went down from the tower and made his way to Catrin's chamber where he found her telling little Alice the ancient tale about the maiden formed from flowers. Frowning, he said irritably, 'I wish you would not fill her head with such fantasy, Catrin. 'Twould be better were you to begin to teach her letters!'

Catrin raised her eyebrows to say with a disapproving sniff, 'Letters, indeed, Edmund? She is too young for such things and my story but serves to mind her of her heritage whilst we pass away these dreary winter days!'

'Mind her of her heritage, Catrin?' he replied tersely. 'Why, this flower maiden of whom you spoke is but a myth! You'd do as well to tell her of those ancients who raised the stones of Bryn Celli Ddu and made the Old Religion out of their study of the stars and who now are long since dead and gone!'

Catrin gave him a knowing glance to say softly, 'They are not dead and gone, Edmund, for they live on in such as that wise old soothsayer, Crach Finnant, who knows more of what the movement of the stars portend than we shall ever learn! Despite the preachings of the Popes of Avignon or Rome, the learning the ancients gleaned over the millennia is with us yet and their ancient festivals of fruitfulness are embraced within this new religion!'

A strange feeling came over Edmund then, for even as he looked at her he saw for a moment, not Catrin, but the elusive Cathy of his dreams. He shook his head as if to rid himself of the vision, yet it was still to the wraith he spoke as he said firmly, 'That is blasphemy, Catrin! You must not speak of such to the children and that for their own dear sakes, if not for your own hope of life hereafter!'

Catrin smiled as she gazed at him serenely, as if bowing to his whim, yet sure in her own mind of where the truth might lie. 'I am your wife, Edmund, who as such must obey your command.' She paused there before, chin raised defiantly, she asserted, 'Yet I am a prince's daughter too and must raise our children in the knowledge of their ancient heritage, one which flowered and thrived before the Saxon invaded our shores. Nor did the Romans, try as they might, entirely stifle that ancient lore which will live on when you and I are long since gone.' She smiled confidently as she continued, 'The seeds of knowledge of the Old Religion, still nurtured by such as Crach Finnant, will flower again when the right season comes and that will indeed be the day when Wales is its own self again!'

Her face was just a blurred image now as he gazed at her mesmerised and though the voice was clear, incisive, it seemed to him that it was indeed the wraith Cathy who spoke. He found himself sweating now as if in the grip of his old fever. Driven by his own fears as to his hold on reality, he replied harshly, 'No such magic, Catrin, will gain Wales its independence, only your father's strong right arm! It is for his success that we must pray, not rest our hopes in some necromancy that properly lies long since buried amongst the stones of Bryn Celli Ddu! Meanwhile, I would have our children reared in the faith of the true religion! Nor would your father argue with me on that!'

That last he knew was something of which he could speak with confidence, for any hope Glyn Dŵr might have of future aid from France rested in changing his religious allegiance to the Pope of Avignon! Turning on his heel, he stalked out of the room and went to his own chamber, as concerned now about Catrin's talk of 'the Old Religion' and the effect it might have on Alice, as he had been about the progress of the war against Henry Bolingbroke.

It seemed, though, that Catrin held no resentment over their disagreement, for going to her chamber later that day he found her in surprisingly good humour. He smiled at her, saying, 'It pleases me that you are happy, Catrin, but have you heard good news that I have not yet shared?' He hoped indeed that it were so, for there had been little enough of that for many months!

'Good news indeed, Edmund,' she replied happily, 'for Alice is to wed!'

Frowning, he stiffened for a moment, then grinned as he asked, 'Your sister Alice, I trust, my dear?'

Catrin gave a little bubbling laugh. 'Of course! We shall have to wait a few years yet before our daughter weds!'

His face suddenly serious, he thought, pray we are all here to see that day, but brushing the thought aside, asked quietly, 'Who is Alice to wed, my dear, is it someone known to me?'

Rising, she walked over to look out of the window for a moment before, smiling again now, she nodded as she replied, 'Perhaps Edmund, for like you, he is an English knight!'

He laughed in disbelief. 'An English knight?' he asked. 'Who is this knight that scorns his king's grace for sake of love?'

Head on one side, she smiled as she replied softly, 'Why, someone much like you, my lord, for time was when you'd have said the king's grace was well lost for love!'

He frowned and shook his head. 'Of course it is, my love. I did but mean . . . well, that there are few English knights who might so invite Henry's displeasure!'

Her lips pursed, she remained silent for a moment before saying with a sly laugh at his discomfiture, 'You may well know him, Edmund, for he is Sir John Scudamore!'

A perplexed frown on his brow, Sir Edmund stared at her in amazement now as he replied, 'Surely not, my love, for he fought bravely when he repelled your father's assault on Castle Carreg Cennen! What could bring him to wed your sister?'

Catrin smiled knowingly. 'Perhaps it was his kinsman Phillip Scudamore, who has long supported my father's cause!' She shrugged. 'At all events, for these last two years Sir John has been the channel through which my father has received money from monasteries in south east England!'

He shook his head in disbelief, wondering what else had been kept secret from him besides Alice's wedding and now this! Frowning, he said quietly, 'This cannot be, Catrin, for it is such treason as would cost Scudamore his head!'

Still smiling, she nodded and put a finger to her lips, then whispered, 'Oh, 'tis true Edmund, for he was so accused, but the king, not believing his accusers, hanged them for theft! 'Tis why the marriage will be in secret, when Sir John will retire to his manor in Monnington,' she gave a little snigger as she added, 'where Alice will keep house for him.'

Still amazed, he replied quietly, 'Then I pray for both their sakes that it remains a secret, for there are few manors where there be no wagging tongues!'

It was a bitterly cold February morning when with Catrin, well muffled up, by his side, he stood in the inner ward to bid godspeed to Alice and her mother, Lady Marged. He put a hand gently on Catrin's arm as she dabbed her eyes with a kerchief. Alice would not be returning, for she was setting out for her secret wedding. As the ladies disappeared through the gateway with their escort, Catrin turned to him to ask, 'Will I ever see her again, Edmund?'

The tears were there again now and he put a finger to her cheek to brush them away, saying reassuringly, 'Of course, my love, when this war ends we shall visit her at Monnington and they shall come to Harlech, or wherever we shall dwell and we shall laugh and talk of this secret affair!'

Two weeks later, Lady Marged returned to Harlech and if she had any misgivings over the reasons for her journeying, she bore them well, saying only to Catrin, 'There child, your little sister at least is safe in England now!'

Shortly after Lady Marged's return, Glyn Dŵr was leaving Harlech again, this time for Pennal, just south of Abermaw, where he had called a council, hopefully to gain assent to acknowledge Pope Benedict of Avignon as the true head of the Church. Upon this any further aid from France now depended.

Glyn Dŵr did not return from Pennal, apparently now busily preparing for a great offensive against King Henry in the spring. Sir Edmund was not greatly excited to learn that, with some opposition from the bishops present at the council, Glyn Dŵr's proposal had been endorsed.

He was disturbed to hear that in Scotland, King Robert III being close to death, had sent his son, James, to France fearing for his life at the hands of the Duke of Albany who would be regent on the king's death. It seemed that the English had learned of this, however, and the young Scots prince had been captured by one of King Henry's ships, leaving the Duke of Albany to rule the Scots now as a client of the English crown.

As if that blow to Glyn Dŵr's hope of gaining a Scots ally were not enough, the spring of 1406 brought Sir Edmund new concern with the news that King Henry was now offering his grace and pardon to all those Welsh rebels who submitted to him.

Sir Edmund's concern was to prove justified. After six long years of a war which had impoverished Wales, the thin trickle of those deserting the Welsh cause increased to a steady flow. In November, no less than two thousand men of Anglesey paid their fines and submitted to the king.

It was a harsh winter that year and, with his own growing concern, he found it increasingly difficult to reassure Catrin that, with the western castles still held for Glyn Dŵr, the children were safe at Harlech, concerns not lessened by the fact that they had nowhere else to go.

With little to distract him from his fears for the future, it seemed a long winter for Sir Edmund, his only consolation being that there would be no fresh incursion into Wales by King Henry, at least, not until the spring.

Spring was not long advanced before he was deprived of even that consolation, for Prince Henry, together with some of the king's most able commanders, laid siege to Aberystwyth Castle. Whilst Prince Henry's attack was not entirely unexpected, Sir Edmund was dismayed that an English force of this size had so freely penetrated so far into Wales as to make a determined assault on one of the western castles.

If nothing else it encouraged him to redouble his efforts to ensure that Harlech's defences were in good order, for if Aber fell they would surely be Prince Henry's next target and if Harlech fell . . . but he dared not think of that! Catrin did though, and when not inspecting the castle's defences, he was endeavouring to reassure her that they were safe enough.

Summer came and Rhys Ddu of Anhuniog, Glyn Dŵr's commander at Aberystwyth, still held out against the English. With growing optimism, Sir Edmund confidently told Catrin that with Glyn Dŵr's army now in Gwynnedd, Aberystwyth's siege would soon be relieved

As the days and weeks passed, with no news from Aberystwyth nor yet of Glyn Dŵr being on the march, he even began having thoughts of sallying out from Harlech to go to Aber's relief. He knew though, that he dared not leave Harlech undefended, knew too, that with his bare hundred men it would be but a forlorn hope, serving only to present Harlech as a gift to Prince Hal: he could but wait and hope. He could not understand though why Glyn Dŵr did not hasten to the relief of Aberystwyth before it was too late.

In Gwynnedd, Idris stood talking with Dafydd Mawr gazing at Snowdon, bemoaning the lean pickings there had been for them so far that summer. 'It's a real campaign we need, Dafydd,' he was saying despondently, 'else it will be a lean winter we'll have from a summer of pilfering along the marches!'

Hearing the clatter of hooves, he turned to see a group of horsemen approaching the camp and asked Dafydd hopefully, 'Do you think they bring us news?'

'Aye, though not good news I fear, Idris,' Dafydd replied drily, 'for that's Rhys Ddu who leads and he holds Aber for the prince!'

Together they watched Rhys Ddu greet Prince Owain before they nosily sauntered over to glean what news they might from his escort. Dafydd Mawr smiled as he asked their gaunt captain, 'Will you have a pot of ale with us, Captain, whilst you wait upon Lord Rhys?'

Grim faced, the captain shook his head as he replied tersely, 'I thank you, but I dare not. We ride straight back to Aberystwyth if the prince does but give us leave.'

Dafydd shrugged before asking innocently, 'What news do you bring from Aber that has such urgency then Captain?'

The captain looked at him with shrouded eyes as though reluctant to confess what that might be, then said quietly, 'Rhys Dhu has made truce with Prince Henry and comes here to ask Prince Owain for leave to yield Aber to the English and thus save his starving men!'

Dafydd Mawr gaped at him in amazement, then asked in disbelief, 'Is that truly the burden of Rhys Ddu's errand here?' Seeing the glum faced captain from Aber just nodding in reply, Dafydd drained his pot and, his eyes ice cold now, said curtly, 'Prince Owain will not have him yield Aber, not for all the men therein, for it is key to his hold on all West Wales! If Aber falls, then Harlech will be the next and who knows where it may end! Nor shall you return to Aber alone!' He turned to Idris. 'Come Idris, we must ready our men for the march!'

They did not ride that day though, for a few days were to elapse before Glyn Dŵr could muster his forces and set out on a forced march to the relief of Aberystwyth. When at last they arrived there, it was with such a show of strength that brooked no attack from Prince Henry. To stiffen the sinews of the castle's garrison, Glyn Dŵr sent Rhys Ddu's captain ahead to assure them that if they did not hold the castle for him, Rhys Ddu would hang. The eleven men within who had also signed the truce indenture with Prince Hal were being given notice of their fate.

The truce now obviously at an end and Glyn Dŵr's forces outnumbering his own, Prince Henry prudently declined battle and departed whence he came, harried constantly by the Welsh along the way. With Aberystwyth Castle secure again and its garrison reinforced, a smiling Idris turned to Dafydd Mawr to say, 'A victory at last, Dafydd!'

Dafydd nodded, then said with a touch of bitterness, 'A victory, Idris? That was one we should never have needed. Whilst we in Gwynedd stood idly by, our comrades here were under siege, yet we did not march to bring them succour! Too many victories like this will yet cost our prince his coronet!'

Chapter Thirty

At Harlech, Sir Edmund remained unaware of how desperate things were at Aberystwyth and ignorant of what action Glyn Dŵr might be taking. He was relieved therefore to receive the message that the prince was making all haste in going to the relief of Aberystwyth Castle with a great army. More than that he could not glean from the messenger who, when asked whether the prince required Sir Edmund to join him, said the prince only desired that he hold Harlech safe. Pausing only to gulp down a pot of ale, the soldier rode off to rejoin Glyn Dŵr, leaving Sir Edmund concerned now as to whether the prince would arrive in time to raise the siege.

Some ten days later there was great excitement in the castle at the sight of an approaching army. The excitement was tinged with more than a little apprehension as all there worried as to whether it was a victorious Glyn Dŵr, or Prince Hal fresh from a conquest at Aberystwyth, who approached. The apprehension was soon dispelled though when Prince Owain's banner could be seen fluttering proudly in the van of the army. Sir Edmund hurried down to the inner ward to await Glyn Dŵr's arrival, anxious now to learn how he had fared at Aber.

His fears were soon allayed though, when Glyn Dŵr came through the portals followed by his two captains, his cheerful countenance evidence enough of a mission accomplished.

Smiling now, Sir Edmund greeted the prince with an eager, 'Aber is yet held for you then, my lord?'

Glyn Dŵr grinned. 'Were you so fainthearted as to ever doubt it, Edmund? Of course it's held and the more secure for my visit there! There are no faint hearts there, not now I've weeded out the one or two who would have infected the whole garrison with their talk of yielding!'

Sir Edmund wondered for a moment what grim action Glyn Dŵr might have taken against the 'faint hearts' but brushed the thought aside, this was no time to question Glyn Dŵr's action there. Whatever that might have been, it had secured the safety of Harlech as well . . . for the time being.

Turning away, Glyn Dŵr walked over to greet Lady Marged and Catrin now, before looking at Sir Edmund to say with a smile, 'It seems that you've been busy at making me a grandfather again Edmund! Come, let me get rid of this armour and we'll share a glass of wine whilst we talk of Aberystwyth's plight, so that you may avoid the errors they made in their defence.' With a sideways glance he added, 'It is as well you learn from their mistakes, for one day young Prince Hal may come knocking on your door!'

Shortly afterwards they were both ensconced in Glyn Dŵr's chamber, where over their goblets of wine, Glyn Dŵr instructed Sir Edmund as to the additional measures he must take for the defence of Harlech. So detailed were these that the wall cressets were being lit without Sir Edmund having had the opportunity to ask the question that had concerned him most over the whole affair. That question might one day be of critical importance to them all at Harlech: why had Glyn Dŵr delayed so long in going to Aber's relief?

The prince was in buoyant mood at table in the great hall that night as he related, for the benefit of Lady Marged and all those close by, all that had happened at Aberystwyth. Sitting alongside him, Sir Edmund listened intently, still anxious to learn from the strategy Prince Henry had employed in his assault on the castle. As Glyn Dŵr had so grimly warned him, the English prince might one day use those strategies in an assault upon Harlech!

He still could not understand though why Glyn Dŵr had not gone to relieve the siege earlier and when having done so, he had not brought Prince Henry to battle. When Prince Owain paused to take breath, Sir Edmund put the question to him as delicately as he might.

Glyn Dŵr turned and glowered at him. 'Sitting snug here at Harlech, Edmund, you have little understanding of the problems the commander in the field might face, be it me or even Dafydd Mawr down there below the salt! None at all!'

Taken aback at the impassioned reply, Sir Edmund could only listen frozen faced to the tirade that followed.

'My forces were deployed along the marches,' Glyn Dŵr continued angrily. 'There was no time to bring them west to Aber and had I done so, t'would have been too late to be of help! No, I had to act quickly and so I did. In days I marched on Aber with two thousand men. Men they were indeed. Men who'd left their pitchforks and grabbed a sword. Young lads, shorter than the bow they carried, their best armour a leather jerkin, their last fight over a friend's wench they'd laid!

'Aye, I took them and brought them home again, with Castle Aber safe! Had I chosen to take them against Prince Hal's battle hardened army with half the nobility of England at its head, how many men of mine would now be on their way to mind their farms again? There is a time to fight, Edmund, a time that I know well, and there is a time to take what you have gained and hold it against all who come!' He shook his head and, to Sir Edmund's surprise, added quietly, 'No, I was glad enough that when Prince Hal saw the size of my force, he fled the field!'

Reaching out to fill his goblet from a ewer of wine Glyn Dŵr raised it to his lips, swallowed it in a gulp then slammed the goblet back on the table. With sudden insight, Sir Edmund realised that Glyn Dŵr's anger was directed mainly at his own self. Understood too the concern he might have felt at taking his hastily gathered army of farm hands against Prince Hal's battle hardened army. Dreading, no doubt, the dire cost of failure.

He looked down at the table, then glanced up at Glyn Dŵr to say quietly, 'You are right, I did not know, my lord.' He shrugged as he added, 'There is nought I can say, save that Harlech is safer for your actions and for that I thank you. For my part, when the time comes, as come it must, I'll hold this fort to the death against all who come!'

There was a shadow of a smile on Glyn Dŵr's face now as he replied, 'Aye, I know, Edmund. You'll hold Harlech as I'll hold Wales, for there is nowhere else for us to go!'

Sir Edmund glanced at him, wondering whether he detected a hint of war weariness in the prince's words. If there had been however, it was not apparent now, for rising, Glyn Dŵr smiled and slapped Sir Edmund on the back as he said, 'Yet I would not change a jot of it for Henry Bolingbroke's crown! Now I must not loiter here but get me to my bed, for I march north at sun up!' With that he turned to go but had only taken a pace or two before he turned to point an admonishing finger and say sternly, 'You hold Harlech well for me, Edmund, for I may not be at hand to save you as I did Rhys Ddu!'

Thoughtful now, Sir Edmund watched him go, wondering at the vitality Glyn Dŵr displayed despite the heavy burden he bore. He was roused from his thoughts by the clatter of dishes, and glancing around him saw that the great hall was nearly empty save for himself and a few servants clearing away the remains of the night's meal. He smiled, thinking that they too would have to be up betimes, for Glyn Dŵr would break his fast before departing. Rising, he walked slowly out of the hall and went to his own chamber, smiling at the thought that he too must rise early, to bid god speed to Glyn Dŵr.

It was a calm moonlit night as Idris stood in the shadows outside the great hall. He had been there for a few minutes now, wondering whether he dare go to her. He had not been close enough to even touch her for what seemed to be an age and yet the old yearning lingered still. Heart pounding, he stood there, his back to the wall, catching an occasional glimpse of Catrin up there on the battlements. He had been coming out of the hall with Dafydd when he first glimpsed her there and, pretending that he had left his knife on the table, had let Dafydd go on ahead.

Plucking up courage, he had been about to step out of the shadows when he had heard footsteps and shrank back against the wall. There was no reason why he should not have been there, yet he felt guilty, felt the need for secrecy. That was heightened now as he watched Sir Edmund step out of the great hall and, head bowed as if deep in thought, walk towards the entrance to the south-east tower wherein lay his chamber.

Breathing a sigh of relief, Idris watched him disappear into the tower before, taking a deep breath, he prised himself away from the wall and walking across the inner ward began climbing the staircase that led to the battlements.

Catrin turned and gave a gasp of surprise as he went out onto the battlements. 'Idris!' she exclaimed. 'What are you doing here?'

He was silent for a moment and just stood there gazing at her and taking in the look of surprise on her face, the wisp of hair that strayed from beneath the scarf around her head, her eyes bright in the moonlight. Nor could the generous cloak she wore conceal that she was heavy with child again. When at last he spoke, his was voice husky with emotion as he asked, 'What are you doing here? It seems 'tis time my lady was in bed!'

Catrin smiled. 'It's where I come when I seek solitude, Idris, some time to think of what has happened to us all!'

He walked towards her slowly, as though she were a fawn that he wouldst not frighten, but she just stood there looking up at him solemnly as he reached out to her. Then, as he bent his head to kiss her, she sighed and resting a hand on his shoulder, said softly, 'We must not, Idris, for it is a part of our past that we must treasure, not sully now!'

He still stood there with his arms around her for a moment, then reluctantly his arms dropped to his side and, hurt now, stepped back from her to say stiffly, 'It was not always thus!'

She shook her head and with that slow smile that fond memories bring said, a little wistfully, 'No, it was not ever thus, Idris, my dear.' She sighed again, then said, 'But Sycharth lies in ruins now amongst whose ashes lie our carefree youth.' She sighed and nodded as if just talking about them had brought the images back to life. 'Yes, I often think about those days, Idris,' she continued, 'and remember how frightened I was when you were going off with my father to fight Lord Grey of Ruthin.'

Smiling now, he said quietly, 'I know cariad, and I held you close and calmed your fears then as I would now.'

She shook her head. 'My fears then were real enough, Idris, but the ones I have now are ever with me. Fears for my children should Harlech be taken, the fear that this war will take my other brothers as it has taken Gruffydd and fear for him lying in chains in London's tower. I have little but fear left now, Idris!'

As he looked at her and saw the tears glistening on her cheeks, his heart went out to her and he said quietly, 'Harlech is well held for the prince, Catrin, and when your father brings King Henry to heel, Gruffydd will be freed!'

The words sounded feeble enough to him and Catrin gave him a sad little smile as she replied quietly, 'You sound just like Sir Edmund, Idris, for he tells me much the same, yet I think that this war will end in nought but sorrow and I am frightened for all those who follow my father's banner!'

He flinched, then gave a harsh laugh. 'If I am lumped together with all those, Catrin,' he said bitterly, 'then fear not for me, for I am paid my due and must face the hazard!'

Head on one side, she moved towards him slowly and as she drew near, rested a hand on his arm. There was a catch in her voice now as she put a hand on his cheek and said softly, 'Oh, most of all, I fear for you, dear Idris.' Suddenly her arm was around his neck as she reached up to kiss him on the lips, then just as abruptly she turned and walked slowly over to the staircase that led to the inner ward. She turned her head towards him there and he could see the tears on her cheeks as she said, 'God go with you, Idris, for I doubt that we shall meet again . . .' She seemed to frown then and perhaps it was only in his imagination that he heard her add softly, ' . . . not in this world!' Then she was gone and all he was left with was the memory of her lips on his and the sound of her footfalls on the stone steps.

The first blush of dawn was in the eastern sky as a bleary-eyed Sir Edmund stood in the inner ward waiting for Glyn Dŵr to appear. For once he was not wishing that he was riding off at the prince's side, sure in his mind that whilst Prince Hal might have been repulsed at Aberystwyth, he would be back with even greater power. The sound of voices interrupted his thoughts and he turned his head to see Glyn Dŵr's two captains talking as they stood together nearby. Dafydd Mawr turned towards him and touched his helmet in salute but the archer Idris just glanced at him and gave the slightest nod of his head in acknowledgement of his presence there. He was about to rebuke the man for his lack of courtesy when Glyn Dŵr appeared, all booted and spurred ready for his journey.

The prince seemed to be in ill humour though for, with a perfunctory nod to Sir Edmund, he stomped over to the two captains to ask the man at arms gruffly, 'Are all the men ready for the march, Dafydd?'

Dafydd Mawr seemed used to the prince's humours though, for touching his helmet again, he nodded to say with a grin, 'All ready, my lord, and eager to get back to their farms and nurse their sheep!'

Glyn Dŵr appeared not in the mood for such repartee, for he replied curtly, 'Well, what are you standing there for then? Let's be about it!'

With that, the three of them were mounting and with a terse, 'Keep a sharp watch here, Edmund, for you may yet have visitors you'd not want at table!' Glyn Dŵr dug in his spurs and led the way through the gateway.

Sir Edmund frowned as he watched them go, knowing that Harlech's security depended as much on their campaigning success as ever it did upon whatever defence he might put up against a siege. Better for them to keep the enemy from the door than for him to try to prevent Prince Henry from battering it down!

Soon after Glyn Dŵr's departure, Harlech and all the countryside around was covered in a white blanket. Nor was the news that came at the end of February any more favourable, for it caused Sir Edmund even greater concern for his sister Elizabeth. From what the messenger said, it appeared that the Earl of Northumberland, no longer welcome in Scotland, had marched south with such forces as he could now muster. Arriving in Yorkshire, he had been brought to battle and killed on Bramham Moor by the sheriff of that county.

Saddened at the perilous position in which the Earl's death placed Elizabeth and her children, Sir Edmund was even more concerned over the advantage gained by King Henry.

With the Duke of Albany a client ruler over Scotland, Henry's northern borders were secure and now the threat of a powerful, rebellious magnate in the north had been removed. Nor was he threatened by France any longer, for the Duke of Burgundy had had the Duke of Orleans murdered and had entered into a truce with England. King Henry was at last free to concentrate on quelling the Welsh rebellion.

Grim faced, Sir Edmund watched the messenger leave the chamber thinking as he did so that whilst Bramham Moor had been but a skirmish, it was as great a defeat as any that Glyn Dŵr had yet suffered.

The coming of spring lent Castle Harlech a more cheerful aspect but it served only to increase Sir Edmund's concern and he anxiously toured the castle and its environs daily, seeking weaknesses an enemy might exploit. His foraging parties were scouring the countryside too for provisions that they might store, for he knew well that the greatest enemy the garrison might face was the spectre of starvation.

Early that summer he learned that the English Prince Henry was marching on Aberystwyth with a powerful force including canonry in its train. Even worse news followed when he learnt that another English force under the command of the Talbot brothers was approaching Harlech. Their visit, he was sure, would be no mere courtesy call.

How long, he wondered, could he hold out with enemy canonry battering at his gate. It was not a question to which he had an answer any more than he could offer reassurance to Catrin and her mother, Lady Marged, who fearful for the safety of the children, constantly assailed him with the same question.

He shared their fears as he stood on the battlements searching for sign of the approaching army. Especially now, he thought, with little Elizabeth having been born only last month. He smiled, remembering that they had named her Elizabeth after his sister. The smile faded, as he wondered how his sister fared up there in Northumbria, alone now except for her children. Sighing, he shook his head, knowing he could not help her or the young Earl Edmund, not with the threat he now faced at Harlech.

Chapter Thirty-one

When the Talbot brothers finally laid siege to Harlech, it was not the size of their force that concerned Sir Edmund so much as whether the great brass cannon that accompanied them could breach Harlech's walls. He was somewhat relieved however, to find that, for what remained of summer, it bombarded Harlech's stout walls without success.

Looking out of Catrin's chamber now, Sir Edmund saw a countryside already tinged with russet, announcing that autumn had arrived. Surely, he thought, Glyn Dŵr must be on the march westwards now. He turned to see Catrin looking at him, a worried frown on her brow. She sighed, then asked despairingly, 'No sign?'

Smiling, he shook his head, to say reassuringly, 'Your father will come soon my love, for with summer over, he'll end his campaigning on the borders and come to our aid. Prince Henry and the Talbots will have no hope of reinforcement then, and Prince Owain will have them at his mercy!'

She looked at him doubtfully now, to ask quietly, 'But how much longer may we hold out, Edmund, with our stocks of food already low?'

He laughed. 'I see no scarecrows on our battlements, cariad! If our stocks run low, your father prevents their baggage trains reaching the Talbots!' His laugh was a hollow one though, for he knew, as Catrin must, that the Talbots scoured the countryside for provender, whilst preventing foraging parties from leaving the castle.

They heard a roar then as the 'The King's Daughter', hurled another missile at the castle walls and Sir Edmund gritted his teeth, anxious now to hide his concern from Catrin. How long, he wondered, before the cannon breached the castle walls, allowing the Talbots' men to surge into the castle. He swallowed at the thought, knowing that with the English outnumbering them, there would be little hope remaining then. He gave a wry smile as he realised that even he saw them now as 'the English'. Pray God, he thought, that they saw him as Welsh, for the prospect of being executed as a traitor brought the bitter taste of bile to his throat. He braced himself, thinking, it will not come to that surely, for Glyn Dŵr will not let the western castles fall!

Over to the east, the thought of Harlech being besieged was something that was worrying Idris. He was imagining it all now, the English storming the castle, taking it and taking Catrin too, for they'd care little whether she were maid or princess in their lust when the fighting was done. He closed his eyes, trying to shut out the images that came to his mind's eye, but they remained there, tearing away at his heart.

He turned to Dafydd Mawr to ask bitterly, 'Why do we linger here, Dafydd, when we should be marching to Harlech's aid? Must we wait, as we did last year when Rhys Ddu came to the prince, pleading to be allowed to submit?'

Dafydd Mawr pursed his lips, then shaking his head in exasperation replied calmly, ' 'Tis always questions with you, Idris bach! Why this, why that! If you do not know, why should I? I am but a soldier whose duty is to obey, as yours should be, not question the whys or wherefores of this or that at every turn!'

Frowning, eyes screwed up, Idris snapped back, 'Must duty stop us from seeing that which is right, Dafydd? There's no great campaign which prevents us now from hastening to Harlech's aid, nor has there been all summer. All we've done this summer is to harass the English along the marches! With nigh on half of Wales lost to the prince, his power thus at an ebb, 'tis time for him to hold on to that which he yet holds 'til the tide turns again!'

Dafydd Mawr sniffed. 'There you go again, Idris,' he said reprovingly, 'playing strategist now you are, when you should earn your pay by playing the soldier. Your guide should be to do your duty, aye, and that without question!'

Idris looked at him askance, to say with irony, 'There you speak the truth at last Dafydd! Let duty be our guide but let it not rob us of the power to think, or we'll both be dead soldiers ere long.'

Head on one side, Dafydd seemed to consider that for a moment before replying quietly, ' 'Tis how a soldier finally earns his pay, Idris, e'en should it arise through another's error! Letting your heart rule the way you fight a war is a soldier's greatest sin. In none of this are your thoughts of Harlech's walls, but of she who dwells therein. Until you can put that aside, let Prince Owain do the thinking for both of us!'

It was early October when the lookouts on Harlech's towers at last saw an army approach. Sir Edmund was at table in the great hall when the messenger came hurrying to him to break the news. Catrin's face lit up and she sighed in relief, saying, 'Thank God, Edmund! My father has come at last!' Glancing at her straight-faced he did not answer her but turned instead to the messenger to ask quietly, 'This army, it comes from the east?'

The messenger hesitated, then shook his head. 'No, my lord, from the south!'

Sir Edmund nodded thoughtfully and said with resignation, 'Then it is Prince Henry!'

Dismissing the messenger, he smiled pensively as he turned towards Catrin and saw the crestfallen look on her face, the tears already welling in her eyes. There was despair in her voice now as she asked, 'Are you sure it's not my father, Edmund?'

He hesitated, then shaking his head, replied, 'No, my love, but it can only be Prince Henry who marches on Harlech from the south.'

It seemed that she still did not understand for she frowned, saying, 'But that cannot be, for you told me Prince Henry is besieging Aberystwyth!'

He wondered how he might break the news gently, but knew there was no such way, so he just shook his head before saying, with a sad smile, 'Aye, my love, and so he was. That he now marches to join the Talbots here means Aber has fallen and that we are your father's only hope in the west!' The tears were rolling down her cheeks now and he went over to her to hold her, to try and give her comfort when there was none that he might offer. His fingers trying to stem the flow of her tears on her cheeks, he said softly, 'Come my love, what's this, tears from a princess? That can never be! This is the time when you must be brave, for our people will be looking to us for strength!' He smiled then as he added, 'Your father's daughter will not fail them in their hour of need, now will she?'

Catrin sniffed, then shook her head, and even with tears welling in those blue eyes of hers and her lips trembling, she said, 'No, I shall not fail them, Edmund, 'tis just that I fear for the children!'

Holding her close to him he caressed her cheek, whispering to her that Prince Henry, though an enemy, was an honourable man who did not take his vengeance out on children. 'Nor will he on you or your mother, my love,' he said reassuringly, before adding with a confidence he did not really feel: 'But have no fear of ought of that for, with autumn here, there is nothing to detain your father from coming to our aid. You'll see that he will not have Henry's banner fly over Harlech's towers!'

The one bright piece of news that accompanied Prince Henry's arrival at Harlech was that he came without his great cannon, 'The Messenger', for it had been destroyed in a self destructive explosion when firing during the final stages of the siege of Aberystwyth. There was some comfort to be found too, in that the garrison suffered from no shortage of arrows, for even the children gathered up armfuls of the spent missiles showered on Harlech from the augmented force now besieging them. It was small comfort to the garrison, for much of those that were salvaged were spent trying to bring down the seagulls that were the only addition they could make to their now depleted stores of food.

There were no fat men around Harlech now and as each day passed the rations were halved then halved again. Seldom were there children to be seen playing or laughing in the inner ward now. Hunger, or more like starvation, was taking its toll on them too and they lay listless in their quarters, kept there for safety's sake. As the enemy's daily toll of the defenders grew, women manned the battlements alongside the men, to present to the enemy the illusion of there being a greater number of defenders than there really were.

No one spoke of hope of relief now, for isolated as they were from the outside world, they knew not whether there was anyone left who might indeed come to their aid. All that was left for them to hold on to was Harlech. Their only purpose in life now a stubborn determination to resist, to survive.

With the new year of 1408, yet another envoy came to the castle gate from Prince Henry under a flag of truce to call on them to surrender. As he stood there across the drawbridge from Sir Edmund, he said arrogantly, 'His Royal Highness, Prince Henry demands you yield this castle to his arms. Knowing that you have no hope of succour from outside its walls and none of gaining provender for your garrison, he offers you this last chance of surrendering with honour. Yield now and you may yet save the lives of those within. Yield not and you damn them to the dire penalty that awaits all rebels!'

Sir Edmund was really only half listening to the man, rather was he thinking of the time when he had stood outside this very gate giving a similar message to the then custodian of the castle.

When the man had finished giving his message, Sir Edmund smiled before saying firmly, 'Pray tell Prince Henry that I thank him for his courtesy, but that since I hold Harlech for Owain, by the grace of god, Prince of Wales, I may yield it to no other.'

The man, his face flushed with anger, retorted, 'I'll give no such message to my prince from an English rebel, Mortimer! You yield or not and that is all there is for me to tell or him to hear. Surrender now, or you shall receive no mercy when at last you yield, as yield you must, for then your head will adorn Ludlow's gate, your four quarters tell towns across England of the reward a traitor earns!'

Sir Edmund smiled. 'Why sir,' he replied, 'with such diplomacy it is a courtier you should be, not soldier! Yet for you to exact such penalties you must first cross this threshold and that you'll find is but a forlorn hope, for it shall choke with your dead 'fore even one gains entrance here! My compliments to Prince Henry and pray tell him to depart whilst yet he may, for we have little room for prisoners here!'

The English envoy glared at Sir Edmund, then without a word in reply turned on his heel to march stiff backed towards the English encampment.

Sir Edmund stood there for a moment, hand on hip, knowing that in the English camp all eyes would be on him, gauging his confidence, wondering what reply he had given to their demands. He smiled, thinking that they would know soon enough and then the assault would start all over again! Turning, he sauntered into the castle again as though he had all the time in the world, had only ventured outside to take the air. As the great gate slammed shut behind him though, he paused to take a deep breath, thinking as he did so of his message to Prince Henry. Brave words, he thought now, but pray God they are not put to the test!

Looking around at the few gaunt figures waiting around to hear from his own mouth what their destiny might be, he wondered how many of them had prayed that he would yield. His eyes clouded as he asked himself how many of them would pay with their lives for those brave words of his which had spurned their hope for life!

He saw them then, Catrin holding Alice by the hand, her frail mother, Lady Marged, standing beside her, leaning heavily on a stick. Megan the nurse, wide-eyed with apprehension was there too, with Lionel and little Elizabeth. Looking at them he wondered now what his rejection of Prince Henry's mercy would cost them all.

He sighed, knowing that there was no turning back now. What was done, was done and they must face the renewed assault together, as they would assuredly fall together unless Glyn Dŵr came soon. Smiling, as though he brought them good news, he walked towards them but, even before he reached them, he tensed as 'The King's Daughter' roared her defiance of his message to Prince Henry and hurled her great missile at the castle's walls. For a moment he faltered in his stride but bracing himself, strode on as the defenceless group watched his every stride.

There was neither accusation nor approval in Lady Marged's voice when she greeted him. 'You did not yield then, Edmund!' she asked.

It was a statement not a question and with a glance at Catrin, he just shook his head.

Lady Marged sniffed again, but there was a hint of approval in her voice now as she said, 'It is as well, Edmund, for I'd have had you cast into the dungeon had you done so! This is my husband's castle and none but he shall give it up to the English and they'll wait long enough for that!'

Sir Edmund grinned. 'Then I am glad my message to Prince Hal meets with your approval, my lady, for I have no more liking for your husband's dungeons than I had for his caves! Perhaps 'tis you who should have spoken with the English envoy!'

Lady Marged snorted. 'Envoy, indeed! He was but a messenger. Should I speak at all it shall be with the usurper's son, not with an errand boy!' She turned towards one of the men at arms standing behind her. 'You may take me to my chamber now, Iestyn!' she said with authority and, taking her by the elbow, the man at arms led her slowly away.

Seeing the other two men at arms who had been standing behind her walk away now, Sir Edmund realised that her threat of putting him in a dungeon had been no idle words. He grinned, thinking that perhaps he might have been safer there! Catrin was coming towards him now and putting a hand on his forearm she said quietly, 'We must hold out Edmund, for my father will come soon now, you'll see!'

He gave a wry smile. 'What need of your father here, my dear, when your mother is in command!'

He stopped there and looked at Catrin in amazement, for there was a defiant ripple of cheering rising from the battlements. Evidently the men at arms who had been at her mother's elbows had spread the word of Sir Edmund's response to the English envoy. For the first time, he felt that he really belonged there at Harlech and not with the English forces outside the walls. Smiling at Catrin now he said confidently, 'Never mind your father's coming, cariad, with such men as these around us we can hold out 'til the second coming of Christ himself!'

*   *   *   *

As the days and then the weeks passed with no sign of Glyn Dŵr, Sir Edmund sometimes looked back on those words of his, wondering with not a little resignation, which of the two might reach Harlech first.

Like all the others, he was always hungry now for there was nothing left in the cellars, nothing at all. Mostly his hunger was only a dull ache, something he tried to ignore, for thinking on it merely made it worse. It was more difficult though, for him to ignore the wasted figures, the hollow cheeks of the children, cradled in the skeletal arms of Catrin and Megan the nurse.

Lady Marged seldom left her chamber now and one day in February he dragged himself up to her chamber wondering as he did so whether, her resolve weakened by hunger, she would tell him to yield. Whether indeed she was yet alive to tell him anything. All was silent when he arrived outside her chamber and knocked hesitantly on the door. Gaining no answer, he gently opened the door and entered the room to find that she was indeed alive, if only just.

Propped up by pillows, her shrunken face the colour of old parchment, she gazed at him with faded blue eyes as he entered. As she lay there still, he wondered for a moment whether she really was alive, then one of the frail hands resting on the bedcover feebly gestured him towards her.

He walked slowly towards her to stand at the bedside looking down at her, wondering as he did so whether the indomitable old woman thought they must submit. He knew in his heart though, that it was all too late for that, for they'd get no quarter now. As Lady Marged opened her mouth to speak, he bent his head towards her, but her voice was strong enough as she told him defiantly, 'You must not yield, Edmund! My Owain will be here soon now!' Her head dropped back on the pillow then and looking up at him, she added, 'Yes, he will be here any day now!' With that confident utterance, she dismissed him with a tired wave of her hand.

Smiling down at her, he nodded and echoing her defiance, replied with more hope than conviction, 'Aye, my lady, he will be here any day now!' Turning, he walked thoughtfully towards the door, wondering as he did so whether Glyn Dŵr's arrival would be soon enough for him to meet Lady Marged in this world.

As day followed weary day the bombardment of the castle continued unabated. Arrows and crossbow bolts fell around them like a deadly hail, interspersed with the fearsome roar of 'The King's Daughter', which vainly tried to breach their sturdy walls. Still they waited with fading hope for Glyn Dŵr's arrival, with the only sustenance they could now gain being to chew on strips of leather softened by long boiling, though seldom long enough to render it palatable. Occasionally too, there was the luxury of a stew made from a cornered rat and grass scavenged from around the battlements. Perhaps it was that which at last brought the fever amongst them and laid so many low.

Making his way around the battlements to encourage those few still able to bear arms, Sir Edmund himself gained strength and encouragement from them in that they greeted him with weary smiles of companionship. Never now did he sense resentment in them, or gain the feeling they saw him as a turncoat, but rather that they saw him as a companion in their adversity. One day, bathed in sweat from climbing to the battlements, a feeling of euphoria came over him and, strangely, he knew somehow that his destiny lay there, one that he would not change for all the comfort and peace of his days in Ludlow. He knew that he belonged here now, knew that it was somewhere he would end his days, with Cathy.

He stumbled then, and as he fell to his knees he was thinking, no, not Cathy, Catrin! Confused now, he seemed to remember her telling him once that she could help him. He was thinking of that and hoping that she would come to him soon, when the swirling mists overcame him and he felt himself sinking slowly but inexorably into oblivion.

He felt a cool hand on his brow, a cold damp cloth wiping the perspiration from his face and opened his eyes to see that he was in his own chamber, his own bed, with Catrin standing there beside him. He gave her a wan smile and when at last he could find his voice, said quietly, 'I'm glad you came Catrin, my love.' He frowned then, as he remembered thinking of her when he was up there on the battlements, hoping that she would come to help him. He tried to sit up, only to find he had no strength and fell back again to let his head rest on the pillow. Frowning again, he asked, 'What happened, how did I get here?'

She gave a gentle smile that did not hide the anxiety in her blue eyes. 'You had a touch of fever up there on the battlements, Edmund dear,' she said with a show of cheerfulness. Looking at him now with a tenderness he remembered from their days at the farm, she added, 'There's been a lot of it around the castle these last few days. You've been doing too much, not resting enough. A day, perhaps two and you'll be well again!'

He raised himself up onto his elbows to say irritably, 'I can't stay here for a day or two, Catrin! There's too much to do, too much to guard against!'

She laughed, saying, 'I fear then my love that it will have to wait, for it was struggle enough to bring you here the once, do you but fall again, then you shall have to lie in the castle yard!'

Even as she spoke though, her face was becoming misty, her voice sounding as though it were echoing along some empty corridor and Sir Edmund, his eyes already closing, let his head drop back onto the pillow.

It was the noise that woke him two days later. Shouts of alarm, running footsteps and the clash of arms. He sat up in the bed, strangely alcrt as thc door to the chamber opened and Catrin came running into the room with Megan and the children following her as though seeking shelter there. Swinging his legs out of the bed, he asked wide-eyed, 'What's happening, what's the matter?'

Horror struck, hands trembling, Catrin hesitated a moment before she replied despairingly, 'The English! They've breached the walls!'

He was already out of bed, standing there on shaky legs, looking anxiously around the room for ought he might wear, for weapons.

Frowning now, tears in her eyes, Catrin cried out, 'You can't go Edmund, mustn't go, you are sick!'

He turned to her as he hastily donned trousers, to say tersely, 'There are no sick or well in Castle Harlech today, Catrin my love, only the quick and the dead!' Already though, he was strapping on the few pieces of light armour that had been discarded when he was brought there from the battlements. Then, grabbing a sword as he went, he was rushing out of the room, beads of sweat already running from his forehead into his eyes. From behind him came Catrin's cry, pleading, 'Don't go, Edmund, don't leave us!'

Outside the door, he stood for a moment, catching his breath and wiping the sweat from his brow after the exertion of the last few minutes. Then he hurried on down the spiral staircase and out into the maelstrom of interlocked bodies into which the inner ward had been turned. Even as he did so he was glad to feel the weight of the sword he had worn at Pilleth in his hand, for this mêlée had none of the daintiness of the fencing master's art but rather the hacking brutality of the knacker's yard.

That one step was all it took for a hulking man at arms to come charging at him, a great sword raised above his head menacingly, his face distorted in anger, blood lust. Instinctively, Sir Edmund raised his own weapon to parry the man at arms' deadly slash before being rocked back on his heels by the fury of the man's attack, his arm jarred through to the shoulder as their swords clashed. Then, the sweat streaming down his cheeks, it was cut and thrust as each tried to gain the advantage, with Sir Edmund, his arm aching, feeling his strength ebbing with each stroke. It seemed that the enemy man at arms sensed this, for his attack became manic now and, his sword raised defensively across his body, Sir Edmund was driven back against the wall of the tower. Snarling, the man at arms pushed his sword irresistibly against Sir Edmund's, to leave him helplessly pinned against the wall. Wide-eyed, Sir Edmund saw him draw a dagger with the other hand and begin to thrust it at his throat.

Despairingly, he thought with anguish of not having told Catrin that he loved her before rushing down to the inner ward. Even as he did so, Iestyn came rushing towards him and, with one mighty swipe of a great battle axe, felled the English man at arms and the man's dagger fell harmlessly to the ground.

As Sir Edmund pushed himself from against the wall, Iestyn grinned. 'Good to see you on your feet again, my lord! Try and stay that way!' Then turning from Sir Edmund he threw his head back to bellow a rallying cry. 'A Mortimer, a Mortimer!' he roared and, to Sir Edmund's amazement, there was a sudden surge by the few scarecrow defenders as inch by inch the English were pushed back towards the gate.

Outnumbered as they were by the English, their rally could not last and step by step they were driven back against the castle's inner walls. Iestyn stayed by Sir Edmund, watching his back. He stayed there fending off assailants until he was felled by a blow from a mace. Sir Edmund watched horrified, as a passing lanceman stuck his lance in Iestyn's throat as casually as he would have stepped on a spider, then went rushing on blindly without pause or thought.

Sir Edmund gave a quick, despairing glance around him to see that there were no longer groups of defenders resisting the English, only in ones or twos were they fighting desperately now with their backs against the walls, no longer it seemed with any hope of repelling the English, but just fighting to survive.

Arms aching and running with sweat from his exertion and fever, he fought on. Not to hold Harlech for Glyn Dŵr now, but like all the other defenders, for survival. Aye, for that and for Catrin and the children too. A man in a leather jerkin came rushing at him, an archer from the wrist guard on his left wrist, but Sir Edmund cared not who or what the man might be, only saw that he was no master of swordcraft. The man's sword was raised now to slash viciously at him, a stroke Sir Edmund deftly parried, before thrusting with all his failing strength at the leather jerkin. A red flower suddenly blossomed on the man's chest as he fell to his knees, his mouth gaping, staring in surprise at Sir Edmund as he fell.

Minutes that seemed like hours passed as Sir Edmund fought on, the sounds of battle diminishing now as one by one the defenders succumbed to the English onslaught. Three men at arms were attacking Sir Edmund now, intent on killing the man who had been the cause of that last rally by the defenders. Still he fought on with desperation, knowing it was his only hope of life, for there'd be no quarter now, not after their stubborn resistance. He parried yet another blow then thrust at an attacker. As he did so he felt a blow on his shoulder as though he had been struck by a sledgehammer. He staggered from the impact and slowly his knees buckled and, eyes misting over, he fell to the ground, still clutching his bloodied sword.

As he lay there waiting for the coup de grâce he knew must come, his eyes cleared for a moment and he saw the tall figure of a knight approach, a sword hanging carelessly from his hand. He was standing there now, looking down on Sir Edmund through the slit in his helmet. As Sir Edmund watched, waiting with a dry throat for the inevitable, the knight slowly raised his visor.

Sir Edmund gasped, to say in amazement, in fleeting hope, 'Geoffrey! It's you!'

The eyes that looked down at him were brittle hard though as the knight replied scornfully, 'It's Sir Geoffrey now, Mortimer, and I've come to see how a traitor dies!'

With that, Sir Geoffrey de Lacey raised his sword and Sir Edmund turned his head, exposing his neck. As he did so he caught a glimpse of Catrin, together with Megan and the children, standing between two English men at arms at the entrance to one of the castle's towers. Her eyes were wide in horror as she stared at him and he thought for a moment that he heard her calling to him, but her voice was cut off by a loud swishing noise that filled his ears and suddenly there was only silence and a darkness which enveloped him completely.

Epilogue

LUDLOW – APRIL 1999

Cathy looked up as the door opened and Idris walked into the living room. She smiled as she put down the magazine she had been reading and rose to her feet to say with a wave of her hand, 'Hi! You been busy?'

He shrugged as he replied, 'Oh the usual: surgery, then my morning rounds.' Cathy watched as he went over to the alcove he called his study and put his black leather medical bag down beside his desk. Glancing over his shoulder at her now, he said, 'Oh, by the way, Mrs Tomlinson has had her baby, a boy. Eight pounds!'

Cathy grinned. 'That's four she's got now! She'll be disappointed! She told me she wanted a girl this time!'

Idris grunted: 'I don't suppose it'll stop her trying again!' He paused, then said, 'What's for lunch?'

Smiling a little apprehensively, she replied, 'Lasagne.' Idris grinned. 'Make it yourself?'

She bridled at that, painfully aware that cooking wasn't exactly her strong point. 'Well, I cooked it anyway,' she snapped, then softening, added, 'and there's a bottle of that chianti you like, to go with it.'

Idris sighed, to say with not a little exasperation, 'You know I can't drink when I'm on duty, Cathy!'

He must have seen the crestfallen look on her face then though, for he relented and grinned, to say with a toss of his head, 'Oh all right! It'll have to be just the one glass for me though . . . and not too many for you, either!'

Her face flushed, Cathy flounced out of the room and into the kitchen. Sighing again, Idris called after her, 'Just a joke, Cathy!' His attempt to retrieve the situation though, was met with a stony silence from the kitchen, except for the rattling of dishes.

It was only a storm in a teacup, for a couple of minutes later Cathy was smiling again as she brought in their lunch and he smiled too, trying to make amends as he sniffed and said with perhaps just a touch too much enthusiasm, 'That smells good. Looks good too!'

Sitting down at the table, he poured a glass of wine for Cathy and a rather smaller one for himself and began eating the pasta. Cathy picked up her glass and took a sip of wine before saying hesitantly, 'Oh, Idris . . .'

He sensed from the tone of her voice that she was going to ask him something over which he was not going to be enthused. A forkful of lasagne half way to his mouth, he glanced at her to ask cautiously, 'Yes?'

She was looking down at her plate, toying with her meal, but looked up at him now to say, still hesitantly, 'I was thinking . . .'

His fork still poised there, he said impatiently, 'Well spit it out, darling! What were you thinking?' Then he shovelled the lasagne into his mouth.

She took a deep breath, as if plucking up her courage, then said, 'I was thinking that its a week now since that business outside the jeweller's in Ludlow and wondered if we could go and see Eddie Mortimer?'

If he were enthused about the idea he managed to hide it very well, for suddenly he was engrossed in his lunch. It seemed to Cathy that he continued eating stolidly for ages before saying with his mouth half full, 'Well, it's a bit of a busman's holiday for me really, isn't it, darling? Only met the chap once anyway!'

He didn't say so, but the look on his face told her more than anything he might have said that he hadn't liked Eddie very much then either, probably because he knew Eddie was on drugs she thought. As she remembered how Idris had helped her get over her own problem she thought that he, of all people, should know that sometimes something could be done about that. Fairly obviously though, it was not going to be done by Idris, not this time!

Disappointed at his reaction to her suggestion, there was a hint of pleading in her voice now as she replied, 'Oh please, Idris! I'm sure he doesn't know anyone around here and it was quite brave of him to tackle those thieves like that, wasn't it? According to the local paper the police caught them because of what he did! No harm in us just going there to see how he's getting on, is there?''

He sighed, then pursing his lips as though about to bow to the inevitable, he said with obvious reluctance, 'Tell you what, Cathy, I'll give the hospital a ring this afternoon from the surgery and see how he's getting on, see if he can have visitors!'

Her face lit up. 'Oh, will you Idris, that will be great! Perhaps we can go and see him tomorrow, if that's all right!'

As he carried on eating his lunch he replied non-committally, 'Yes, perhaps so.' Even as he said it though, it seemed he was already beginning to regret his concession, for he added, 'Of course, perhaps Mortimer has already been discharged.'

That evening, as they were sitting down to a snack supper, Idris looked up at her. 'Oh, whilst I remember Cathy, I did ring the hospital about that chap Mortimer.'

She smiled. 'Oh, thank you darling! What did they say?'

In between mouthfuls of ham sandwich he told her. Mortimer it seemed had been more or less unconscious for the best part of three days, much of which time he had been in delirium, rambling on about the Glyn Dŵr rebellion which he seemed to have read about in a book about the Mortimers of Ludlow they found in his rucksack.

Frowning, Cathy asked, 'Was his delirium caused by the beating he got from those thieves?'

He avoided her eyes now as he answered her, 'Well, it seems he had more problems than just that!'

Cathy lowered her eyes to her plate, then looking up at him all innocent now, asked, 'Why, was he on drugs or something?'

He looked at her appraisingly for a moment, as though he were thinking, as if you didn't know! He didn't pursue it though, just nodded and said, 'Yes, something like that.' Thoughtful now, he chewed on his sandwich for a moment before asking her, 'Do you remember when he had lunch with us at Worcester and nearly fainted when David slapped him on the shoulder? He wouldn't let me look at it then, but John Humphries, the doctor who's been looking after him, is a Territorial Army medic and saw right away that what was obviously a battlefield wound on his shoulder was badly infected. It must have been as much because of that as from the blow he got in the raid on the jeweller's, that caused him to pass out.'

There was a horrified expression on her face now as she remembered that night in the barn, when she had seen those terrible scars on Eddie's shoulder and chest. Subdued now, she whispered, 'He must have been in awful pain then, Idris, even when we saw him!'

Idris must have noticed that Cathy was not exactly surpised by any of that which he had told her, for he commented drily, 'Yes, no doubt! I knew there was something wrong with him that day in Worcester, but you can take a horse to water and all that sort of thing! Anyway, I've said we'll call in and see him tomorrow just before lunch. John Humphries said we'd better make it before twelve because Mortimer might be getting discharged then.'

He had hardly finished, before Cathy was smiling happily and saying cheerfully, 'Oh, that will be splendid, Idris. I hated thinking of him lying there in that old hospital thinking that no one cared whether he was dead or alive.'

Sardonically now, Idris replied, 'Oh, he's alive all right, but he's going to have to change his ways if he's going to stay that way!' He changed the subject, saying, 'By the way, I've arranged for us to view the Old Vicarage in the village on the way back from the hospital. It's up for sale and this cottage is a bit small . . . for the two of us!'

She was dressed all ready for him and having coffee with Big David when he came into the cottage's sitting-room the next morning. He stood just inside the front door looking at them in surprise before saying, 'Hello, David, nice to see you! What's brought you here?'

Rising, David smiled that slow smile of his. 'Oh, Cathy told me you were going to see Eddie Mortimer this morning, Idris,' he said, 'thought I'd come along, if that's all right and if there's room in your car for me as well!' He grinned now as he slapped his leg and added, 'Just thought that wounded old soldiers like me and him must stick together!'

Smiling now, Idris nodded as he replied, 'Of course! Delighted to see you anyway, David!' He grinned now as he added, 'You sure you can hobble to the car?'

There was that slow smile again as David nodded, saying, 'Aye, sure enough, Idris! The Falklands and the Sir Galahad may mean I don't run so well anymore, but I'll still walk you off your feet!' He glanced at the engagement ring on Cathy's finger and stroked his drooping moustache thoughtfully before adding with a knowing smile, 'Anyway, Cathy tells me you're going to see the Old Vicarage afterwards, so I s'pose we'd better be on our way!'

Idris grinned. 'It wasn't exactly meant to be a secret, David, we just haven't got round to telling anyone yet!' He paused, then contiued, 'Yes, if you're fit, I suppose we had better get going.'

Big David nodded understandingly and with a courtly wave of his hand showed Cathy to the door then, limping, followed her out of the cottage and waited whilst Idris locked up.

It didn't take them long to get to the hospital at Ludlow and, after Idris parked in a space marked 'Doctors Only', they walked into the reception area where Cathy and David waited whilst Idris spoke to the receptionist. A few minutes later a white coated doctor, stethoscope around his neck, came hurrying into reception and shaking Idris by the hand greeted him with: 'Good to see you, Idris!' Idris briefly introduced him to the others as Doctor Humphries and with that, Humphries was leading them along corridors smelling of antiseptic, talking quickly to Idris as they went. They were at a glass panelled cubicle now and Doctor Humphries was saying, 'Well, I must dash, Idris. Anything else you need to know, just give me a bell!' Then he was hurrying off down the corridor.

Looking through the glass panel Cathy could see Eddie sitting on the hospital bed with his back to them. Suddenly hesitant now, apprehensive, she turned to Idris, who waved a hand towards the door. She stood there for a moment looking into the cubicle, surprised to find that just seeing Eddie sitting there made her heartbeat race. Taking a deep breath to steady herself, she walked through the door that Idris was holding open for her. As she did so, Eddie looked up from the book he was reading then, his eyes widening in surprise, he was saying, 'Catrin! what are you doing here?'

Eyebrows arched, she looked at him for a moment then smiled as she said, 'There's formal! Nobody calls me Catrin these days though, just Cathy!'

Still looking surprised he shook his head, before saying, 'I could have sworn you told me to call you Catrin!' He shrugged then smiled. 'Doesn't matter!' he said dismissively. 'It's good to see you again.' His eyes were running over her now as though taking in her presence, her appearance. 'Yes,' he said again, 'it's good to see you again . . . and looking so well too!'

She frowned briefly, wondering what he meant, before saying quietly, 'I don't know about me but you are looking much better than when I saw you lying in the road outside the jeweller's! I thought those men had killed you . . . and the jeweller as well.'

Eddie grinned ruefully. 'Yeah! As I was passing out, I thought they had, but thanks to Doc Humphries I think I might just survive! Oh yes, I went to see old Mr Roberts the jeweller yesterday, when the doc told me I was walking wounded, he's in the next ward. He was still a bit shaky, but getting on fine he said.' Reaching over to the bedside cabinet he picked up a small leather trinket box and showed it to her, saying, 'He sent this over to me this morning!'

He opened the little box then to reveal a heavy gold ring nestling in its bed of blue velvet. Wide eyed, Cathy asked, 'That's nice, what is it?'

Eddie smiled. 'It's a ring I'd sold him before the robbery . . . an antique ring, he called it the Mortimer seal, something the Mortimers of Ludlow Castle used for sealing documents and that sort of thing! It seems that it was recovered from the thieves along with all the other bits and pieces they'd stolen, when the police caught them. Mr Roberts gave it back to me as a thank you. Nice of him, wasn't it? He told me that I'll probably get a reward from his insurance company too!'

Cathy nodded. 'That was very nice of him Eddie, but no more than you deserve. You could have got yourself killed!' She smiled now, as she asked him, 'Did you see what they said about you in the Gazette? A "soldier have a go hero" they called you!'

He frowned and rueful again now, replied, 'Yeah, I know. Trouble is, I'm just an ex-soldier now!'

David had come into the cubicle now and Eddie smiled in recognition as he greeted him: 'Hello, Dafydd Mawr!'

David smiled in return as he said, 'Been learning Welsh whilst you've been in that bed, have you Eddie?' He winked, as he added, 'Or should I call you, Sir?'

Eddie gave a toss of his head. 'I've never heard a sarn't major call an officer "sir" as though he really meant it, David! In any case I'm not a serving officer now!'

Head up, shoulders back, David smiled at him knowingly and said, all regimental now, 'Still on the retired list, though, aren't you, sir?'

Eddie nodded, acknowledging the truth of the remark, but with a wry smile replied, 'Yes, and likely to stay there too!'

David gave him that look of superior wisdom which is apparently acquired when the royal coat of arms badge is sewn on the tunic on promotion to regimental serjeant major. 'Not if what Doctor Humphries told Idris is true, sir! He said there's nothing wrong with your arm now. Not now he's taken out that scrap iron they couldn't get at in the military hospital. Seems the infection helped make it more get-at-able like! Now that you're being discharged, he said he'll give you a letter that might get you a review of your medical discharge from the Army. Not that he's making any promises like!'

Eddie looked at him with disbelief on his face for a moment, then his eyes lit up as he said in amazement, 'Did he really say that, David? That's great news!'

Cathy looked horrified though. 'Are you mad?' she asked. 'You'd go back to that, after all that you've been through?'

The two men were grinning now as Eddie replied, 'It's what I'm trained for . . . what I do best Catrin. Dafydd would too, even with his gammy leg, if he could!'

David just stood there grinning, either at Eddie's slip of the tongue over their names or in agreement that he too would rejoin the colours if he but could.

Cathy, however, just shook her head in exasperation. 'You're mad,' she said emphatically, 'the pair of you!'

She was only looking at Eddie though, as she said it, then flushed as she saw that he was looking at the engagement ring Idris had given her. Heard him asking her then, his eyebrows raised quizzically, 'What else should I do then Cathy, stay here in Ludlow, hoping for handouts, perhaps get a job in a supermarket or something?' He shook his head. 'No, Cathy, I'm best back in the service, if they'll have me. It's where I belong!' He was looking into her eyes now, as though he would reach into her very soul as he said quietly, almost wistfully, 'Yes, I'd be best off back in the service. There's nothing for me in Ludlow, now.'

She averted her eyes away from his steady gaze, to glance at David who was still standing there smiling, as if he knew that her mind was in a complete turmoil, knew that she loved Idris, needed the security that Idris could give her and yet . . . She braced herself, then as if brushing all such thoughts from her mind she said calmly, 'Well, I suppose, if that's what you want . . .' she paused and Eddie looked at her is if wondering what she might say next, but she just hurried on with what she had to say, must say, ' . . . well, if it's what you want then . . . er, I mean, go for it, man!'

Determined to remain dry-eyed, she looked away from Eddie, almost holding her breath now in an effort to control her emotions. Looking out of the cubicle, she saw Idris and the other doctor approach. Turning back to Eddie, she had her voice under control now as she said calmly, 'Must go, Eddie, good to see you looking so fit again. Good luck then!'

Eddie was looking at her now, a quiet smile on his lips as if he knew what had been going on in her mind. She hesitated, wanting to give him a farewell kiss, but knew that she daren't.

Hand raised in farewell, she turned away, then hurried out of the cubicle, trying to get out of there before the tears came. As she went out she heard David say, 'Nice to see you again sir! Good luck with getting back into the mob!' So anxious was she to get out of there she didn't even hear Eddie's reply.

As she stood outside the door though, she heard Doctor Humphries saying to Idris, 'Yes, I thought so too at first. Thought his delirium was just part of the withdrawal symptoms, but not so! If he's been an addict at all, it seems he's been clean now for a very long time!'

As soon as he saw Cathy standing there however, he changed the subject quickly, saying, 'Yes, I'm discharging him now, Idris. Usual forms for him to sign, then he'll be off.' He waved an envelope, then added, 'I'll give him this, then make a few phone calls and if he has any luck he'll be back in uniform. No reason that I can think of anyway, why he shouldn't!'

Idris glanced at her. 'Everything OK?' he asked and as she nodded, tight-lipped, he smiled, saying, 'That's good! Let's get off and see that vicarage place then!'

A few minutes later Eddie Mortimer stood on the hospital steps, breathing in fresh air which had absolutely no trace of antiseptic. He was breathing deeply too, because he'd hurried there hoping to catch sight of Cathy before she left. There was no sign of her though, so he just stood there, wondering whether to get a taxi or walk to the railway station. Suddenly he heard Idris's voice behind him: 'Sorry about that, dear,' he heard Idris say. 'Had to have a quick word with John Humphries again about a patient of mine!'

He turned and Idris gave him a cool smile as he said, 'What's up, couldn't wait to get out?'

Eddie grinned. 'Yeah, something like that!' he glanced at Cathy and opened his mouth to say something but he'd said his goodbyes and there was nothing else to say now. Goodbye had a sort of finality about it that left one with little else to say.

Idris was looking at him as if waiting for him to say something, Cathy was just standing there looking anywhere but at him, with Dafydd Mawr just standing there massaging his thigh. It was Idris who broke the silence: 'Can we give you a lift anywhere, Eddie?' Adding hopefully, 'The station perhaps?'

Eddie hesitated a moment, thinking of sitting next to Cathy in a warm car, thinking of her struggling to find something inconsequential to say, before another final goodbye when they got to the station. He smiled at Idris, then shrugged. 'Thanks,' he replied, 'but after being cooped up in there for a week or so, it'll be good for me to walk.'

Idris nodded. 'Yes, I can imagine. Take it easy though, don't be doing too much too soon!'

Eddie grinned. 'Thank you, doctor, I won't!'

He stood aside then to let them pass and watched as Cathy walked away from him with Idris on one side of her and Dafydd limping away on the other. They'd only gone a few paces before Cathy turned and, with a wave of her hand said softly, 'Bye Eddie. See you!'

For a moment he imagined he saw three little children standing beside her and frowning, closed his eyes as vague memories tried to surface. When he opened them again he knew it had all been an illusion, for there was only Cathy, with the two men standing beside her there in the carpark, waiting for him to reply.

Smiling again now, he waved, saying as he did so, 'Yeah. See you!' Even as he did so, he was thinking, yeah, see you . . . I wonder where!

An Ancestral T

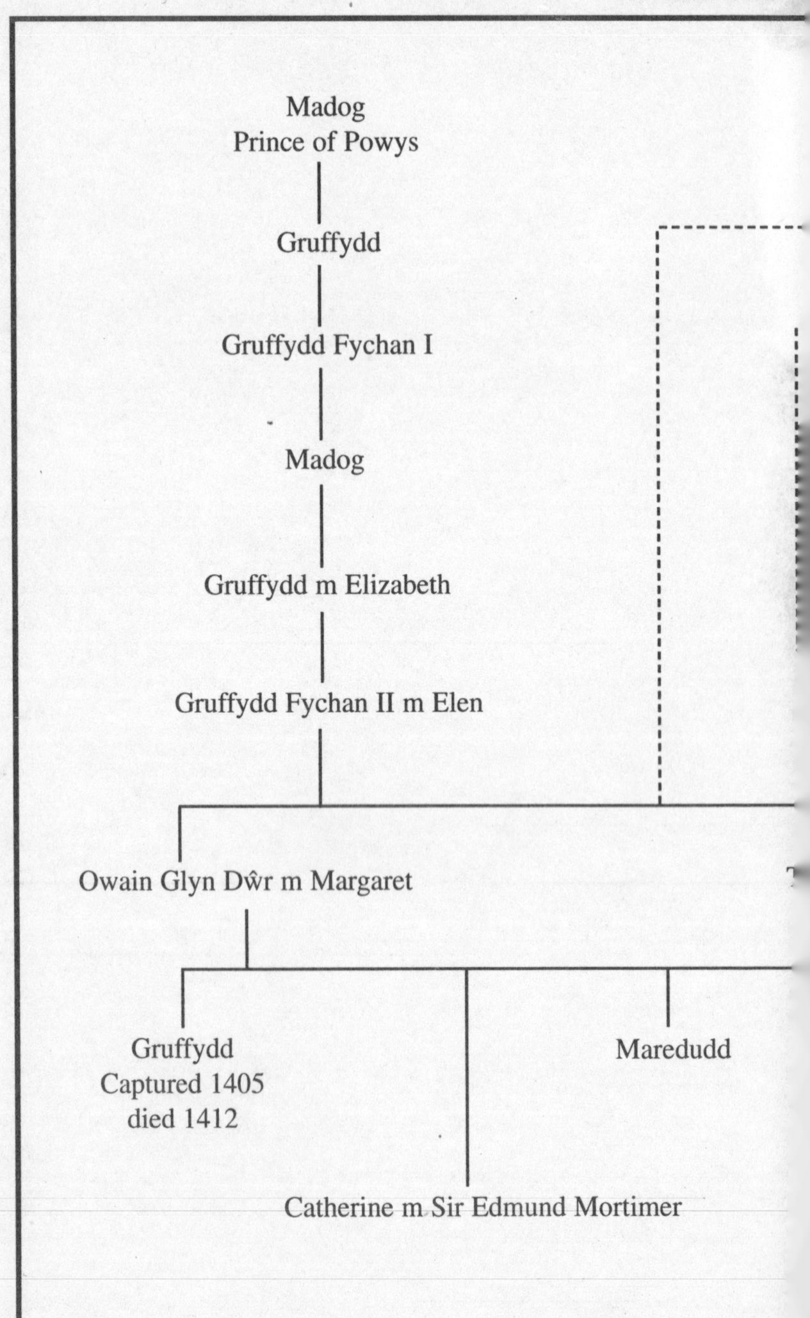